Praise for Michael Griffin's *The Lure of Devouring Light*

"Mike Griffin skillfully works the rich seams of quiet horror and contemporary weird. *The Lure of Devouring Light* is a superb selection of strange stories. It's the kind of debut that should command attention from genre fans and critics."

—Laird Barron, author of *The Beautiful ~~~ vaits Us All*

"Michael Griffin's fiction is sleekly ┆ With this debut collection, Griffin establishes ┆ sensibilities, fiercely dedicated to the explora┆

_____o, author of *Animal Money*

"Often, Mike Griffin's stories isolate an extraordinary dynamic between individuals who can only sustain the strange world they inhabit, secretly and together, with abject devotion to it. Anything short of passion will cause a rift in the narrative they've created, disclosing uncertainty, selfishness, ambition. Opening old wounds, or asking new questions. (For example, is love worthwhile or even possible set against a natural environment we've degraded beyond recognition? Or, what kind of integrity will we maintain if the monsters come for us?) At his finest moments Griffin achieves either a luminous grace or a breathtaking plummet into the unknown. In both cases the shock is earned by the tale that precedes it, and the stakes are as high as they can get. What I admire most (and there is plenty to admire in his writing) is an unforced, elegant ability to make his characters matter to us, in all their preening desire and almost magical expressions, like people we've known, loved, and left behind when all the bad shit happened—but with deep regret."

—S.P. Miskowski, author of the Skillute Cycle

"The focus in these stories is often on relationships that cause the characters to analyze how they intersect with the lives of others, and to contemplate their lives as individual beings—these examinations reflected outwardly in an environment of nightmarish disorientation and dreamlike transformation. This is dark fiction of a rare literary refinement, crystalline and poetic, that never sacrifices the frisson of the weird and horrifying. A highly impressive collection."

—Jeffrey Thomas, author of *Punktown*

THE LURE OF
DEVOURING LIGHT

Other books by Michael Griffin

Far from Streets

THE LURE OF
DEVOURING LIGHT

MICHAEL GRIFFIN

FINKELSTEIN
MEMORIAL LIBRARY
SPRING VALLEY, NY.

WORD HORDE
PETALUMA, CA

3 2191 01001 1301

The Lure of Devouring Light
© 2016 by Michael Griffin
This edition of *The Lure of Devouring Light*
© 2016 by Word Horde

Cover art © 2013 by Jarek Kubicki
Cover design by Scott R. Jones

Edited by Ross E. Lockhart

All rights reserved

First Edition

ISBN: 978-1-939905-19-2

A Word Horde Book
www.wordhorde.com

TABLE OF CONTENTS

To Joe Pulver,
who taught me how to open the vein.

SCORED, SCOURED, SHINING: MIKE GRIFFIN'S SURREAL INSCAPES

I t seems fitting to me that I first met Mike Griffin in Providence, Rhode Island, at the 2013 Necronomicon Providence. This was a convention intended to bring together writers, scholars, editors, artists, filmmakers, musicians, and fans of weird horror fiction and film. The event featured a number of well-established figures within the community: S.T. Joshi, Jeffrey Thomas, and Wilum Pugmire, as well as several whose stars were on the rise: Laird Barron, Michael Cisco, Richard Gavin, Cody Goodfellow, and Simon Strantzas. There was a third group there, as well, consisting of writers and artists whose works were beginning to appear in print and online: Selena Chambers, Anya Martin, Scott Nicolay, and Justin Steele. Mike Griffin was part of this third group. His story, "Diamond Dust," had just been published in Joe Pulver's Thomas Ligotti tribute anthology, *The Grimscribe's Puppets*. I hadn't read the story, yet, since the book was only just out, but Mike struck me as a pleasant, gregarious guy who was quite comfortable entertaining the other writers who coalesced around him and his lovely wife, Lena. (We found out at a room party later that night that he had excellent taste in single malt scotch, which, while no guarantee of his writing ability, spoke well of his general character.)

It was during a joint fiction reading given by Laird Barron and Joe Pulver on Saturday morning of the convention that I think the convention attendees got an early idea of Mike Griffin's talents as a writer. Laird and Joe had been scheduled a long block of time, ninety minutes, but rather than using it up themselves, they chose to invite Mike and Scott Nicolay to join them in reading. No doubt, it was a generous gesture, but there might not have been much more to say about it had both Mike and Scott not delivered fine readings of fine stories. For the remainder of the weekend, those readings were part of the conversation among the attendees, one of those events to which you overhear people referring ("Did you hear those guys?"). Given the chance to share his work with a considerable audience, Mike Griffin took it, as he had taken chances in writing the story that he read.

That piece, "Diamond Dust," is among my favorites in *The Grimscribe's Puppets*, which is no small thing, given that the book won a Shirley Jackson Award for best anthology and seems, with each passing year, an ever more substantial achievement. It wasn't the first story Mike had published, but it strikes me as one that highlights his particular concerns and gifts. Its focus is on Max, whose marriage, it is clear from the beginning, is on less than stable ground. While he continues to work an office job for a local company, Cassandra, his wife, fashions large sculptures from metal and fire. The contrast between their respective professions dramatizes Max's feelings of growing estrangement from Cassandra. Opposites may attract, but if that attraction is to continue, some measure of mutuality is necessary, and whatever Max and Cassandra once shared is rapidly crumbling. Relationships, frequently romantic, are at the heart of Mike Griffin's portrayal of character. He does not give us protagonists struggling alone against a hostile universe; instead, he gives us characters struggling within relationships whose contours are shifting to seismic degrees. This change in the characters' most intimate situations filters outwards, to find echoes, or perhaps consonances, in other aspects of their lives.

In Max's case, this means his job. The place he works undergoes a transformation, expanding its physical plant apparently overnight, its interior office space reconfiguring just enough to leave Max disoriented, struck with the nightmare sense of having missed important information, a memo, a meeting, crucial to his continuing employment. If Griffin is concerned to show his characters in romantic relationships, he frequently follows them to work, too. This is not work as it's often represented in fiction, either bold entrepreneurship or mind-numbing labor. Rather, it's work as a significant percentage of the populace experiences it, which is to say, somewhere between the poles of ownership and menial drudgery, the employee given enough responsibility to feel anxious about it.

And anxious Max must be, as he learns that his company is engaged in a bizarre project unlike any they have undertaken, a cyclopean tower whose fiery construction recalls Cassandra's sculptures, and which he takes at first as a fabulous device for communicating with the stars. As Max learns that his wife is in fact involved with the structure, he also learns that its target is not outwards but inwards, into the Earth and strange entities gliding through its molten blood. In the end, everything points to the interior, to Max, who is left facing the strange world he has spent the story uncovering.

Diamond dust is, of course, used as an abrasive, and it's hard not to use the term to describe Mike Griffin's prose. It eschews hypotactic excess for a kind of stripped-down elegance, mixing shorter sentences with sentence fragments, studding both with precise, vivid details. It's as if the language of the story is performing a kind of scouring of the story and its characters, buffing both until they shine.

"Diamond Dust" paved the way for Mike's next important achievement, the significantly longer story, "Far from Streets," which was published in a standalone edition in 2014. It can be more difficult for a writer to move from the short story to its longer siblings, the novelette and the novella. The short story allows for an intensity of effect, to the extent that it can approach the tone poem. The novelette and novella demand an investment in more traditional narrative techniques and strategies. "Far from Streets" succeeds because it demonstrates that patience. Here, Griffin focuses on another married couple, the unexpected inheritors of a significant parcel of land outside the limits of the city in which they live. Together, Dane and Carolyn decide to construct a cabin on this inheritance. Reenacting a familiar, even archetypal, American story, the couple builds a home in the wilderness. Almost from the start, however, something is off about their new dwelling. Time, Dane remarks, feels as if it flows differently while they're there, more slowly. The two of them encounter strange fauna, sudden violence. Worse, in this strange place, their relationship becomes increasingly dark, sinister.

Whenever you have a story in which a small number of characters are alone in the wilderness, confronting weird forces, it's no surprise for comparisons to the fiction of Algernon Blackwood to be made. Indeed, the back cover of the "Far from Streets" paperback makes them. In Blackwood's stories, though, the natural world is the site of the sublime other, terrifying, awful, awe-inspiring. In Griffin's narrative, the natural world is a location where what is inside can be made manifest in bizarre and surreal fashion. It's as if the streets of the story's title are the boundaries that maintain the order in Dane and Carolyn's lives on any number of levels, so that to move far from them is to enter a space where all manner of breakdowns in order, from the interpersonal to the ontological, may occur.

If "Diamond Dust" indicated Mike Griffin's ability as a writer, then "Far from Streets" confirmed it. At the same time, the longer story demonstrated that there was more to Griffin's talent, a willingness to dig deeper into his characters and their experiences. With *The Lure of Devouring Light*, these stories are joined by an impressive selection of Griffin's other fiction. Together, the contents of this collection map the districts of a locale that is distinctly Mike Griffin's. It is a place where you realize that the world around you has changed, has already changed, while your life has become disjointed, fragmented, your closest relationship become opaque. It's a place of strange and frightening visions, of unexpected and startling insights. It's a place where you are scoured to a polish, where the light that gleams on you consumes you.

—John Langan

"Soon we will plunge into the cold darkness;
Farewell, vivid brightness of our too-short summers!"

—Charles Baudelaire, "Chante d'Automne"

"By believing passionately in something that still does not exist, we create it.
The nonexistent is whatever we have not sufficiently desired."

—Franz Kafka

"With a kiss let us set out for an unknown world."

—Alfred de Musset

THE LURE OF DEVOURING LIGHT

ONE

Lia eases the vintage blue Impala down the meandering gravel drive. She's sightless in one eye, which makes it hard to gauge proximity to the looming Douglas firs, but she's so familiar with the place she could navigate blind. All through her twenties, the cabin's been her off-campus retreat. The last month, she's stayed away.

She parks clear of the trees and quietly shuts the car door. No amount of psyching-up is going to make this easy. It's partly her fault, she knows. Bringing Mészáros in this term may not have been her idea, but nobody forced her to invite him out here. If he'd stayed in the Visiting Masters campus apartment, he might've stayed focused.

God, how excited she'd been, meeting him that first night. The great man, János Mészáros. At first she saw similarities between them, despite the age gap. Both composers, cello specialists too rough-edged for the classical milieu. Lia, the pierced and tattooed punk, with a style more Velvet Underground or Killing Joke than Bach and Brahms. Mészáros, the mad silver-haired libertine, in constant worldwide demand despite vulgar behavior at every stop. Until the latest outrage, at least. The dark cloud left behind in Zagreb, he might never outrun.

The door to the cabin stands open. No music, for once. Part of her dares hope he's gone, though her reason for coming is to bring him back. Lia absently kisses the crescent moon tattoo on her bow-hand index finger, a habitual good luck gesture.

Inside, the cabin's a wreck, not just the door open but every window, too. A tornado of strewn clothing, empty champagne bottles. An exquisite cello lies before road cases containing Mészáros's electronics gear. Microphones, PA speakers. A tangle of cables converge on a portable mixer and audio interface attached to a scuffed silver laptop. Beside that, an injection kit. Syringes, rubber tie-offs, glass vials of clear liquid.

"Great," Lia mutters.

Mészáros arrived in Oregon seemingly clear-headed. His early lectures were brilliant, but those weren't why the Dean had brought him in. The point of his visit, the capper, is supposed to be tomorrow's performance of Stockhausen's twenty-nine-hour opera cycle. The university is billing it as the first complete, continuous performance of Licht in North America.

Since Mészáros started missing commitments this week, the music department's built into a cacophony of rumor. Then his no-show at this morning's media sessions sent everyone into full panic. Had Mészáros fled the day before the show?

Finally, Lia told the dean she had some idea where the man might be hiding.

On the kitchen counter rests a drinking glass half-full of what can only be blood. In the sink, a spray of red, as if someone's been sick. Liquid only, no trace of food. The place smells toxic, a mood of degeneracy looming heavily. Her quiet getaway, now repository for the grim karma of a madman.

At the table Lia reads Mészáros's notes. Mostly music transcription, including cello parts Lia herself will play, if the show happens. Interspersed are dated, diary-like entries. One outlines Stockhausen's ritual prescriptions for Goldstaub, not part of Licht, but a notorious bit of the composer's real-life craziness. Isolation, fasting and sleep deprivation as preparation for a music performance. A kind of "summoning the muse," a phrase Mészáros repeated and underlined.

The final page addresses meditation, which triggers a memory of Lia's time here with him. He loved the forest, especially Monk Point overlook, where he meditated in the mornings. She remembered those days, a giddy rush of possibilities. What doors seemed about to open?

So eager, then. So trusting.

TWO

Paths, worn by feeding deer, climb until the slope grows too steep halfway up. A small waterfall gives forth a white stream, which descends a hillside overgrown with lush green vegetation. Lia climbs diagonally over fallen clumps of crumbled earth. The umber soil sparkles with tiny flecks like gold dust. Those childhood summers, when Lia played here alone, Aunt Janet told her wood spirits sprinkled gold to mark their way.

Lia crawls, pulls herself up by roots and vines. She knows there's poison oak but isn't sure she'd recognize it. To get under the fence at the top, she hangs from the sagging wire. Her feet dangle above the waterfall. When she was young, none of this seemed dangerous. Now she can't believe Mom and Aunt Janet allowed her up here alone. If she dropped, she'd be washed over in a foamy rush. Lia grips the rusty wire fence, swings under. She finds footing on a tree fallen on the far side and tightropes up to the flat. A trail curves along the ridge toward a river overlook clear of trees. Monk Point.

There János Mészáros sits cross-legged, nearly naked, eyes closed in emulation of yogic posture. He's shaved his head and looks much younger than his sixty years. His eyebrows are also gone, and every trace of body hair.

"János," Lia says, then yells, "János!"

Nothing. Eyes closed, placid.

She approaches, meaning to shake him out of his trance.

Mészáros's eyes open. He smiles blissfully and pulls out earplugs. "Silence of four days, it sensitize the ears. The brain."

"You wouldn't be smiling if you—"

"The opera, tomorrow. Or do you come here to make love again?" He rises to his knees and reaches for her, delicately as if she were a butterfly.

Lia flinches, disgusted, but doesn't want to insult him. "No. We can't do that again." She collects herself. "That's something I shouldn't have done, Doctor Mészáros."

"Doctor." He laughs. "When we first meet you call me Doctor. By the end of the night, you call me János. We drink American wine under this moon. We fuck with your back in the mud. You remember all the mud."

"Stop it," Lia says. "Your scandal's blowing up online, on TV. Dean Vermer thinks you've run away. Says he should never have brought you here."

"What do you say to that?" Mészáros asks.

Lia exhales. "I told him nobody knew you were a predator at the time he booked your visit."

Mészáros grins, intending to charm, but over-wide eyes make him look demented. He stands, skeletally thin and nude but for a dirty towel tied around his waist. One of her bath towels. He gropes her breast, grinning that infamous leer, resembling the menacing close-up all the news outlets lately use to illustrate stories about the music world's sex criminal. His animal masculinity, once attractive, now makes her ill. Still, she wants to ensure the show goes on, not least for her own prominent role.

She backs away, as he shimmies toward her in a loose-hipped thrusting sort of dance. Angry, she pushes back. He falls, yowling and wailing, and his towel flips up. He's vulnerable, wounded.

Lia wants to hurt him. "It's time for you to leave here. It's your choice whether you perform tomorrow, as you promised. I hope you will. People are counting on it. Not only that. I'll be blamed, if it becomes known I brought you here, where you came…unwound." Lia pauses, afraid she's gone too far. She crouches, softens her voice. "Your staging of Licht would be remembered a long time."

"Forever." His manner shifts as at the flick of a switch, now humane, even polite. He covers himself and stands. "Of course the show goes on. Now, it helps me if we talk through some detail before. Especially with you who understand my vision. And vision of Stockhausen." Mészáros bows.

"We'll talk at the cabin while you get your things together." Lia notices a deep gash inside his forearm.

"Is nothing." He covers the cut with his other hand. "I took out my own blood to see if I could drink it."

She flinches. "How's that working for you?"

"I try." He shrugs. "But it make me sick."

Mészáros leads her back to the fence and swings under with the light grace of a boy, not an aging academic of decadent lifestyle. He descends the slope with vigorous confidence, and Lia recognizes how she fell for him six weeks ago, before anyone knew the wreckage he had left in his wake at Academy Zagreb. Before stories emerged of a string prodigy, resident at the university despite being too young to drive. Lia may have long since given up seeing herself as a youthful genius, yet thinks she understands the girl. What she sought to become. How Mészáros led her to hope. To trust.

THREE

Mészáros straightens the cabin's disarray with a casual air of normalcy. Without comment, he closes the injection kit, washes his face in the sink and rinses down the blood-spew. "I don't hide here because of this news story. The young lady of Zagreb." He gestures as if he's forgotten the name Celia Popp, though everyone else knows it indelibly. The story's all over the news. At least he's still behaving, as if the hike gave him time to remember how to talk to people. "It is…preparation ritual. You know Goldstaub? Meditate with silence."

Lia looks around for food, sees none. "Going full Stockhausen, then?" Somehow the craziness bothers her less, knowing he's gone days without sleeping or eating. She almost speaks the opinion that no ritual's likely sufficient to purify him, but holds silent. For someone like him, the muse may be entangled with more savage impulses.

Mészáros picks up the cello, an Amati worth fifty times the price of the cabin, and replaces it in the stand. On the cello's body are painted figures like tattoos on a woman's torso. He wheels a cart of sound processing gear closer, takes up the cello and plays a few notes. "You appreciate this, I know. Cello we share, more intimate that the other sharing. Which we discontinue. Your choice, not mine."

He flicks a switch on a silver panel mounted in the rack. Vacuum tubes brighten and glow, visible through a tiny window. Preamplifiers emit a resonant hum, which rises when Mészáros turns knobs on a massive pair of Bryston block amplifiers. The stand-mounted PA speakers on loan from the school bear the silver spray-paint imprint UO Music Dept.

Slightly hunched, he plays a figure. The melancholy is so effortless, so achingly profound, Lia shrugs off any concern for Mészáros's morality. Faced with this, how can she focus on a man's failings? Notes of distilled sadness, silent interstices of perfect timing and duration. Volume swells to fill the cabin and drift beyond open doors into the wild air. A bass note's deepest harmonic strikes her low in the gut.

Mészáros stops playing, sweeps toward her as if dancing, and offers a plastic pill bottle. "Ecstasy. Is both the drug name, and the experience we give together." He pops a white capsule into his mouth.

Lia shakes her head. "Is there any wine?"

He drifts into the kitchen and comes back with an open bottle of room temperature white. He pours two glasses. Lia takes one and sits to listen as he resumes. Time passes, and distance, all measurement is swept away. The journey varies, with periods of introspection and melancholy interspersed with utmost vividness and energy. The experience is like a tour of an infinite museum of the greatest masters, both known and imaginary, being allowed to see the paintings close up and touch them with fingertips.

At the bottom of her glass, Lia tastes bitterness. She swirls the yellowish dregs. Listening to him playing in rapt oblivion, she managed to drink most of whatever he crushed up in the wine. Mészáros pauses between notes, catches her eye and shoots a look toward the table. A plastic baggie of yellow pills sits open. A moment of panic before she realizes whatever he spiked the wine bottle with, he drank most of it before her. She goes to the sink, pours out the remaining grit. She rinses the glass, runs the water ice cold, and gulps until her stomach clenches.

Behind, Mészáros stops playing. Lia turns, expecting another lunge and grope, but his attention is focused on adjusting a microphone.

FOUR

At the dining table again, listening to him playing, Lia tries to gauge if she's feeling any different. Her head's maybe half-clear, and getting muddier. "I thought you wanted to talk through some ideas."

Mészáros spins to face her. "This is how I speak."

His sound thickens, grows darker. The microphone feeds a mixer and from there, a vintage spring reverb and some kind of modular filter bank. Some of it's familiar from the electronic music lab, some from Lia's brief, regrettable relationship with Robert, nicknamed Synthesizer Guy by her friends. Most classical players have no use for electronics. Lia takes a more modern, experimental approach. Sometimes, for solo performances, she uses looping delays and harmonizers, but even for her, Mészáros's stacks of gear seem too self-consciously rock and roll. One equipment rack within arm's reach allows Mészáros to alternate playing figures on the cello and tweaking a loop playback device. He adds layers and counterpoint to his own playing, effectively accompanying himself.

Lia's trying to pay attention, learn something from his tricks. Everything's grown foggy, her mind too sluggish to fathom what he's doing. The atmosphere inside the cabin feels swampy and damp. Is it night?

A choir of mixed voices, a layered wall of electric guitar. Pipe organ. The pills may be coloring her perception of the sound, but most of these effects arise from electronic treatments. Lia looks up, finds he's not even playing. The sound field sustains, deepening in resonance and depth. Mészáros is on his hands and knees in front of the speaker, the woofer energetically wobbling inches from his nose. So much for days of silence leaving his ears sensitized.

"Stop now, János," she says. "Doctor."

He stands, oblivious to Lia, head bobbing to rhythmic low frequency oscillations. On his way back to the cello, he notices her and grins like a naughty boy.

"You act like other people are nothing," she blurts.

The smile vanishes. He's adult again, his face lined, silver-stubbled. "You are talking about yourself, or the poor little girl?"

Lia wants to cry, wants to scream the name. She won't let him manipulate her. He knows the name.

"The needs other people have, that is not my needs." Mészáros approaches. "I need to devour. You know it, Lia. I devour you." He stands over her, mouth a thin black line, the merest trace of a smile. "You gave me yourself to devour."

She shakes her head so vigorously her black-brown hair flies into her face. "Big deal. I was star struck by the hot-shit genius. Thought I'd have an experience." Lia wants to storm out, but finds she can't rise.

Mészáros, too, shakes his head, more slowly, grin widening. "I took you. Another victim, like her. Do you think about her name and yours? Lia? Celia? That's how I knew you were for me to take."

"You're a monster, a child rapist," she spits. "Worse than Polanski."

"Much the worse. Polanski, he sodomize the girl. Celia, I fuck her mind. I unwind her from the world. She stop to exist." Mészáros's eyes go vacant and he looks away, toward an empty corner of the room, as if searching for a ghost. No sympathy, nothing at all for the girl lying in a hospital bed she'll probably never leave, victim of her own futile gesture to recapture the maestro's attention. He drifts away, into the bedroom, and comes back holding a metallic gold robe similar to the white robes he insisted all tomorrow's performers wear. This is the first time Lia's seen what Mészáros plans to wear. Not just the color differs. Mészáros's has a great monk-sized hood. Everyone else will go bare-headed.

Mészáros approaches, face glistening sweat. Minutes since the last note was played, the soundscape continues. Overlapping loops degenerate and fragment. "I fuck you before. Then you don't care what I am. You think maybe I help you." His eyes narrow, venomous. "Now you never unfuck yourself."

Before Lia knows what she's doing, she lashes out, strikes him high in the face. Mészáros blinks rapidly and tears spin down his cheek. Blood trickles from his nose, over narrow lips. Huffing, he lunges, sprays her with his blood. Lia falls back, tries to catch herself. Mészáros presses her down with his body's weight, his breath an awful, rotting stench. He writhes on top of her, between her legs. Lia's woozy, afraid she can't fight him off. Part of her escapes, races back in time to the first night she brought him here. Her ambition, her greedy curiosity, wondering what spring fed his talent. Repeatedly she insisted he was welcome here. Use the place. Make it your own.

On some level she's aware of Mészáros fumbling the buttons of her shorts.

His music lulled her into susceptibility. She thought him sensitive, even delicate, but she was wrong. He's a monster. He devours.

Lia weakly tugs against hands loosening her shorts. They slide down over her hips, past her knees. She tries to struggle but lacks strength. She's disoriented. How can she stop him? So stupid to come here. Cool air brushes her uncovered skin. He rises, grips her face between his hands and stares close into her eyes, both sighted and blind. He rasps noisily through teeth red with his blood. She pulls back, strains her heads sideways to avoid his stink. She feels him convulse. From deep in his gut he roars.

The cloud of his darkness drifts over.

Lia sees someone else in the cabin. Watching over Mészáros's shoulder, ghostly white and tall. Female, ivory breasts bare. Transparent crystal eyes drip black tears, a stream of ink over pale cheeks. On her head, a mantle of horns covers narrow braids, glistening black.

The woman looms over Mészáros and lowers a hand. As if he senses the looming touch, Mészáros rolls off Lia and stands away. Though he seems not to see, he moves away from the presence, irritated. He returns to his instrument, followed by the bright goddess, or muse, or whatever she is. Something has come between them, shifted Mészáros's intentions. Lia rests, vacant and bereft.

FIVE

Eyes open. Minutes later? Hours? Lia's vision has a strange quality, amplified, surreally sharp. Maybe a lingering effect of the drug?

The cello plays a familiar line, differently accented. The same passage once placid now churns, aggressive and hard-edged.

I let him in, Lia thinks. He wants to unwind me. Eat my soul. She finds her shorts, pulls them on.

She's not alone. The ice-white creature stands by the door, regal in her helm of antelope horns, keeping watch. Not quite a muse, Lia's sure, even if summoned by Mészáros's ritual. She sees and protects, deals vengeance where needed. A spirit seeming dark to some, light to others. Lia won't shy from Mészáros again, won't shrink away, crushed beneath him like Celia Popp. She'll face him down, unflinching. Might even learn something worth keeping, some useful takeaway. Lia only wishes that something could have visited

Celia, who needed protecting more than herself.

The room swirls with Mészáros's toxic cloud, a cyclical wall of cumulative noise built on a foundation of elements from Licht, thickened and elaborated by layers of improvised ornament and undercurrents of brain-melting noise. Interstitial gaps of silence specified by Stockhausen overflow with the growl of industrial tumult.

Lia stands, midnight weary. Mészáros sees her and stops playing. He offers the cello, takes up a trumpet instead. She decides to play, accepts his instrument and drags a chair near the microphone. Lia plays the string trio parts on the extravagant cello, while over her shoulder the white one hovers, alert. Just barely she nods in time, as Lia plays, with the knowing gaze of a teacher, or fellow player.

Mészáros adjusts a second microphone, plays left-handed trumpet while his right works a road-worn Kurzweil digital piano. The cabin overflows with sound. The potent vapor drifts out open doors and windows, dispersed by the wind, inhaled by trees. An infernal rendition of Licht, bent and deepened by spiritual derangement. Does Mészáros's genius elevate him, Lia wonders, more than it sickens him? Is that something she wants?

Hot wind swirls, a cyclone formed of noise. The white creature stands amid the mayhem at the center of the room, both arms extended at her sides. Thin braids, black and sticky as tar, buffet her face. They break free from her white head, fly around her like a storm of black leaves, dry and weightless. The black shapes flutter away from her and swirl around Mészáros, active living creatures of malign intent.

He initiated this, but can't possibly stop it. The white spirit fades, though as her light dissipates, her wrathful heat accumulates into a new sound-world. Night-blackened air thick, stifling. Sonic mayhem is all there is to breathe.

SIX

Morning. Sun above the trees. Lia wakes, naked and shivering in dewy grass at the driveway's edge. Her body aches, a hundred bruises, a thousand cuts. She rolls over. Gravel pierces her flesh.

The cabin door stands open. Quiet.

No idea why she's naked. No memory of these abrasions. Every inch of skin burns. One image, a midnight climb to Monk Point. Memory, or dream?

In the center of the driveway, between her car and the cabin, a mound of black ash smolders. The remains of burning trash, or leaves, a black pile knee deep.

Lia rises to her knees. Pain shrieking, she stands, hobbles to the cabin. No sign of Mészáros or most of his gear. Only the cello remains, the glorious Amato, and the gold hooded robe draped over a chair. Why leave the robe? And this rare cello, is that his gift? She could sell it, unburden herself of lingering grad school loans, fund a world tour. No sign of her clothes. She drapes the robe over naked skin and takes the cello out to her car. Her cell phone's still charging in the console. Keys in the ignition.

Before she leaves, she locks the cabin door and stops at the smoldering pile. Is it possible Mészáros burned his equipment before making his escape? He owns no car, but could've called any number of local worshippers glad to retrieve the Great Man from this rural exile. The smoke stinks of burned hair and Mészáros's rancid breath. Mingled among the ashes are broken fragments of bone, still white. This is him, Lia's certain, consumed by fire. Celia's retribution. Purifying rituals and summonings are tricky, especially with karma that's blackest of the black. Hard to find the muse among all the shadows.

On the road back to Eugene, she makes a call. The Dean sounds like he was asleep.

"Good news," Lia says. "The show goes on."

"You found him? Where?"

"The woods. Seeking inspiration or something," she says. "He'll make quite an entrance, this flashy gold robe. White's good enough for us, but too mundane for him I guess."

"God, I hope this goes off." The Dean pauses. "You hear the latest? Celia Popp died."

Lia should be surprised, yet somehow she already knows. She recalls the white presence, a ghostly yet tangible participant in the sound. "Someone let me know." She looks at her own eyes in the rear-view mirror, closes the left eye, then opens it and closes the right. Clear vision in both, for the first time since she was young. "Her spirit will be with us tonight."

SEVEN

Yellow backlight subtly lifts the blackness. At the rear of the stage, white pinpoints blink like stars. A figure in a loose gold hooded robe climbs to prominence before assembled players in white.

Lia feels no fear. She carries with her something of Mészáros, his morbid darkness mingled with aspects of last night's brighter spirit. She feels in herself a new complexity, an urgent illumination shining through places burned to transparency.

The audience stands. Lia raises the famous Amato cello to applause, careful to use her left hand to avoid revealing the distinctive tattoo on her bow hand. She feels a tear fall and reaches to wipe it. The fingers come away ink-black.

Lia follows the beacon within, feels herself buoyed up. Follow the cloud of gold dust that leads into light. Let it widen and disperse, cover everyone. She'll judge no more, criticize no more, only listen. The stage is a universe of glittering stars newly made, where no language exists but music.

DREAMING AWAKE IN THE TREE OF THE WORLD

I came back to life high in the Bigleaf Maple, my naked skin mottled green and brown like the leaves. Sometimes a flash of sunlight penetrated to where I hung suspended in my hammock, but rain never found its way in. My sanctuary among the branches stayed pleasantly warm, protected from the weather and rich with the smell of truffles and rain-dampened bark.

I felt Nomia nearby long before I saw her. She spoke to me, laughed alone, and flitted from branch to branch like a tiny weightless animal. The luminescent canopy was a universe encompassing wider space and deeper time than all the world outside. I slept to her wild earthy laughter, her many-voiced mutterings. I wanted to answer, heard the sentences in my mind before I tried to speak, but my mouth produced nothing intelligible. The effort left me exhausted.

While I rested Nomia prowled, ran up and down among the branches as another climbed stairs. She disappeared for hours, then approached to rub her body against me. Every day she would tangle field grasses into a mesh sodden with mushroom paste and crushed leaves. With this she wiped my body, painted me with colored liquids which dried to a coating on my skin.

"Tomas!" she said, over and over.

My eyes opened. Nomia brought me back to wakefulness from confused sleep, soothed my burns with salves of her own making, calmed my terrors with potions green and brown, distillates flecked with golden root pulp. She fed me a tangy mash of black occult fungi sprinkled with white seeds. She cleansed my memories with tingling iridescent yellow tinctures, soothed my fears with mud-like poultices of powdered lichen so active with living bracken spores they burned my eyes. My body's smell merged with the ubiquitous vegetal ferment. I no longer noticed heat or cold of days, of nights, of seasons. My burning skin soothed, my mind clarified and calmed.

I suffered no hunger or thirst, desired nothing but the green flitting creature who cared for me in her blissful hidden refuge. She moved on all fours, her skin vivid green, hair long and brown, interwoven with thin vines. Her face, smeared in earth tones, grinning wild-eyed.

She loved me, and asked the same question every day for what must have been years before I could answer. I felt her loneliness, her desire, and tried to summon the clarity of mind to speak. My slurred noises made no sense even to me. When she heard them she turned away. Always later she returned, fed me with her fingers from the wooden bowl. Granted me more time.

"I'm glad you found me." She leaned close, smelling of mint, tomato vines, catnip. "It's hard to live outside, just one alone." She poked out the tip of her tongue, gave my face a tiny lick. Her teeth were straight and white.

Evening tilted toward darkness. She watched me with those vivid dark eyes, pupils so dilated her irises seemed black, rimmed with sizzling gold electricity.

"Will you stay with Nomia?" This was what she always asked.

I sat up in my hammock and breathed deep. I saw her so clearly, a vision burned into me forever. My fingertips grazed her hand.

"I will never leave," I finally said. "Nomia."

I knew very little beyond what I could see.

Nomia showed me the contents of the wallet she'd found on me. According to my Oregon driver's license, I was Tomas Levin, twenty-eight, from Eugene. My University of Oregon ID card was date-stamped, but I didn't know what the year was now. Was I student, former student? Professor?

When I asked Nomia about places outside, or dates, she only smiled and shrugged. Then she might place her body against me so I felt her warmth and breath, saw deep into those dilated, boundless eyes. Eternal and encompassing. With fragrant green-stained fingers she fed me dark paste wrapped in Amaranth and Sorrel leaves. This soothed me, dispelled any wanting for things outside. I relinquished my questions, my selfish wondering. She draped her hand possessively over my chest.

I noticed she no longer spoke to herself, and told her so.

She smiled. "Now I have you."

What little I recalled from before my rebirth in Nomia's tree was inadequate to flesh out the life I knew I must have had. Usually I didn't care. Sometimes I returned to my few memories, especially on solitary afternoons when I rested in my hammock while Nomia worked somewhere above. I lay back, soaking in the green-gold light and wondering whether the lingering echoes would fade, or multiply.

In blackest nights, when Nomia left me alone, these memories spoke. They persisted and nagged, ghosts trying to become solid.

One thing I brought with me was an encyclopedic knowledge of plant names, both common and botanical nomenclature. Genus and species flashed to mind with perfect certainty at first glimpse of root or fungus, seed or leaf.

Nomia's domain combined qualities of treehouse, greenhouse, and herbalist's workshop. Within the canopy, on beds made of moss and soil in parts of the tree where the rains could reach, she grew exotic greens, thick mushrooms the size of apples, aromatic twisted bracken. Some of these fed us. Most, Nomia shredded or mashed, tasted or sniffed. The only thing she ever wore on her naked body was, at times, a pouch strung over one shoulder for carrying stems, leaves and roots.

Once I could speak, I surprised her by naming every plant I saw. At first I thought the Latinate names amused her. Then she retrieved seedpods of two varieties of *Portulacaceae* and handed them to me.

"Which comes from Miner's Lettuce?" Nomia asked.

I held up the *Claytonia perfoliata* pod. She clapped her hands and laughed. Her smile thrilled me, so natural and joyfully wide. She was a higher being, an exotic beauty. An evolved, leaf-eating nymph of the trees.

"I'm a student," I said. "I remember a thesis, Herblore and Phytotherapy."

The look on her face. She knew these words.

The second thing I remembered was my father. Not his name, or where he lived. I knew he owned a lumber mill, which gave him wealth and made a rift between us.

"You hate your father," she said, when I told what I recalled. "He cuts down trees."

"How do you know about that?"

"I showed you, your identity." Her smile dimmed. "It was in your pocket when I took you out of your clothes."

"But how did you know about his lumber mill?"

She lifted herself by the branch above and swung lightly, playfully. "Maybe you told me before."

"I just remembered."

She stopped swinging. "Tomas." Her eyes narrowed, two black slits. "Do you need to open every locked door?"

"No." I knew she had saved me. "You gave me new life."

This satisfied, and Nomia went above to prepare our food. As I ate, she noticed how long my fingernails had grown, and trimmed them for me with a scalpel-fine blade. I licked the last of the black paste from the bowl. The foods she made were more than nourishment. They relaxed the mind so the whole world fit comfortably, exactly as it was.

I felt ready to sleep.

Nomia circled as I drifted in my hammock, dream-traveling in ageless delirium. As she passed near, the smell of her comforted me like a loving touch. So strange, to drift in and out of narcotic sleep, to accept the transference of her essence. To feel it permeate the dream.

One other thing I felt sure of, not a factual memory but an emotional one, was that I had always been alone. If not forever, then so long it seemed that way. Whatever brought me here, the home I left behind was now quiet. No one lingered. Nobody missed me.

That night she washed me. When she finished, she asked the same question she continued to ask every night, even after I had become able to answer.

"Will you stay with Nomia?"

I told her again. "I will never leave."

She rubbed her body against mine, smeared my new, clean skin with her scents, her colors. I began to drift.

After I gained enough strength to move confidently beyond my hammock and table, Nomia showed me her workshop. Her splicing and grafting techniques were unorthodox, more mystical than scientific. I told her some of the pairings seemed impossible. This made her smile.

I wanted to go higher, see more of her private space, but this seemed enough for now. Nomia suggested I explore outward and down. She gave me a lozenge, large and sticky brown as a candied fig, with a smell like molasses and pungent truffle. "Suck this while you explore. It will help you learn the tree."

The dense plug sizzled my tongue, left me buzzing even after it dissolved. I climbed until afternoon and finally stopped to rest on an outer branch overlooking sloping meadows, my hands raw, shoulders aching. Below, a muddy path cut through fields of *Urtica dioica*, stinging nettles. This recognition stirred a memory of my burns. Vivid pain. I flashed back to lying agonized in my hammock, twisted by delirium, unable to speak.

At the far end of the field, a figure approached, hairy and shambling. It too was familiar, and triggered a recollection just like the nettles. As the thing neared, I saw it wasn't a monster or even an animal, but a very tall man completely covered in loose animal skins. His face was bearded, suntanned. I'd seen him before.

My skin burned. I remembered running, chased into the nettles by this giant shrieking monster with mud-caked fur. Was that how I'd come here?

"Nomia!" I muttered, and hurried up the tree to her workshop where I found her bashing root-bark in a mortar. I pulled her outward, toward the tip of a precariously flexed branch, and pointed down through an opening.

Nomia smiled. "That's my friend, Greenwood." She flung herself earthward, branch to branch, in a barely controlled plummet.

I reached the lowest limbs as Nomia greeted this Greenwood, who was pulling off mud-smeared animal skins. This wasn't the twelve-foot monster that lurked in my memory, but he was very tall, especially beside Nomia. Neither of them seemed uncomfortable about her nakedness.

Nomia looked up to where I crouched above them. "Greenwood's an alchemist," she told me. "Has a shop in Troutdale, comes to trade."

I jumped down. How long since my feet had touched earth? Being out of the tree seemed perilous.

"Greetings, bud." Greenwood shook my hand, then went back to stripping off hides, down to a loin cloth.

I understood the skins, finally. Protection from nettles and blackberry vines. So the monster was just a man. The memory so vivid, so alive, my heart pounded. The nettle poison nearly killed me. Somehow I was susceptible, probably allergic. In that state, senses distorted, he'd seemed twice as tall.

My head was spinning from the brightness of unobstructed sunlight, or maybe from resurgent memories.

"Troutdale?" I asked. "I saw you before."

"Saw you too, bud, having bit of trouble." Greenwood looked uncertainly at Nomia. "Good to see you're OK."

"It was so long ago," I said. "How long has it been? Seems like years."

"Not so long, bud." Greenwood grinned through his beard. "It was my last time out here, that's every two weeks. Saw you run, fall in those stingers."

Two weeks? Not possible. Hundreds of nights passed in delirium. Weeks, months, I struggled to come back to the world. How many nights did she ask me to stay before I even opened my eyes? Until I finally managed to speak?

I jumped, grabbed the branch, and pulled myself up.

Nomia came after. I paused, let her press up close. Everything seemed familiar again, comfortable, as she breathed in my ear and we balanced together on the limb. She started up again, and once I followed she sped effortlessly ahead.

Greenwood remained below, barefoot, nearly naked.

At my hammock Nomia turned serious. "Wait here while I finish trading." She leaned into me, her skin more brown than green. The skin wrinkled at the corners of her eyes.

"Two weeks," I huffed. "And he's from Troutdale? Why didn't you tell me we're near Portland?"

She ignored me, turned away and climbed above to fill two burlap sacks with clinking glass vials, dry bundled herbs, and pouches of refined leaf and powder. Then down again, past me without a word, to the ground.

I ventured toward the edge and watched through the leaves.

Greenwood exchanged banded stacks of cash for Nomia's bundles. He tied these around his waist, then put the skins back on.

I climbed up to her workshop, then higher, to a platform I hadn't seen. A laptop computer, and battery arrays trailing wires up the canopy. Higher, a pole affixed to the trunk extended a satellite dish far enough outward for line of sight to the sky.

Back in my hammock, I reassessed the hours she spent above. Splicing, I thought. Nurturing. Mixing our food and drink. I closed my eyes.

I felt a shift, soundless. Opened one eye. Nomia stood over me.

"It's better this way," I said. "Now I know how things really are."

"Tomas, stop." She placed fingers over my mouth.

I stood away. "In the real world, we have to make money. Land's expensive near the city. You've got to pay for all this hidden technology. Solar panels. Satellite internet."

"Not hidden. Separate." She stepped toward me, tried to close the distance between our bodies. "Real life is our tree, not out there. What matters is what you and I create."

"I'm not disappointed," I clarified. A lie. "You just aren't what I—"

"Did you think this was all magic? I lived without need of money?"

I shook my head, but she was right. I'd convinced myself she was a tree nymph, a Dryad. Who was she really? Just a hippy girl botanist who lived in an old maple?

She held out her palm to reveal two compressed pellets of dry mushroom. Her eyes lifted, sparked gold again. One edge of her mouth tilted up, a half-smile. I opened my mouth, allowed her to take care of me. She placed one pellet on my tongue and my saliva opened the dry fibers, brought them bitterly to life. I swallowed and the world's dimensions began to change.

In a dream I found pieces of myself.

At the edge of Riverbend Park, just beyond a sign. PRIVATE PROPERTY - NO TRESPASSING.

There they were, so close. Growing in moss and dead leaves around the roots of a dying spruce. Not just mushrooms, but the first *Amanita veneficae* ever found in Oregon. Just a few steps over the line, seen only by butterflies. *Veneficae*, no question. Snapped photos *in situ*, zipped specimens into a bag.

Something drew me on, into the meadow. A sound, like a dying, struggling animal down the hill. It turned out to be the creaking of a strange wood statue beyond a fence at the bottom of a slippery mud slope. It moaned and swayed, some kind of Pagan effigy, loose boards draped in weathered burlap. The statue stood guard, behind the ragged fence, over cultivation beds full of mushrooms. Not just *veneficae*. Many illegal to cultivate, some I didn't recognize. Someone's hidden crop.

The mud was too slick to climb back the way I came. Decided instead to circle down, come around to the park on the flat. Found a muddy path with brackish puddles. Nettle plants leaned inward along the path's edge. Most hikers recognized them, and as a botanist I knew all about *Urtica dioica*. I zig-zagged around the murkiest stagnant water, slipped and nettles brushed my leg below my shorts. The tingle came on, worse than expected. Toxic stinging, enough to blur my thoughts. My ears buzzed. I staggered, slipped in the mud. Brushed a leaf, another jolt.

A noise behind turned me around. In the path, a giant inhuman creature, fur caked with mud, pushed toward me through the vines without harm. Twice my height, and growing. It raised its arms, mouth twisted open, and let out a distorted scream. The ragged maw extended tendrils like grasping fingers, raw and bloody red. I tried to run, but the sticky mud held me. The shrieking monster was coming.

Panic. Had to find another way.

I left the trail, split off to my right, into the nettle field. My only thought was to reach the park. A forest of delicate leaves painted me with poison. Brutal pain. The tide of panic rising.

If I fell here, I'd never be found.

My tongue swelled, a wet, meaty rag filling my mouth. I spewed slimy foam. My skin, my lungs, burned black.

When I woke gasping from the dream, Nomia stood over me, eyes radiating light.

I barely halted my impulse to immediately tell what I recalled.

"I want to stay," I said, "but you need to tell me…"

Her eyes narrowed. "What?"

"Did you change the nettles, make them stronger?" I still felt the phantom burning from the dream.

"Crossed with Death Cap toxin," she said. "So nobody can come through and bother us."

I felt a botanist's curiosity about how she did it, but didn't know how many answers she'd give.

"Is what Greenwood said true?" I asked.

She looked relieved and nodded. "We're seven miles from Troutdale. You've been with me fifteen days. Medicines made it seem longer."

I considered. What did I most need to know?

"You almost died," she added, "even with my antidote."

"All the potions, medicines," I said. "Do you give me something to make me want to stay?"

She seemed to shrink. No answer.

I refused to look away. "How do I know my feelings are real?"

"Real? What's real?" Her eye released a single tear. "Isn't it enough, being happy? I admit it, Tomas. I'm trying to make us happy."

"It's all manipulation," I said. "The breeding, mixing. All for the effect you want."

Her eyes moistened and their light went out. "Is that how you see me?"

Finally I looked away. "Even if we stay high all the time, both of us, forever, that doesn't change reality. Just makes it look different."

"The only way to make reality fit is to transform yourself." Her smile was gone, her forehead deeply creased. A vein stood out on the side of her neck, pulsing. "I'm shaping a new world, just for us. I thought you were with me." She turned and climbed away.

The next morning, I accepted the wood bowl Nomia offered, drew it to my face. Oily brown fungal musk and the weird alkaline of *Salvia divinorum*. She watched me sip.

After she returned to her workshop, I poured out the rest.

I closed my eyes, tried to hide in dreams. Sleep always came easily. Not today.

Nomia's body, her scent. I couldn't stop my imagination, my desires. Both were beyond discipline, kept under a spell by her potions.

No more. I resolved to eat nothing, drink nothing, unless I could see what went into it.

Late morning, my thoughts clarified. A veil lifted. Objects appeared more solid.

By mid-day, panic sweat flowed. My hands trembled. Skull, about to split.

Nomia climbed down one-handed, carrying another bowl. "You look like when I found you." She showed the bowl's contents. Salad, not the usual unidentifiable liquid or mash. "Do you want wild greens with honey and vinegar?"

I made no move to share, and she dug in, watching me. Hunger flared, more powerful than lust. I went for the bowl, plucked out glistening spiced leaves, and stuffed my mouth.

"The things I feed you, Tomas. Once you start, you can't go without," she said. "A smart college boy understands addiction."

I stopped chewing, almost spit it out. She held out the bowl so I could see into it again. Harmless. Sweet and sour greens flecked with, what? Pepper, coriander and hot basil I could identify. Also her designer herbs, I imagined. It tasted wonderful. I swallowed, took more, chewed hungrily.

"You aren't the first man," she said. "Others have disappointed me. Some before you were born."

I scrutinized her face, wondered at her age. Pigment obscured her skin. She never mentioned dates, the passage of time. We couldn't discuss music, movies, anything to give a cultural point of reference.

My vision blurred and slanted.

"What did…" I slumped, eyes open. Aware, yet paralyzed.

"An inventor keeps trying solutions, failure after failure, until something works." She straddled my chest and held forth a pair of pliers. "This will make things easier for you. Less temptation to go back."

She gripped one of my front teeth and wrenched until it tore loose. Blood ran, warm and salty. One tooth, another. No pain or struggle, just the horror of understanding. She took them all. The blood overflowed the corner of my mouth, streamed down my cheek, through the porous hammock, the leaves, and down to earth.

Her fingers glistened, blood spattered up her arms, over her chest. It washed away the colors she wore like clothing, revealed her pink natural flesh. For the first time I saw her truly naked.

"I'll make root syrups for the pain," she said. "And mushrooms so you won't mind. A perfect balance."

Time swept past the motionless world.

I tried to remember what used to be wrong. A gauzy curtain trapped me inside my wilted, tired core, a translucent membrane between myself and everything outside.

Sometimes a thought flashed—*run away*—lacking reason or urgency. Why leave this luminous sphere, this green heaven of rustling leaves?

"You're remembering how happy we were," Nomia said, feeding me spice tea and watery amber pulp. "Creating a new world with just our bodies and minds. So many possibilities. Pleasures not yet brewed."

Over and over I apologized, clutching, grasping. I missed her in my hammock, wrapped around me in perfect yin and yang. I begged her to sleep beside me. She tried, but my sweating restlessness drove her off.

Alone after midnight I flew upright, seized by tremors. Usually the elixirs calmed, but sometimes their effect reversed. One minute euphoric, the next despondent. Bitter sweat burned out of me. My knees wobbled. Vision tinted yellow like a broken TV.

Then I felt my toothless, damaged mouth and remembered myself. I had to get out.

I staggered past a rack of drying herbs, grasped a handhold, swung down. Moonlight hinted within the tree's core. I descended blindly, by habit. Touched ground, and carefully quiet, I ran.

The mud path cut through the fields where once I fell. From above I'd seen the narrowest sections of blackberry bramble and nettle. Beyond that, only grass separated me from the world. Riverbend Park, I remembered it now. So close.

At the edge of the blackberries I hesitated. Verdant juices seasoned my naked skin. Protection from elements, but not thorns. As I climbed in, my flesh shredded. I stifled a scream, trying to part the inflexible vines barehanded. Every step tore deeper, like wading through razor wire. Up my legs, my torso. Every inch, torn bloody.

I pushed on. Pain was intangible. My will was stronger.

The last vines gave way and I fell clear, into a gap. My skin tingled, streaming hot blood. I stood panting.

Only the narrowest section of nettles remained. I planned to hurry through, maybe twenty quick steps. Still I trembled, anticipating the burn.

I backed up, then surged into the stinging barrier. It hit me, worse than I imagined. Not just pain, but mortal terror. I tried to press on through the burning. Another step, two. So far to go. I fell to my knees, gasping, heart racing. Pressure burst within me. I was trapped. Poison all around.

A sound, rustling from the wall of nettles. Coming closer.

Nomia pushed through the greenery and stood over me. Moonlight glistened off her body, wet and darker than usual.

Couldn't breathe. Constricting. I gestured at my throat.

"Unfaithful men." Nomia's face contorted. "I must be so terrible. You'll crawl through poison to get away."

I gasped, my toothless mouth opening and closing like a landed fish. She knew, yet turned away from me, toward the star-sprinkled horizon.

She'll let me die right here behind her, I thought, then drag me into the park. They'll find me, toothless and naked, no ID. A homeless guy strayed in, ate something he shouldn't. Probably happens all the time. This is how she ends it.

I tried to relax, stop struggling. Gave in to suffocation. Detachment lessened the pain.

My eyes stared, blank as the dead.

Nomia turned back to watch me. She stood perfectly still, skin black with mud, protection from the Death Cap poison. Then she stepped over me and ran soundlessly toward the tree.

I managed to draw a little breath, or maybe that was just a dream. The sun seemed to hint at the horizon. My hand moved, just barely. My leg. I crawled through, toward the park. Straddled the fence, near the PRIVATE PROPERTY sign. The burning, the paralysis, all gone. I felt no pain. When would I be able to tell, I wondered, if my escape was real or not? Whether I really breathed again, or Nomia had granted me a final, blissful dream?

FAR FROM STREETS

1.

Dane and Carolyn's life together followed an unremarkable, almost blandly linear trajectory.

From college in Eugene to jobs in Portland. Acquaintance to dating, cohabitation to marriage. Twenties, thirties, forties. One unremarkable suburban tract home, then a second. Career stood foremost in both their minds. Carolyn did contract technical writing from home, while Dane was a financial analyst for a heavy industrial business across town. Carolyn grew fond of having the house to herself every day. Dane gradually came to realize he quietly despised his job, for no reason he could name.

Their life was straightforward, perfectly usual and unremarkable until Dane inherited, from an uncle he had barely known, a parcel of forty-nine wilderness acres. No one in his family had ever seen the plot, nor had heard the uncle mention it. Carolyn voted to sell the land and use the money to move from their starter home near John's Landing to a much bigger place, her dream house in a new development on Portland's easternmost edge. The object of her desire featured purple marble countertops and granite floors, high ceilings, and tall windows overlooking the lushly varied green of an undeveloped hillside.

Dane was driven by a wish for fair compromise. He hoped to chase his dream without depriving Carolyn of her own. Their finances could stretch to manage the big suburban home, without selling the acreage. He had

important plans for that land, and though Carolyn shared none of his interest in that direction, he believed she might come to see the value in what
he had planned.

So it was that Dane ordered designs to build a cabin, and undertook research in earnest. He purchased books explaining centuries-old techniques
of artisanal construction, and found online sources for old-style craftsman
tools such as felling and hewing axes, adze and awl.

A little tightening of the belt wouldn't hurt; in fact there could be pleasure in sacrificing to fulfill one's lifelong aspirations. They would be first in
their social circle to own both a showcase city home and a weekend getaway.

The purchase of the new place was a simple matter of paperwork. The
mortgage was a big commitment, a daunting sum measured against their
combined earnings, but everyone agreed, even their realtor. It was sensible to
buy the most house they could afford. The market could only keep going up.

Their life of weekdays continued. Work, routine.

Dane's other plan could only be realized through time and sweat. From
their first visit to the land, his imagination thrilled at possibilities. Nights
at home, he lay awake obsessing, never questioning the effort and sacrifice
would be worth it. Their forty-nine acres abutted Mt. Hood National Forest, a vast expanse of mostly wild and inaccessible public land. Effectively
this was an annex of many thousand adjacent acres, unlikely ever to be
touched or seen by anyone but themselves.

For Dane and Carolyn to change their lives would require a sacrifice of
weekends.

2.

The setting chosen was an area where thick old-growth forest met a field of
wild grass verging on a stream too small to appear on maps. Dane insisted
on referring to the stream as "our river," so a river is what it became. The
water anchored this section of land, provided gravity for it. At the river's
edge, where grass trailed off into shoreline, was a flat section of firm, dry
soil where they would build.

Dane sought to convey the strength of his obsession, to make Carolyn understand his hunger for the quiet land. A passion almost like physical lust compelled him toward certain notions: to remove himself from the city, to retreat to this private refuge in the shelter of Oregon's tallest mountain. What he kept hidden was the depth and urgency of this wish to be absented from civilization, to leave behind society, culture, obligations. He imagined what she'd say if she knew how he ached to leave behind all they'd known. In his vision, they would relinquish everything they owned, all they'd worked for, no matter the cost. This included even the new suburban house.

Such was the pull of the vast sky and untouched miles of ancient pine and Douglas fir. Had any human ever walked this land? No streets delivered their property to the world outside. The site was four miles from where they hid their car among the trees, off Fire Road Six. They traversed public forest land to their own parcel. At first, they camped in a simple tent, enjoyed the river, explored fields and forests. Their footpaths wore trails. Dane carried in tools, built a lean-to beneath which to shelter materials between weekends, then moved on to the felling of trees of appropriate size and straightness. These he hewed into beams, or sawed into lumber. In lieu of foundation he sunk piles held firm in premix concrete, fifty-pound bags from Home Depot hauled in one at a time. The concrete was Dane's sole concession to modernity, to expedience. The piles, he crossed with beams, which formed the base on which all else would rise.

Where possible, Dane preferred doing the work himself. Carolyn was physically strong, and willing to assist with tasks requiring more than two hands. Mostly she lay sunbathing upriver, working her way through a stash of pulp and noir paperbacks she'd collected since college. In no time, she finished the complete Dashiell Hammett, moved on to Raymond Chandler. After Chandler, she moved on to Goodis, and Cain. Summer saw her reach the bottom of the dusty crate of old paperbacks, two or three every weekend. She'd been carrying them around for a quarter of a century, and finally plowed through the whole lot, all in a row. She needed the books to keep her busy.

Carolyn possessed the pale skin of a natural redhead. Since her thirties, she'd cultivated that whiteness, believing it fit with her intense auburn hair.

After so much time reading under the sun, Carolyn's complexion gradually darkened such that Dane barely recognized her. He remarked over and over that she looked more like the girl he'd met in college.

Self-sufficiency was foremost among rewards Dane sought. Out here, he was self-guided, and in a sense, alone. Often he cut, hewed, and hammered sixteen hours on Saturday, and again Sunday. His body, soft and white from twenty years manipulating spreadsheets in a fluorescent cubicle, tanned and hardened. His back grew straight, shoulders square. Cords of forearm muscle bulged.

They both transformed, not as a primary intention, but a pleasant side effect, into younger and more vital selves.

Dane insisted that sleeping within the cabin should wait until it was completely finished. Airtight, as he liked to say. Even when the cabin had walls and a roof, they slept in their tent beneath open sky, anticipating.

3.

The weekend of completion finally arrived.

Dane framed two small windows and set the door on hinges. Now the place could be closed against weather. An end to rain blowing through, squirrels nesting. Their second home was about to become a real home, smaller certainly than the Portland place. More humble.

The cabin, though, was entirely self-made.

Dane went outside at the end to survey what he'd built. From conception to final realization, he'd created something following only an inward drive, a compulsion of his own without regard for anything else in the world. Here amid rustling firs and the river's mellow churn, was a refuge for himself and his wife. A place of purity. Dane's hands trembled. When he tried to speak, to tell Carolyn it was finally done, emotion surged, threatening to overrun him. Such relief, and yes, pride of accomplishment. He waited to speak until he regained control.

Carolyn approached. "You should take a break. You never stopped to eat anything all day."

"It's finished," he said. "It couldn't be more perfect."

Through long construction, she'd seen the place in and out. Still he wanted to present it to her formally, as if the place were never before seen. A humble sort of ceremony. Dane straightened, mindful of his posture and the position of his hands. He stood on the small porch threshold, looked significantly at his wife, and swept open the door with a flourish.

Carolyn stepped up, was about to enter when a bird swooped out of the darkening sky, past her, and into the cabin.

Dane conceived in a flash that this was an almost mystical good fortune, proof of nature blessing their presence here. When he entered, though, he found the swallow ricocheting madly, striking walls and windows. "No. Stop."

The bird slammed a window, reversed wildly. The glass didn't break. Wings fluttered, out of control.

Dane flailed his arms, trying to scare the creature toward the door. "Go out!"

The bird ping-ponged in escalating desperation, back and forth, ignoring Dane's efforts. Finally it thumped again into a new window and fell motionless to the floor, amid a disarray of feathers, blood and shit.

Leaning in from the threshold, Carolyn surveyed the scene.

"It got confused," Dane said. "Found windows where it's always been able to fly through."

"So you don't think that's a bad omen?"

No bad signs here. No mishap of nature would ruin Dane's plan so easily. "I'll clean this up." He went outside, took off his shirt and dampened it in the river.

He returned to find Carolyn sitting atop the picnic table, chin on her knees, watching as if in judgment.

Already the sun verged upon the treetops.

Dane went back inside, swept out loose feathers, and then scrubbed away what he could see by the lantern. Many times he returned to the water, rinsed clean and wrung out the shirt, then continued inside.

Eventually Carolyn stepped past where he knelt, and climbed into the sleeping loft.

Dane wanted to repair all that had gone wrong, worrying how it would look by tomorrow's harsher light. The place couldn't be perfect any more. Already entropy was underway.

His eyes strained to discern drops of blood on unsealed wood. Outside, the sky was fully dark. Lantern light was sufficient to reveal obstacles in the night, but inadequate to reveal the sort of fine detail over which Dane had obsessed during construction. Of course he was missing some of the blood. The bird seemed to spray death over every surface in just seconds. One minute flying weightless, then a flurry of panic and it lay there broken, extinguished without warning.

Dane decided to quit, went to the river to wash his hands and rinse his shirt before hanging it to dry. On the way, he remembered leaving the dead bird out in the grass while he'd sorted the mess inside. He took up the adze, and beside the bird's body dug a suitable grave. The tool found hard stone a few inches down. He excavated around it, and pulled out a flat rock, perfectly round as a saucer. He dug a little deeper and placed the bird in. It seemed too light, too insubstantial, to have ever been a living thing, pulsing with blood.

Briefly he paused, considering whether he should offer words. Nothing came to him in his exhaustion. He grabbed the round stone and returned to wash in the river.

Water so cool, black and endless. Flowing away all the blood, the dirt and feathers. Everything disappeared downstream. The contamination of death, cleansed away.

Invisible beneath the water, his fingers rubbed the stone disc, traced indentations in its surface.

Carolyn, he remembered. Maybe still awake.

Taking the stone along, he went inside, found Carolyn already sleeping. So much for his plan, the ceremonial christening. There would never be another first night. Despite disappointment, he couldn't blame her. It was just that he kept looking, hoping for ways to make her part of this.

Dane angled the lantern so its light revealed the disc's surface. Inscriptions or carvings, like an oversized coin or medallion, lined the edge. He couldn't read the words, wasn't even sure the shapes were letters. In the center was a sculpted shape, more symbol than representation. Fascinating, but Dane wasn't sure what to make of it. He placed it next to the lantern, and then extinguished the light.

Carolyn's breathing in sleep was unmistakable. Dane relinquished the last of his plans, and settled back, lulled by the rhythm of inhalation and exhalation. The gravity of profound fatigue surged up, surrounding him.

4.

Nudged awake. Someone… Dane opened his eyes to perfect blackness. A moment of head-spinning terror. He was blind, buried alive.

He remembered the cabin.

"Something's moving," Carolyn whispered. "Outside."

Dane sat up slowly, careful of the loft's low ceiling. "What's wrong?" He felt around with his hands, orienting himself. Such perfect darkness. No up or down, no sense of time. Like staring into an abyss.

"Shuffling footsteps," she said. "And lots of murmuring."

"Care, no." He shook his head, trying to wake up. "Animals are scared of us. All those nights we slept in the tent, nothing bothered us."

She sat silent, breath held.

He too tried to listen, but heard only blood pulsing through eardrums. Such deep quiet.

"What about… other people?" she asked.

"Nobody lives within ten miles," he said. "It's a rough hike even in daylight."

"You said this would be peaceful, out here. You knew I never liked camping, but you made me—"

"I didn't—"

"I thought at least when the cabin was done, we could feel safe." She shivered, as if to make a point.

"We're safe—"

"How is this peaceful, Dane? Pitch black, and a million miles from people. If something went wrong here, we'd be dead." She reached, clicked the lantern on. Her fingers brushed the stone disc, but she didn't seem to notice. "Aren't you scared?"

"I was sleeping." Dane reached past, clicked the lantern back off. "Nothing's here. If there was something, it can't get in. Go back to sleep, and you won't be afraid any more." He lay back.

She shifted beside him, and then was still. Soon she breathed, a gritty respiration almost like snoring. Asleep again.

Dane felt the forest's weight above him, around him, as if it might bear him under like a wave. The night oscillated like slow breathing, deep in the chest of a black shuddering void.

5.

Pale blue luminance pulled Dane from sleep. Still early. Not enough rest, but he wanted to get up. Wanted to see, before Carolyn. He put on jeans, boots and shirt, grabbed the stone object he'd found last night.

He shut Carolyn inside, still dormant. Out in the shivering dawn, he found the clearing about the cabin marked by many scattered footprints. Not animal. Human, barefoot, and in various sizes. A milling crowd, in the perilous quiet of midnight, while he and Carolyn slept within, protected only by thin panes of new glass.

Imagining the worst was no help, though. This was the forest. There were no barefoot multitudes wandering at midnight. Maybe yesterday he'd gone barefoot, after working. Usually he wore boots, and he didn't recall taking them off, but he must've. Maybe it was Carolyn.

Whatever this was, he couldn't let her get the wrong idea. She'd been so afraid. He'd dismissed her.

For the first time, she'd admitted to not enjoying the place like he did. What would happen if she no longer wanted to come? Her first idea had been to sell the land. She couldn't take this away. The only reason she ever wanted to sell was for money to buy the new house, but they'd gone ahead and bought it anyway. Sure, it was a stretch. But now that Carolyn had what she wanted, shouldn't he have something, too?

Part of Dane wanted to blame Carolyn for how things went last night. Not for the bird, but for how she made him feel foolish and inept afterward. Like somehow he should've known better. The way she sat glaring while he cleaned up.

With the sole of his boot Dane scrubbed away the footprints, first outside the door, then the clusters by each window.

By the time Carolyn emerged, he'd eradicated all signs. He'd packed everything for the trip home. If she noticed any signs, any hint to prove her fears were justified, she said nothing.

6.

Most often they returned to the city Sunday afternoon. Sometimes they waited until Monday morning, before dawn. Dane needed little time to prepare for work, and Carolyn telecommuted. Usually staying over was Dane's idea, trying to squeeze more hours out of the weekend. Another night. The longest possible break from real life.

He never needed an alarm. Some subconscious voice always knew when it was time to return.

Gradually as he drove, Dane returned to himself, like waking from anesthesia. A slow crossfade, one existence slipping away, all the logic of that way of life relinquished. One matched set of priorities and assumptions gave way to another, like swapping one self for another. One home, separated from the other by a permuted sequence of turns and stops. A code to be cracked.

"Out there, I have this sense of time stretching." Dane hadn't spoken since they left the fire road where their Audi wagon hid among the trees.

Carolyn startled as if she'd forgotten him.

Dane continued. "In town, a day's just a day. Out in the forest, everything dilates."

Carolyn glanced at him. "Maybe it's your brain that's dilated." Dark circles under her eyes made her look older.

Near the top of their hill, he turned left onto Suffolk, a street lined on both sides with houses in subtle variations of gray. Some upstairs bay windows were on the left side, others on the right.

"I'd rather stay out there," Dane said, pulling into their driveway. It was one among many, neither first nor last, highest nor lowest. "Some unmeasured stretch of forest time, versus two normal days here."

The garage door hummed, a curtain rising on a stage.

They idled in the driveway.

"You worked twenty years," Carolyn said, "fighting for a good position, a better salary. Is crunching numbers at a desk really so hard?"

What did she know about whether it was hard or easy? He was the one who'd been doing it twenty years. "It's hard, but not the way you mean. Why should I have to justify it to you? My job isn't so much difficult as torturously dull."

Carolyn blew through pursed lips. "You're a suburban guy who likes to go out and play in the forest. Drive the fifty-thousand dollar SUV out to the cabin, play pioneer in the wild land. How do you think you'd survive if that shit was real? If you had no other choice?"

"We'd do great," Dane said. "Everything would be perfect."

"No, Dane." The set of Carolyn's mouth indicated something sour on her tongue. "Once we're accustomed to luxuries, having health insurance, money in the bank for treats, then maybe it sounds fun to pretend your life is actually primitively simple. That you're this pure-hearted being, immune to modern bullshit. Go out to the cabin, don't bother shaving, don't even wash yourself. Spend all day hunched over the river to catch six dollars worth of fish. That's fun sometimes. I get it. Not as much fun as you think it is, but fine. The point is, if we didn't have the Audi parked in the trees, and this other house forty miles away, and your job to go back to with its 401k, and all my clients lining up to hire me and pay me to do unpleasant work for them, without all those things, nature would just be hardship. Just... doing without. Basically, suffering."

Dane considered. He understood what she meant about living without a safety net. Yes, that had to be scary, at least at first. But he believed the fear indicated proximity to the primal. Just let go, and drop through to authentic existence.

"It's not suffering I want," Dane said. "Through suffering we come out the other side, to an existence simpler and more profound. That's what I want, some day."

"No," she said. "I got used to the good stuff, now I'm not giving it up. I love a nice peppery Shiraz, a tart, lusty Pinot. Chocolates from Au Fait. A nice stinging hot bath, heavenly candles and perfumes. All my books, the trashy and the serious. Hi-def movies on the big projector."

These facets of their other life, the looming realization that it was back to going through motions, made Dane tired, heavy-limbed. She always asked what was so hard about it. It wasn't dangerous, or physically strenuous. The hours were moderate, the office climate controlled. Monday through Friday, Dane sat in a nine hundred dollar ergonomic task chair. Which aspect should cause this weight in his chest, this sense of facing terrible doom? Everyone had obligations. Work was the price, part of an exchange to enable brief getaways.

The garage light blinked out. Dane clicked off the Audi's headlights. The black rectangle gaped before them, a void of unknown depth.

"Isolation does something to me." He always struggled to convey the important things. "Reading by lantern, instead of staring at computers and TVs."

"Mmm. You can read at home." Carolyn was looking away.

"It's more than reading." He gestured at the house. "I dream of giving this up."

Some component of the car ticked, keeping time. He switched the headlights on.

Carolyn sighed. "We can't subtract ourselves from our world, Dane. The world we're born into is the one we get. Ours is modern, it has technology. People work and drive cars around, use phones and computers." She paused. "How do you go back to a world without those things? Dane, you can't."

"You don't want to."

"Yeah, I don't." She waved the back of her hand at him. "We can retreat, pretend the world's all rivers and trees. No matter how long we sit out in that cabin, this world doesn't go away. It remains, waiting for us, until sooner or later, the weekend is over."

"I'm just sick of all the bullshit and noise. You work here, not in an office. You don't know, the cubicle chatter. I'm trying to zero in on what's real."

"Out in the trees, maybe that kind of talk sounded poetic," Carolyn said. "Sitting here now, it just sounds ridiculous. I'm dirty, and I stink. I want a shower."

This wasn't ridiculous. Dane tried seeing her way, remembering all she sacrificed, spending weekends outside. It cost him nothing to let her go inside, get cleaned up. Later, he could figure out a better way to explain. For tonight, they could relax, watch a movie with a bottle of wine. Carolyn always had some impressive new bottle.

He'd get by until Friday.

Dane pulled into the garage and pressed the remote. The door slid down.

The house was windless, neither hot nor cold. It smelled neutral, as if no living had ever occurred within. A strange artificial locale, furniture showroom or movie set. Someone else's concept of the ideal life.

7.

Dane held his rod and reel in the shallows, trailing a line downstream. Perfectly transparent water took on the green and brown of the rocks, with distortions where the water curved. Sometimes it was possible to see a fish holding in the still places downstream from larger rocks. Most often no fish were visible, even when present. The trick was envisioning places fish might likely hold.

Carolyn approached after spending the heart of the day on her own. She peeked into a wood bowl left resting on a flat rock. The bowl contained dark purplish berries Dane had picked, some unfamiliar hybrid neither blackberry, boysenberry nor black raspberry.

Guessing her unimpressed by the berries, Dane placed the pole into a notch between rocks and crouched to delve into the stinging-cold water of an eddy. He pulled out a metal string holding the morning's catch, five glistening trout of good size. Along with the berries, today's haul, which was the best he'd seen, ignited a thrill of potential self-sufficiency.

"Fishing and foraging this good," Dane shouted over the current, "we can haul in less food."

He grabbed the pole, reeled in, and joined Carolyn on the bank. From his pocket he produced a cloth bundle which he unwrapped to reveal mushrooms. Bent, thin stems and slightly crushed caps.

Carolyn looked puzzled. "We can't eat those. Don't you recognize—"

"Of course, in college." He grinned. "Finney's boat, the reservoir. We drank mushroom tea and tripped under the stars. You, me, Finney's girl. I think her name was Zo."

"Like you said, Dane, college. We have jobs now."

"There's still time," he protested.

"Tomorrow's Monday. You want to show up to your kick-off meeting tripping on psychedelics? Puke on your boss?"

"We still might—"

"You have to be up at five tomorrow," she insisted. "We're not those people any more. It's not Nineteen-Eighty-Whatever."

He shook his head. "God damn it, what's the point of working if we can't—"

"You're going to rebel yourself right out of a job, Dane. You scrambled so long for a little security."

"Security." He kicked a shore rock into the water. "I'm only making money now because it's a job nobody wants. Jobs people actually want don't have to pay as much."

"Please. We'd be better off impoverished? I've been poor, remember? Have you forgotten all the brutal jobs we climbed our way out of?"

"College grads line up to work in record stores, book stores, for nothing. Nobody's lining up for my job. They have to pay six figures because it'll drive you fucking crazy."

"Your work has value. Your company rewards you for it."

"Jesus."

"You'd be happier if you saw it that way."

He approached as if in reconciliation, perhaps conceding her point, and wrapped one arm around her shoulder. His free hand brought the mushroom pieces near her mouth. She shook her head. He pressed between her lips, trying to force past her teeth and tongue. He laughed, still trying to be playful.

When she resisted, he pushed with more force.

Carolyn squirmed free. "Are you crazy?" She spat brown fibers and wiped her mouth. "No, Dane. I said no. And you're not doing it either." She swatted the bundle, knocked it out of his hands.

Dane squatted, picking bits of the psychedelic mushroom out of the dirt. In one palm he separated the good pieces from fragments of leaf and twig.

"God damn it, Dane!" Carolyn tried to kick his cupped hand.

He held the mushrooms protectively up near his chest. She jumped on his back, swatted at his hands. He extended his hands beyond her reach, resisting until she became frustrated and climbed off.

Breathing hard, she stood away, and resorted to toe-scuffing the section of ground from which he'd already retrieved most of the mushrooms.

"Fine, I get it." Dane stood back. "You think you don't need this."

Carolyn lunged, drove a flat palm into the center of his chest.

He backed off, heart pounding.

She ran into the cabin and emerged with a sleeping bag draped across her shoulders like a vagrant's blanket. The sun was still bright, hours from setting. She meandered up the shore, over uneven sandy soil and rocks made round by lifetimes of persistent streaming. Usually she took a paperback when she wanted to read. This time, no book.

Dane watched her slow progress until she stopped where he expected. The flat section of clean sand was protected from wind by a grassy berm. Carolyn spread out the sleeping bag, untied her shorts and pulled them down, then stripped off her T-shirt. If she noticed Dane watching, she gave no indication. He took voyeuristic pleasure at first, seeing his wife like this. At such a distance, it was like watching a stranger, some unknown woman disrobing and preparing to recline in the sun.

Soon he resumed feeling angry, both at himself and at her.

8.

Dane put the string of trout back into the stream to cool while he fished. He needed to clear his mind. The repetitive motions of casting and reeling took on a meditative aspect. So unaware of time, he might have continued on and on, despite having taken an excess of fish, but the stringer only had hooks for twelve. With nowhere to carry the thirteenth, he had to smack its head on an exposed rock, and carry it with the others to the flat shelf-like stone where he gutted and cleaned his take. The last fish wasn't a trout at all, but something strange, exotically striped. He didn't bother gutting that one, just set it aside. A dozen rainbows would be plenty. Dane took the cleaned fish to the picnic table and built a fire.

After the food had been going a while, and just as worry about Carolyn began edging into Dane's thoughts, she returned. Fully dressed and pink with sunburn, she dragged the sleeping bag behind her. She glanced into the cook pot of lightly boiling red stock, and sniffed.

Dane stirred chunks of white fish, diced onion and garlic, celery and spinach. "Fisherman's stew, if you're hungry."

Carolyn leaned toward the clearing's edge. "What's that?" She pointed toward the thirteenth fish, eel-thin and black with yellow stripes. It lay dead in the dirt, a step or two from where he'd buried the swallow. "Eww. Fucking demon fish. I'm not eating anything that came from the same river as that."

Dane shrugged. "It looked weird, so I left it out."

Carolyn approached and leaned over the dead thing cautiously, as if it might leap up. She reached, almost touched it, but backed away, making retching sounds.

"Fine, I'll get rid of it." Dane used a discarded scrap of foil to grasp the slippery thing. The horned black skull looked weirdly human. Though tempted to hold it up to Carolyn, tease her squeamishness, he himself disliked the eel-like slipperiness of it. He took it to the river, flung it in, then returned and dropped the foil in the fire. It hissed and sputtered. "The stew just has the good river trout we always eat. You like those."

Carolyn popped a cork and poured white wine into a plastic cup. She sat back on the top of the picnic table, looking unconvinced about the stew.

Returning to work, Dane juiced four limes into the pot, and then hand-shredded cilantro. The smells drew Carolyn near. Though sometimes Dane was clumsy in his thinking about his wife, he often perceived what would reach her.

She refilled her wine, poured a cup for Dane, and brought two bamboo bowls.

They sat on the picnic table top, overlooking the river. Neither spoke as they ate. They paused only to sip the crisp Pinot Gris or study the bottle. When their bowls were empty, Carolyn poured more wine while Dane removed the cook pot from its frame and stoked the fire.

The fire intensified, broadening and stretching toward the steel gray sky.

How long since he'd spoken? Dane stood, stretched his back. "Drinking wine outdoors makes me feel like Hemingway." He grabbed the wine bottle, now empty. The green glass seemed luminous, a trick of evening light, or his eye compensating. The Salix Vineyards label was metallic, round like a coin depicting a bird encircled with rough symbols. He felt a sudden impulse to throw the bottle into the river. Though he was sure he wouldn't, that the impulse would pass in an instant, Dane wound up and lobbed the bottle.

"Dane!" Carolyn said.

As the bottle spun thirty feet through the air, Dane cringed, wishing he could take it back. He didn't want broken glass in the shallows, where they waded. Carolyn and he both were scrupulous about never leaving behind trash.

The bottle plunked, made a small splash. No breaking sound.

At the moment the bottle left his hand, Dane had felt certain throwing it would come across as a clear, decisive gesture, an expression of a kind of sense, or an utterance of philosophical truth. Even the instant he released the neck of the bottle, he already knew it was a mistake. He couldn't even remember what he'd meant by it.

"I'm just glad it didn't break," he said, wondering at the two minds within himself, neither understanding the other.

Carolyn stood, head down. In a wide stance, she wobbled, one hand on the table. "I feel dizzy. Something's wrong." She staggered into the shallows, fell to one knee, and vomited. She threw up into the water, again and again.

Dane sat watching.

When her stomach was empty, Carolyn moaned and retched unproductively. Finally she was still, quiet. She splashed her face and swished out her mouth.

Dane went halfway to the water, and then sat roughly where the grass ended.

Carolyn crawled back to him, scowling. He laughed.

"What's funny?" Her irritation broke, and she too laughed. "Your fucking stew made me puke."

His laughter quickened, briefly manic, rapid-fire, then stopped. Dane stood, crossed his arms across his gut and hurried to the shallows Carolyn had just left. He leaned forward, and as if it were expected and perfectly natural, vomited in the river.

His gut clenched and released, and though he tried to let it come out of him, tried not to fight, he felt his head might burst like an overfilled balloon.

He rinsed and spat handfuls of river water, then dropped to his knees on the shore and crawled back to where Carolyn lay waiting, as she had minutes earlier crawled to him.

"I mixed in the shrooms, chopped up teensy-tiny." He tried to giggle, but the impulse was spent. "I keep trying to explain. I know I keep failing."

"What?"

"I didn't just want to change our setting, coming out here. I wanted to change everything. The shape of our life. The size."

She nodded, despite lying on her back. Did she understand?

"I feel good right now," she said. "I feel carried away. Do you think it's one life or two?"

"What is?"

"You just said, Our life." She rolled her head side to side. "I feel good, right this minute, at least."

"Maybe it'll stick. You think it might?"

"I'm not sure I can go all the way," she said.

He rolled on his side, faced her. "All the way, where?"

"Where you want." Her voice was flat, exhausted. "To completely drop out."

Dane remembered that night, those stars above the reservoir, imprinted vividly in memory, a cinema he could revisit at will. Twenty-five years, a different planet. Those stars were psychedelic, full of portent and dazzling promise.

He was the one who'd changed. Not Carolyn. Not the sky. He didn't care to recapture youth, as she believed. All he wanted was to briefly recall how it felt. An unworried mind. To be blank slate, free of the clutter and overhead of age.

"It's scary," Carolyn said. "The sky, I mean. How high does it go?"

A sprinkling of clouds elongated, stretched thin by an atmosphere wide and deep as infinity. All that moving complexity above persisted, indifferent to whether anyone watched or cared.

"We're the ones," he said. "Moving."

Eyes closed, everything still drifted.

"This is like…" Carolyn's voice, a dry-throated croak. "…like a nightmare. When you can't come out."

She shifted nearer, arms and shoulders trembling. Her skin felt dead cold, inhumanly strange, like fish straight from the river. She's not cold, he thought. She's afraid.

"I wish you could see how it is for me." Dane spoke with such desire, such heartfelt ache, wishing he could convey some part of what he felt.

Tomorrow, she would forget.

Dane rolled over, crawled across rough ground toward the fire. The half-full stew pot cooled on the table. He stood, wobbling absurdly as he sipped from the ladle. He lost his balance and fell. His head struck the ground so forcefully his teeth clacked.

Her faith always slipped. Mood, always swerving toward doubt. He didn't want to let her poison him, was afraid there was no other choice. One of them always had to drag the other back down to earth.

9.

New light flowed overhead, a sky-filling cinema. Slipstream passage of time. Hypnotically beautiful, alternately jarring.

Something flew near? He twitched. A vision of the swooping bird. Gone now. Dead and buried.

Could the world shake him loose? Spin away, adrift in aether space. Was

Carolyn right? Her fear of night's looming threats.

Unanswerable questions in such a dark place. Terrible things lurked, more or less half-solid. Night moved forward and back. The place beside the river, the reservoir with Finney and Zo. Other places, the future or clattering machines. Everything ran faster despite grinding gears misaligned.

The ground was hard beneath him. Sand stuck to his back, sweat-damp, hypersensitive. Chill wetness, a puddle of whatever Carolyn spilled earlier.

Oh, I fucking pissed.

Sat up, where? Outside the cabin.

Terrible light pierced, too bright.

Look up, always up. Pinpoint stars, the newborn kind, not yet tired. But he didn't know enough yet to show the way.

"Open the door!" he screamed.

When universes were born, what happened to the old ones?

"The door's already open," someone said. "This way."

"There's no seeing!"

When we shed ourselves, what happened to the old skin?

He crawled, blind. Tried to stand, fell flat. Hands and knees climbed cabin steps.

Underground machines still hummed, bitter and malign.

A door slammed.

10.

Scuffling brought Dane upright, angry mutters answered by squawks or shrieks. He looked around, too groggy to understand.

Carolyn was out of bed, scrambling naked on the floor below, as if trying to catch something.

Dane rubbed his eyes, swung his legs over. Found the ladder's top step.

Again she lunged, bare feet slipping. Her body concealed whatever she'd captured. She forced some flailing creature, raging loudly, into a canvas duffle bag.

"What are you…" he began.

She kicked the door open, lugging the bag two-handed, shoulders back against the heavy burden, and disappeared outside.

Dane waited, listening. Nothing.

"Carolyn?" He climbed down, also still naked.

She returned through the doorway, bloody from hands to elbows. "It was clawing through the bag. Or maybe biting."

"What?" he asked. "What bit you?"

"This animal." Carolyn displayed deeply sliced wrists, and backs of hands. Nothing like a bird or house cat could do such damage. Blood streamed down forearms, dripped from elbows onto the floor.

"So much bleeding," he gasped. "Let's clean you up."

"You're always cleaning blood." She laughed, with a tremor. "Ever since we came here."

He grabbed yesterday's shirt and led Carolyn outside.

At the clearing's edge, a fresh hole had been dug, very near where he'd buried the swallow and unearthed the stone disk. The newer hole was larger.

Dane sat her on the edge of the picnic table and wetted the T-shirt in the river. He returned and started clearing away the blood. So much running blood had created the impression of dire injuries, but the truth was less serious. At his touch Carolyn jerked as if startled. Tears flowed, as if something upsetting had returned to mind. Dane kept working, wiping her clean. As the blood was cleared away, her tears diminished.

He left her alone a while. After she'd come inside and was mostly dressed, he questioned her again. "What was it? Another bird?"

"Are you stupid?" Carolyn stopped, shirt barely pulled down, one arm still overhead, striving into the sleeve. In this posture, she glared. "Did that thing look like a fucking bird to you, Dane?"

"I didn't see what it looked like."

She pulled down the shirt and shrugged. "It sure as hell didn't have feathers."

He decided he'd rather stop wondering than ask again.

11.

Hiking out Sunday evening, Dane felt a certain heaviness. That was normal, despite how much less they carried out than in. After lugging consumables like wine and liquor, nuts and vegetables, all they ever took home were clothes to machine wash and the odd piece of trash they couldn't burn or bury. Hikes back to the car on Sundays were always lighter, at least in terms of physical burden.

What he felt settling upon him was different kind of weight. A few steps short of following Carolyn into the tunnel-like opening where the path entered the trees, Dane's toe kicked something solid in the grass edging the trail. A partial glimpse reminded him of the stone disc he'd found buried, and since hidden to avoid questions.

Ahead, Carolyn continued into the trees.

Dane knelt, and was unsurprised to find something like what he'd guessed. Another artifact of carved stone. This too was encircled by symbols around the rim, but these surrounded a monstrous humanoid face.

"Care," he called ahead.

She kept walking, didn't look back. Either didn't hear, or didn't want to stop.

He was willing to show her, Dane reasoned, to share what he found. It wasn't his fault if she had no interest. He slipped the stone disc in his pocket, and hurried into the trees.

Secrets multiplied this way, every concealment growing upon prior, festering deceits. At some point a threshold was crossed, more hidden than shared. Every old lie interlocked with a thousand before it, an interdependent structure of deception. So much to protect. It was easier to offer further shadings, omit mention of complicated truths, than to try fitting them into existing patterns already agreed upon. What needed protecting grew larger, less stable.

With passing time, barriers grew higher, more numerous. To speak up, to explicate, was riskier than silence.

In his pocket, his hand found the object. Maybe some kind of ritual artifact. It seemed ancient, yet here it was, on the verge of a path he'd walked countless times before. What brought it to the surface now? If it had been dropped more recently, that would mean others nearby. The dark, occult face. Hard to deny the hint of something sinister.

"There!" Carolyn shouted. She'd stopped ahead, pointing off into the trees.

Dane caught up. "What?"

"Someone…"

He too strained to see. The sun was high, bright, but the forest here was dense. No hint of movement. No people. Just trees. "What do you see?"

She started walking again. "Nothing here."

Though Dane had seen nothing himself, he was less certain they were alone. Recently this place had revealed new aspects, hints of deeper significance, or resident intention. His first impulse was to fear such revelations, but he believed this was because life had made him soft, and too cautious. Growing up in a city, college in another city. Nothing had prepared him for the possibility of meanings deeper than office toil, with short breaks for television.

Time streamed past. Only the tug of its passing triggered awareness of all he'd missed. That revelation carried him here, delivered the impetus to open his eyes, start paying attention. He only had so much time. He could pack some living into the days he had left. Weren't they happier now, already? Carolyn was having trouble, but she'd catch up.

Such thoughts occupied him on the hike through the trees. He never questioned which way to go, even when he led and Carolyn followed.

On the drive home, Dane got lost. He followed streets that turned out wrong. He missed signs.

Carolyn barked at him in frustration and impatience.

"Help me, then," he implored. "Tell me which way."

She looked around, finally admitted she wasn't sure either.

He drove, drove until night. In darkness, the signs were less confusing. Certain patterns and angles became recognizable.

The neighborhood. Even when he found their street, Dane was unsure. He hesitated, idling outside the driveway, began to wonder if this was right after all.

12.

The deepest reward came after Dane had caught enough fish, completed all repairs and upkeep. Such a pleasure to slow down, to simply stand motionless, present amid such beauty. Beautiful surroundings, beyond anything he'd hoped for. Sun slipping behind mountains. Blue-gray sky shifting to burnt sienna.

Carolyn still hadn't returned.

Dane tried reading a while, until the words dimmed on the page. Feeling hungry, he searched upriver, across the grass, toward the trees. Downriver, though she never went that way.

At first, Carolyn had spent her days reading outdoors. After a while, maybe when she'd finished that stash of books, her routine changed. She began to wander, exploring for an hour, maybe two. More recently, she vanished all day.

Dane went inside for the lantern. He climbed to the ladder's second step and reached, right hand braced on the platform of the sleeping loft. His fingertips found an unexpected texture beneath Carolyn's side of the mattress. Some kind of packet in a Ziploc bag. Inside, a stack of photos.

They'd never had a camera here. Dane had never seen Carolyn with any snapshots, or albums, either here or back in town. No framed photos. She wasn't close to family, really. Just him.

Hard to make out in the failing light. The lantern didn't help much. Most of the images were dark, blurry.

A half-submerged face peering up from green liquid. Carolyn's eyes. Where was this taken?

Another, himself and Carolyn posing naked by the river. Dark clouds partly obscure the mountain. Texture of raindrops on the water. Dane had no memory of the scene, no idea who could've taken this. Segments of his own life, lost to him. If he hadn't seen the photo, how would he have ever known there was something he'd missed?

Another image. Carolyn standing nude, blurry as if in motion or vibrating.

The only part of her sharply defined was her hand resting on the shoulder of a taller figure covered in something like black fabric, too dark for the camera to capture. The shape appeared larger than Dane himself.

What else had vanished from his mind? Experiences lost, clouds drifted away. Lately he'd wondered about Carolyn's missing time, how forgetful she'd become. Tonight, still not home. Was he forgetting too? Like these photos—

Outside, splashing. Carolyn. Always she seemed to reappear when Dane began to focus on her absence. An aspect of marriage, maybe. Connectedness. Sensitivity to another's thoughts.

He wrapped the photos, returned them to their hiding place.

Outside, he found Carolyn meandering along the bank, naked and deeply tanned. Her dark red hair coiled in long springs, unchanged by their return to nature. Her body's voluptuous softness had been whittled down by time and exertion into a keener firmness, still entirely feminine. Dane found her more appealing than before. Strangely, it was her wandering in avoidance of him, which transformed her body in a way he found more desirable.

She brushed against him distractedly, like a cat greeting her owner by rubbing past his ankle. "I want breakfast," she said.

"You've been gone all day." He wondered if she was kidding. Hoped she was. "I ate without you, three times."

She turned. "You didn't wait?" Hand on hip, and a pout.

"Care, it's night. You stayed gone." Dane took her by the shoulders. "You want smoked trout?"

She started to argue, then seemed to notice the darkness and stopped herself. "No wonder I'm hungry." She drifted to the clothesline, unpinned a hanging sundress and stepped cleanly into it. The looseness of the dress clarified the change in her physique.

"Carolyn, every day you wander. Every day, come back naked."

"It's OK." Her eyes darted, searching for a response.

"You're always confused, like you forget where you went, and how long it's been."

"I'll just have some wine."

"Then you drink some wine, and everything's almost normal for an hour, and we sleep."

"That's not true." A hint of anger, readiness to fight. "This is the first time. Where's my clothes?"

"It's not the first." He handed her the glass.

"Too bad if you don't like it. You're the one who wanted to ditch out. What about what I want?" As she sipped, her eyes sharpened. "We met in college, Dane. Not the forest. The deal we made, you changed it."

"You wanted the big house, four fucking bathrooms. I helped you get—"

"We're not some frontier-born couple."

"—everything you asked for, and just wanted one thing for me."

"That would be different, but we—"

"Back home, Portland, weekdays, that's for you. Weekends, I get the forest."

"If it was only weekends," she said, "that would be fine."

"You keep losing track of yourself out here."

"Me? It's this place," she said, "it's taking us over."

He glared. "You're trying to wreck this life I made. This place. It's all that keeps me going."

She opened her mouth, said nothing.

Every angle, every tangent, had been argued a million times. Any possibility was exhausted. He wanted answers to arrive from, where? Probably she waited for the same rescue, or the wine to take hold, bring forgetting. He'd grown accustomed, knew it was the same for her. With every argument, to end in stalemate offered no solution, and did nothing to head off the next conflict. The only effect was to increase the length of mutually-acceptable silences.

Seconds. Minutes.

"I'm hungry," Carolyn said.

Dane headed toward the solar cooler, seeking anything to serve as distraction. At least a change of subject.

An idea surfaced. He turned to Carolyn, approached with a confused mixture of hatred and desire, each strengthening the other. Her dress, pulled on so casually, hung twisted across her body. One strap hung off her shoulder, the opposite breast exposed. Her skin seemed new. He reached out.

She moved closer, then fell with him in rapid escalation. Desire, animal aggression. Sudden sweat. Hard ground beneath them, wild prickling grass. Above, the sky.

Afterward, they went inside, feeling connected. They took what pleasures remained. Smoked fish, stale crackers. Tart berries Carolyn had gathered.

Dane remembered half a bottle of gin cooling in the river shallows. He went to retrieve it. Brief focus on stars, on sky.

Was it wrong to knowingly sidestep real problems, distracted by pleasures? No. It was the only way to survive. Maximize pleasure, minimize pain. Keep going. Forestall the inevitable.

They sipped gin, laughed, forgot arguments.

Back outside, they sat together beside the fire's sunlike core, like planets in orbit, beneath a sky spinning new stars while old ones fell.

Dane thought, This can still work.

Carolyn said softly, "This life can't go on."

Inside he ached, wanted to cry, to protest. How could any wound heal if endlessly torn open again, always in the same place?

Just keep going. The longer they remained, the harder Carolyn would find forcing a change.

13.

Connections reformed and unraveled, too transient to be dependable.

Days without words. At times, the universe itself seemed coldly indifferent. No greater separateness existed. The knowledge Carolyn too was alone gave no comfort.

At times they connected in ways almost tender, and unspeaking, held one another. They listened to the gauzy rush of clouds, the river's murmuring churn. Two bodies shared a single bloodstream. No distinction between one reaching out, one being touched. In some brief interludes, a semblance of closeness convinced Dane they would never again misunderstand, never argue.

All certainties were delusion. Everything was changeable.

When she removed herself again to a degree impossible to ignore, he voiced grievances. Bonds reformed and rebroken too many times could never be fixed. Being only two, they always drifted back into proximity.

Increasingly one or the other gave physical hurt. Harder than playful, yet short of true desire to injure. Slaps, inflicting sensation. Bites, escalating intensity. Then always grappling in the dust, or tumbling in the grass beside the water.

Legs pressed apart, lips pried open with tongue. Without conscious realization of the shift, what had begun as one thing became another. Always this resolution, this grunting and fever-mad denouement of sweat and anger. Hostility and pleasure, hard to distinguish.

This foundation kept them together. Always after, sleep reset all values to zero.

14.

Dane flicked the line upstream and followed the fly's drift.

Movement near the cabin drew his eye.

Sometimes Carolyn returned mid-day for something to eat. She always announced herself. This was different. Lately, she'd hinted at seeing people around. They never found anyone, never even saw tracks.

This time, Dane saw. A crouching, slinking shadow.

He dropped the pole and raced to the cabin door. As he rounded the corner, someone emerged. A shirtless boy tried to run past, wearing only brown pants, torn and ragged around the ankles. Dirty feet stained green from grass fields. Ribs and shoulder blades stood out sharply.

Dane seized his wrist and spun. The skeletal boy yipped, struggling wide-eyed in animal fear, free hand trying to stuff something in his pocket. Dane grabbed the boy's other wrist, shook it until he dropped smoked trout filets into the dirt.

Dane shoved him back. The kid fell, started crab-walking toward the grass.

"Stop!" Dane jumped on him, held him pinned. The kid's skin was greasy slick.

Footsteps coming around. Panic flashed, wondering if the kid wasn't alone. Without letting up, Dane twisted.

Carolyn, arriving clothed, for a change.

The boy cringed, tried turning his face into the ground, like a beaten dog.

Dane pulled the boy's face around, trying to get a look. "I caught him stealing food."

She stood over them. "Give him something. We have plenty."

"I'm not having this little wild animal thinking this is the place to come when he wants to steal food."

She lowered to one knee, touched Dane's shoulder, and half-hid behind him. "We have extra. We've got to head home."

"Home?" The boy's ragged voice was inflected in a sort of drawl. "Home, where?"

"Just hand over what he wants?" Dane's brow wrinkled. "That'll teach this rabid fucker not to steal?"

Carolyn leaned in as if she might examine the boy, and then turned to regard Dane, nose to nose. She seethed through gritted teeth. "Those times I was afraid, you said nobody was within twenty miles."

"I just went on errands for mama," the boy rasped. "Must'a lost myself is all."

"So your mama just sent you out for milk?" Dane asked. "Where's the nearest store?"

"Kept searchin', such long time." The boy's eyes flitted, looking for an ally. "Tryin'a find the milk."

"You've been watching us," Dane accused. "From our own land."

"Just try," the boy said. "Try'a go home. You'a end up like me. Nobody believe you, even when they'a lost the same."

"We go home every weekend," Dane said. "Leave, and come back again just fine. We park on the fire lane near Romar Quarry."

"Dane, don't tell him that!" Carolyn said.

"This place ain't a'meant for us. It for things a'run in treetops." The boy wrenched his face from Dane's grip to look sideways at Carolyn. "She know what I mean. You get a'losing track."

Carolyn's nails dug into Dane's shoulder. "Get off him now." She backed away, and softened her voice to address the boy. "We'll give you food if you go away."

The boy tried to nod, still gripped under the jaw. "Food now and more tomorrow. I'a help you find the way."

"No. If I give you food, go. Don't come sneaking around."

The boy considered. Finally nodded.

Carolyn went in the cabin and returned with an orange, half a loaf of dense brown bread, and a cold potato wrapped in fire-charred foil. She held out this offering, both hands outspread, mouth contorted as if at an unpleasant taste.

Dane stood, then the boy. Dust and dry grass coated the boy's back and shoulders.

The boy lunged at Carolyn, snatched the potato, and shied back. He peeled back the foil and choked down half in one feral bite.

"If I can't show a ways out…" He paused for another bite. "For sure I a'tell you some a'them's names."

"Names of what?" Dane asked.

"Night things here." The boy nodded at Carolyn. "She know."

Carolyn handed over the bread and the orange, and stepped back.

"You're scaring her," Dane said. "Take it. Go."

The boy swallowed the last of the potato, giving no indication he'd heard, then looked at the orange like he'd never seen one before. His mouth opened, as if he might take a bite, peel and all, then he reconsidered. His appraising squint made him appear very adult. In stature, he appeared younger than Dane's first guess. Maybe ten or eleven.

Dane clapped. "Move, now."

The boy stood rooted. Dane guided him by the shoulders around the cabin's perimeter and toward the river bank. The boy allowed himself to be led. When Dane took his hands away, the boy tried to circle back.

Dane blocked the way. "Go!" He gave the boy a shove.

Looking surprised, the boy took a couple steps.

Dane herded and nudged until the boy stood ankle-deep in the shallows. Upstream a bit, Dane took a small rock from the shallows. He aimed short but threw close enough to splash the boy, hoping to scare him downstream.

The boy stopped after two more steps, and Dane lobbed another rock. Instead of staying near shore, the boy kept backing into deeper water every time Dane lobbed a warning. The boy stood up to his chest. Dane chose a heavy rock, lobbed it two-handed from his chest like a shot put. When the splash startled the boy, this time his footing broke loose. He drifted, floating, hands raised to keep the orange and the bread out of the river.

Carolyn approached where Dane stood watching from the shore.

"What's wrong with you," Dane asked, "making him think he's welcome here?"

Carolyn's face tightened in angry irritation, then eased. "You're okay with no human contact. To you, everyone's a threat to be driven off. That's not human, Dane. We're social creatures. We help each other, if we can."

The boy was almost out of view. He drifted passively, giving no hint of trying to leave the river.

"No, you were right before," he said. "It's more dangerous out here than I could admit."

Downstream, the boy disappeared around the bend.

"The river's broader now." Dane felt by naming it a river, his conscious intention had manifested a change in the physical world. Stream had become river. The water sounded thick, rushing deep and vigorous over rocks, lapping the shore. A greater flow extended the river's reach, allowed it rise above what had once constrained it. The river subsumed the sandy soil at its margins, and washed it away.

"When did it get so deep?" Carolyn asked.

"Must be the thaw," Dane said. "Can that be right, spring already?"

In some aspects, this place was not precisely what he hoped, and never would be. In other ways, his hopes were exceeded. The most pleasing surprise was the degree to which the world was malleable to intentions. He might live forever, if reality could be shaped this way. The tangible, fortified by desires.

Even after the boy had gone beyond seeing, Dane stood wondering, dizzy with awe at how much had already changed.

15.

One hot and windless night, as Dane and Carolyn lay in the loft looking out through the window at the round moon, he drew the outlines of his theory.

"In earlier times," he said, "we could walk safely into the deepest, black heart of the forest, at midnight on a moonless night. That place now would seem to us perfectly dark, but then we would have been able to see. Our hearing and other senses also would have dilated to perceive the layers now hidden all around us. Everything's invisible now, but it's not gone. We've lost the senses we possessed. Not vision exactly. More like attunement, sensitivity to different energies. We were part of a connecting flow, of time being born, dying, being reborn again. Trees are aware. And the wind guides us with intentions, sometimes."

Carolyn leaned on one elbow, looking down into her wine.

"Before civilization, the greatest influence on people was the natural world. Not culture, not language, not neighbors. Long before television, the internet, even before newspapers, our minds were differently attuned. Eyes saw other wavelengths, different colors with lost names."

"It's normal, darkness causing fear," Carolyn said, visiting as always on nature's terrifying aspects. "Because we've always been scared of it, we collect into town or cities. Keep each other company."

"Dark is sacred," Dane insisted. "Drifting into towns, we focused on each other. We learned to fear solitude and darkness, but we don't have to."

"I know you don't actually believe that," Carolyn said.

"I do."

"Then why not hike into the forest without a lantern? There's no moon. Try having yourself a real primal experience."

He stood. "I will."

"Come on, Dane."

"I'm going to see what it's like, deep out there," he insisted. "Maybe the old senses will spark up." He stepped out the doorway into the hot night.

Carolyn stood. "I can't let you go alone." She picked up the lantern. "Not after I teased you into it."

"No lantern."

She hesitated, apparently considering arguing or recanting her offer, but left the lantern on the table.

Outside, Dane led them across the neighboring grass field, purposely avoiding the worn paths, high-stepping instead through deeper grass and tangled weeds.

Once in the trees, the going was even slower. He'd forgotten how rough the forest undergrowth used to be, having become accustomed to getting around on their own network of paths and trails. Past the forest's outer boundary, thinner undergrowth made for easier footing. Darkness clung thick, like a tangible obstruction on every side. Dane pressed outward, beyond the more familiar territory nearest their cabin. North was a direction they rarely ventured.

"Are you sure?" Carolyn asked.

Every tree clutched, moved beyond and left behind meant he'd penetrated the forest that much more deeply. These unfamiliar surroundings felt threatening. That was the whole point. Such pure, absolute darkness made the territory seem strange. If he went deep enough, some aspect of his senses might flicker awake. This atmosphere seemed resonant, the very spaces between trees vibrantly alive. So much time spent out in nature, and they'd only brushed the most superficial edge. Just a mile or two in a truly new direction might reveal land never walked by human feet.

Passing each tree, Dane felt the solidity of the trunk, rooted motionless to the ground at the same time the upper limbs strived toward the sky. His eyes cast up, he imagined the sparkling sensation to be innumerable silver stars glimmering in the gaps between trees.

"Look up." His eyes, so attuned, perceived the sky's dark canopy as velvet blue.

"New wavelengths," Carolyn intoned. "Forgotten colors."

She was seeing it too? Dane opened his mouth, eager to ask what it was like for her, only to stop himself. He realized she only meant to tease him about what he'd said earlier, in the cabin.

Carolyn nudged his shoulder, first with her hand, then cool metal. He turned, strained to see. She was a black shape, the same black as the backdrop of forest, yet standing apart from it. She held a subtly luminous metal flask in one hand, the cap in the other.

"Something I made." She sipped. "A concoction."

He accepted the flask, took a taste. The first sensation was the threaded opening, like a penny on the tongue. Then a surge of peppery heat and the spicy tingle of fermentation. Fumes heated his sinuses. "You made this?"

Her featureless outline nodded. "Been maturing quite a while. A bitters, technically. That's a liqueur of spices, roots and berries."

Dane took another eye-watering swig, exhaled, and handed back the flask. "Yow." The flavor had a complex, aged quality. Powerfully concentrated as a Laphroaig single malt, like distilled earth, moss and smoke, astringent on the tongue.

Carolyn screwed down the cap. "You like?"

"Yes. It's strange."

Incense overtones seemed to promise a visionary effect. If not hallucinations, at least a subtler alteration. Even before the drink, his world had felt strange. All within felt perfectly still, attuned to the without. Each infinitesimal moment extended in unhurried detachment from obligations. Dane was unsure what to name this sense of existing beyond reach. He used to believe the word to describe what he sought was Quiet, but that was wrong. This place was alive with sounds. Sometimes the rain tapped, a million impacts on all sides, different sonic characteristics where raindrops struck trees, grass, water, stone. Wind through the firs and pines, the call of birds. Morning deer bounding over the stream, half-weightless. This place never lacked sound.

They couldn't continue walking forever, heading away from their home. Rather than turn straight back, better to shift trajectory into a gradually narrowing curve. He could continue exploring, yet wind down like a spring, emerge downriver from their place and return along the river, upstream. Though they were somewhere they'd never been, part of Dane knew where they were. He envisioned a map, and saw their place on it.

Nobody could remain here unchanged. The transformation Dane had undergone was as profound as if he'd discovered he could breathe underwater. So much was new.

A downhill slope steepened. Gaps opened between the trees. This wasn't an emergence. They remained in the heart of the forest, deeper than ever.

Across the open space, more trees. Overhead, a lavender circle of sky. They were in a clearing.

A light sensation touched his face. Whiteness moved, like a firefly sweeping past.

"It's snow falling." Carolyn raised her palms, trying to catch fluttering white pinpoints.

"It's too hot."

"Then what?"

Dane shrugged. In another time, he might have been irritated by the mystery, troubled by not knowing. Stumbling through the unknown, he decided not to be afraid. He moved on, continuing their trajectory through the night forest.

16.

A scream brought Dane awake. He jolted upright, found himself alone in the cabin. The door stood open. Cold, misty dawn. Another scream outside, faint and distant.

She must be out beyond the clearing.

"Care?" he shouted. No answer. He climbed down from the loft.

Outside the ground was frosted white, slick and cold under bare feet. Over the hills beyond the river, sunrise hinted. The sky bled orange into the gray.

Dane turned back to face the trees, west and north. "Carolyn?" His shout echoed away.

He turned, ready to try another direction, when an answer came. Another scream, wordless and raw, from the broad field between him and the trees. He ventured in. The waist-high grass was punctuated by thick, wild tufts taller than himself.

"Where are you?" Dane shouted. As he passed one of these mounded growths, he spotted Carolyn in the near distance. Standing amid deep grass and weeds, she wailed in distress, looking down at something he couldn't see. He ran as best he could, diagonally through the field.

He came upon Carolyn at the edge of a broad flattened area, like part of a crop circle, where the field grass had been pressed cleanly down. He imagined a herd of elk or deer stopping here to sleep.

Dane's relief at having found Carolyn was offset by her obvious distress. If she noticed him, she gave no sign.

"Carolyn, what happened?" he asked. Though he'd seen emotional outbursts from her, this was new. "What's wrong?"

Despite the cold, she wore only a white T-shirt full of cuts or tears, and smeared with bloody handprints. Shivering, she rubbed her arms, spreading blood from many tiny cuts. In this state, she'd probably stumbled through blackberry vines and sliced herself up.

As if she'd noticed Dane for the first time, Carolyn pointed and gestured toward the flattened circle. She grasped Dane's hand, tugged him nearer. Though her attention mostly focused on the clearing, she kept glancing back over Dane's shoulder at the direction from which he'd come.

Her manic, dissociated affect was bizarre and frightening. Dane gripped her shoulders, brought her around to face him. "Carolyn!" His heart thudded inside his chest.

Her hyperventilation arrested with a gasp, as if the sight of Dane's face startled her. "You!"

He started to shake her gently, but realized she might be hurt. "You have to tell me what's wrong." He pulled her close, wrapped his arms around her.

Carolyn moaned, shaking her head. Such violent trembling, like a frightened animal. Despite so much blood, the cuts on her arms and legs looked superficial. The T-shirt was soaked red.

Dane backed up, giving her room. Something had terrified her. She reached down into the matted grass at her feet and snatched up something metal. It looked like a knife. She clutched it against her chest and ran past him, back toward the cabin.

Dane was able to catch up, but remained a few steps behind, not wanting her to feel threatened.

Back outside the cabin, she seemed confused. Maybe if he gave her some room, she'd calm down. Get her talking, find out what's wrong. Sometimes she got confused like this, but always came back to herself. This was worse than ever before. Carolyn seemed incapable of speech. If he couldn't help her pull it together, he'd have to get her dressed, help her through the forest to the car. Her doctor in Portland was at least forty miles away. Maybe there was an urgent care clinic in Sandy.

"Should we go inside?" he suggested. "You need to warm up."

As if a switch had turned off, Carolyn stopped shivering, climbed up on the picnic table and sat with her feet resting on the bench. This was encouraging, seeing her sit the way they often did at sunrise, surveying the stream and the fields with a glass of wine. The object she'd picked up in the field, she half-concealed between forearms crossed over her chest. Dane kept telling himself it wasn't a knife.

Shifting in agitation, Carolyn regarded him. Her face cycling between wariness, confusion and despair. She uncrossed her arms, dropped both hands to her sides. Dane saw clearly what she gripped in her right hand, sticky blood on the rainbow pearlescent handle. The ornamented hilt and blade were dull gold like tarnished bronze, the blade a foot long, thinner than a hunting knife, slightly tapered at the tip. The tarnished metal was speckled with dirt, as if newly unearthed after long burial. Carolyn extended her arm and made slow, distracted swipes.

Better be careful, Dane thought. She didn't seem overtly threatening, but she was so far removed from her usual self. The blade might be sharp. He sat back, out of range.

Carolyn's sobs began to ease. She wiped her tears and dropped the knife on the table. "I've been… trying…." She broke off, then started again. "Trying to talk to you." She managed to look at Dane, shook her head, and looked away again.

Dane scooted closer and took her hand. "Care, the knife. Where did you…" This time, it was he who trailed off, when he saw for the first time what Carolyn had been screaming about. His mind reeled, trying to deny the possible truth of what his eyes told him they saw.

17.

The rising sun revealed impossible devastation. Thousands of massive, ancient trees had been cleared overnight. At least a highway's width of land extended like an airport runway into the mist. Not a single fallen tree was left behind, no brush or debris, not even stumps. The dirt was perfectly smooth, scraped into a pristine, almost glossy-smooth plateau.

Mouth gaping, Dane extended a hand, pointing dumbly at what Carolyn had already seen. "What... I never heard—"

"You wouldn't wake up." Carolyn was calm now, quieted by his recognition. "I shook you, slapped your face, kept screaming your name. I thought you must be dead. So I was alone out here, all alone. So, I went out." Her mouth stretched into a grimace. "The sounds were so terrible, Dane. Like some end of the world movie. I felt so scared, couldn't see anything at all. It was so dark. Just the vibrating sounds. Roaring, tearing, and this awful rumble."

Dane climbed onto the tabletop, straining for a better view. The clearing almost paralleled their path toward the quarry and fire road where they always parked. It was like a clean and perfect line between themselves, and civilization. Beyond both side boundaries of the cleared strip, forest resumed untouched, lush and natural as ever before. It seemed impossible. How could anyone sleep through a procession of giant earth-moving machines? Yesterday there'd been no sounds of clearing or grading, no hint anything like this was coming.

He jumped down. "I need to see where this leads."

"Dane, no!" Carolyn snatched up the knife and leaped up. "We're not safe here. What more proof do you need? I went into that... darkness." Her face broke at this recollection of trauma. She showed her blood-smeared hands, indicated the cuts on her arms and torso. "This is what happened."

"And this knife." Dane extended his hand, palm up. "Where'd you get it?"

Lip jutting like a girl who didn't want to give up a toy, Carolyn shook her head. Suddenly then, as if something more important just occurred to her, she set the knife aside on the table, already forgotten. She lifted her shirt front, pulled it up over her breasts, to reveal at the center of her belly a gaping fist-sized wound. White flesh ended in a perfect, clean edge. Within the cavity where her organs should be resided a dark cluster the size of an apple, like a mass of nuts and wood chips bound up in dark molasses or umber pitch. The sphere glistened like lacquer.

Dane looked at her face, then back down. This had to be a dream. What he saw just couldn't be true. With each inhalation, Carolyn trembled. Goosebumps on her breasts, and the reaction of her nipples to the morning cold, convinced Dane he was still awake. This really was the daylight world. Not a dream. He had to accept some mysteries were true. Lately, so many confusing adjustments.

He knelt closer, looked inside her. Something cancerous, necrotic? Maybe she'd been driven mad by illness, and tried to cut it out. The scent wasn't what he expected. Not sickness or rot, but a fragrance reminiscent of autumn, of pumpkin spice and fermented cider and orange mounds of fallen leaves disintegrating in the grass. The fibrous mass inside her, which closer up looked like pine cone seeds bound together with black pitch, smelled sticky sweet and alcoholic. Familiar. The spiced liqueur Carolyn had made.

He extended his fingers and slowly reached, afraid to tear her open wider. When he hesitated, she grasped his hand.

"What are you…" he began. "Carolyn, I won't—"

She squeezed hard, as if trying to crush his bones. "Feel it." She forced his hand in. The opening seemed to expand to encompass him.

The slick mass in her belly was hot, seething with tiny movements, vibrant with life as a cluster of insects. A tiny rattling, chittering sound. "It's like…" He trailed off. *A new form of life*, he wanted to say. The sensation was unprecedented, too foreign to comprehend. He'd never touched or even seen anything like it.

Her eyes fixed him. When she spoke, her tone was deadly serious. "I want you to cut it out."

"Wait." Dane looked away. He wanted to evade.

"Now!" Her free hand reached, snatched up the knife.

He trembled in panic. "Wait! How did this happen?"

She yanked, and his hand came free of her gut with a slurp. She slapped the knife handle into his glistening palm. "Dane, do this for me." A sob shook her. "Cut it out!"

"We have to…" He tried to think, to imagine alternatives. "You have to tell me what's really going on."

She glared at him hard, then looked away. "I've been eating seeds I found. I liked how they made me feel." She smiled, and then her face darkened. "Dreamy, like I used to get from wine. Like the difference between a bad day and a good one."

"How long—"

"Does it matter? Dane, this is why I kept secrets. You always want me to justify everything."

"That's not true," Dane said. Of course, she was right.

"Everything has to be the way you decide. Just… at least help me."

He tested the blade with his thumb. Deadly sharp. Despite appearances, this wasn't some dug-up relic. Such a honed edge wanted to cut.

Leaning close, he confronted her opening, at once a tumorous disfigurement and a beautiful, an almost sculptural arrangement which fit perfectly within her as if by design. So fragrant. He imagined the taste of it. Sweet.

Dane extended the blade.

A flood of memories. Wreathes made from pine cones, tree trunks dripping pitch. Halloween spice, cider hot enough to burn the tongue. Rum cake with sugar and cinnamon.

He delved inside her, and cut.

Carolyn screamed. His hand twitched in hesitation, as he tried to interpret her response. Not pain or torment, but a cry of letting go, almost like childbirth. Relinquishing. He cut where sticky seeds joined flesh. No blood, just that fragrant, molasses-dark pitch. Withdrawing his hand, he wanted to taste his fingers. She was watching.

As soon as he removed the cluster of seeds, it ceased trembling. Quickly it began to cool. So unmoving, it no longer seemed a living thing. The slick coating, drying, became tacky.

Breathing quietly now, Carolyn pulled down her shirt and reclined on the tabletop.

Dane looked for someplace to dig. "Always burying, here."

A fresh place, apart from prior holes, along the edge of the clearing.

He returned to find Carolyn's eyes closed, hands covering her shirt front. No signs of trauma, just the dried smears of blood she'd had when he found her in the field. Her chest rose and fell, the slow breathing of sleep. Herself again.

Concerned, Dane sat next to her. Would she recover?

She looked up, smiled slightly and sat up.

"You still have a wound," he began. "We should—"

She snatched the knife from his hand.

"Put that down," he said slowly.

She stood. "No, I'll hold onto it." Her voice was flat, with none of the earlier strain. "Until you tell me we're getting out of here."

"Carolyn." Dane stood, backed off a little. Slowly, he ventured a reaching hand.

She screamed an angry warning.

He knew she wouldn't hurt him. To be sure, he took another step back toward the river, kept going, looking for an angle to take the knife. She advanced, blade arm extended, body angled sideways. He remembered the girl he'd met, a nineteen-year-old champion on the University fencing team. How different—

She lunged, forward knee bent, arm extended.

Dane contorted, angling his torso away from the blade. "What are you doing?" Breathing hard now, fully alert. No longer amused at her knife play, just angry, confused. She'd seemed to be kidding. Just minutes ago, he'd done what she'd asked. He helped her. Now he'd have to take the knife away. Dane measured what it would take. Could he strike quickly, grab her wrist?

Maybe she was just sending a message, letting him know she was serious about leaving. She lunged again, her expression so relaxed, lacking any outward hostility.

Dane was unconcerned until he felt the blade cut through his shirt and bite his chest. He yelped before he realized what had happened. "What are you..."

His fingers came away from the wound bloody. He pulled up his shirt to reveal a belly wound a hand wide, mostly a shallow parting of pink dermis and epidermis, but in the center, a deeper slashing. Where these layers were penetrated, pulpy subcutaneous fat pushed up like blood-seeping cottage cheese.

Carolyn looked unsure, yet still held the knife extended. Her face gave no hint what she intended. With her free hand, she flicked a strand of curly red hair from her eyes.

Dane backed up until he found the cool of the shallow water. His feet penetrated soft, muddy sand. He remembered the boy, how he'd backed him into the river just the same. He kept waiting for Carolyn to stop, to apologize. If not that, then to advance again. Nothing. No indication. Slowly she followed him into the water.

Standing knee-deep, he abruptly lunged, struck Carolyn's wrist. He expected her to evade, to cut him again. The knife, loosely held now, fell loose, dropped into the shallows and clinked off a submerged rock.

Dane wrapped his arms around Carolyn and clutched her to himself. Arms pinned to her sides, she struggled, trying to get loose. He lifted, raised her so her toes touched nothing but water, splashing the surface as he carried her out deeper. The cold flow rose around them. Where their bodies pressed together, he felt raw stinging. Her own wound, in almost the same place as his, was much worse. She gave no indication of feeling pain. Even now, he wondered what she felt in that vacant, bloodless hollow. How could he have failed to notice, before now?

Her growl in his ear built to a shriek of emotional release. Then quiet, her face pressed against his cheek.

"I'm setting you down," Dane said.

Her feet fluttered, and then she stood in thigh-deep water, one hand on his arm for balance.

"Dane, you're hurt." She looked confused. At least she sounded like herself again. "What happened?"

His fingertips felt the cut through his wet shirt, then reached up under. Pain burned. Fresh blood trickled. He was afraid to look again.

Carolyn grasped him to herself, clutched him so tightly he flinched at the pain. She must be suffering too. They wobbled, efforts at mutual support working at cross-purposes, until they fell sideways together into the water.

The cold stream surged into Dane's mouth. Choking, he turned and knelt.

Already Carolyn stood, dripping. She reached down into the water, and came up with the knife.

So quickly, trust turned to fear, and back again. "Not again. Please." Dane raised both hands, palms forward.

As if remembering, Carolyn's face contorted, and she broke into new tears. She handed Dane the knife, handle first.

"We'll be OK now." Even holding the knife, he was afraid.

"No. It's too late." She shook her head, covered her face with both hands.

Dane felt ashamed. She'd suffered so much, finally brought to this. He broke down, eyes burning. Tears came. How could he let her slip so far, leave his wife completely on her own, adrift? Many times he'd held himself blameless for her pain, told himself he didn't understand why she was unhappy. He'd made this place everything. The cabin, the river and trees. Those had been the entire focus of his desire.

Dane embraced Carolyn, mindful of both their wounds.

The sun stood high and warm. Mist burned away, all illusion stripped, the landscape stood nakedly revealed. Dane had come seeking mental quietude, some respite from life's nagging overhead. In this place among the trees, he'd tried to sever connections to a litany of demands, expectations imposed from within and without. His head still rattled with the accumulation of a million trinkets he never needed, no longer desired. There was no giving these away.

Cautiously he led Carolyn from the water. Together they found the shore. She knelt on the firmer sand away from the riverbank, then reclined on her side. Now that most of the blood had washed away, she looked more cold and tired than wounded. As if she only needed sleep.

Dane rested beside her, watching her face. His fingertips traced her arm. Just a few tiny cuts. He had too many questions, so asked none.

So still, Carolyn appeared already asleep. She surprised him by speaking. "No more fighting." Her long fingers, now river clean, went to the corners of her eyes. They wiped away the last of her tears. "Please, no more. I just want to go."

Dane clutched her, feeling bitterly aware just how alone they were. Two together, in a rough land far from streets, beneath an expansive, gold-shifting sky.

"I'll take you back." He closed his eyes. "Back to your life. Just rest a minute. Then we'll go home."

18.

Dane woke face down in crusty sand, Carolyn beside him, one arm draped over his back. As he turned, her hand dragged across his wound. He winced at the pain. The front of his shirt was heavy with blood thick as pudding.

Remembering Carolyn's injury, he gently lifted the front of her T-shirt, wincing in anticipation. He was shocked to find no wound, no opening at all. Just a flat surface, skin scraped raw and bloody, possibly infected. His fingers still recalled the slick-hot feeling of cutting loose that vibrant, living lump. No trace remained of what had happened.

A glance upriver told him not all this morning's memories were imagined. The broad strip of forest remained stripped bare of trees. That seemed more unbelievable, a greater transgression, than whatever had come from Carolyn's belly. His memory of the morning was full of contradictions. This beloved place was falling apart. Carolyn wanted to go. Maybe that was for the best. Dane stood, trying not to disturb her.

The sun had advanced beyond mid-day, yet not quite as far as evening.

He recognized it had been irresponsible to ignore his wife's cumulative distress. Marriage meant an obligation to help each other. He had to do everything he could to keep her safe, and as fulfilled as possible. Too self-focused, centered too much on his own desires, Dane had managed to convince himself she was merely forgetful, just harmlessly wandering on her own. Things had degenerated too far. By the time he'd recognized trouble, it was too serious to ignore.

Now he'd said the words, made the promise. They had to return home. Had to make it work.

Dane could rededicate himself to the other life, focus again on long-neglected priorities. Carolyn always said if Dane displayed half as much determination at work as he showed building the cabin, he'd make Vice-President in no time. The problem was, being VP was never something he wanted. She always persisted, as if the idea would eventually take hold if he heard it often enough. Maybe there were elements of truth in her suggestion. Certainly a man capable of building all this out of raw land could rework a suburban home and an office career into some tolerable shape.

Carolyn murmured, stirring. He waited for her eyes to open, expecting the question. Are we still going?

She didn't ask, just stood. "I'll pack a few things." She started toward the cabin.

Dane lifted his shirt. Dark, thickened blood crusted over the wound, concealing the gory opening in the flesh. Probably needed stitches, though. He followed Carolyn inside, and as she stuffed items into her day pack, he found the toolbox and fished out a padlock.

"Out here, we never need locks," she said. "You told me."

"Who knows when we'll be back?" He slung his own pack over one shoulder, thinking how worn and dirty it looked in high sunlight, and then slipped the lock through the door latch.

Their departure felt different from all before. Hiking was always comfortable, natural. Today, both moved slowly, stiffly. This Dane attributed to their injuries, the emotional aftermath of wrenching confrontation, added to the shock of awakening to find the forest vandalized.

Dane started out following that gap in the trees, trying to get a better look, though the direction diverged slightly from the optimal line toward their parking place. By daylight, this appeared less like road-building or construction, more like the angry eradication of a strip of forest by some titan-sized scraper. A whole swatch of varied life, of trees and soil, ferns and grass, had been abruptly erased. What remained was flat soil, lacking any trace of what had lived there before.

After at least a mile, seeing no variation ahead, Dane scrambled up the bank and angled through the trees toward Romar Quarry fire lane. It seemed they'd detoured farther off the path than he'd realized. He kept thinking, here we are, believing he recognized the way, only to realize the ground was too overgrown to be their trail. They pushed on, trusting in the direction of the sun. Progress was slow in the heavy brush. Hours passed in quiet exhaustion, high-stepping through thick, weedy growth. While Dane had first tried to enjoy the meditative silence, this evolved into full avoidance of the reality of fear creeping up on him. The nagging possibility, they might be lost. Would his relationship with Carolyn ever recover? He worried about her, both her physical and mental wellbeing. The world seemed to have shifted, a rug pulled out from beneath them. All was doubt, worry, fear. He considered admitting he was lost, asking Carolyn which way she thought they should go. If he did, probably she'd accuse him of pretending, of not wanting to go home.

Two trees sagged together into an arch. Dane brightened at this familiar formation, despite plodding fatigue. What he thought of as the A-frame trees were less than a mile from their destination.

Though neither of them spoke, when they stumbled into the humped gravel of the fire road, not far from the yellow bolted gate, Dane could feel Carolyn's relief was as great as his own. As always, their Audi remained sheltered behind a broad, slumping tree. The SUV was almost unrecognizable, dark green paint thickly layered with dust, and an array of words and symbols in Day-Glo yellow spray-paint. One side was shot up with rust-ringed bullet holes, and a fire set on the hood had burned the paint away to reveal bare metal. The side and rear windows were smashed out. Only the windshield and moonroof were intact, though marked with yellow graffiti.

Carolyn's door wouldn't budge, so she went through the driver's side before Dane, and slid across. The ignition gave no response at first, then the engine lurched, hesitated, heaved again, and silenced. Another turn of the key. Nothing.

"Please get us home," Carolyn pleaded, obviously exhausted.

The car had never been any trouble before. Dane tried the ignition again. The engine gasped, hesitated, and finally roared smoothly to life. The Audi rolled up from the shallow ditch onto the gravel.

19.

Dane stopped at a T-intersection, feeling stuck. Two choices. The roads within Mt. Hood National Forest had passed easily, feeling familiar. Nearing Troutdale, on Portland's outermost edge, Dane first perceived his own mind fogged by confusion, his nerves jittering with panic.

"That way." Carolyn pointed left, across the bridge.

"This is the Sandy River?" Dane asked.

Should they keep going? They always crossed the river here, he was sure. This was the back entrance to Troutdale. He started, hesitated and stopped again, blocking the outbound lane of the historic highway as well as the narrow bridge's east end.

"What's wrong?" Carolyn asked.

Which direction? He scanned for road signs, some kind of help. Cross the river, or continue along? "It's like I've read about this place, heard it described, but never seen it."

"Isn't it this way?" Carolyn asked. "How could you forget?"

"Do you remember?" he asked.

She turned away as if something beyond the window caught her attention.

He chose at random, drove past houses, turned corners.

"Remember the brick house, that first corner," she said after a while. "That's our neighborhood."

"We're nowhere close. Have to get in the vicinity first."

"We can't spend our lives in between," she said.

Every intersection meant a new decision. He couldn't keep stopping, second-guessing. Outside the car, people stood outside houses, on sidewalks. Dane considered asking directions, but when he tried to formulate the question in his mind, he couldn't imagine how to describe where he wanted to go. Better to stop worrying, drive without intention. He trusted his subconscious to find the way.

"Body knows better than mind," he said.

Dane was as much as passenger as Carolyn, both taking a ride. Through suburbs, along highways, down streets like Burnside and Foster. Numbered streets, markets and strip malls. So many buildings, signs. None familiar.

Then, a neighborhood. A brick house at the front corner. The development seemed familiar, yet changed.

"Is this it?" Carolyn asked.

"Yes!" Dane pointed.

The Wood Gardens monument sign. Jefferson Street's uphill corkscrew. The little park, always vacant. No lights, no cars. Strangely faded. Many houses abandoned, some gutted by fire or vandalized, many overgrown with purple vines. The crest of the hill. Left turn onto Suffolk.

Their house, charred and windowless, dripped with decay. In the yard stood a faded and weathered realtor's sign on a post.

Dane parked, stumbled out dazed. "How could this…"

Carolyn ran up to his side. "It says foreclosure."

"That's not possible," he said. "If we missed a payment—"

The very structure tilted, like a rotting barn about to fall. Paint flaked away to reveal naked wood, not the living golden boards from which he'd built the cabin, but weathered gray, warped and splitting along the grain. This was a dead house, penetrated by wind and rain until the rottenness inside had bloomed outward like a flower of decay.

"Should we go inside?" Carolyn asked.

Dane stepped through the doorless entryway and led Carolyn up the creaking stairs. None of the steps were missing, but most flexed weakly, on the verge of breaking through.

The master bedroom furniture was all stolen, broken or burned. Clothing in the closet and books on the shelves dripped, grotesquely swollen and black with mold.

Nothing left, at least nothing he recognized.

Carolyn ventured into the corner. The bed was a collapsed pile of disrupted springs connected by a web of haywire cords. Sodden half-burned scraps of fabric intermingled with leaves, mounded in corners, fading into the same black mold growing up the walls, reaching for the ceiling. Their room, overtaken by raw, violent nature. Every surface made unlivable, stained and rotten. Everywhere, heaps of unnamable decay, their own deteriorated possessions intermingled with dead leaves flown through missing windows, and those arterial purple vines.

"All lost." Carolyn cried over the bed. "Nothing's left."

She crossed the room, retreated into the corner farthest from the open front windows. There she knelt in the deepest pile of half-dry leaves, delving in as if trying to shelter or hide. Dane followed, huddled beside her. Their bodies fell into a kind of accordance. Stunned quiet, hearts pounding into forgetfulness, they lay still.

In darkness, despite tension and chill unease, Dane whispered, "Try to sleep."

Then a glimmer, wakefulness. Dane rose, back aching, stiff. A different light. Dawn.

At the big window looking over the street, Carolyn stood, feet amid bent mini-blind slats, fallen into a mad tangle of white metal. Her head turned at the sound of his movement. "We just need someplace safe." Her teeth chattered.

Dane nodded. "Pick a place, then we'll stay." He stood, stepped stiffly toward her.

She approached, met him halfway, holding something extended. A wine bottle. "I found this."

He was about to say he didn't feel like drinking. Her expression stopped him. The dark green bottle looked familiar. Salix Pinot Gris, round label, silver like a coin. "Why do I—"

"That night you made fish stew, laced with those mushrooms. That was the first time I bought this wine."

He nodded. "I threw the bottle in the river."

"This specific bottle, I only bought once. I remember."

Could memory be trusted? The bottle was distinctive, not so much the dark green tapered glass, but the label. Circular, silver, imprinted with the image of a bird, a swallow in flight. He'd lobbed it into the river. Had never thrown anything in the river, before or since. "You're saying it's the same bottle?" he asked. "What, I threw it in the river, and it floated here?"

Her eyes held him motionless. "Everything's changing, since that first night." She thrust the bottle into his hands.

"The river flows the other direction," he said. "Away from Portland. And that's forty miles."

"I don't care. Outside, the world changed." Her face was calm. "Inside, we did."

"It makes no sense," Dane protested. "If it were true, what would that mean? Would it make you want to go back, again? Or stay here?" And what did he want? What place was a better fit? Civilization turned wild, or a forest cut away, a bit a time? At first he'd pulled her one direction, while she pulled the opposite. He'd thought they could have both. They had to choose.

Carolyn's face was drawn and pale. She looked older than Dane had ever seen.

He dropped the bottle. Took her hand, held it.

"The trees," she said.

He was going to suggest the same, if she hadn't.

20.

The explosive burst of tires brought Dane to awareness. He fought to regain control, too late. The vehicle skewed sideways, off the loose gravel shoulder, and crashed with a metal shearing thud, nose down in a drainage culvert. Carolyn flew out of her seat. Her head snapped the rear-view mirror loose from the windshield, and she slumped heavily back. The car ticked.

"How'd we…" Dane trailed off. How had they gotten there, he meant to ask. Something was missing. Sprocket holes torn loose, too many jump-cuts past important scenes he needed to remember. The road looked familiar. A lightning-split tree sagged halfway down to the road, a hundred feet away. Not far from their usual parking place. The fire road.

"We're back," Carolyn said.

"I was trying to drive us home." Dane struggled to make sense of disjointed events, to discern connections. Like memories from a fever dream. "Only we're facing the wrong way."

"This is home, remember?" Carolyn touched a trickling forehead contusion, examined bloody fingertips. "The house isn't ours any more. This is all that's left."

The ticking engine slowed, skipped beats.

Dane's door was jammed against the ditch wall. He contorted through the glassless window frame. Standing on the hood, he helped Carolyn out.

"I remember now," he said. "The cabin I made. The forest."

No choice but to hike. Try to find the way.

Gaps between trees opened, enticed passage, only to close again, blocking the way. The forest seemed to shimmer, to expand and contract. Trails narrowed, seemed to press in, then abruptly opened upon white, brittle sky. The ground became a jagged spill of freshly shattered rock, dynamited remnants of some vanished mountain. This gave way to an area of intense burn, all flora eradicated. Only black stubs remained. Amid such featureless areas as these were more dramatic constructs, constrained to geometrically perfect segregations. Circles of asphalt, square drainage pits filled with brown-black liquid giving off waves of heat. Between such features, the land opened, became more wild again. Familiar pines, fields of beargrass and wildflower. This land they'd known so intimately seemed changed, both in general shape and in details of plant, rock and soil.

"I keep thinking," Carolyn said, walking behind. "What if we're dead?"

"We're talking to each other. That proves we're alive."

"Everything seems fine now. But remember the times you wouldn't wake up? Even when I shook you, and screamed."

"I'm awake now. We both are."

"Maybe it's hell. We're stuck, trying to leave." She looked up. "End up floating forever, near the tips of trees."

"No," Dane said. "We just lost track of things. We were stuck a while, like a record skipping." He was feeling the difficulty of the walk. Heart pounding, weak in the knees. He didn't want Carolyn to know how much trouble he was having. Every muscle ached, every joint. The chest wound wasn't the worst, in fact it already seemed to have faded into history. What about Carolyn? How was she able to hike, after he'd cut her open, only yesterday?

Over wet, spongy moss, every step a conscious effort. On both sides dewy ferns waved, taller than a man's head. Ancient firs strained skyward, vying for a taste of light. Dane was looking up, trying to see the sky, when a sudden grassy downslope tumbled him out of the trees. He slid sidelong into a perfectly smooth plateau, dry and unnaturally flat and linear as a ten-lane highway.

This at least he recognized.

Behind him, Carolyn approached the drop-off.

"Careful," he shouted. "It falls away."

His hip screeched painfully as he rose to help her down.

The featureless corridor extended ahead, roughly toward the cabin, as well as backward in very nearly the direction from which they'd come. Dane hoped they'd found the way they'd come this morning. No, yesterday. When was it?

After a while, he noticed at frequent intervals, narrower street-like pathways branching away. This wasn't the single, straight runway he'd imagined, but more like a grid. Each offshoot, precursors to lesser streets, stretching off the broad, central spine. Each corner, where digressions split away, was marked by a post. All these lacked any sign.

Carolyn said something behind him. At that moment, his attention flitted to a bird in a diving trajectory. Dane ducked, raising a hand to fend off the bird, but felt nothing. He looked up, expecting to see the bird winging off into the trees, but couldn't find it. He remembered that first night inside the cabin. Like the confused swallow, he felt lost. If everything was always changing, how could he know which direction to head? Only the momentum he'd carried out of the forest bore him on, despite aching muscles and a mind fogged with fatigue.

The trees to both left and right thinned, growing smaller and too sparse to be considered a forest. Along both sides of what Dane had come to think of as a dirt highway were elevated fields, intermittently mounded with tangled grass and vines, some of the heaps dry and partially burned, others damp and rotten. Jagged shards of pale wood protruded from humps of mounded dirt and rock, detritus of leaves and stripped limbs of trees littering the forest's edge. Further on, forming a barrier against the deep and now-distant forest, a row of dead trees stood inverted, trunks jammed into the ground, roots skyward. Water collected into irregular stagnant green pools. Still no sign of the river Dane had hoped would guide him to the cabin.

The land was profoundly changed, almost unrecognizable. His heart thudded weakly under cumulative panic and disorientation. He sought any landmark, any reference point at all. Mt. Hood was visible even from their back yard in Portland, but from here, no sign of it. No mountains in any direction.

Dane could only press on, ignore the dizziness.

Finally he discovered, to the right side of the cleared space, what had become of the river. A chalk-white trench amid rounded rocks, an alkaline scar upon fields overrun with brown weeds. He turned back, excited to show Carolyn what he'd found.

She wasn't behind him. As far as he could see, both directions, even up on the bank, there was no sign of her.

"Care?" he shouted.

Irritation flared, certainty she'd followed her own path, left him to drift. He shouldn't be angry. Hours had passed since he'd talked to her, lost in his own things. She must've thought better, split off and followed her own path. That would be nothing new. They'd both promised things would change, but he couldn't blame her for falling back on old patterns. Certainly she knew these fields well enough. She'd probably already found the cabin, and waited there to tease him for falling behind.

21.

As he walked, Dane was surprised at how keenly he felt his solitude. He tried to keep in mind he was walking toward Carolyn, not abandoning her behind. So much of their time lately had been separate, Carolyn reading or wandering while he fished or worked. Now her absence pained him, not only out of worry, but selfish concerns as well. What if her disappearance hinted at some threat to both of them?

Following the line of the dry river grew difficult. The rocky bed sunk beneath chalky soil shot through with grass and thorny weeds. Seeing a rise ahead, Dane thought he might have found Carolyn's sunbathing windbreak. What he found instead was a standalone, crumbling stairway, made of concrete and river rock, leading up to nothing. He climbed to the uneven platform, steadied himself, and looked around. No movement, no sign of any path.

Feeling hopeless, he descended. Just then, the wind whipped up, pulling at his clothes. It seemed to impel him onward, in a direction he still thought of as downstream. As dehydrated as the lost river, and so pained with fatigue that he walked hunched and limping, he gave in to what he imagined must be a trick. He would follow the wind's guidance.

Daylight failing into dusk, Dane stumbled past a rectangular pad of deeply cracked asphalt which formed the base for an installation of playground equipment sufficient for a school full of children. Stainless steel posts supported structures lacquered green and yellow. Beyond the swings, whose chains swayed silently in the wind, he saw his cabin.

At first Dane didn't recognize it, took it instead for someone's abandoned shack. The grass perimeter was overrun with thick weeds, the wood exterior weathered gray, both windows glassless. The door squeaked half-open on rust-shot hinges. He found the interior overrun by withered leavings of nature's cycle of growth and decay. From spongy floorboards grew a vein-like tangle of dark vines. In the loft, some animal had made its den. No longer Dane and Carolyn's bed, but a beast's abode of shredded hides and varied skeletons, some dry, some meat-flecked, others stretched with drum-like yellow skin. An accumulated perimeter of gnawed, leafless tree limbs formed a giant nest, upon which a desiccated creature sprawled. It resembled a great cat, hairless and grey-skinned, oversized skull jutting serrated tusks, massive rear legs jointed the wrong way. This had to be an assemblage of found parts. The bones of several creatures, someone's idea of an affront to this abandoned home.

He ascended to the ladder's second rung and reached beneath the mattress's disintegrated base. The plastic-wrapped cache of photographs remained where he'd left it, how long ago? It seemed forever. He'd always meant to ask Carolyn to explain.

The packet, thicker now, contained images he hadn't seen.

Two men, faces covered with dark handkerchiefs, stood by a deformed trophy animal hanging inverted from a rope.

A clear snapshot of Carolyn reclining nude and smiling on a steep fall of jagged rocks, glossy black as obsidian.

A burlap-swaddled baby, face and shoulders crisscrossed with angry scratches.

Dane himself, reaching into the slit belly of a large animal, oozing tarry blood. No memory of this, or any others.

Most were abstract, lacking recognizable pictorial content, yet shimmering with a vibration of memory. Such vague recollections were accompanied by hallucinatory sounds, smells. Echoes of meaning, just beyond reach, sufficient to terrify.

The last photo, Dane and Carolyn posing shoulder to shoulder, naked before the river. Faces, much older.

Who'd taken the photos?

He remembered her absence. "Care," he whispered. He went to the door, alert for sounds of her. The transformation outside disturbed him. So foreign. Nothing made any sense. Upturned trees in a fence-like row. Miles of stripped land, half-developed, yet vacant. Concrete beginnings for absent houses, unmade neighborhoods, invisible schools. The outline of a world, without content filled in.

"Carolyn!" No movement, no sounds. Not even an echo.

Between the graded landscape and the forest, the grass field remained as it was, perhaps slightly overgrown. There his eyes drifted, saw movement. A shape, hiding behind a clump. Dane ventured in. As he neared, the human silhouette peeked out. Not Carolyn. Someone taller. As if they'd seen Dane, they crouched back. Adrenaline surged, enough to overwhelm fatigue. He ran, trying to curve around, gain an angle on the hiding figure. His foot caught on uneven rocks concealed in grass. He stumbled, stopped. Not just a few rocks, but a mound. Someone made this.

Behind the clumped grass, the figure stood, moved into view. Not Carolyn. A thin boy, the food thief. Older now.

Without thinking, Dane knelt, picked up a rock to throw. He stopped, frozen by what he saw beneath him, amid the smooth gray stones from the river. At one end of the mound, a rectangle of wood, polished. Carolyn's name carved into it.

He didn't understand. Who would put Carolyn's name here?

The abandoning sun left only a rim of antique orange above the flat horizon, overwhelmed by a broader lightless sky.

Why hadn't he found her?

He looked up. The boy stood motionless, nearer than before.

Dane took up the board, traced fingertips through indented letters. Beneath the board hid the long-bladed knife. The rainbow metal handle still shone.

He'd missed something. Time passed, more than he realized. Nothing left of all that had fled. He looked back, tried to measure. Impossible to count what he'd seen.

The boy stood just beyond arm's reach. Still ragged and dirty, but now taller than Dane. Broad in the chest. Not a boy.

"We don't have any food to give," Dane said.

The other approached in timid half-steps until he knelt next to Dane. He took the wooden sign from Dane's hands, straightened the disturbed stones, and replaced the sign where Dane had found it, first picking up the blade. He made a small, careful adjustment to the angle at which the board rested.

This was a burial mound.

The other was an adult man, Dane now saw. He looked Dane in the eye and offered the knife, handle first.

Without stopping to think whether he wanted the knife, Dane accepted. He didn't need knives, though. He needed to remember where he'd lost Carolyn. The last thing he remembered, he was cutting sickness out of her belly. There was something about returning to the city. So much had happened in the short time since they'd first come here.

His plan, seeking for something indeterminate.

A breath of nature, maybe. He never wanted to cut loose from everything. Maybe he had.

No matter what, everything fled, especially time.

The man picked up a flat stone disc from among the others. Dane hadn't noticed it before. It was smooth, like the rest, but flat. When Dane accepted the offered stone, his fingers discerned markings in the surface. The shapes were too faint to read in the dark, but he could almost read them by touch.

The man stood and moved very slowly in the direction of the cabin.

Dane remained alone at his wife's grave, chilled by the black air. Breathing it in.

Soon he became aware of light flickering. The other man had built a fire in the pit outside the old cabin. He sat on top of the picnic table.

Dane approached, more easily now that there was light. Tall trees made a jagged horizon, black against near-black. The sky's expanse deepened to reveal millions of spinning stars, seeming to vibrate brilliance against pitch black infinity. His eyes believed there was little difference to see, between day and night.

Nearing the radiant fire, Dane shivered. As he held out hands to the warmth, he realized he still grasped the stone disc. Turning it against the fire light revealed perimeter lettering, like a coin. The central image was a swallow in flight.

The first night. He remembered that, sharp as yesterday. The swallow had swooped in, just as he presented the cabin to Carolyn. Found itself trapped, confined where it had expected wide open air. Dane wanted escape, even still. Where to, now?

The words around the stone's edge finally made sense. He felt the words with fingertips as much as he saw them with eyes.

"While you look away, the stream is moving past." Dane's voice sounded strange, as if he hadn't spoken in a long time.

In this inconstant light, the cabin appeared new. As far as the firelight extended, everything remained just like before.

Squatting barefoot in the packed dirt, Dane set the stone aside, freeing both hands for that most primal human gesture. Palms up, he absorbed the fire's heat. His skin looked ancient, spotted and wrinkled. White crepe over a network of purple and blue. Dane wanted to see his own face, to see if he was still himself. He had no mirror.

He looked up, caught the boy watching, with Carolyn's eyes.

THE BOOK OF SHATTERED MORNINGS

1. The perpetual birth of morning

Mind is nothingness at the instant of solitary waking. Transparent lack of essence gives way as pain already present rises to my full awareness. A wave of agony crashes over me. At the sight of my destroyed body, skinless and bleeding, panic surges.

Hands and wrists abraded, chest and abdomen scraped raw, oozing scarlet. Nerves and muscles sensitized yet lying vulnerable on the surface, drying in the hostile air. Extremities a map of pain, ruined, left dripping.

Who abandoned me like this? Try to remember.

A sun-bright room, silvery reflective walls, windows full of morning's garish light. A new day, unformed as myself. Shapeless, undifferentiated potentiality. The wall opposite the window is decorated in projections sprayed by the blast of brilliant sun through imperfect glass. Every blemish casts a shadow. Specks of dust so enlarged blur like gigantic amoeba, trembling.

What do they call me? I know nothing of myself. Someone's nameless victim, left dying alone.

A black wood table against the wall supports a massive leather book on a stand, resting open. A red satin ribbon marker drapes across the open pages and dangles almost to the floor.

Someone marked the spot, but why? I can't decipher what's written. Not from here.

For the first time, I feel moved to stand. Not sure I can. Will this ruined body, torn apart to display inner workings like a transparent machine made for demonstration purposes, obey my command?

I manage to bend, raw nerves screaming. Pain intensifies, then recedes to the accustomed low-level screech.

Sit up, lift my legs. Feet on the floor.

To stand seems impossible. First step wobbles, tentative.

There's so much I don't remember. Not even sure what I'm becoming.

The second step almost steady. By the third, the fourth, I move across the room, almost gliding, quick as intention. Even the pain recedes, despite visible proof of gruesome damage. Hands glisten, wet with gore, skinned as if by delicate surgery.

I wonder at the work of these hands. What purpose?

The light, which seemed harsh before, now enfolds me in blank, unthreatening whiteness. I stand over the open book, hoping to understand. Forms on paper. Words, pictures. What do they mean? Even close up, none of this makes sense. The smaller shapes must be letters. Whatever part of me grasps the concept of language cannot elucidate. Larger figures, illustrations? It's all sharply in focus, yet lacking meaning. A problem of interpretation, not vision.

I flip pages, back toward the beginning. This should mean something. Whatever that may be escapes me. I start over from the first, hoping for some key or hint, but find only confusion.

I'm about to turn away, when something changes. Recognition. Shapes in series, some repeating. Connected, they form ideas.

I finger-trace a line, barely touching the page. Abruptly I remember the blood and snatch my hand back. Only then I notice the skin of my fingers is healed. Palm smooth, back of the hand pale, dry, as if never injured. Intact skin extends as high as mid-wrist, above which injury persists, as far up the shoulder as I can see. Chest, belly, still oozing gore. The rest of me drips, raw and vulnerable.

Did the healing begin at extremities? Was it initiated at the paper's touch? I don't understand the cause, only that the paper's pristine white remains unstained. Black words assert themselves against a virginal surface. Increasingly I find sense within these, like vague chatter from another room cohering into conversation. It's as if I've seen the words before. This is how a story is made. At least I understand that much.

Whoever created this, it's a gift of wisdom. Whispers of some personal voice.

I lay the ribbon marker across the page and close the book. The cover is heavy dark leather, a purple wine-deep, almost black. Exotic and rough textured, as if rubbed by oil and charcoal, aged many seasons. The massive tome possesses an imposing density. It seems impervious to change. Timeless.

I'm drawn back to the text inside, lines of ink, varying thickness. I follow the thread, delighted to build upon hints of coherent intention.

Who made this?

As I read on, I find that earlier ideas linger in mind long enough to be elaborated by subsequent lines. Each word, perhaps only barely significant in itself, plays a part in a flow of emergent meaning. The cumulative value of the word and the sentence is not additive, but exponential.

2. A history: The boy's softness annealed by fire

Narrative unwinds like a tendril of smoke, the tale of a boy born similar to others. In time his unusual nature was revealed by speech and ideas judged strange by those around him. Eventually the truth became plain. This boy, unnamed in the story, showed frightening auspices. One they called Father made the decision to keep the boy apart from the group, either tribe or family. Father was massive, brown and impenetrable as the ancient oaks, hands dry, strong, and textured like bark. In anger, Father's gestures threw off red sparks, which sometimes set fires in the woods. He made all the children and women afraid.

If there were other men, the story did not tell.

The story summarized in list form the many violent acts undertaken by the boy at Father's insistence.

Devoured a nearby village of simpler beings as they slept.

Killed every animal in the forest, created more, and killed those too.

Descended into the hell pit to learn the secret of throwing fire.

The boy did as he was told. Each morning, returned to the village's edge. Was sent out again. He hoped Father might be gratified by these efforts, that some point would be reached, after which life would return to the more pleasing simplicity of childhood.

Alone after each lesson, the boy rested at the top of Bittergrit Mountain, beside Mirror Lake. There he wondered, when will I be old enough?

He yearned for everything to stop. Each day, another trial. Cycle without end.

One morning, the boy refused to come down from the top of the mountain.

The Father found the boy where he remained by Mirror Lake. This was the place the boy loved. His escape, and one solace.

Father told the boy to remove all the water from the lake. Leave behind a dry, barren hole, Father commanded, and departed.

The pristine water reflected an azure circle of sky rimmed by trees. Visible also was the mountain's very tip, the snow-blasted summit. The boy waited out the day, took no action at all. He sat unmoving until the sun set and the reflections disappeared into darkness.

Under black sky the boy descended the mountain, returned to the edge of the village and admitted to Father his defiance. The task remained unfinished.

Father cursed, struck him, and ordered him back.

Climbing again, the boy's anger grew. Rage built within him to a smoldering internal fire bright enough to light the mountainside. By the time he arrived at the lake again, the boy burned with terrible heat, made of an agony of conflict such as he had never known before. He submerged in the crisp water, breathed it in, and exhaled steam which bubbled to the surface. He sank to the bottom, drinking and drinking, trying to cool the horrible resentment within himself. The boy tried not to think about what must result. To destroy this most beautiful thing made him sick.

Morning returned to find the boy standing within a dry crater of jagged rock, in the place where always before Mirror Lake reflected a white peak set against a perfect sky.

3. Man is made, father destroyed

Words on the page tell of confusion and hurt. Destruction of peaceful, harmless beauty, never to be seen again.

I'm still waiting for Father to tell me finally it's enough. If that's true, if I've done enough, he should tell me.

I mark the book and turn back to face the room. It's the same, silvery-white and open, yet somehow changed.

A ringing sound. A telephone I hadn't noticed before, on the table beside the bed. A heavy gray phone, old-fashioned plastic, with a curled cord.

Another ring. Who's calling?

A third ring. I know it's him. Father's found me.

I go to the phone, reach out my hand. Don't pick up.

So sick of waiting. So angry. Inside, I burn again.

I snatch up the phone, not just the handset, raise the entire phone over-head and throw it down. It smashes on the floor, bursts into shards heavy as stone. The impact cracks the seamless floor like a broken eggshell.

The ringing stops. Echoes linger.

What happened at the lake? Try to remember. What happened after? I don't understand what brought me here. The book. This room.

Mirror Lake, dead and dry. I can't go back.

The crack in the floor widens. Dark brown fingers reach up from below, through the opening. Dry hands, coarse as the bark of a bitter tree, push up, invading the room. They open the gap wider. Wrists, then arms reach in. The crown of a head sticks through. Father. His eyes find me. He's smaller now, less substantial. His shoulders struggle upward, breaching through.

I rush toward him, kick his chest, his forehead. Stomp his hands. He draws back, bits of him chipped away. Dry flakes flutter loose from blood-less wounds. So full of rage, heart pounding. I can't stop. Keep kicking his face, his shoulders. Drive my heel down, again and again, on top of his skull. He flinches, withdraws, further down. Still I'm kicking, trying to kill. One foot, the other. His cries fade, grow distant. Wailings of the fallen. I send him back, push him down, wailing into nothingness below. Whatever elder realm will have him. Oblivion.

The narrow gap in the floor knits together, a wound rapidly healing. Small pieces of him remain, detritus I try to scatter underfoot. His last essence. Old Father, conquered. Fallen. Nothing but dust. I realize my feet are healed. Freshly grown skin, pale and pink, from foot to ankle to shin. Above the knee, healthy again.

I stand in that spot, Father's authority destroyed, rendered impotent. Final redemption for the lost Mirror Lake.

I'm bigger, now. Stronger. Still I don't know my name.

I return to the book.

4. A history: The allure of forgetting

A young man encountered a young woman of singular, striking beauty. Though the village had grown into a small town, he wondered how he'd never noticed her before. He was beguiled at first glance by her poise, a mysterious complexity beyond her years, an exoticism totally unfamiliar.

Their eyes met in the market, at riverside gatherings in summer's heat, and in the Firehall on winter eves. Obsessed with her routines, he fabricated excuses to encounter her. She too seemed frequently to be waiting in his path. They lingered in these moments. He tried to ask questions. Where was she from? Her smile enticed, yet she spoke only evasions.

The young man lacked experience managing such powerful desire, and reeled under its influence. Despite certain longing, their coming-together transpired slowly as a flower seed planted beneath soil's surface takes time to break through.

On the first yellow afternoon of spring he saw her, shoulders uncovered in the sun, skin vibrantly alive. Alone she danced, movements odd and utterly singular. He stood transfixed by her fleshwork, provocative designs in ink beyond the skill of any local artisan. Still dancing, her eyes spoke to him of clear intent. When he neared, her body's warmth, a tangible aura, pulled him closer.

Then she reached out. Her fingertip gently brushed his arm. Final culmination of the many significant glances.

After this touch, he stopped denying the special meaning she held. They met intentionally, whispered plans. Slipped away, found privacy. Stared in silence. Ventured to touch. In a room nearly dark, he watched her strip away garments, saw the full magnificence of her fleshwork, an intricate narrative in ink, illustrative of impossibly long experience and exotic travels over many lifetimes. By increments she revealed all. So he believed.

Some hints he ignored, choosing to focus on other things.

They withdrew from public life, insistent in their burgeoning intimacy upon solitude. Friends and neighbors whispered speculation. She introduced him to pleasures so amplified as to seem to transcend the real, to derive from places unknown. Together they collected a perfect diversity of intimate secrets. Focus narrowed, turned inward.

In time, he showed her the home he was constructing, suitable for more than one, in the shelter of trees far outside town. There he moved his possessions. She did the same.

Part of him that had always desired to explore, to venture widely in the world and be tested, was tamed. To remain apart with her satisfied him. Gladly he made the exchange, forsaking potential new discoveries in favor of familiar, recurrent ecstasies.

One evening the beautiful young woman did not return to their new home at the expected time. Hours passed without a sign. Worried, he searched the places she used to go, wherever she spent time before their lives changed. He couldn't find her.

What happened? She couldn't possibly abandon him.

Days passed. Nights sleepless at the window, eyes burning. Turmoil churned his gut. No answers.

Exhausted, he finally dropped into sleep.

He awoke to find the pain slightly dulled, surmounted by hunger. No choice but to venture out. In small ways, he resumed trying to live.

Another evening he returned to the empty house, and found a note.

Don't misunderstand, her writing urged. Please don't jump to wrong conclusions. Nothing's changed. I'll be home soon. Later tonight, the note promised, we'll have dinner and I'll explain.

The handwriting was hers.

So he waited again, evening into night, heart pounding. Back and forth anxiously between the chair and the dark window. The moon climbed, surpassing the trees.

His waiting heart became a black, acid hole.

How late could it be? He was afraid to look.

Sunrise cut off all denial. It wouldn't matter if she returned, left another note. He imagined her with someone else. Another man's fingers tracing her skin's designs.

So much time had passed. He'd forgotten all that set him apart, lost everything distinctive in himself.

Now he was ordinary, and painfully alone.

5. The way back to forgotten self

Words on the page, out of which her face appears. I blink the image away. Stomach rages, hands tremble.

I replace the marker, close the book.

How long has it been?

Her voice intrudes. "I was never away overnight," she says. "I came home. You must have been sleeping."

I shake my head. Still hear that voice.

"You misunderstood," she says. "I love you more than anyone else ever could. Please don't lose the beautiful thing we share."

Can't let her keep inflicting pain. Not after all this time.

She's back again. Here in the room, beguiling face, overlarge eyes, flesh traced in decorative ink lines. A smiling intruder, enticing me out of solitude with the promise of warm encircling arms. More beautiful than ever.

I'm angry at myself, angry for desiring. Still my heart longs.

Her smile. She moves in closer, that way she has of spinning, and reaches out a weightless bloodless hand. Another trick she uses. Heat radiates from fingertips.

A spell is cast.

I shy back. "Answer my questions," I say through gritted teeth.

She vanishes, reappears, just like memory. Identical in all details. Lost love. Seductress. Through transparent beauty shines something else. The shrill distortion of excess. Disproportion, imbalance. Eyes shocking blue, inhuman. Lips, the garish red of broken television.

Repulsive.

I turn my back, she vanishes. A moment's solitude, she returns. Always behind me. I turn, find her there. Features outsized, amplified.

So angry, I want to kill. She's not solid.

Want to scream, banish her. She won't hear.

I do scream, for myself. Don't care if she listens. Shake my head, close my eyes. Hands pressed over both ears. Alone within my screams, in the black void of mind.

Then I realize. Every time she returns, I've summoned her.

My fault. All of this. Only I can shut her out. Purge the memory. Free myself.

The sharpest pain is the tearing away. That pain will fade. The echo of ancient suffering creates pangs that never die.

I was alone before, never suffered. Why such torment now, loneliness verging on breakdown? In the mythology of mind, she's a villain who destroyed me. But she's neither monster nor mystery.

I'm only broken if I allow it. I pre-existed her. Some intrinsic aspect hasn't disappeared.

We diverge. No more tragic hero crushed beneath a temptress's boot.

I pull myself loose, cut threads, struggle free. Feel the skin tearing. Separation shreds every nerve. Cut away lips that used to smile, to kiss. Gouge out eyes that made me weak.

Claw my way back.

6. A history: Ghosts arrive on dreamcurrents

A chapter in solitude, deep in the forest's cool shadow. The man lay weak, broken in despondency, in an agony of self-doubt. Reduced to lowest depths, he delved into fundamental questions of being.

Why? What if?

Fragility left him susceptible to intrusive spirits. As he wandered aimless in dreams, or a state perhaps more akin to meditation, a ghost appeared, a reflection of the man's own shape, yet luminous and perfected, smooth of skin and symmetrical of feature as the man himself no longer was. The vision was semi-transparent, less than fully tangible.

Even in this state of mind it occurred to him that phantoms of legend could often be seen through. Could this be projection of his greatest need: a being possessed of answers?

As if responding to this notion, the apparition approached forcefully, flitting in a way that seemed hostile. So close as to merge with him, it spoke words painful to hear, berated him with accusations, and mocked contradictions inherent in the man's excuses and assumptions. Most intimate beliefs spoiled, world view utterly shattered, the man broke down. He tried to hide. Found nowhere to escape.

He cried, Aren't dreams a refuge? Let me rest and heal. He wailed, clutching his head. Let me hide.

Instead of answering, the ghost attacked, darting and piercing at the speed of thought. The man's cumbersome body couldn't evade. The ghost penetrated his flesh, which in this realm was actually spirit.

The sensation chilled the man, left him sickened. Broken, trembling, he lay waiting for his mind to wake. If not sleep, what was left to him? He'd grown up, become a man, followed the path he was supposed to, yet now struggled with more terrible uncertainty, greater pangs of self-doubt, than anything ever suffered as a helpless child.

Eventually he returned to wakefulness, feeling worse than ever. He lacked the perspective to see how much he'd already changed. The spirit's accusations had broken loose his calcified mind, set him free of immobility. Lately, he'd retreated to sleep as often as his body allowed. There he'd sought to repair intangible aspects of selfhood, like healing a wound.

Now he hated the very need to sleep, and dreaded the next time he must visit that place. Sleep, the thing he needed most. Even that was poisoned. He hated what he'd come to.

"I need your help!" the man screamed. "Not more torture."

The ghost ignored him.

The man lay awake in torment, wondering if the ghost was really himself, perhaps his future self looking back yet unable to speak, or his past self projecting forward to divine what may come.

7. Every story has a beginning

Words on the page find me back in the room, sunlit through windows. I've been aware of the glass. Only now I imagine the world beyond. Whatever must be out there is useless to me. Memories, too far removed, cease to hold interest. So many things no longer apply.

I feel myself watched, eyes out there somewhere, invisible, yet seeing. I find the shirt and pants. For the first time, feel a need to cover myself.

From the book comes a murmur, a deep and significant rumbling of disturbance. Out of open pages, a human shadow drifts into the room.

I open my mouth, ready to ask the usual questions. To plead for help.

The ghost, anticipating my entreaties, simply watches. Its eyes never leave me.

This time, I don't speak. I don't protest, or look away.

I wait for the flood of criticism. This never comes. The shadow, whether reflection of self, or transient spirit of judgment, merely hovers. Weightless and darkly luminous, it quivers at the mercy of invisible, aetheric winds.

I step closer, mind blank, so it won't anticipate what I plan.

When I'm close enough, I thrust both hands into the gut of the phantom body. The motion disperses, renders formless, the cloud of sooty smoke. It disappears in a white flash so bright I'm left blind. I keep blinking until I'm able to see again. The spirit has left me. No trace remains. I'm alone once more, in another empty room.

I see, next to the book, a small glass object left behind. I approach, pick it up. A bottle of ink. I hold it up to the brilliance streaming in from the window. The liquid is so dark, even sunlight can't penetrate.

I turn the cap, dip my finger, smear the ink over my thumb. The stain spreads, dark, but not quite black. Hidden color revealed. Purple, dark as midnight.

What can I do with this? Nested within the book's pages, I find something else, something I need. An empty pen. Anticipating, I load the chamber with ink.

The room is not a place, but a setting. Backdrop for dreams.

I flip through pages in recollection. A book of my own making. Even when I'm destroyed, reduced to some protean thing forced to start again from nothing, this book remains. Proof exists, witness to all I've learned. Impetus for ruined nature, introduction to the pain of first betrayal, mirror revealing every defect of self.

Read on. Visit unknown tales, turn pages until I'm near the end. Where the scrawl leaves off in blankness, I touch pen to paper. Lines unfold, newly emergent realms. Fresh life, words and pictures, even music.

I fly toward a future that bursts into creation the moment I arrive.

The stain of purple midnight, so nearly black, spreads past my fingers, across my knuckles, and covers itching hands. The ink, so powerful, starts to burn. Where it touches, my skin tingles. Increase of pain.

Soon, drops of blood run from skin disintegrating at my fingertips.

I remove these white clothes, drop them on the floor before blood spoils them, and set back to work, naked at the page. Faster I push as my body slowly fails. Wounds form where ink burns away skin.

Onward through the pain.

The bleeding comes faster, heavier. All this blood should stain the pages, but it doesn't. It makes the tale more potent. More real.

Soon I'm breathing hard, dizzy. Have to rest. Want to keep going, but have to stop. I lie on the bed.

How did my body get like this? Skinless, bleeding. The sight of me stretched out is horrifying. Nothing left but a single, viscid wound.

Need to sleep.

Next time, I'll remember what's possible. Just have to remember. The story's more than real. I'm a god in a world self-made. I have no name.

Nothing outside matters. Here, I have blue sky overhead, a lake, a perfect mirror. Limitless.

I will never die.

ARCHES AND PILLARS

I only remember ever feeling at peace in the museum's Great Hall, drifting through the Rothko exhibit where the orange sun of evening spins through skylights and scatters across polished stone. Only here my mind settles, among vivid color fields. Stepping soundless on the marble floor, I'm alone, unheard, unseen. Nothing to prevent me circling forever.

I've worked here so long, I don't remember when I started, or when this wing ever contained anything else. What excuse did I use to avoid my desk before this exhibit arrived? These canvases, this place, irrevocably linked. As far as I'm concerned, this is the Rothko Room.

Brushwork softens transitions between color fields. Blood red and aubergine, grass green and lemon. Such defiant minimalism. Simplicity taken to uncompromising extremes. Genius lies in these indefinite boundaries. The impossibility of discerning where one world gives way to the next.

My thoughts cycle, the usual obsessions. My need to assert myself with Robin. I can't face another evening of missed opportunity. The same chance might not come again.

Among all the museum staff, I'm the only painter, the only one here for the art. The rest might as well be selling widgets. At five, without stopping in my office, I glide down a broad stairwell fit for a castle and pass the front desk. The attendant must be new, a girl in flapper dress, bright blue hair in a boy cut with spit curls. The kind of look you remember. She doesn't notice me going past.

On my way through the heavy brass doors I feel a strange pang, like nostalgia for a place long departed. Outside, a mental shift. Time to plan, get my head straight. A walk through the park blocks, toward the University campus, then downtown to meet Robin. The Brasserie at six, as we've done every evening for... how long? Our relationship. Is it a relationship? She must want it to be. If we both want it, that's what it is. It's a relationship already. Of course. Maybe a new one, certain words never yet stated, but routines established. Dinner every weeknight at the Brasserie Montmartre, that's proof of something. Interdependence.

If it's not real yet, tonight it will be. Just have to figure out when to speak up. That's all. What to say.

Then it occurs to me, I've told myself all these things before. So many times... This realization's interrupted by movement behind, feet skipping on the sidewalk.

"Thought I'd surprise you." Her voice, close and familiar. Robin pulls me around, holds my arm possessively against her.

It's a surprise, yet totally expected. Happening again.

I'm not ready yet, not until the restaurant. Plans aren't complete. Maybe I'll just have to try again. Another time.

But the plan's not so complicated. I just need to move things forward. Speak up, when the time comes. It's what we both want.

Damn it, wanting isn't enough. Desire counts for nothing unless I act. Make it real.

"Startled me." I tell her what she wants to hear.

She smiles, waiting for more. Excitement at the surprise? I've looked forward to seeing her all day, obsessed over nothing but Robin, Robin. Now she sees my concern. I needed time to get my mind right.

I'm absurd, of course. Ridiculous. It's not about planning. Just look her in the eye when it comes down to it. I know what I've done wrong before. Just need to change it.

We're still heading away from the restaurant.

"The park's so pretty in October." Robin's mouth forms the words. I anticipate them. Which comes first? She watches me as she speaks, not the scene, which we both know well enough to describe with eyes closed. A row of barren trees fade into mist. Fallen leaves glisten, a rain-damp blanket like a decaying golden snow of autumn.

I lead her in a gentle arc northward, back toward the Brasserie. Orange glowing buildings shelter the failing sun. Black-suited men course the side-walks and students cluster faceless, no more than background to our passage. I pause at a shop window. Italian suits. Stainless steel rods draped with silk neckties. Blood red and saffron. The barely blue silver of dying autumn sky.

"I like that one." Robin points.

I fail to note her preference, distracted by memory. *That one.* Her precise inflection, a memorized song. Don't we always meet at our table in the Brasserie? Did she surprise me on the way before? More than once?

The restaurant's white door stands open beyond a sandwich board announcing musical performers. Plates and crystal glasses chime counterpoint to the upright bass's oblong growl. Too soon, we've arrived.

Our table in the rear sits apart from the rest, on the same raised platform as the stage. The players warm up only a few feet beyond a rail at my elbow. Music isn't due to begin until six-thirty but already the bassist and pianist tease with warm-up fragments, brief surges of song momentum which threaten to become tunes, only to halt abruptly without reaching an end.

The waitress hurries by, aiming for the hallway to the kitchen. I wave but she passes without notice.

Otherwise somewhat formal, the restaurant affects playfulness by providing butcher paper in lieu of tablecloths. Crayons encourage casual expression. The walls are adorned with a selection of more ambitious efforts in museum-grade frames, the products of the occasional diner possessing artistic skill combined with seriousness of purpose.

Robin foregoes crayons, pulls from her purse a hair-thin Rapidograph drafting pen. She scribbles the barest framework of lines. Looks up, those swimming-pool eyes catch me watching. Despite ghostly paleness and a determinedly monochrome wardrobe, she avoids severity by virtue of sculptural cheekbones and those brilliant eyes. Short curly hair upswept like a flame.

Too much beauty, I think. Overwhelms the senses.

She resumes sketching. "What's new today at work?"

I shrug. "Mostly hid out. Swam around in the Rothkos."

"Mmm. I love those."

"They're like a tranquilizer. A warm bath." So much time spent at work, and all that comes to mind is that bright stone floor ringed by vivid splashes of color.

Her sketch draws me in. Geometric forms, architectural, delineated with crosshatch shadows. Romanesque columns and arches, an open courtyard. The corners hint at statues and obelisks. The scenario unfolds upon our table, frozen in ink, draws me out of this place to another. Pulls me in.

I'm not really hungry but wonder why nobody's come by to take our order. "Where's the waitress?" I ask.

"They can't see us, remember?" Robin continues drawing. "I'm sorry, we always talk about that now. Just trying to steer clear of the usual."

What she's saying, it starts to make sense, especially as I'm lost in her inkwork. Arches and pillars, a dreamland realm. A destination. Somewhere we belong.

I still want to be here, with Robin. What she's saying makes no sense. She says it like I should understand. Like I—

"Just draw with me." She touches my hand.

I try to pull my eyes away from the drawing, afraid it's sucking me in, away from here. She notices me staring, covers the sketch with her hands. What other vistas has she seen, and now reside in her imagination? The more I try to forget the drawing, the more I'm attracted to it. What's in store for me, if I ever find it?

I blink, look up. Into her eyes.

From our table by the wall, our spot ever since we found it, I see the whole room. How long has it been, Robin and me together? Weeks? It feels like an old marriage and a new thing, both at once.

Plates of food whirl past on trays. I'm hungry, or at least feel I should be. Expectation is worse than hunger. Smoked salmon fettuccine, seared scallops with basil and garlic, linguine drizzled in olive oil. At every table a fresh basket of mini sourdough baguettes. Every table but ours.

The baritone sax guy moves as if he's playing, the drummer too, but I can't hear the music any more. It's strange. I know what this should sound like.

"Something's wrong with the music," I say.

"I know." Robin looks resigned. "That bothers you every time."

I begin to protest, then pause. "I do... I always say that." Shortness of breath. Dizziness. "What's happening? We're just re-enacting, aren't we? Going through motions."

"It's OK, Julian. Don't get upset. You keep forgetting—"

My chair squeaks on the tile as I stand. I want to apologize to the band for interrupting. They're still playing, but without a sound. Nobody notices me except Robin.

I have to get hold of this. Another chance might never come. I take Robin by the hand and head out. She follows. I feel confused, like I should pay first, then remember we never ordered.

Urgency tugs. Inevitability, pulling me along a line. Maybe it's just my desires, fermented by now into desperation. I just need to get her alone, away from the restaurant. Everybody's watching.

But nobody's watching. Nobody sees.

If we could just be alone together. That's what's wrong.

Outside, Robin takes my hand. "Everything OK?"

"Nothing's wrong," I protest. I've felt disoriented, displaced, ever since she surprised me after work.

She backs up against a stranger's parked car. Waiting for me to speak. Finally she shakes her head. "My car's by the Mission. I'd better go. Same time tomorrow?"

My mind spins, seeking anything to suggest. Go for drinks? But where? I have nothing planned. We never go for drinks. Anyway, that isn't what either of us want. It's my fault, taking things so slow. Need to snap out of this.

"Can I show you my loft?" I say. "Do you want—"

Her face brightens. "I've been hoping."

Such relief, I feel weightless. I walk a few steps ahead, spin and walk backward, looking at her. This girl, going to be mine. For so long this game. She approaches, I evade. Feels like forever. Her long coat sweeps cape-like behind her, revealing toned legs in black tights, a form-fitting silver-white

sweater. I'm immersed in buzzing thoughts, the implications of her phys-
icality. The promise of carmine lips. The scene around us vacant, background to her outline. Automobiles pass, soundless. The terrible burden of
desire, looming large.

I trip backward from the curb into the street. My trance breaks. Sudden
thrumming rush of cars. People on the sidewalk abruptly become aware of
us, startled as if I've dropped out of nowhere into their midst.

Robin kneels at my side. "Are you all right?" The world shrinks. She
touches my arm gently, as if I'm injured.

My keyed-up excitement still now, I stand. "Fine."

We walk slowly, in our own world again, across streets, bridges. A silent
accumulation of tension until my building looms, forest green, more modern than the neighborhood.

"I like this area," she says. "Kind of hidden between The Pearl and the
crazy parts of Northwest."

The certainty rises in me, a sense I don't belong. Reaching for the outer
door, I doubt my key will work. Maybe I lived here long ago, but time has
moved on. The knob turns, the door swings open. Up the narrow stairway
to the second floor, my mind spinning, seemingly intent on discovering
some way this must be wrong. Will my place be how I left it? What if my
things are gone? Someone else living here, looking at us like we're crazy?
I'm already nervous, now terrified what she'll think. At my apartment door,
before I reach for my keys, Robin turns the knob. It opens and the door
swings wide. She enters before me and sweeps through the place, taking
everything in.

"So nice," she says. "How many square feet?"

Everything familiar. My paintings on the wall, shot glass collection on the
concrete bar between kitchen and great room. Home.

"Twelve hundred. Open floorplan makes it seems bigger."

Robin ventures past the bar toward the corner of the great room, where
an opening leads to the enclosed bedroom, left dark unless I'm alone here.
That's where guests usually stop. To my mind it's unequivocally private,
despite lack of barriers. Robin continues into the unlit corner where I paint
and sleep and lately dream about her. I start after, ready to pull her back

from the brink, but she turns back on her own. Several terrible, aborted canvases are still up. Until now she's only seen finished work, tiny photos online. So disconcerting to be glimpsed in the banality of my private world. I feel exposed, compromised.

If anything Robin seems impressed. She's on her way over to check out my glass collection, and says something.

I'm too distracted to catch her words. "Sorry?"

"I asked how you found it." She toys idly with a Danish vodka decanter at the end of the shot glass row. Slender fingers beguiling, somehow too sexual. I look away.

"Advertisement." This is what you want, I tell myself. Isn't it? "Can I make a drink?"

She lightens perceptibly. "Rum and Coke." Is she nervous too, needing that drink? Or just relieved I seem ready to break through this stalemate?

I round the bar, briefly in control. Nothing so lasting as true confidence, but a semblance at least. I see my next move ahead of me, and I'll cling to that, build on it. I glance up, find her backlit by an overhead halogen, a luminous silhouette. Sometimes she startles me with this sudden unreal loveliness. I should revel in it, be glad this beautiful girl seems drawn to me. Instead I freeze, self-consciously dwelling on this idea, *Will it be tonight I dismantle her mystique?*

Trembling hands stir the drinks, black with ice. We know each other, in some ways intimately. So many long talks, dinners, yet this distance remains in spite of all desire. Before her I've desired others, and after intimacy no longer saw them as this ineffable mystical beauty. Wanting and having, two different things. Having kills wanting.

I hold out her drink, planning to hand it over and move up close. If I hold back we'll stay stuck.

I look at her, intending to close the gap, and then… I can't go all the way. Want to, but can't. She looks at me with those eyes, bright piercing out of the dimness of the room. I leave her glass on the counter, midway between us. She moves nearer, reaches, takes a sip. Looks at me over the edge of the glass, eyes barely open. Lips on the edge, sipping. She must calculate that glance, summoning me, aware of my struggle.

So overwhelming, this build up. Too much. I retreat to the kitchen, turn on the faucet. Grab a sponge, dish soap, start washing dishes. Only a few, not enough to bother with. My back is to her and I'm not thinking really.

She must be watching. Waiting.

I grit my teeth. Don't blow this. You can still say something.

"Julian." Ice shuffles and her empty glass clinks on the concrete bar. "I'm worrying about my car. Kind of a bad spot, by the Mission."

Finally I turn.

Flat resignation in her eyes. "Do you mind walking me?"

Over her shoulder, my bedroom so near, darkly concealed.

"Of course." I shut off the water, dry my hands. I'm angry, though not at her.

She's talking, but I can't focus. We're stuck in this loop, nearly coming together, somehow failing. It'll smart later. Too late to try again tonight. Maybe next time I'll do better.

Robin's still speaking as we walk toward Old Town.

I force myself back to awareness. "Sorry, what?"

"I asked why you behave this way toward me." She glances at me then away, perhaps afraid I won't like her question, but nonetheless willing to force the issue.

We walk a long time while I consider my answer. I'm sure she thinks I'm angry, that I won't respond.

"Predetermination," I say. "Tonight's the night we go back to my place after dinner. The universe tries to guide us, ensure things go a certain way. It's automatic. No way to change what comes next."

"So it bothers you that sometimes dinner dates lead to intimacy? Two people relating to each other? There's nothing predetermined. It's on us to move forward. Determine to make it work."

My life before Robin seems infinitely distant, another person's memories. I want to protest that I've tried what she suggests. Pushed aside all doubts, only to come up against the expectation gap. A magic ideal always outshines dull reality.

She's watching me as we cross over 405, a weird reminder we're in a city, despite the quiet. The highway below is empty. Dead asphalt waits for absent cars.

"Is it better to float through the world like a ghost," she asks, "so afraid of the let-down, you never connect?"

The surreally vacant Pearl District passes in our wake. Darkened restaurants, locked boutiques. Signs painted-over in some letters I can't read. Familiar gibberish, a language once fluent, now forgotten.

I want tell her everything, open my guts, hope she understands. My problem isn't lack of desire, but too much.

Within sight of the Old Town Mission, Robin stops. In front of a brick apartment tower she looks up and I follow her gaze. On the fire escape, a flurry of movement. Instinctively I pull back, drag her with me.

A gang of manic-looking speed freaks loom overhead on the steel latticework. A half dozen sweat-slick men, all tattoos and grinding teeth.

I remember this fire escape. The memory's clearer more vivid than anything I've seen all day.

The alpha freak, their leader, leans out over the second platform's edge. The raised stairs are cantilevered a dozen feet below and it's fifteen more to the sidewalk. He swings over the rail, hangs by his hands from the base, and dangles over the tip of the extended stairway. He lets go, lands on the steps as if he's practiced a thousand times. Knees flex to absorb the shock and he rides the ladder down, then jumps off just before it reaches the sidewalk. Metal strikes concrete with a great metallic clang. He pulls from his boot a length of heavy rebar, one end wrapped in cloth tape for grip, and grins a mouthful of gaps. More than sweaty, he glistens as if dunked in oil.

I stand frozen until Robin moves, and I start after her. She takes off running toward the river, and civilization. Her car must be near.

She looks back at me, both of us sprinting, and in that flash of eye contact we share the awareness: *This is how it always ends.*

I'm catching up because she's wearing boots with heels. She stumbles, crashes scraping to the ground. I stop. My instinct is to check on her but he's right behind us. I step in front of Robin. Raise my arm.

Nothing I can do. A blur of motion, the flash of awareness, violence impending.

I always think we'll have more time. Opportunities don't vanish but just loop around, offered up again and again like dishes in one of those conveyor belt sushi restaurants. We can always—

Black steel swings a blurred trajectory, then silence.

Empty sidewalk, quiet street. Try to remember. Where did this begin? Stop light changes, hyper-slow. Eternity from red to green.

Just want my heart to stop pounding. I walk until I recognize something. A line of trees naked of leaves. Marble stairs to monumental doors, bronze and glass.

The front desk girl must be new. Short blue hair, spit curls, flapper dress. I expect she won't recognize I belong, that she'll tell me admission's eight dollars, but she doesn't notice me passing. Never even looks up.

Up the stairs I'll find silence. Space to breathe.

I move in circles, waiting for some trigger, some hint to tell me what's next. Eventually something will come along. I'll recognize it when I see it.

Time passes. Finally calm again. Pass the same checkpoints, again, again. There's comfort in that, also sadness. Tightrope walk a sunbeam alongside the subtle vibrations of Rothko. Blood red and aubergine, grass green and lemon. I bathe in pools of color, swallow every hue. Drink them like wine.

DIAMOND DUST

Max climbs in the echo chamber of the concrete stairwell, every step rhythmic time with earlier footfalls. Fifth story, one from home. Already, a tickle of sweat under his arms. Maybe Cassandra won't be working tonight. Maybe for once he can relax.

From the next landing above, a eruption of clangs and clatters. Two brutes barreling down, lugging an ungainly burden of welded steel. The massive construct shrieks against the metal rail and caroms into the outer wall, tearing a jagged trench in the concrete, pluming dust and scattering chips. Max covers his ears against the racket, hesitating. No way he can turn back in time. No way the twin hulks can stop their momentum. He flattens, flings up his arms to cover his skull. The avalanche of metal passes over. Jagged edges shred his suit, slicing skin.

The thundering terror rounds the corner below. Max straightens, pulls together the torn jacket sleeve, as if the edges, like a wound, might somehow heal.

Max resumes his climb. Blood trickles from gashed forearms, drips from fingertips, leaving a trail to the sixth floor. Home.

Through the apartment door, the smoke alarm shrieks over the pulse of industrial music at nightclub volume. He enters, finds the entry hall billowing smoke, walls and ceiling dark with soot. In the living room, most of the carpet is burned away, the rest blackened. What color was it before? An area near the dining room, still smoldering, churns out eye-watering murk.

Cassandra leans over a heavy steel plate, firing her plasma torch one-handed. Her denim shorts and tank top are shot through with pinhole burns, every one the aftermath of a spit of molten steel trajecting toward skin. No safety gear but a single glove and unlaced steel-toed boots.

An afternoon wasted in daydreams of home, hopes of a quiet night. What was he thinking? When is this place ever quiet?

Max disables the smoke alarm and stomps smoldering carpet. Cassandra's still cutting. He turns down Einstürzende Neubauten, a band he always loved, at least until Cassandra started blasting them every waking moment. Finally she looks up. The cut form breaks free from the half-inch slab, clanks onto the pile. She kills the plasma cutter, snatches a black-smudged liquor bottle and swigs. Whiskey runs a rivulet from the corner of her mouth, cuts a clean trail through ash-dark skin. She backhands it away, a delicate gesture that hints at what Max used to find appealing in her. What if they could clear away all the wreckage, the noise? Just two of them again, like the beginning?

He reaches for the fire extinguisher. Cassandra snatches it up first and gusts a chilly white cloud at his feet.

"Got tired of stopping to put it out." She shrugs. "So I just let it burn."

Stifling a cough, Max examines his bleeding forearm. "I passed two guys on the stairs, lugging a new sculpture of yours."

"Furniture!" Cassandra glares. "Why can't you respect my work, just because it's *avant garde?* It's furniture. Not sculpture. Not experiments."

Max raises both hands in surrender. "Just noticing you've been busy. This enormous piece I hadn't seen before." He tries to be discreet, scrutinizing her latest geometric absurdity. Nothing but angles, sharp edges. All her earlier work's comfort and familiarity vanished. Same as their relationship.

Cassandra loops a thick cable over her arm. "I need patrons if we're ever going to rent a place with a workshop." She throws a blue tarp over her work, picks up the bottle and finishes it.

"Hope we make it before you burn the building down," Max says. Part of him wouldn't mind being rid of all this. Being forced to start over.

Max doesn't tell anyone of his obsession with the new neighbor, because there's no good explanation. It's just that every morning on his way to work, no matter what time he leaves, Max glimpses the neighbor for only a split second. Most days, the neighbor disappears behind the adjacent front door. Sometimes the guy slips down the stairwell, and vanishes by the time Max follows. Lately Max thinks a lot about timing. The turn of the knob, the opening of the door. Better to hesitate, or open right away? Whatever he chooses never makes any difference. It's become a game, maddeningly unwinnable. The neighbor, like a ghost, lingers just long enough to eliminate any doubt he's been seen.

Try not to think about it, Max resolves this morning. Just turn the knob. Open the door.

Outside, perhaps six feet away, is the neighbor. He doesn't look surprised to see Max. The man stands there with his ordinary face, giving Max all the time he wants to look back. How could this have been something to obsess over? Max notices the man's right hand and arm, revealed by a short-sleeved dress shirt, are gruesomely scarred, disfigured by burns. The neighbor finally offers a nod.

Max proceeds toward the elevator, as he does every morning. Some robotic aspect of himself seeks the path easier than stairs, forgetting the elevator's broken. It's been broken for years. Some other part of Max reasserts control in time to redirect toward the stairs. Most days Max spends the drive to work thinking about these two minds within himself. The part that day after seeks the elevator, despite years of futility. The lagging mechanism that recognizes, only slowly, stairs are his only option.

He drives the four miles to Portland's industrial district and finds the entire Boaz Industries parking lot replaced by acres of fresh-poured concrete foundation. Tractors shift the earth. Cranes lift tilt-up walls in as far as the eye can see. This abrupt transformation is unexpected, Max's position in Boaz management making him privy to all upcoming projects. More than that, it's impossible, weeks or months worth of construction labor completed in a single night's darkness. It would take a vast workforce, not to mention organizational planning of the kind normally handled by Max's own department. He's heard no mention of this. Not a whisper.

Am I the only one out of the loop? he wonders briefly, then extinguishes the thought. Implications too awful to consider.

Many employee cars are parked along Lorraine Street, though not nearly enough for Boaz's six hundred employees. Max finds an opening across
from the abandoned brick factory. The return walk takes him past flashing
lights, police cars and ambulances surrounding three cloth-draped bodies
on the median strip. Police officers regard him suspiciously. One scribbles
Max's license plate number.

The offices are so nearly vacant, Max checks his watch to make sure he
hasn't mistakenly come in on Saturday. A cluster of strangers murmur
near the coffee dispensary. Others click away at desks. Overnight the cubicle grid has been reduced by hundreds of workspaces, compressed into
a much smaller area. The reclaimed area, bordering the steelworks floor,
is blocked by an intimidating row of scaffolding covered in black fabric.

Max finds his desk in the usual corner of the grid, near Mr. Boaz's office.
At least this much hasn't changed. He's too distracted to focus on prepa-
ration for his early meeting. What's going on behind the black scaffold?
Plant expansion? He should've been in the loop.

Max commands his trembling hands to stop, clenches them into white-
knuckled fists.

"Maxwell." Boaz pops in, too short to be seen approaching beyond the
partition.

Max jumps. "Meeting still on, sir?" He grips the seat of his chair with
both hands.

"Always. Why wouldn't it be?" Boaz plays the tips of square, stubby
fingers against each other. "No time for second-guessing, Maxwell. What's
business without information?"

"True, sir." Max concentrates on projecting a look of control, while
inside he churns. Surrounding cubicles, though outfitted with computers
and expensive ergonomic chairs, remain vacant. He's alone in the Planning department. Someone's making plans, just not Max or his team.
"Where are my people? It's after eight."

"Retasked. Special projects." Boaz looks down at his feet, despite the
company's mandatory eye contact policy, his own initiative. "Melt shop,
most of them. Meeting at nine, as usual." Boaz spins, retreats to his office
in a flurry of tiny steps.

Though he doesn't know who'll be attending, having seen none of the management group this morning but himself and Boaz, Max processes the usual sixteen report copies.

Twenty-three minutes left. Still alone in the cube grid, apart from a few milling strangers. Heart pounding, Max picks up the phone, dials Cassandra.

"Everything's changing here," he whispers.

She exhales audibly. "Yes?"

"Construction, staff reorg. All my guys gone." Max pauses. What has he called about?

"Max, I'm working!"

"The guys in the stairwell yesterday…" He trails off, aware she hates questions. She does this intentionally, overreacts so he'll never question her about anything. "Last week, I saw those same two guys outside, loading something big, covered, into a truck. Maybe another of your scul…. Your furniture?"

"I told you, patrons. They're taking several pieces."

He regrets calling, but he's already interrupted her. "I'm not going to tiptoe around this!" Max catches himself, his voice escalating in sudden urgency. "The truck had a DRG logo. Our competition, Dyno Resource Group. Boaz hates them. Hates. So if you're using steel I bought you to make sculpture—"

"Furniture!"

He grits his teeth. "—Furniture, with Boaz steel, and selling it to Dyno which is Boaz's bitterest enemy, he wouldn't just be mad. I wouldn't just get yelled at, or merely fired."

"Oh?" Her amusement conveyed with perfect clarity. "What would he do?"

Visions of the apartment ablaze, a wild clashing inferno. Bodies gutted by the cronies Boaz hints at, but nobody ever sees. The two blackened dead lying there, blood sizzling in ashes.

She giggles.

Max slams down the phone.

On his way to the meeting, Max passes Boaz's office at the very moment another taller man emerges. Preoccupied, Max doesn't register at first that the man's wearing short sleeves, forbidden at Boaz. Something familiar grabs his attention before Max is fully aware what it is. His neighbor. Those terrible burns. By the time Max looks back, the man's gone around the end of the cubicle row. Curiosity urges Max to follow, but there's no time. He races to the conference room. Empty. He sits, waiting quietly, alone.

"Not here!" Boaz stage whispers from the doorway.

Max grabs the report packets and follows, past empty cubicles, inactive document centers, a vacant break room. Near the edge of the construction scaffold, Boaz stops and opens a janitorial closet. What's this? Max hesitates, then enters the narrow supply closet. Boaz joins him and shuts the door. High shelves force Max into uncomfortable proximity with his boss. Boaz straddles an empty mop bucket. Max leans back against stacked toilet paper rolls, struggling to avoid encroaching on the man's personal space. Boaz loses balance and almost falls. Max steadies him by the jacket lapels and Boaz ends up standing on Max's foot.

"This is the meeting," Max observes. This should be funny. So why this hollow ache in his stomach?

"Secrecy's increasingly important. Stakes escalating." Boaz's lips narrow. "Gigantic things underway."

"I see we're scaling up for something but I—"

"I'm trying to bring you onboard, Max. Make you part of this." Boaz leans in. "Just seeing if you're up to it."

Again Max wants to laugh, an urge quelled by the queasy hint of malign insanity. Every muscle tense, rigid with fear, as if in response to some looming threat. "With a major project underway, shouldn't we have all hands? The brightest members of my team—"

"Yes, yes, but I have to weigh risks." Boaz grips Max's shoulders. "Our people, they're good boys, most of them, but with the normal tendencies." His lip curls as if in suppressed revulsion. "To resist radically new ideas."

Max nods. What to say? "Acknowledging these concerns, sir, how can we ramp up, let alone service existing customers, without our human assets?" Maybe he's overextending? He almost changes the subject. "Newton's one our smartest guys, and loyal. And Palomar?"

Boaz seizes the doorknob without turning it. "They're involved. Most of them, busy in the melt shop. Don't worry, we'll leverage everyone's capabilities. This new thing, it transcends business. Like Manhattan Project, or Apollo. Changes everything!" Boaz wipes beads of oily sweat from his hairless scalp, then rubs slippery palms together. Finally he opens the door.

Returning to his desk, Max tries to calm down. He wants to manage this, take stock of facts. What might all this mean? He keeps feeling this new way of things is something he'll never understand. That he's being left out. Still oblivious, walking blindly toward... What?

He wants to call Cassandra. Probably she's working. The thought makes him angry. Why should he play along with her pretense about furniture? These weird constructs of hers have nothing at all in common with the little tables and chairs she used to make. Next time this ridiculous notion of *furniture* comes up, he'll force the issue. What exactly are you talking about? Tables, chairs? This makes him so angry. Everything disintegrating, both home and work.

The walls of the cubicle constrict. Max tries to focus on routine tasks, duties which always seemed intrinsically valuable. Yesterday's priorities feel absurd, distant, faced with an office of empty desks, vacant but for a few loitering impostors. Vast overnight construction, undertaken without oversight by the management team. It's too much. He's too far outside the loop to see any way back in. One terrible thought keeps looping, like a broken record: *Maybe I'm left out.*

Max sits at his desk, mind racing, unaware and unconcerned that he appears to be doing absolutely nothing. At that moment someone walks past his cubicle opening. The short-sleeved man. No mistaking the burns this time. It's Max's neighbor! He passes, giving no hint of having seen Max, enters Boaz's office, and shuts the door.

Max tries to stand, knees weak, and almost falls. It's too much to comprehend. This mystery belonging unquestionably to home, the faceless always-aware neighbor, somehow colliding with this place. The whole world's flipped. Boaz unrecognizable. Cassandra acting like his enemy. The new neighbor shows up here, today of all days?

Heart thudding, steadying himself against the desk, Max cranes to watch through Boaz's window.

The man turns, sees Max. Expressionless, he flicks the blinds shut.

On his way up the stairs, Max tries to fortify his resolve. When did Cassandra's lies begin? He can't remember when things changed. Lately when their eyes meet, both of them know something's broken. Before opening the door, he pauses, the way he always paused on his way out. He needs to confront her. Max takes measure of his emotions. Too angry. Too frustrated, ready to blow. Too raw, made vulnerable by his wanting. The love he still feels, though distorted and fragmented, exerts such force when he tries to deal with her. Cassandra. When he says the name, he still sees the face of the years-ago girl.

Max opens the door. The apartment's quiet, no stereo blasting, no plasma sizzle. No smoke. Cassandra must be gone. He relaxes, slightly relieved, then hears shuffling papers. In the living room, she's hurriedly piling design drawings. On top, she places a heavy art book.

He pretends not to notice. "No fires today." Smiles feebly. Before she turns away, he sees her eyes. Dark circles, skin pale and transparent. "Wait, Cass. We have to talk, then I'll leave you to it."

Cassandra faces him, slump-shouldered. "Too much to do. We can eat something, if you want. Maybe around nine." More than tired; she's hollowed out. Just reaching for the torch, an obvious effort.

Max crosses the room. "No, we need to talk first." He jerks the plasma unit's plug from the outlet.

Instantly feral, she presses up in his face. "Do you realize how easily I could leave you?"

First he backs up, then stops himself, exhales. "I've supported your art. What you're doing affects my career."

She lunges for the plug. He sidesteps to block. She turns left, reverses right, and frustration boils over. Inchoate rage finds release in a wordless scream. She throws her glove across the room, storms out, slams the door.

Pulsing throb in Max's temple. Breathing hard. First time she's threatened to leave. He takes a look around, thinking it's the first time he's even been alone in their apartment. Such quiet. Dust motes hover in still air. He's a stranger in his own place. An intruder. The urge to run, to flee home, pulls hard.

Her pile of drawings are weighed down under *La Poupée*, a book of Hans Bellmer's surreal puppet photography. Eroticized constructs of mismatched doll parts. Inanimate sexual invitation meets body horror. Concealed under a few of Cassandra's drawings, pencil sketches of the sort of furniture she used to make, are numerous professional engineering plans not in her hand. These resemble the weird, gangling structures she's lately been assembling. The names and part numbers mean nothing to Max. One of the plans appears to dictate the assemblage of thousands of moderately-sized components into an enormous whole. An overview depicts a multi-leveled structure tapering from a broad base, each ladder-like rung narrower, something like the Eiffel Tower but vastly larger, judging by tiny human forms provided for scale. Could she really be building something, using steel Max purchased from Boaz, helping somebody assemble pieces into this sky ladder, whatever it is? What if it involves Dyno Resource Group?

At the top of one code-like text document, the name: DIAMOND DUST PROJECT.

A nightmare, like waking up buried under suffocating weight. Too hard to breathe. One dark revelation after another. Level after level of secrecy. At home, at work. Sickness manifesting in her eyes. Cassandra always mentioned a plan. A way out of this apartment. A better future. She never mentioned becoming a cog in some secret machine.

The front door clicks, squeaks open. Max flips back the papers, replaces the Bellmer puppet book, and stands away. Cassandra enters from the hallway. She looks at him. Says nothing.

His chance to speak. How often has he resolved to force some issue? Each decision to bring matters to a head trails off somehow, ends in nothing. An intolerable status quo extends, on and on, his concerns swept aside whether or not he uttered them. Max wants to scream, somehow break through her impenetrability. He's part of the problem, he knows. Inertia, passivity, when it comes to her at least. Unwillingness to cut free, even from something he's no longer sure he desires.

DIAMOND DUST. Whatever it means, the name makes him think of "Diamond Dogs" by David Bowie. Max finds the CD, puts it on without a glance at Cassandra. Too long she's dominated the stereo with her soundtrack for collapsing buildings.

He sings the opening line, raises his fist on "genocide!"

Cassandra crosses the room to check her pile of papers.

Max sits on the charred futon, reading lyrics in the CD booklet.

She approaches, sits beside him and sidles up close. She keeps her palms flat on her thighs. Despite this, her version of physical affection, he senses her formulating plans from which he's excluded. A creaking ladder into a sky opaque with the blackness of soot and metal dust. Cassandra wandering, part of some industrial doomsday. Himself alone in this place, ashen black, cold and still.

So close. A thousand tiny scars on her face and shoulders, each a pocket of metal that burned into her and cooled beneath the skin. Such tiny disfigurements, so many in number. Enlarged, in too great proximity, even the beautiful can seem ugly. All Max's friends, especially the men, everyone commented on Cassandra's beauty. Impossible to ignore. They all say he's lucky to have someone like her.

She drapes an arm across Max's shoulders and he shudders at her emptiness.

The next morning a new executive office has appeared out of nowhere beside Boaz's own, the company now two-brained in control of the cubicle-dwelling segments of its corpus. Max sees within the new office his neighbor conversing with three policemen, probably about the bodies they find every night along Lorraine Street. So many dead. No explanation.

Boaz stays shut away, alone in his office, even after the police are gone.

So much changed. What's the point of giving up dreams for salary if it doesn't come with some promise of security? If it can all be taken away, in times of upheaval like these? All Boaz's promises, hints really, probably useless with a second boss balancing the scale.

Max keeps trying to stamp out his fear before the embers ignite. Despite lacking adequate information, he remains determined to keep up the appearance of forward motion. Someone will let him know what's going on, or he'll figure it out himself. He'll get back on top.

The corner cubicle, Newton's until last week, is again occupied. Max has already forgotten the new guy's name. Legs asprawl on his desk, pant legs riding up to expose white skin over black socks, the man endlessly mutters into his phone, so monotone Max doubts anyone's on the other end. Within the droning monologue, the words: "…DIAMOND DUST…"

Electrified, Max leaps up, stumbles into the next cube. He spins the man's legs off the desk and grabs him with violent urgency. Max leans in, nose to nose. "What do you know about it?" He mouths the words: DIAMOND DUST.

The neutral-faced man thumbs the disconnect button. "I thought you were inside." The man's lips are pale, grayish. He looks around. "This is Planning unit, right?"

Max nods. "Boaz spoke to me yesterday."

The man looks skeptical.

"The janitor's closet," Max whispers.

Recognition. The man's face relaxes.

Max takes a seat. "The thing is, Dyno. I thought they were the ones getting the bid on Diamond Dust?"

The guy inclines his head toward the new office. "This new man, Fabrizio, he says Diamond Dust is so big, for the first time it's not Boaz… I mean us, versus Dyno. We're in it together, every engineering firm in town, every structural fab, every melt shop. And it's not just Portland any more."

Max still isn't sure what it is. He want more, something to flesh out the projection he imagines from Cassandra's plans, briefly glimpsed.

Boaz emerges from his office and starts toward Fabrizio's. He sees Max and stops. "What you said about Newton, I've been thinking. See if you can find him on the melt floor. He's too valuable to be slinging coal, or who knows what." Boaz mimes shoveling, a motion which unavoidably becomes a golf swing. He gives it up.

There's sense in what Boaz suggests. It's what Max wants. Why does it feel like being sent to Human Resources for a layoff?

Passage to the melt shop is blocked by the black-draped scaffold. Max finds a seam, slips through, and navigates a web of crossbars and platforms. Once beyond the layer of fireproof carbon blanketing the inner scaffold wall, a wave of fierce heat waters his eyes. Vision adjusts to a darkness mitigated only by a distant red glow. The factory he estimated doubled in size is closer to ten times larger than before, the expansion covering not just the old parking lot, but north and east as well, where days ago stood empty fields and a crumbling brickworks. A space so vast, walls recede in haze like the desert horizon. Machines hum and churn, the heartbeat of mechanistic life newly birthed. The melt pool a demonic ocean covering acres, serviced by a fleet of giant cauldrons.

So unfamiliar, all this. What insight can Max offer. The perspective of decades, worthless now.

Dead-eyed laborers plod step to discordant clanging. Rows of sullen hunchbacks, faces featureless, powder black. How will he find Newton, let alone recognize him? Drifting, drawn toward the central vat as if by gravity. A seething orange lake, millions of liquid tons, a city-sized repository of thermal energy. Ordinary melt pools are terrifying enough. This is like standing near the surface of a tiny, remorseless sun. One slip, and all that energy unmakes you. Fall in, leave nothing behind but a puff of ash and a tiny pocket of impurity soon churned away, dispersed. So easy to disappear. To be devoured by all this.

Max has visited steel mills around the world. Twenty years. He's seen nothing like this.

Too hot, stifling. Wants to move closer. Drawn toward an area of blinding intensity. Luminescent currents swirl just below floor level. What is it? Within hypnotic patterns of yellow-hot eddies, he perceives familiar shapes. Human forms. His mind reels. Yes, a pair of bodies. They swim and frolic together in molten steel. Impossible, of course it is. Max leans, grips the railing, squinting against the heat. Not just the two of them, intertwining in a fluid sort of dance. Beyond, others in the background. So many. All moving, unharmed.

One of the pair resolves to greater solidity, a set of proportions familiar as a face. Max gasps. His heart rattles painfully in his chest. It's Cassandra, enfolded, writhing with another. Max wants to turn away. Even in such shock, he can't deny what he's seeing. Everything's changed. It's all unknown, not just Boaz, the factory, Cassandra. All solid ground vanished. A world of deadly fluidity.

Her face rises from the glowing steel lake and turns to confront him. Any doubt, erased. The second shape, still touching her, Max recognizes as well. Fabrizio, it must be. Cassandra and the neighbor. The new boss. Too much. Max can't bear watching. None of this makes sense. He backs away.

The Cassandra shape disentangles from Fabrizio. Her movements change, from fluttering easily like a swimmer in a pool, to the slower motions of struggling against resistance. She climbs, as if stepping out of thick mud. Finally she steps free, the flow seemingly fully solid and able to support her, as if responding to her desire that it do so. Air cools her to reddish orange, standing there atop the steel, then climbing stair-like ridges at the vat's edge. As she reaches the concrete floor she's becoming flesh again.

Fabrizio remains behind, watching nose-deep from the pool, which remains fluid for him.

Cassandra approaches Max, her body some evolving intermediate between steel and naked skin.

"You aren't…" Max begins. "I thought we were…"

Cassandra lifts her arms, demonstrating for Max her new form, unblemished white, free of the many tiny scars. She turns and glides off toward darker realms beyond the pools, motioning for Max to follow. Eyes adjust, until he discerns the edge of a vacant space, a deep cavernous pit.

"I saw plans in the apartment. Some kind of sky ladder." His gestures, indicating uprising levels, stop abruptly when he realizes his closeness to the precipice.

Cassandra stands on the verge, toes extending into emptiness. "Wrong direction." She raises a thumb and points it emphatically down.

Max tries to look down. Such dizziness, he almost swoons. The yawning scale of the abyss. "I came looking for Newton," he gasps. "I don't even know how I—"

"You've been meant for this all along." Cassandra reveals a smile he's never seen before. It's terrifying. She isn't what he thought. Maybe never was.

A great descent is underway. A metal latticework of trusses and beams penetrating the earth. Rungs on which climbers probe the deepest dark, some of them colleagues, members of his team.

"H-horrible," Max stammers.

"No." Her smile broadens, disproportionate. More than ugly. Monstrous. "Progress. Culmination of our utmost destiny."

Again straining toward the threshold, Max cringes at the bottomless infinitude, desiring at once to turn away and to behold the alien construct of parts made by Cassandra and others like her. Pieces interlock, held in place by anthropometric steel fixtures. Workers swarm the metal grid, suffering at the tension. Ever more join the effort. Machines link in, ratchet lower, and hammer foundational stone. Diamond-tipped burrowers swarm, glistening as they spin.

Fabrizio approaches from behind. Slowly cooling, he stands beside Cassandra. Max feels a possessive reflex. He's aware this is absurd.

"The bosses like you, Max," Cassandra says. Always hinting, tenuous. Never quite a promise, not tangible enough to grasp. That's all she's ever given.

"We're ready to bring you in, Max." In Fabrizio's half-metal state of flux, his speech is slurred, guttural. "Just stop resisting. Do what you're told, and you'll run this. Otherwise…" Grinning, he extends an arm in a dramatic, balletic gesture toward the pit. His skin is clean and white, free of scars.

Max gives no answer. None is needed. He has no alternative.

Creatures barely human climb slippery hot from the melt pool, pass without stopping and slither over the brink. Each descends to an ordained position and slowly hardens in place. Bound together in an agonized realm of ash and steel, their relinquished dreams and forgotten pleasures form underpinnings of a new, transformed world.

The trembling ladder vibrates, emits a head-splitting tone. This resonance harmonizes like an infernal chorus with moans of torment echoing from the depths. Cinder plumes rise, black orchids blooming against seething red. Eyes water and burn, stung by primordial dusts which swirl up from the bitter dark.

Nothing to see or hear but a hellish roar. The future, unknowable. Max drops to his knees and crawls blindly toward the heat.

THE ACCIDENT OF SURVIVAL

We're driving, or really Beck is. I'm just a passenger. The world flies past my window, a series of inaudible visions which seem unreal in my detachment. Beck rests one palm on the wheel, watchband dangling from his wrist, sized loose on purpose. He wears driving moccasins without socks, and khaki shorts. Summer's over so he has the heat blasting so hard it stings my eyes. The stereo spins quiet electronica.

Pumpkin Ridge Road curves a shallow corkscrew and shifting forces reorient my body away from the door, toward Beck. To our left, an uphill slope of trees and moss. The road's opposite edge drops away to a brittle stream. The road flattens, begins to rise. Inertia acts upon us. The impulse to lean against the pull is automatic.

Beck jerks the wheel, an adjustment small in degree, yet forceful. Urgency seizes my attention. Sudden, heart-hammering life surges within me.

A massive truck looms ahead, a leviathan of silver and black metal hurtling. My impulse is to shout a warning, but Beck knows. In his face, urgent clarity is etched in deep lines. His mouth gapes. So unlike him. So unguarded.

The truck, too fast for this corner, straddles the line.

Beck adjusts, holds steady. Nowhere to go, no way to avoid this. Can't rewind.

Thoughts flash, concurrent with awareness of their absurdity: *James and Marcus will be disappointed—they'll think we forgot—their place so beautiful, that view—they'll think we stood them up until they find out—*

I scream, cover my eyes. My hand burns, spilled coffee. Forgot I was holding it. Yellow paper cup with chartreuse lid tumbles.

Another flurry, thoughts flitting weightless on hummingbird wings: *Last chance to see Beck—too late to turn, it's coming—so many places, always meant to visit—too late, now we'll never—what were we waiting—too late to—*

Shuddering rumble breaks the car apart. Universe trembles.

We vibrate—disintegrate—wait—

Shrieking tires. WHOOOOOSHHHH, jet scream overhead. Rumble fading. Tremors settle.

My eyes open. Beck beside me, driving straight. He lets a small exhalation pass pursed lips, a soundless acknowledgement of significance just passed.

Somehow, no crash. Is this possible? It missed us.

Inhale. How long since I drew breath? "What happened?" My voice. Lips numb, Novocaine slow.

Beck's face, too tan for winter. Hair too blond. That yacht captain sweater. His lips move to form a response. Nothing comes. I can't even guess what's he thinking.

"We almost died," I say.

"Everything… went so fast." Beck's voice is level, calm. "For a second, thought we were done for." He flicks a brief glance at the rear-view mirror. A minuscule shrug. Readjustment.

"Thought we were done for?" I ask. "Of course we were."

"Don't dwell on negatives, Ryan. You always do that." That dismissive little shrug again. "Anyway, remember? We've got this incredible weekend coming up."

Coming up. Future? He's right, weekend plans. James and Marcus's place, perched on a beautiful wine country hillside. Marcus is an architect, designed their place himself. James runs the winery, Lethe Hills Vineyard. I remember. That's where we were going. It's Saturday morning.

Beck grins at me sideways, as if it's all behind us. "Great dinner, wine. Hot tubbing. Then tomorrow, all day touring. VIP treatment at every stop, with James's connections. Every luxury, my dear. That'll set you right." He puts a hand on my thigh.

I look the other away, out the window. Still see him reflected, watching me as he drives. Evaluating.

"Maybe you're in shock. Poor baby." Trying to act like it's nothing, deny the reality of what happened. "Try to relax."

Something in me has fled. He must feel the same, despite trying to bounce back. At least enough of him remains intact to keep him propped upright, mouth set in a jaunty half-smile, as if this were just another morning, and today just another increment of time.

He's living out a story with no room for collisions.

Trees fly past. Time flits. Miles. I'm adrift.

Shouting brings me back. Beck's angry.

"What's wrong?" I bluff.

He's been yelling. Took me a while to answer. Too long.

Beck breathes audibly through his nostrils. "You were muttering. Scared me." Knuckles white on the steering wheel. "Some nonsense. I don't know what the hell that was."

I can't remember. "What did I say?"

"Nothing sensible." He shakes his head.

I remember thinking, I'm staring at a wall. Featureless, white. Nothing on the other side. Afraid to touch. Seems solid but I'm afraid it'll pop like a bubble. We brushed against death, passed near enough to smell its sour breath. That millisecond of contemplation, facing what awaits. Thoughts need only an instant to spin out, to elaborate new possibilities, like an epic dream in the five minutes between snooze button postponements. To come so near an ending is to pass some threshold. I've seen what comes after. Where my life, Beck, our home, none of that exists. In retrospect it all seems absurd, this preposterous, overacted stage play. Old pleasures break apart, interlocked beams of a construct that no longer holds. Pieces hit the ground and scatter. No outline is left behind, no hint of the shape that stood before.

Whatever I thought was me, nothing's left but wondering.

Far away, Beck's talking. I begin to respond, then realize he's on the phone, talking to someone else. Marcus, maybe James. Something about me. He's worried. At least we're safe.

He says those things.

Are we safe? What does that word come from?

I flinch. Shift amid shattered glass. Where is this? Barefoot, in the kitchen.

Beck runs in. He's wearing shoes. What kind of person sits around the house in shoes on a Saturday night? Is it still Saturday? Darkness beyond the windows.

Somebody's screams split my ears. It's me.

"Stay there," he says.

My feet are pierced amid glass shards and blood.

"Ryan, don't walk in it. I'll go get something."

How did we get home? I'm swimming in blood, tiptoeing on the edges of a thousand blades. Aftermath, blood pumping, soaking. Can't breathe. How do I fix this? I want to come back.

Beck runs back in with plush, charcoal gray bath towels. "Hold still." He tries to lift me, carry me out of the circle of shattered glass, but I'm taller and heavier, so he can't. He gives up, lays out one of the towels folded double, and gestures for me to walk on it. Glass stuck to my soles. Each step, a deeper cut. Beck flinches, reaches for me, draws back.

I walk the path made by Beck's towels, through pain and blood. Then I remember. "James and Marcus's. Why didn't we go?"

Beck looks grim. "You were upset. Wanted to come home."

I didn't want to be here. I don't. "The truck," I remind him. "It was right there in front of us. No way it missed."

Clear of the glass, I sit on the clean tile.

"That was this morning." Beck uses the second towel to wipe my feet. Blood. Sticky razor-edged glass bits. "And tonight, obviously, we're still here."

"Oww!" I flinch, pull my foot back. "There was no room."

Beck hands me the towel, stands away. "You're trying to create a crisis." His voice takes a new edge.

I stand. "A crisis happened. I didn't create it."

"Yes, you're creating one! Out of nothing." Beck never loses his cool. It's more than temperament. Control is his identity, restraint his philosophy. Now his voice shakes. "Why do you do this, Ryan? Look for things to be upset over."

"We died today. Smashed to pieces." Streaks of blood on the cream tile. My feet smear the blood around.

"If you're smashed to pieces," Beck says, "you don't stand around after, dropping wine glasses and arguing over bullshit."

I have to admit that point seems reasonable. "Who knows how it works?" That's all I can think to say. Maybe we die and some part of us continues where we left off? Continues the story in the direction we were headed? A new outcome branches off to convince us that we're still going. That life keeps spinning.

I say none of this out loud, but Beck glares at me as if he doesn't like whatever I must be thinking. "Why can't you let it go?" He seems resigned, tired of arguing.

"I feel like I've been shaken loose from life. I want to get back, but I can't." I'm angry, ready to sleep. Maybe tomorrow everything will be normal. I think of asking Beck to stay downstairs, in the spare room. Even angry, I realize that's a bitch move. I'm the one who's upset. Anyway, he'd refuse. I realize I'm trembling. My fists are clenched.

Beck opens the cabinet and takes out a trash bag. He stuffs in the towels, full of glass and blood, then washes his hands and pours a glass of red almost to the top. He moves up against me, hip to hip. "Come on." Suddenly playful, he lightly bumps my forehead with his. "Let's be buddies again. Wanna?"

His arm slips around my waist. I pull out of his grasp. Though I don't look back to make sure it's true, I visualize myself trailing a vivid stain across the kitchen tile, the dining room, then the carpet of the living room. I slam the guest room door.

Past midnight, still awake. Cold room, shitty cheap bed. How can we expect guests to sleep here? Why haven't they complained?

I'm alone. Not just now, in this room. I inhabit my own reality, out of phase with Beck. Walled off from everyone.

The night is dark enough. The room is quiet. Just waiting for thoughts to still. The chatter persists.

I flip back covers, roll out of bed, and climb stairs to the room where Beck sleeps. I sit right up next to his body, swelling and contracting like a giant lung in the radiant dark.

I slide open Beck's nightstand drawer. Within a folded cloth, his gun.

His breathing sounds nasal. Nearly middle-aged, mild asthma, a little too heavy. I heft the gun. Always surprises me, how heavy it is. That proves it's real. If I only imagined myself holding a gun, it would weigh exactly what I expect.

Of course it's loaded. No need to look. An unloaded gun, Beck says, that's an expensive paperweight.

I touch the barrel to his chest. Just barely, no pressure. It's easy to time the rise and fall to that wheezing rhythm. Trace the metal up his collarbone, his neck. Aim higher. Jawbone. Where would it do the most damage? The temple, thinnest layer of bone over brain.

I'd never hurt Beck. Nobody could ever want to hurt him. He's impossible to hate, but none of this matters anyway. None of it's real. Beck, Ryan, they're somewhere else. This metal feels solid in my hand, but it's not. It's malleable, a cloud shifting in the wind. Objects take any shape ideation commands. All of this, subject to change. Nerve impulses twitch, and everything's remade.

I pull the trigger.

Click. Was there a click? No burst of fire. Intention without effect.

Did I really pull the trigger? Hear the sound? Feel it?

A rush of doubt. There's no way to be sure, to go back and observe. My recollection is that I heard the click. Felt it.

What could stop a gun from firing? What could stop a crash, too late? Trigger leads to bullet. It's impossible to perceive the end. Shroedinger's cat slips around a corner. One version goes on living, another dies into quiet, eternal blindness. Consciousness follows the living, forever thinking, *How?* Thinking, *Something must have intervened.*

Then forgets.

You only think you pulled that trigger.

Turn the gun. Look down the barrel. Try it. Nothing will happen. I put the barrel in my mouth, feel the tip of the barrel with my tongue. Close my lips on the metal, tasting oil. Finger trembles on the trigger. Pull it. Eliminate doubt.

Wait for this to register. Feelings will come. Wait.

Beck, myself. We shouldn't die. Not today, not ever. Want my life again. Not just that, but to feel myself living. Feel the world a solid thing around me. Feet on the ground, a sense of the world around me. Air to breathe.

Take the barrel out of my mouth. Aim at Beck again.

What is this? Why am I...

So tired. Tired of everything. Fading from nightmare to absurd wakefulness. What if he caught me like this, looming?

Limbs heavy. Takes all my effort to slip the gun back, soundless. Shut the drawer. Climb across Beck's rising and falling body, rattling breaths the only proof of life ongoing.

I let go, and fall into our bed.

In a vaulted gold wood dining room, Marcus stands at the head of the great table, mid-sentence bragging about James's brilliance, his boundless energy, his new offshoot of the vineyards and winery.

James grinning, embarrassed but still very pleased, those amazing white teeth. He offers Marcus the first aperitif glass, pale amber. Pours for the rest of us, passes around.

This dining table is a huge, old world thing, a half-ton slab of oiled oak, down at the end nearest the window that overlooks that million-dollar view. That's the life they live, entertaining the wine industry people, hosting dinners and tastings. The plan this weekend was just us, a pair of couples. Acres of divergent strands of planted vines, green and brown. The richness of the land, growing things embedded in this gently sloped paradise. This might be my favorite place on earth. Lethe Hills Vineyard. Sunset across the valley.

I'm confused. We were on our way here, but turned back, went home. Maybe argued, then returned?

Dinner plates pushed aside. Four empty bottles of the '05 Pinot. Now James is explaining his newest thing, this artisan distillery, subsidiary to the winery. Lethe Exotic Liquids Division. Pear brandy. Grape vodka and grappa. Eau de vie.

All these details. Do I remember this? Did it happen? Is it happening?

Tiny glasses on a tray. James pours from another bottle, passes. Beck sips, offers words of praise.

The others look at me. Waiting for me to taste. Haven't I already? I'm supposed to taste, and smile, and tell James how wonderful.

I watch Beck sitting on the floor of the day-lit living room. I'm gone, he's alone. Watch his reaction, measure his pain. What kind of sadness is this? The suddenness of forced change? Recognition of an end? Bitterness of remembering some intimate detail, significant to him alone?

Must be dreaming this. I'm dreaming.

Bent in anguish, Beck moves to the couch as if lacking coordination, or compensating for bodily pain. He reclines, covers his face. Keeps twitching, rubbing his eyes. Can't sit still. Tears acidic, toxic. I smell them from here. Leans over for wine, sips, picks up a book. Puts it down. Looks around, as if he can sense me watching. Feel my presence.

The room is full of changes. It's not our house any more. A tree blooms in a giant clay pot where the floor lamp should be. Absurd pink lemons dangle from the branches. Impossible to read without the lamp. I try to spot the other changes.

Birch wood floors gleam absent the rugs, mirror bright like a TV commercial, unreal. The smell of lemons is false, more like furniture polish. Real lemon trees don't smell like this.

Everything glaring dream light. Not home. Some new place.

Beck rises, crosses to the stereo. Our old system, from when we lived in Seattle, not the high-end new gear. No red lacquer turntable, no planar speakers taller than me. He slides out scarred vinyl, deftly flips it. The surface reflects the shrill glare from the dining room, then he drops the platter on the Technics and places the needle. Just then, he's the guy I first met a quarter century ago, me DJing at The Vogue and Starlite, Beck spinning at raves. Life was so different. Pet Shop Boys, Donna Summer, Depeche Mode. At the clubs, all shirtless, dripping sweat. Our bodies, everything so alive. Drinking Red Deaths at Frontier Room, before and after.

I wonder if Beck's remembering it this way. His tears stream, glistening wet.

Our dark room. Beck breathing next to me. I try to sleep. I want to dream

Beck's the one who died, that I'm the one left alone. Want to know how that feels. Compare my grief to his.

Vibration in my skull. Eyelids flutter. Up against a cold wall.

Living room again, this time fluffy white area rugs like cotton balls ankle deep. Beck's gone, lost to me. Alone I stare out the dining room window. Down the slope of Capitol Hill, beyond yellow trees scattered among brick buildings, the city is cold and wet and soundless.

Aloneness is impossible to imagine until it's real. Then there's no going back. This was ours. It's worth nothing without him. Don't want to go on. Want to run, leave it behind.

Flicker of awareness. See what I'm doing? Trying alternate potential outcomes.

If I ever settle on one path, will it become true?

Eyes burn in the darkness. Awake. Am I really? What is it that signals not a dream? A feeling? A flatness to the real?

Hint of sunrise. Alone in bed, Beck's side rumpled, vacant. Mind fuzzy, thoughts lethargic, like after too much Cabernet.

Neglecting something important, but what? Lying here in bed, I'm missing out on something. I remember what Beck said. James and Marcus. We can still have Sunday, if I feel better. I should want to go. It's the kind of thing I live for, that gets me through the work week. Winery tours, the green misty landscape of Yamhill County. Walking the rows of vines. To be indifferent to that is insanity. To just lie here, missing out.

Maybe we already went. I'm having trouble.

All memory is the same. Memories of life, of dreams, wishes. All indistinguishable after the fact.

I think I remember being happy, wanting this. Choosing it.

My eyes press against the wall, trying to penetrate the veil. Ghostly inertia, emotional deadness. Thoughts scatter, body parts in a crash. A spray of blood. Atoms dispersed, the heat death of the universe. The tangible turns ephemeral.

Memory dies. Reality ends when no eyes remain to see.

I remember where this started. Pumpkin Ridge Road, the morning, sipping coffee in a yellow cup. A truck came around too fast. When was that? Yesterday?

Everything's behind me.

Maybe I died, Beck's in mourning, and my mind or whatever defines me came unglued and scattered like drifting seeds.

Maybe we both died. No way to survive that truck. A holding pattern. Purgatory. An echo of life that seems almost real.

Maybe I've been dead all along, and it took thirty crushing tons to break the spell. To reveal the hallucination at the hollow core of being.

Pause at the bedroom door. Look back at Beck in the bed, still breathing. It's my side of the bed that's empty.

The floor creaks under me on the upper landing. Careful on the second step. Don't want to wake—

Leave the garage standing open, the house vulnerable to the world. Anyone could walk in.

Start the engine. Drive.

Beck's dreams, or mine. A torment of repetition I can't stop. Not sure I want—

Dawn mist settles, a pale river winding the valley below our hill. Driving alone, I rise from the stream. Leave Portland behind for the hills thickening with trees. Ride the roads west. Germantown, Cornelius Pass, Skyline. Toward the end.

Human settlement trails off into a world so nearly natural I'm able to forget all the people. So many trees, most intact, others fallen, dead and rotting. Trucks barrel at first light down these roads, out of the raw hills of Scappoose and Vernonia, carrying trees away.

Someone cries for me. My name repeats. Beck, at home, crying in our bed. His anguish should pain me, should feel immediate. Emotions are remote, cold and damp, like obsolete newspaper stories left out in the rain.

I drive, in flight from a dawn always pending, never to reach the fulfillment of morning despite perpetual hints at the horizon behind. The last of night won't relinquish.

Trailing cries of anguish persist. Slamming doors, searching. Beck's bare feet on tile. He calls my name, finds the house empty. The garage, open.

I'm never coming home. I see that certainty ahead of me.

Jangle of car keys. My name. My name.

Eyes closed, I navigate by feel. Recognize my path ahead of me. A line through the curves.

I turn off headlights. Veer over the line.

Beck speaks as if he's beside me in the car. My last chance to look, but I feel the truck coming. Rumble of air compressing. Vibration. Then the sound.

When will I know if this has happened before?

Beck talking. Thirty tons of steel hurtling. Coffee burns my hand, I flinch. I have no coffee. The yellow paper cup with the chartreuse lid falls from my grasp, turns slowly in the air, never falling.

I feel peace. It doesn't matter what I do. Nothing—

This is real. Beck is present, in the passenger seat beside me. Nowhere to swerve. Nothing left but another tangent, a skewed divergence from where we left off. No new beginnings, no avoiding the end.

I have been driving all along.

Reach for his hand. Briefly I feel comfort. No longer alone. I close my eyes.

NO MASK TO CONCEAL HER VOICE

I'll go anywhere I want. I'm Lily Vaun. Just try telling me *No*.

Hear enough *Yes*, that's all you hear anymore. I've got enough *Yes* stored up to last me.

Sure, you know the Lily Vaun story, the ups and down. My glamor years, the envy of Hollywood. My later crashes, humiliations.

Once you're a star, though, once you've shined bright enough, that never fades. A certain level of fame, that sticks. Every time I disappear into some place like Alderberry Hospital, I get out and find the world's still hungry for my story.

Agents can drop me. Studios can nullify contracts. After that shit, maybe you give up.

Not me. Demand may be on the decline, but I'm still Lily Vaun.

I haven't had a screen credit in five years. I'm still worth eleven million.

I've wasted more luck and money than most people get in a lifetime. I still haven't run through the last of it.

I'm forty-two years old. Men in the eighteen-to-twenty-four demographic still want to fuck me.

So you go ahead, just try telling me *No*. I'll be heading for my next big *Yes*.

This time, my recovery's for real. I'm ready to kick ass again. All the king's horses, all the king's men, they finally wrapped up the unravelling threads of my psyche. This morning I ended a nine-month stint in Alderberry, which despite abundant luxuries, is a dreary place. All beige, not a single pleasure. No sharp edges.

Walk out that door and the very same day, I'm on a plane for Paris.

De Gaulle's a weird airport. Countless times I've seen it, always wrecked on something. Seeing it sober is a first. I mean sober, not counting my one prescription, Doc Sennett approved.

The place is all white lines and glass, the desolate futurism of a *2001* space station. Or *Ballardian*, that's a word I haven't thrown around in a while. Back in '99, I co-starred in *Concrete Island*. Used to drop *Ballardian* into interviews all the time.

I walk the long hall, past yellow lights which flick past evenly spaced in hypnotic rhythm, like staring into a dream machine. Something I've noticed, just since I'm sober. The rhythms of the world sort of rub off on me. Brain waves fall into sync. Not sure I like it. The last thing I want is to be too susceptible. You won't survive this world, being too influenced by what's around you. Always waiting to be done-to.

For so long, I was always in demand, even after hospital stints, rehabs. At some point, one crash or another became too many. How do other people get jobs without an agent? I've never had to try.

Still in Alderberry, I got an envelope from the director, Leer Aster. Serious A-list, but strange, reclusive. French postmark.

A brief note. "The new Aster production needs Lily Vaun's magic."

A cashier's check. US dollars, lots of zeroes.

No signature. Just "NO TIME FOR WORRY," hand-scrawled across the bottom in lavender pen. Fucking weirdo, no question. The money's exactly what I needed. The flattery aspect, I mean. I don't exactly need the funds.

Paris sounded just right. Doesn't Paris always sound like that? A solution?

Now that I'm here, there's this little voice whispering, "Uh-oh! What the fuck are you doing?"

I block out the voice. *Na na na*, not listening. By the time I'm done, the trades will announce Lily Vaun's out, she's working. Then I'll fly home, interview agents. Keep pushing, moving forward.

First thing, *la livraison des bagages*. That much French I remember. Baggage claim.

A side-lit chauffeur awaits glittering, decked out in yellow-gold sequins, jacket and pants, hat and gloves. A real Siegfried and Roy vibe, typical Leer Aster bizarre. He holds a sign, my name beside some three-armed yellow symbol, the same that appeared on Aster's letterhead. Must be the production company logo.

I walk past without stopping. The chauffeur grabs my rolling tote, carries it easily, and surges ahead. He's no taller than me, narrow through the shoulders, but his movements are confident. Strong. On him, the spangly outfit seems theatrical, not fruity. I catch no more than a glimpse of his face, register no expression. He says nothing, just keeps walking so fast I have to hurry, trying to catch up.

"They gave me a hard time at customs," I say to the back of him, really projecting so he can't pretend he doesn't hear. "I mean, snotty, like, *quelle purpose* was I for *visitez* to *la France*. Anyway, what do you think I gave her right back? Just the shitty answers she deserved. But she wasn't having it, and I start thinking uh-oh, is this bitch seriously about to turn me away? I mean, they're going to border block Lily Vaun? Luckily, the next booth agent recognizes me, comes over all grinning, both thumbs up. You know what she says?"

The chauffeur doesn't slow, doesn't turn. Doesn't answer.

"Guess it's time to hit the road!" My voice rises, delivers the famous catch phrase in a girlish pitch. "The whole world still loves my Amber movies."

He turns toward me, still walking. I think he's about to speak. Instead he offers a slip of paper, a folded note.

"Inform the chauffeur of any chemical support required," I read. Then the little symbol, and *Aster*.

He flicks a glance back, again so quickly I get no sense of his features.

"Avoiding that shit, that's half the reason I'm here. Just read the trades. If I had access to my old scripts, I'd be dead in a month. Ha ha, scripts, that's funny, right? Actors, we reads scripts. Then to get drugs to fuck our lives up, we need other scripts."

Still no response. Why won't he speak? If he's got some problem, I can't figure it.

"Anyway, no pills, just the one stabilizer I brought with, Doc Sennet approved. I could use red wine, though. My last tango in Paris, they had all the *vin rouge* a girl could want."

Aster's gold glitter limousine, an absurdly opulent converted hearse, idles outside a 5th arrondissement late bar.

The chauffeur returns, hands me a bottle already uncorked.

As the limo pulls away, the sun roof retracts. Night sky feels dangerous, like it might pull me out of here, lift me away. Black stars shimmer against perilous depth.

The world spins fast, too much to absorb.

Trying to mellow, I lean back, sip wine from the bottle.

Paris. No midnight traffic, just palpable antiquity and whispers of suicide poets. Each inhalation carries fragments of disintegrating statues, dust from crumbling mausolea. Tourists find this evocative. People like Aster pay fortunes to mingle among blowing spirits, monuments to saints, museums for dead artists. Statues of Balzac, Voltaire. The dead hang on, refuse to let go. They inhabit every room, linger around corners. Like my memories.

Who needs reminders they're dying? Maybe people who've already lived enough don't mind the specter looming. That trembling curtain, threatening to drop.

Not me. Nine out of ten shrinks agree, that's my whole fucking problem. Unwillingness to accept reality.

Bullshit. I've got too much unfinished business. Addictions set me back, plus a few bad decisions. Just need to stay clean and work, finish projects, rack up credits. Some comeback recognition, maybe a nomination.

The clock spins, spins. There's still time.

I lean forward, shout, "Which hotel?"

I'm hoping not the Ritz. Too fussy, and they know me. Jesus, I do not feel like being recognized.

The chauffeur turns, grants a quarter profile glimpse through glass.

Will he answer?

Again, nothing. His face seems unreal, like a porcelain mask. The merest hint of eye creases. Smooth, too pale. Frozen, incapable of expressing emotion.

It's a look I've seen too often in the mirror.

Traffic drops away. We turn into a district I don't recognize. Gilt perimeter walls reflect golden light, transmuting the midnight scene into sunset.

Gates swing open. We pass through the barrier wall, like a castle carved into the heart of Paris. Otherworldly, extravagant, like a slightly more tactful Las Vegas. Not French, not American, more a liminal fantasyland, all lit fountains, luminous canals. Statues loom, seeming alive.

The car stops, my door opens. Light spills in, reveals large pearls scattered underfoot on the limousine floor. My hand goes to my throat. The pearls, not mine, roll minimally in unison, as if the car were still in motion.

I step out, Charlie about to explore Wonkaland, or Dorothy verging on colorful Oz.

Guarding the entry ramp of pale yellow brick are two upright mummies sealed in glass, bandages unwrapped and dangling, desiccated forms preserved with gold powder which glistens under spotlights.

I follow the chauffeur inside. An impressive exhibition of curiosities lines the foyer, and the many halls divergent from the center. Bizarrely obscure memorabilia, fabulous costumes and props anyone would recognize. Nic Cage's snakeskin jacket from *Wild at Heart*, Lecter's restraint mask from *Silence of the Lambs*. Rosebud. Yoda. A man-sized *Gojira*.

Jesus, Dorothy's ruby slippers.

Even by Hollywood standards, it's a statement of determined excess.

The foyer's central fountain lacks the showstopper quality of the rest, yet it's the fountain that transfixes me. The sparkle of the water under piercing lights, like weightless diamonds. So brilliant. Fragile. Water falls, keeps falling, never damaged or diminished. An endless cycle of bright, undying renewal. The world drops away. I don't mind being alone.

Everything's quiet, all but this falling water. I guess the chauffeur must've gone, then I look up, find him there across the mist, watching protectively. That face, that pale mask, betrays nothing. I keep thinking he'll excuse himself, leave me alone. He doesn't move.

Is this piercing sharpness just a matter of the light? Maybe this isn't water, but some dazzling liquid designed specially for illuminated fountains.

More likely it's my bent perception. An artifact of a mind's ruined chemistry.

Stop. I'm clean, can finally claim that achievement.

Not quite feeling it.

"I want to sleep," I say, unsure who I mean to tell.

"No." A voice behind surprises me. "Time for work."

Finally the chauffeur speaks?

I spin. Not the chauffeur.

"Welcome to my home." Aster grins as if my presence delights him, then closes the gap between us. He runs his hands all over me, wherever he finds bare skin—shoulders, arms, hands, even my face. He's wearing eyeliner, a hint of blue eye shadow. Glossy lips.

All the notions I have about the man standing before me come from magazine articles and gossip. I've never met Leer Aster, or don't remember if I have. Everybody knows his look. Always silver suits over rubber S&M shirts, spiky hair prematurely white. The man's barely older than me, late forties. He lived on food stamps, working as a night watchman, while he scraped together his surrealist Seuss-meets-Cronenberg debut, *Flowers in the Shuttermaze*. Uncompromising and darkly perverse, it lit up Cannes and cemented his reputation.

Next, he took his swing at the Hollywood mainstream—megabudget, A-list cast—and despite pressure to succeed, expectations he'd fail, *The Spectre of Memory* topped 2008's box office. Wowed critics, blew everyone's minds. In lieu of salary, Aster took points. Variety put his take at $190 million.

Since then, everyone with an opinion, which in Hollywood means everyone, tried guessing: *What will Leer Aster do next?*

Return underground, self-finance a DV-shot guerrilla production with a small cast of unknowns?

Or swear everyone—from execs to catering, from d-girls to talent—to the airtight secrecy necessary to shoot Hollywood's first completely covert, leak-free big budget tentpole picture?

Nobody really knows.

I know he's got me in mind. That lovely note, all praise and poetry, sent at a time when nobody would touch me. His resources, his reputation. Aster can do any project he wants.

He wants me.

We're in France, so of course I kiss both cheeks. "I shouldn't impose on your home. Perhaps a hotel?"

"You'll have the place to yourself," Aster assures me. "I'm never home until production wraps. I'm only here now to take you to the studio."

"Work, now? It's the middle of the night. I'm game as anyone, dear, but I've been traveling days."

"You imagined sleep?" he asks.

I smile, striving for lighthearted charm. "Sleep, yes. It's something I try to do most nights."

Aster leans in, grinning perversely. "Fatigue puts one in duress. Discomfort weakens restraint."

"Restraints can be fun, used correctly." I'm not sure what I'm saying. Defaulting to flirtation? Despite this smile, I'm determined to kill this idea of working straightaway. I really am bleary-eyed, stale from flying.

"The unique mood of my films, my special trick, let me tell you. It's shattering control." He smiles, not at me, and claps his hands forcefully as if declaring a scene's end. "If you need espresso, the chauffeur will provide. Now, to work."

I follow.

Wide open darkness. How broad is the universe? Boundaries too distant recede into invisibility, lose any function as limits. Walls should hold us in, prevent wandering off to infinity. Everybody needs tethers to prevent that inevitable drift.

I follow Aster into the void, alone, the chauffeur left outside with the car.

What does Aster have in store? Somehow he gets away, disappears. I'm left dangling.

A moment, a flash of indecision. Panic.

POP! A loud, amplified, emission from an unseen public address speaker.

"Is she ready?" The voice echoes, accented and slurred. Not Aster, but a strange masculine voice.

If this is the soundstage, they can't possibly be ready to shoot. No lights, no cameras. Just emptiness.

As if reading my thoughts, Aster speaks, somewhere near me in the dark.

"Filming is ended."

A yellow light flicks on, illuminates this outsized madman striding toward me in exaggerated haste. Cinema's great eccentrics, Jodorowsky, Lynch, Almodovar, they have nothing on Aster. The manipulations, the groping hands. Obscure proclamations shouted from strawberry-frosted lips.

Filming, ended. Must be a joke.

Look around, consider what I've seen. No sets. None of the machinery of filmmaking.

Leer Aster has no intention of shooting me.

He draws me nearer a pair of shed-like boxes, unfinished wood, like Swedish saunas. The larger, a glass-fronted control room, contains sound recording gear. Opposite stands a smaller vocal isolation booth with a tiny viewport.

"Only this remains." Aster guides me, right hand across my lower back, left grasping my nearer forearm.

Through the window of the control room I see a wide mixing board, walls hung with rolled microphone cables, tall stacks of rack-mounted electronics. Some glow with the warmth of vacuum tubes, others with digital LED displays. Against the wall, an ancient Moviola editing table, spooled with 1" mag tape and 16mm film. This isn't pro-level Hollywood gear. Reminds me of the experiments and student projects I worked on back in the '80s, before my break.

Memory rushes back to one early project. I stop myself. Don't want to recall.

"Sound!" Aster shouts. "Get out here."

A narrow figure stands behind the mixer's eerie glow, thin face hidden behind oversized bug-eye glasses with white frames. The mantis-like man gropes his way out of the booth, moves vaguely in my direction.

Aster tells me, "Sound, he's another of my secret weapons."

I take a few steps toward this man Sound, meaning to shake his hand. He continues stiff-legged past me, as if I'm not even there. For an instant this registers as a snub, intentional, then I understand. His dark lenses, the maneuvering by touch.

Sound is blind.

I turn, glide up next to him, and take his elbow. He jumps. I close my hand over his. There's a quiver in his next inhalation.

"I'm Lily Vaun." At least for a moment, back in control.

Aster pushes me into the booth, prods my body into the narrow space, muttering oblique instructions. Apparently I'm to do overdubs, voice work for picture already shot. I've seen no script.

On the tiny screen, unedited rough footage runs, snippets lacking any kind of continuity. A young woman is featured, a different type from myself. Pixie blond hair, like Jean Seberg fifty years ago, when she stormed the screen in *Breathless*.

I turn to Aster. "What am I supposed to do with this?"

Her mouth moves in soundless closeup. A blur of hair, or skin texture in macro. Lips move, responding to another actor I'm not seeing. They give me only this woman, no reactions, no wide shots. Even her, I haven't seen clearly.

"What I desire is your guts," Aster says. "Raw emotion, the real spice. Kick the audience in the heart."

"There's too much missing." I feel unsettled, insecure. "These aren't scenes, just flashes. Who is she?"

Sound leans in, adjusts my microphone by touch, then returns to his booth.

"You've gone deep." Aster runs hands along my arms, then grips my shoulders. "You've lived it. Now, for film."

The footage stops. All lights die except in the booth.

I'm helpless. Where's the Lily Vaun confidence? I wait alone in the closed booth. No sound.

Yellow light flickers in the control room. Are they watching footage on the Moviola? Hot tungsten, celluloid and dust. I can smell it from here, the heat of the lamp, the ozone burn. The old way.

It's crazy, what Aster suggests. Part of me believes. Nothing but my voice, the microphone, and fear in my gut. I have to dig out what I can. Manage my nerves, and get ready. Try to bleed.

***

I'm beyond exhausted, flat on my back in bed. Who knows if I even accomplished anything? Just confused myself, frustrated my director. He's still at the studio, working.

I should want to sleep. Keep obsessing on this one thing.

I'm alone here. For the first time I can remember, real solitude.

So long, shut away, surrounded by a flock of loons. No silence. Too many cracked-bulbs, shrieking away the night.

Quiet.

When was the last time I slept behind a door not locked from outside? Nobody screaming. No obligation to bear witness to some neighbor's agony. If anyone's crying tonight, it'll be me. Nerves rattle like chattering teeth. Sanity teeters on a blade's edge, ready to cut. Will I slip?

No. Just rest. Lie motionless.

It's coming. See it coming, feel it rise? A wave hits me full on. Pounds me down, buffets, washes over, presses me down.

Memories.

Isn't this what I wanted, to get back to living? So much time wasted, pining for release. Nights obsessing on getting out, on freedom. Why do we lust for money, more than love or sex? Because money buys freedom. Freedom like this, to lie trembling in anger, in fear, unable to sleep. Wealth, fame, isn't that what everyone wants? That's power. Imperviousness to *No*. The right to live without rules.

And all I can think, since I got out?

Someone please tell me what to do.

So much yearning, striving. To climb over bosses, taxmen, voting members of the board. Fucking executives with their notes. Sacrifice everything to get free. Then what?

This terror.

I want a drink. I want pills. Not Doc Sennet's mellow ones. Fun, jazzy pills. Something to light me up.

Anything but lying here, facing myself. Straight, no chaser.

I wobble out of bed, find myself meandering down unknown halls. This enormous house, all statues and sculptures, memorabilia under spotlights. I'm a bleary-eyed kid shut overnight in the museum. It occurs to me, maybe

Aster left staff behind. That'd be great, meet his old footman, me wearing just this sheer T-shirt. He could snap an iPhone pic, sell it to the highest bidder, and there's my ass on TMZ.

Another corner, another dim hallway. The hall widens to an alcove, centering around a headless statue. A stone figure in yellow robes of real fabric, trailing to the ground. I step high to avoid tripping in the accumulated yellow fabric, which fills the hallway in tangles. I squeeze along the wall, press onward.

Just a dead end. A panel made of some reflective pale gold metal, like the shield Perseus used to gaze upon Medusa. No doorway. In its center, the three-fingered insignia, vaguely triangular. Aster's sign, from his letter, and the chauffeur's airport sign.

I search for seams, thinking some latch must be hidden. Some way to open this wall. What's Aster hiding?

The gold wall seems immovable, merely decorative, like a shrine or monument. Finally I give up, begin to drift away, and hear a voice behind. A woman, on the other side of the metal wall.

"Lily," she cries.

Did I really hear my name? So tired, can't be sure. My heart pounds, like a nightmare revelation.

I hurry back, past the enrobed figure. Despite lacking a head, it seems to watch me. The way it stands, scrutinizing, reminds me of the chauffeur.

I wind back to a more comfortable part of the house. Less museum, more home. Passage to the kitchen. Industrial range, walk-in freezer. Glass door refrigerator.

This isn't snooping. Just look without touching. Don't open anything.

Would if I could.

No, just wandering, observing. Thinking of wine, even beer. No, I won't drink. Just obsessing. Is it something I should be officially *not thinking about?* Probably.

Maybe if I know there's nothing here, I can stop thinking about it. Maybe sleep.

Of course, I could always go out, buy my own. We're still in the city. I don't have any local currency, whatever that is now. Francs, Euros? I could find a shop, offer to pay triple in dollars. They'd recognize me. Five years I haven't been onscreen, but my train-wreck life kept me on magazine covers. Probably in France, too. They like their films, the French. Isn't Depardieu Mayor of Paris or something?

Behind the glass, a row of clear bottles chilling, like champagne. Clear glass, liquid contents brilliant gold.

I swing open the door. Curious. Not planning to drink. I reach.

Remember what happens if you get started. That last crack-up, pretty unglamorous. Hysterical days, raving tears, finally found wandering, drunk and pill-wasted in the hills above Mulholland. Barefoot, mostly naked. So much blood, the cops who found me thought I'd been shot.

How does life go so badly wrong, when almost everything is right? Just the downside, maybe, to being someone who doesn't believe in *No*. Sure, I'm not great at respecting limits. I get that.

I need someone to apply the brakes for me. Long hours, pressure, endless vodka tonics. Abundant chemicals, prescription and otherwise, all to avoid a reckoning. A ruined heart, the gangrenous death that never heals. Before success, when all ahead was upside. Nobody knew my name.

I fell hard, so hard. My own fault I walked away.

Tried so many ways to salve the pain. A million A-list beaux, names like Brad and Jack, Bruce and Robert Junior.

I should've taken better care. You would've given me strength to survive, whatever fallout. Me and another girl. Would my career have risen like it did? Probably not. I could've handled it. Riding high from Amber, we could've weathered it together.

How did I convince myself to stay away?

I fall back into bed, afraid what I might do, where the memories might lead. Adrift, too much feeling.

What scares me most is I'll stop fearing the edge. That next time, I'll just keep walking.

I keep exiting the booth, requesting direction. I'm trying to act my way into something I can't see, don't feel. It's hard to overdub blind, to envision reality from only hints.

"Show us your desire," Aster commands. "Moaning, kissing. Let passion boil out of you."

Overhead, the daylight panels are open. Polished concrete reflects brittle light in all directions, piercing bright like Aster's fountain.

This place, not a living world, but dead aftermath. All sets struck, shipped away. Lighting rigs packed, cameras returned to rental agencies. A sunblasted vacancy. This tiny booth, a satellite to Sound's studio, bound by nothing but strewn cables, overseen by mad god Aster.

So exhausted. Nothing left but pain.

I can't work in solitude, but this is all I have. A desolate factory, no props to help pretend. No fellow players, no scenery. Some actors have real chops, can call forth the perfect emotional note, even in solitary reshoots. Once I watched Malkovich, alone in a soundstage like this one, work himself up to a trembling, sneering, perfectly-pitched retort to a line delivered months earlier. Alone, after everyone else had moved on to subsequent gigs.

I'm not that actress. To be jealous, I need to look into the eyes of someone and pretend they did me wrong. I need to project a relationship, motivations, shared history. I work off people. They're the only way I can summon real emotions.

Obsessing on *Can't* isn't going to help me do this. I have to try. I'm just setting up for failure. Pre-excusing another crack-up.

It's hard, though. This place is insanely hot, so bright I can't see my monitor. Am I supposed to dub blind, isolated, dripping sweat? What am I even seeing? Some impersonal embrace, supposedly passionate, fumbling toward a sex scene. Who are these people? Which one's me?

I want to hide. Sweat pours down my back. I'm swooning against the wall. I could die in here.

Nightmares of unpreparedness are universal. Show up for the final exam, don't know a single answer. All the questions written in code. Today feels like that dream. I'm trying to give what he wants. All morning, Aster has me acting short voice loops, without any visual reference. I'm supposed to speak a short bit based on description alone.

In response to his come-on, she hums a few notes.

How the fuck am I supposed to play this?

Seductive, playful growl. Carnal laughter.

It's impossible for me, and he doesn't care.

Disrobing. Spanking. Penetration.

That's Aster's focus. It's my discomfort he wants. My agony. Keeps opening the door between every line, screaming at me. He knows it's impossible.
He's bullying.

I go silent, stop reacting.

Finally Aster just stares. "No bonding company in Hollywood will cover
any production you're part of. Same in Britain, Australia." He leans in grinning, breath warm on my face. "You can only work here, with me. A genu-
ine madman."

I try again. Today, I'll give Aster all I can. Tomorrow, I'll bring a knife
from his kitchen. Either I'll wow him, or if that's not enough, it ends here,
in this box. He wants degeneracy, total breakdown. I'll let myself shatter
and bleed.

A dying star. A last performance to burn the screen.

Commotion wakes me. The bedroom, blue silver dawn.

Light from the hallway outlines a gold statue, now moving. He enters my
room quickly, determined, as if pursuing some urgent plan. The wardrobe,
he withdraws something. My clothing.

I'm out of bed, standing barefoot in my sleep shirt, rubbing my eyes.

The gold-uniformed chauffeur approaches carrying my white sleeveless
silk top and pleated black skirt.

"Doesn't matter what I wear," I say.

He throws these on the bed, grabs the bottom of my shirt, and lifts.
Without thinking I raise my arms, and it's up, over my head. He hooks
thumbs into the waistband of my panties at both sides, pulls down. I step
out.

Before I can object, I'm standing naked before him.

"Hey," I protest, barely awake. "I can dress myself."

I have no sense he's looking at me. He avoids eye contact, as in the airport and limousine, averts his face. I barely catch a glimpse as he kneels
before me, stands again.

I want to resist. Instead, I freeze. This conception of myself as an unstoppable force? Maybe it's just that usually, nobody resists me. I'm used to getting what I want. Everything I ask for.

"Stop," I say.

The chauffeur bends, holding the skirt, lifts my right foot in, and gently presses sideways against my hip to shift my weight. As I lift my left foot involuntarily to balance, he slips the other side of the skirt under. It shimmies up, past knees and thighs, over hips.

Briefly he stands before me. So close, his face appears artificial, immobile white, like the mask in Franju's *Les Yeus Sans Visage*. In an instant he moves, grabs the blouse, shifts behind. He guides my right hand into an armhole, then my left. Silk glides over my shoulders. He fastens the lowest buttons, leaves the rest to me.

He returns to the bureau. It occurs to me I should feel molested, but the coercive element of our dressing game feels playful, like a couple in wordless agreement acting out a violation fantasy. I'm not angry, just a bit stimulated. A sensation, a rushing tingle, sends me back into memory.

On location, no rules. The boundaries of actors give way to those of characters we portray. Looser, often justifying the indulgence of appetites. We use this game to approach things we're reluctant to admit we desire.

That's how it began. 1988, a certain co-star. Trading vodka shots, listening to Duran Duran in my trailer. Playful wrestling gives way to pinching. Exaggerated name-calling.

Bitch.

Kisses, bitten lips.

Whore.

Torn fabric, spanking. Bare skin.

The chauffeur drops a pair of black strap-heels next to the bed. I step in.

He takes my arm, drags me after him. Away from Absolut Citron, my "New Religion," and her.

On the way out, near the fountain in the broad central hall, we pass a gilt statue that wasn't there when I arrived. Hooded, with a great, flowing mantle. It's the same yellow-robed statue I saw two nights ago, headless then. Now it stands watch over the bedroom hall.

I struggle to button up as the chauffeur pulls me down the stairs, toward the limousine waiting at the driveway curb. My blouse flutters open, reveals my breast in the pale dawn. I laugh at such a scene, an actress half dressed, half asleep, rushed by her driver to an idling car. This drama makes more sense when I imagine it onscreen, not something happening to myself. I wonder where the story leads?

Then I realize, there's no paparazzi, no eager public. We're still within Aster's gates.

Aster's fingertips trace a line down my sweat-dripping arm to the back of my hand. I feel his frustration. I'm stuck, incapacitated. The heat makes everything worse, despite frequent ice water breaks.

Finally he removes the silver jacket, down to that absurd yellow rubber shirt. His skin's so dangerously pink I feel sorry for him, despite the way he torments me.

He closes the door, goes back to berating me through the viewport. Tiny dots of spit spray the glass. My attention divides between my screen, the headphone cues, Aster's lips moving.

"Soundproof, dummy. I can't hear."

I know his abuse is just manipulation. Still it stings.

The next time Aster throws the door open, Sound's behind him. One leans in, then the other. The booth fills with the odor of their sweat.

"Sun-wasted hag."

"Filthy prostitute."

They alternate taunts.

"Washed-up junkie."

"Talentless bitch."

Hands grope me. Prod, pinch.

"Frigid."

"Slut."

This jolts me. "Stop!" I'm angry, breathing hard.

"That's what I want," Aster says. "That's the Lily Vaun I paid for."

I feel myself slide. Can't let myself.

"I smell it," Aster hisses. "Some real emotion you're hiding."

I shake my head.

"What? Tell us!" he roars. "Into the microphone."

He doesn't understand.

"Love," I blurt. "True, real love. Pushed it away. It haunts… every dream."

He laughs, giddy. "Who was it? Who has power over you?"

I cover my face. He thinks he can do this to me?

"Say the name," he taunts. "You were on top, now you're ruined. Who?"

"Nobody." I want to say her name. *Saffron.* "It was me. I should've been stronger."

"It's Ferdinand Toth, isn't it? That weirdo. You love a gap-toothed man with long hair? Those red pants?"

"No."

"Everyone knew about you and Gianni Ross, through all the Amber movies. You ruined his marriage."

"He ruined his own marriage. I was just toying with him. Never love."

"Who? Everyone you dated, loved, fucked, they're all famous."

"Not all," I say. "Not before."

Everything flows back, 1988 again. Playful flirting in my trailer. Smiles, cherry ice cream. A first hint of what the lust would become.

Back then, my desires ruled.

Now, I let Aster take over. I give in, shriek my rage, vent a bitter flood into the microphone.

Sound rushes back to the booth.

I growl like an animal, eyes wild, tears streaming hot. Trembling in my chest, acid rumbles in my gut.

"Yes!" Aster roars. "Sound, you better be getting this."

If I faint, die, have a stroke, I don't care. So sick of holding it in. I need to be rid of this.

Aster's smiling, pleased with me.

I lash out with fists, shove him away. Eyes sting. Ashamed I've given in.

Aster takes me gently by the shoulders. "If you're broken, Lily, use it."

I grip the microphone, shriek and rage, spew all my poison, ventilate all the buried anger, all the pain. Give in, summon everything. The blackest emotion, the bitterest depressive cloud. Shame, self-hatred. Craving for death. Worst of all, my biggest fear, that all this is bullshit, suicidal ideation no more than a ploy to get back on talk shows. Fuel for a comeback. The thought makes me hate myself.

Trail off. Try to breathe.

"Saffron," I gasp. "My secret, twenty-five years. Saffron Page. Before the world knew me. Before I was Amber."

"Mmm, Saffron," Aster says. "Haven't seen her, not in any movie of yours."

Tears burn. My eyes sting from the poison. "A small film, artistic. Erotic. Me, with a woman." Starting to breathe again. *"Diamond Starshine."*

"Lovely title." Aster grins. "Why haven't we heard of that? Or your Saffron?"

A heart full of pleasures. Fucking, love-making. Soul-tearing orgasm. Blissful, wet kisses. Things I used to know, forgotten by memory. Remembered only in the gut.

I start to speak, caught in the momentum of release, of revelation. Try to stop myself. "Saffron didn't get much work after. Once I had power, I tried to help get her a few roles."

"So you stayed in touch," Aster says. "It's not a case of missed connections. You could've found her."

I climb out of the booth. "For a while. I lost track. She vanished after her agent, my first agent, cut her loose."

"Now, I recall a rumor," Aster says. "A lost jewel of sublime artistic perversion, early in Lily Vaun's career. Occult weirdness, explicit lesbian smut. You made your Amber millions, bought all the prints. Ensured it never came out on video."

I know what I did. Saffron's big chance, starring opposite Lily Vaun, about to become the big star of the '90s. What would *Diamond Starshine* have meant to her career? I should have helped her, not abandoned her.

"My new agent said I had no choice." I look down, can't meet his eyes.

Who else knew the story? My second agent, and the first I shared with Saffron. Who else?

Aster grinning. He knows all this.

"Saffron," I say. "You know her." My mind leaps, an electric jolt.

Aster shrugs. "Who do you think recommended you? Whose story do you think you've been dubbing?"

I look around, frantic. "Where is she?"

"Soon, my Lily." Aster cups my cheek in his palm, looks at me with utmost gentleness, with perfect understanding. "She's almost here."

From behind his back, Aster produces a book.

I've asked for the script I don't know how many times. Aster always laughs. Now I stop asking, and he hands it over. Plain black cover, perhaps a dozen blank pages. Then I come to the title.

"*The King in Yellow*." Flip ahead. "Act One."

"Are you sure you want this?" Aster whispers, watching. "No going back."

I jump pages at a time, skimming, until I find something familiar. "*Song of my soul...*" A girl, young, innocent. A cloaked yellow figure follows. Lust in the air, mingled with death. "I remember some of this."

"Maybe better if I just show you the next clip," Aster says. "Come, time to see what you've been performing."

He takes my hand, pulls me into the booth and presses up beside me. We're smashed together in a space meant for one, sharing a little wobbling bench. The monitor flickers up.

Click, hum. Snippet of argument. Then no sound.

I feel Aster's breathing quicken beside me, shallow and fast. So close, he keeps shifting, moving against me.

Picture flares to life, high contrast black and white. Abstracted bodies, too close to identify. The extreme closeup is intimate, uncomfortable. Fine details like skin texture shift in and out of focus.

"I keep dreaming this..." I trail off. "Where it started. Before it went wrong."

Images familiar, teetering madness. A cinematic nightmare imprinted on the mind. Such craving. Terrible hunger, fit to extinguish sanity.

The camera pulls back. A woman's hand moves across skin. Another breast. Two women. Reverse angle, hands trace the curve of a hip. Shoulder blade, upper back. Such proximity forces the viewer to take part in the intimacy.

A yellow sign. Brief flashes, more explicit. Tongue on nipple. Curve of hip blends into shadow, transitions to black. Fingers delve, the figure turns.

Illuminated feminine roundness, seen from the side. Darkness of the cleft, absolute.

On one set of hands, nails long, painted black. The other has thin, white fingers, nails short and natural.

Closeup on bodies of two women, lovers. The imagery is explicit, shockingly transgressive for a director like Aster. His work has always found a mainstream audience. For something like this, that's impossible.

It arouses, stirs me deep, in a place pornography can't reach. Thoughtless, instinctive, the hot and turbulent provocation of lusty dreams. I feel confused, watching headless bodies writhe and stroke. Despite this stirring, I'm trying to decode, to gain all the information I can.

Then I see the paisley-shaped birthmark under her small, pale breast.

I gasp, speak her name. "Saffron."

"No," Aster says. "Saffron was her screen name. That person faded away."

Her face fills the monitor. No older. No less beautiful.

Movement in the control room catches my eye. I look up, expecting to see Sound.

There in the yellow neon flicker, the chauffeur holds up a clear glass bottle of the gold wine I saw in Aster's refrigerator.

I realize I'm still acting for the microphone. Emotion without thought, words and tears in perfect sync with scene.

No need for script. Now I understand.

The chauffeur unbuttons his jacket, pulls it open. Beneath, no shirt, his skin startlingly pale. Perfect ivory white, like the mask he wears. Is it a mask? He shakes the bottle once, thumbs the cork loose, and amber wine erupts into white effervescent froth. It rises, overflows.

The jacket falls from shoulders, drops away. Narrow waist, small pale breasts. The birthmark. I'm stunned at the shape, the body of a woman. Somehow I failed to see.

The seething layer of milk-white foam settles away, leaves behind splendid radiant hues, veins the color of opal, skin like diamond.

I gaze on her face, finally able to study it. Why did I think this was a mask? Too smooth, too pale?

I wasn't looking at her face. Now I see.

She pulls back the hat, reveals a boyish platinum blond flip.

Still I'm acting, voicing guttural cries and carnal moans as I watch her move in a slow-shifting dance, as if she perceives music I can't hear. Both of us perform our separate pieces, eyes locked.

The image of her dancing repeats on my monitor.

I have to break through, see her in the flesh. I open the booth door, rush to the control room.

There is no mask. Long black eyelashes, blood red lips. Eyes, familiar, so clear. Her face, straight out of dreams.

"My Lily," she says, eyes intent. "You haven't changed at all."

"I don't feel…" I breathe. "I don't recognize myself."

Saffron, lost to the long winter of my insanity. Poisoned by my betrayal.

"You never knew my name." She leans close, extends her hand. "I'm Camilla."

I take her hand. It's like a first meeting. A new beginning. "I'm Lily Vaun." Am I, though? Still?

Movement in the doorway behind. Aster, now changed, cool and impervious. "You completed my great work." His voice is gentle, his gaze far away, as if he sees through us, to another place. "A gesture across worlds. Voice of Lily, image of Camilla."

"How do we—" I begin.

Aster raises two fingers of his right hand. Above the fingertips appears a pinpoint star of pure yellow light, more brilliant and penetrating than the light of his fountain. The light burns bright and cold, shining over a face I thought I would never find.

"How do you beat time?" he asks. "Let me show you."

My tears again. This time they don't burn. These tears wash the charred pathways of all that have fallen before.

My love leans closer, so near I smell her skin. "It will be far," she whispers.

Life comes undone. All my worn threads unwind.

"Carcosa," Camilla says.

Already I see, and recognize. All else gone. All but Camilla, who remains.

THE JEWEL IN THE EYE

1.

"The jewel resides within the eye, not without.
Covet not outwardly. Look to the mirror."
—Viso Mievske, *The Jewel in the Eye*

What bothers Sibyle is knowing her husband Lukas is in their bedroom down the hall, fucking a younger version of herself. The other women of her book club seem not to notice as Sibyle circles the grand piano at the center of the condominium's window-dominated living room. The others sit chatting among themselves as their hostess hides, concealed behind the upraised piano lid, staring into it like a black mirror. Even as she feels contempt for such absurd self-absorption, she looks carefully, tries to appraise herself objectively. She wants to relinquish her own preconceptions, truly see herself the way others see her.

Sibyle hates any aspect of her life which resists her control, worse when such factors reside within herself. What she desires most is to settle this anxiety within her, a wave which threatens to carry her away, beyond distraction into… she's not sure what. She might scream. The possibility strengthens her resolve. This shouldn't get the best of her. Wayward emotion shouldn't interfere with the life she's trying to create for herself, and for Lukas.

The situation—not a problem, merely a situation—is this newest occupant of their condominium. Not a roommate, exactly. Not another woman in any true sense.

No, the thing in the bedroom with Lukas is the shaper Sibyle made, a gift she created from her own design, a woman shape, intended to resemble a younger Sibyle. She still believes it's a good idea, the best thing for them both. Last night when it was done, when it began to move and speak, she felt real delight. And later it giggled and grinned in a way so familiar, just like the college sophomore Sibyle had been when she met Lukas. English 411, Romantic Poets. That Sibyle, a sun-lightened blonde who liked to go barefoot, read Byron and Shelley. She picked flowers in the memorial square, wove them into wristlets. Had skin so flawless, it seemed nothing external might ever touch her.

It took Sibyle until dawn, many hours of concentration and creative strain, before she refined the shaper so it was exactly the way she wanted. It seemed at any moment ready to recite poems Sibyle used to know, the old words imminently about to spill from that new mouth. So vividly Sibyle recalled how it felt, memorizing those words three decades earlier.

The new arrival forms a third point in a newly-created triangle, a shift to a relationship that has always been a straight-line mutuality. Sibyle calls the thing "Si," her own college nickname. She was so different then. It's hard to imagine the new Si, who isn't even exactly a person, might be very much like her old self. More likely it resembles Sibyle's conception of what she used to be.

At this moment, she's trying not to think about Lukas, behind the second door down the hall, shut in the bedroom with Si. Not another woman, just something resembling one. This is Sibyle's idea. How can she complain?

She wonders if this tendency toward obsession is influenced by the book, that its themes might be influencing her. Image, identity, and the way self-concept shifts through time.

The book they're meeting to discuss is *The Jewel in the Eye* by Viso Mievske, equal parts novel, poetry and philosophical tract. Some consider it an elegant rhapsody on unorthodox love, while others might call it a nihilistic and obsessive rant on loss and disappointment as the primary constituent parts of life. Such a broad spectrum of tone and mood, Sibyle supposes, resembles human existence itself. As with every book discussed by the group, some women take it seriously, while others merely use it as an excuse to meet, to gossip and drink wine. All four are over forty, married, and seem at least outwardly to love their husbands. Sibyle has permitted herself covertly to wonder if one or more conceives of themselves as stuck, believing extrication might be more painful than course-staying.

Sibyle is sure of one thing. Each finds within the group some reward they can't obtain at home.

What Lukas is doing is similar. It's nothing to do with lack of love, or loss of intimacy. Sibyle and Lukas must both seek the broadest possible range of experiences. Sibyle gives Lukas all she can, and he does the same for her. To do otherwise would be worse than selfish. It would lead to stifling and resentment.

It's true, there are things husband and wife can't provide one another.

Sibyle looks up from the mirrored lid of Lukas's glossy Bösendorfer, straightens and heads for the kitchen to break open a case of the new Pinot Noir. One aspect of book group ceremony is the closing of the lid, the placing of a folded tapestry on the piano top, then glasses, and bottles of excellent wines. Always something new, sourced from one of the worthy labels of Oregon's wine country in the quiet hills between Portland and the Pacific.

Other than during book group, the piano lid remains propped open in the event Lukas wishes to play. Over a quarter century, Lukas Novak has accreted an imposing fame, first as soloist and accompanying performer, in a straightforward manner, of the established piano repertoire. His subsequent and greater notoriety developed with the emergence of his own artistic idiosyncrasies, as he began to perform his own compositions, ultra-minimal tone poems of glacially-shifting piano chords overlapping, seeming always on the verge of fading delicately into silence. Early on, Lukas admitted to Sibyle his hunger for greater success and renown, worked hard in that pursuit, only to find his fame swollen beyond all control, despite later efforts to rein in or even reduce it.

Sibyle returns, rests the pair of bottles on the floor, and lowers the piano lid quietly. She places the folded tapestry onto the piano, then the bottles, and returns to the kitchen for glasses. On her way back, she hesitates. To her left, the hallway to the bedroom. She could disappear, listen at the door.

The others might notice. Would they wait? Group talk hasn't even started yet.

What would be the point? Foolishness. This was all her idea.

She places four glasses on the tapestry, and finds herself leaning over, staring again into the piano's mirrored surface. Her eyes have changed. One mirror attracts, one repels.

Damn Mievske. His philosophy seeps into everything. Accept disintegration of self, detach from external demands. Shrug off the perpetual torment of death-fear.

Why should she look, what need would it fulfill? She knows what she'd see. The other body, familiar in every detail. Not Sibyle herself as she looks today, but before, an image more familiar to mind, more truly alive in her self-conception, than her present self. She's sure self-concept arrests at some stage, never changes again. Anyway, the two of them are indistinguishable, separated only by time. Sibyle now exhibits qualities refined by diet, exercise and weekly visits to ZYX, Portland's best boutique. Her black dress fits impeccably, shows off the womanly hourglass shape she never had in youth. Hair once golden, now dark, flowing in thick curls past the center of her back. At wrists and throat she glistens. Jewels—*the eye*—lend their beauty.

Some flaws apparent in proximity become invisible with distance. Because of this, others dismiss her insecurities. They envy her lips, her shape, compare her to Isabelle Adjani or Monica Bellucci. Such perfect skin, they say, not seeing the lines, the unwanted blemishes, the tiny imperishable hairs. Friends see flaws in themselves, yet remain blind to imperfections in others. Everyone, forever convinced the rest of the world is more perfect than themselves. The ultimate curse, proximity to self.

She stares. Always another mirror.

Someone behind her in the room says: "Even insoluble grace disintegrates before the lens of self-regard." A quote from *The Jewel in the Eye*. Must be Maud, clever Maud.

The others laugh. They've caught her staring at the reflection.

Sibyle looks up, turns and smiles. She uncorks the first bottle, fills empty glasses.

Four copies of Mievske's book await on the table. On the cover, a face in profile confronts a mirror, an eye reflected back on itself. The eye, a perfect opaque transparency, self-reflective. Which is the jewel, the true eye, or the reflection? The book attracts Sibyle, draws her to approach. She wants to be among the others. Window light glares, brightness in late afternoon extreme, intrusive. She leans against the piano, afraid to trust her legs. She wobbles, thinks she might fall.

The important thing is to avoid picturing what's happening, elsewhere. No harm acknowledging that certain acts must be transpiring, but no need to confront the reality. Better instead consider the benefits. For Lukas, for herself. This accomplishes several things at once. Giving Lukas a new gift, opening possibilities for herself. The luxury of control, of broadened horizons. Lukas requires privacy, yet the contradiction is that sometimes in his most withdrawn state, he craves contact. He suffers terribly, trying to force himself to create the next piece.

Sibyle has her own shaper, a cipher used for housekeeping, faceless by design. An entity of pure functionality. This new one, Si, may differ in the sexual aspect, but the featureless, unnamed other isn't really so different. It's a matter of practical utility. Tools allow the enlightened to extract more from life.

Si's laughter. Sibyle remembers. The familiar way it looked at Lukas. Affection.

2.

"What a forceful and penetrating mechanism is scrutiny.
The uttermost power is to exert judgment upon all one sees."
—Viso Mievske, *The Jewel in the Eye*

Others in the group make similar accommodations.

Autumn permits the affairs her husband acknowledges openly.

Bellamy advocates open marriage, a flexible arrangement both for her husband and herself. Their relationship welcomes a rotating cast of thirds, sometimes also fourths, more often women than men.

Maud was first to give her husband a shaper. The idea was not hers, originally, but worn down by arguments, exhausted by Franklin's persistence, Maud gave in. The passivity with which Maud allowed the balance of marital power to shift out of her favor evokes in Sibyle a pang that aches whenever she contemplates it. Worse, Sibyle considers problematic that Franklin, in envisioning his own ideal, crafted a stereotypical bombshell right out of mainstream pornography, completely opposite his petite, almost boyish wife. Of course, Mievske says we all contain manifold desires, many submerged as far beneath consciousness as lava churning beneath a volcano. Still Sibyle cringes, thinking how Maud must feel, being made so aware how far removed her own appearance is from Franklin's ideal.

Sibyle's determination to stop this fretting is not about conformity with relationship patterns of friends, but a desire to relieve Lukas from a persistent state of suffering. Beyond mere existential unhappiness, Lukas anguishes in particular over his process of creation. The birth of each new piece drags him through a course of terrible anxiety, even physical pain. Over months of composition, editing and refinement, he fights through a painful trial of self-loathing and depression. Even after he's finished, the black cloud persists, sometimes for months. From build-up, to creative struggle and aftermath, lately his entire life seems occulted by the shadow cast by some massive threat, invisible but looming.

Lukas requires time undisturbed at the piano in order to create. Without his labor, Sibyle understands, their life would be nothing so fine. This corner condominium, with its view of city and sky and Mt. Hood's white summit. Each time he recovers, muttering vows of suicide and *never again* along some path to rest and gradual recovery, even as Sibyle persists in believing he'll finally gain some respite of mental peace, she wonders how long until next time? The recurrent cycle of cigarettes, tired red eyes, gray hair hanging lank over his face. Nights sleepless, sometimes hours without a single key struck. At times in the dark while Sibyle tries to sleep, Lukas sits weeping at the piano bench, raving that he'd rather die than produce another note. All this anguish to create something intended to give peace, to create for the listener a pure, crystalline mental state.

Suffering must be a necessary component of the process. Dive into pain, rise again to the surface. Breathe, then dive again.

Sibyle has often considered herself different from her friends, less prone to weakness, less likely to compromise. In proximity, such differences seem to eradicate, distinct lives gradually bleeding together. Now, she's like the rest. But they're happy, at least comfortable. They convey, to the eye at least, a semblance of contentment.

It was Sibyle's idea to give Lukas something, to create in particular a shape similar to herself. She thought it might be fun for them. Lacking children and pets, the condo seems too spacious at times, sometimes almost empty, even as they reside within it. Sibyle liked the idea of this new creature fluttering about, skipping barefoot through the kitchen, leaning out over the balcony rail to discover the city. Perhaps they might talk. An independent reflection of herself, separated only by time.

Time.

Entropy outworks all efforts at clean living. Sibyle fights the temptation to eradicate flaws artificially. She's still beautiful. Not only for a woman near fifty, but judged against anyone, she stands out.

Time to snap out, to engage. Her friends are still here, waiting to discuss the book. She's glad to have these friends.

Sibyle sees Maud note her distance and distraction, Maud's mind already working, making connections. The look Sibyle knows must color her face. The many past jokes, hints and questions. Her attention focused unusually down the hallway, past the door.

Maud seems to apprehend something.

"You did it, Sibyle," Maud proclaims, to the others more than Sibyle herself. "You finally gave Lukas a distraction."

Sibyle's mouth freezes. Her eyes scan left, right. She can't speak. Something's wrong.

This non-denial cements the matter for the others.

"You let him take a mistress?" Autumn, half-smiling, tosses her curly pile of garnet red hair.

"No, that's too uneven," Bellamy says. "Get something for yourself."

Autumn giggles. "Or at least reserve the right."

Sibyle waits until they settle. "I made him a shaper, yesterday. He's with it now." Her eyes point the way.

This silences them, at least for a moment, then after a pause, the chatter of excitement surges. Brief argument, laughter, schoolgirls talking over one another.

"Is it like a real person?" Autumn cries.

"Or one of those swoopy porn girls?" Bellamy flits a covert glance at Maud.

Autumn looks confused. "What are they anyway? I still haven't seen yours, Maud. I mean Franklin's."

"Shapers, I don't really understand," Bellamy admits. "I keep hearing people say the word, but how do you make one?"

"Yeah," Autumn says. "I wonder too. Is it like something you can buy?"

Too many questions.

Sibyle and Maud look at each other. Sibyle made the housekeeping cipher as a trial run, before she made Si. Months before that, Maud was already exploring possibilities, all the while telling Sibyle her plans. Designing new features.

"Nothing like that," Maud says. "You can't buy one, I mean if you made one and tried to sell it, it wouldn't work for anybody else. It's from you. Like a private idea."

Autumn and Bellamy look at each other, more confused than before.

Maud continues. "Think of it this way, our lives are missing something. I mean, everybody, we all have a lack. Just conceive of what you'd want, what it would look like. How it would feel. Then you're most of the way there."

Bellamy looks confused. "I still don't… There's lots of things I want in the world. I want to spend January in Belize, July in Amsterdam."

Maud lifts an eyebrow. "That's not how—"

"I want to write beautiful poems, and climb mountains," Autumn says.

"I want the tits I had when I was twenty." Bellamy grins. "Really, I'd settle for thirty."

"Your imagination shapes it," Sibyle says. "Intentions focused enough, they become solid. As real as you or me."

"It's exactly like something from the book," Maud says, nodding.

Autumn raises her hand before she interjects. Her upper lip curls at one edge. "I'm not trying to judge, but isn't it safer just letting your man find himself a girl?"

"Remember, Maud and Franklin did it," Bellamy adds. "They're okay, seems like."

"Everyone calm down." Sibyle wants to head this off. Their doubts only worsen her uncertainty. How can she control her emotions, facing such questioning? She look from one friend to the next, squares her shoulders. "I gave him one that looks like me."

Silence.

Sibyle can't tell how they're taking it, what they're picturing. Are they pitying her? Her smile hints at strain. "This way, no jealousy. You could say it's me in there with him, right now, even while I'm also here with my friends." Sibyle's not about to let anybody get the upper hand. Not in her own home. Nobody can make her a victim.

The silence continues. She decides they're neutral, not judging. Just wondering. This gives her time to retake control of her smile.

Maud touches Sibyle's arm. "Of course that's right, Sib dear. Win-win."

"Anyway, husbands and wives both need to give each other a little slack," Bellamy says, as if trying to find a way to reassure Sibyle. "Room for new flavors. It's the enlightened way to live." Bellamy's always last to leave book group. Her husband spends Sundays away, and she hates going home to an empty place. Sometimes she stays over late, drinking with Sibyle, and crashes in the guest room at sunrise.

Autumn shrugs. "Just work it to your advantage, sweetie." Autumn stands, goes to Sibyle's side and puts an arm around her shoulder.

Maud looks around. "Your own, Sibyle, your shaper for cleaning. Where do you keep it? Why not transform it? Make a boy-toy of your own."

"It's not like that, boy or girl," Sibyle says, flustered. "Not even so much like a person, really. It's very basic, just cleans up around here. Otherwise it sits out of sight."

"Still, you created the thing," Maud insists. "So maybe improve it. Use the raw materials."

"I agree," Autumn insists. "Give it a man's name. Start thinking of a face. A body, you know. Muscles." She sticks out her burgundy painted lips in a pout while pretending to flex. "Maybe that'll get you into the spirit."

Sibyle considers. "Have you ever noticed we all advise each other to make exactly the same choices we've made ourselves? Like it validates our path if we convince somebody else to follow." This realization helps her feel a bit better.

"Is that from the book?" Bellamy asks.

"Oh, come on, think of your desires!" Maud insists. "Make something good, here. What's stopping you?"

"What I desire is this." Sibyle leans to the table, picks up *The Jewel in the Eye*.

The face on the cover confronts a mirror, corroded antique silver.

3.

> "These capacities make us like gods:
> To create wholly from concept of mind,
> and to judge how existent things should be improved by alteration."
> —Viso Mievske, *The Jewel in the Eye*

Sibyle reads aloud the passage highlighted on the marked page.

There's no need to prod the others into offering interpretation, volunteering how they feel. Having done this so long, the group's members conduct themselves like English Lit grad students. They know how they're expected to respond.

"M's talking about self-regard," Bellamy offers, her voice smooth, like honeyed cream. "The ways you can change yourself."

"The bit about self-regard is later." Maud recites from memory: "'Self-regard is a long, narrow tunnel. We exist perpetually too far from both beginning and end, and lacking desired points of reference, ever fail to find objectivity.' No, the line Sibyle quoted is from the scene where M debates whether Viol is someone he loves, or raw material to be transfigured to his own design."

"M says, judge how existent things should be improved," Autumn says.

"It's about looking at ourselves, figuring out how we'd like to become different."

Bellamy says, "But they've just finished making love—"

Maud interrupts with a snort. "Making love. First, in Mievske, there's no lovemaking. Only fucking."

They all snicker and laugh.

Maud continues. "OK, M and Viol spend three days and nights in his mountain hideaway, alternately fucking and discussing the traumas that formed them. M keeps retreating to the attic to write philosophy, while Viol lounges by the fireplace making poems about the erotic implications of suicide, or when she gets restless, going out to walk around Lake Arretrato, where wild animals always lurk in the trees, whispering at her. M is frustrated by the magnitude of his own desire. Beyond a certain threshold, does lust get upgraded into love, or are they different in kind? M admires Viol's beauty, they have Earth-shattering sex, they satisfy every desire he's ever felt. The world, experienced together this way, becomes new. Does this automatically mean love?"

Sibyle has said nothing since she read the first quote. She's wondering what all this means to her. Within the book, there must be clues.

Eyes confront the mirror. Remember staring, the piano reflection, friends all around, excellent wine, a beautiful home, a million-dollar panorama. Still her mind remains preoccupied, wondering what Lukas is doing. Why such possessiveness? Lukas belongs to her, she to him. Si isn't a threat. Not more or less beautiful, just different.

No, the same.

The discussion has stopped. The others sit silent, watching Sibyle.

She doesn't want them looking at her like this. Sibyle raises the book, finds the next passage. When she reads, her voice trembles. "Body is crude matter, hurtling without pause from womb to breakdown. The sole beauty that persists is the inevitability of looming decay. We are not pure concept, not luminous ideal, but concrete machines, doomed by the intransigent vying between growth and decay."

This time, a longer pause before Bellamy jumps in. "That's about enjoying youth while it lasts."

"Then we're all fucked." Maud, of course.

General laughter.

"No, it's our material bodies that are the problem," Bellamy says. "Our minds remain pure, maybe even sharpen with perspective. But our bodies become weak. Matter disintegrates, not just our own flesh, but people we love. We hate our own disintegration, but it's worse seeing it in the object of our love."

"Or lust, anyway," Autumn adds.

Maud looks pleased with the discussion. "Is M saying desire is good in the present, but love is pointless because we will always fall apart?"

"Is love mostly physical?" Sibyle asks her first question. "Lust is."

All go silent, pondering this crux of Mievske. Some discern profound romance in his fatalistic reverence for desire, while others argue he knows only bodily urges, nothing of deeper impulses like respect or love.

"The most powerful love definitely includes an element of the physical." Autumn punches one fist into the other palm with an exaggerated, masculine growl. "In the stories people want to read, overwhelming lust turns into tenderness and respect. A story about quiet love, respectful from the beginning, that's for the birds. Maybe when I was seventeen, I wanted some polite boy." She makes a brushing motion. "Now I need a little contrast, both in books and in life."

"I'll admit to fantasies of ravishment." Maud widens her eyes, bares teeth in a show of animal ferocity, growls. "A man mad with lust, incapable of stopping himself. Wild, physical, whiskey-fueled fucking." Her expression sweetens, her voice softens. "Only then... he comes to realize I'm also delightful, and unique. He mellows, treats me with kindness, and we make a home together. Still with plenty of crude fucking."

Squeals, laughter. The girls love Maud in this mode. It feels good. Everyone needs to laugh.

Sibyle realizes what's bothering her, more than Si's youth, reminding her what she's lost. The problem is, Si will never change. Sibyle and Lukas will age, further torn down by gravity and decay. Si will only ever be exactly what she is now. Of course blaming Si for this is like blaming the piano for having black and white keys along its front. That's its nature, not a matter for judgment or envy. Everybody's handed an assortment of good and bad they must live with.

There's no transition, no in-between. Everything's fine, perfectly under control, until suddenly it's not. Her own laughter shrill, becoming a cry. Fingers tremble on her tear-streaked face. The others gather around before Sibyle realizes what's happening. Only then she understands, like a child walking along happily, who suddenly falls and feels only confusion, unsure what's happened until the parent runs over, shrieking concern.

What about the book? She's been trying to focus. She wants to delve into story, subtext, philosophy. Wants to quest for the book's bloody heart, along with these friends, who now crowd around, fretting, trying to comfort.

"This was my idea," Sibyle protests, anger surging. She wants to lash out, shove them back. "Even when I'm not in that room, I'm the one in control. I made her the way she is. Whatever experience Lukas has, I gave him." She pauses, gasps, tries to catch her breath. She fumbles the book open, wants to read another line, something to reset the scene, to connect this emotion to something within the book, not herself. Somehow she can't, can't breathe. Gasps again, choking, wondering what's wrong.

Maud goes to the piano for wine. She refills Sibyle's glass, lifts it to her friend's lips.

Bellamy steps in with a palm-sized ivory inhaler. "Here, this is better."

Maud looks, lowers the glass away as if reconsidering.

Sibyle feels reluctant, fearful. "I never take powders. Lukas does. I don't even know what's in it." She looks around at the others, unsure if it's something all of them do.

"It's medicine," Bellamy says, "very natural. We'll all take a little."

"Yes, it helps," Maud agrees. "Sibyle, the powder's made of the same stuff as our shapers."

Autumn comes around to sit on the arm of the sofa. Bellamy consoles Sibyle, one hand on her shoulder, the other offering the inhaler.

Sibyle is grateful for the attention, yet simultaneously mindful of loss of status, not to mention control. She sees in her friends relief that she's been brought nearer their level, her marriage no longer some philosophical exemplar, like something in a novel. As long as Sibyle and Lukas stood apart, living a certain way, the others couldn't fully believe their own compromises were really impossible to avoid.

Now, everyone's the same. Only minor variations remain.

Bellamy charges the inhaler with a hiss, presses the mouthpiece to Sibyle's lips.

The air she breathes is clear, mostly natural, with a hint of flavor. Exotic, like chai spice. A slight tingling, but no urgent need to exhale. From Sibyle, the inhaler passes around. The tension in her chest eases. That sense of heaviness, the lead blanket oppression, vanished. Instant mellowness, a calm smile. It feels good, sitting among her girls.

Autumn moans lightly. "You have to tell me where to get this powder, Bell."

Bellamy shrugs. "The monk in self-defense class turned me on to it. Now I think I'm addicted."

Maud laughs. "Oh, nobody gets addicted."

"You can get psychologically addicted." Bellamy bursts out with an involuntary giggle, tries too late to hold it in. "Like dependent in your mind, even if your body isn't."

"Shit, we can't avoid that damn book." Autumn's voice deepens, imitating how she imagines Mievske's. "The body... the mind!"

Maud snickers. "Bell, you don't even know what's in this stuff."

"I do! It's something like fungus medicine, cultured or..." Bellamy stutters. "Oh, you're right, I have no idea!"

She laughs, they all do. It's easy. They laugh at everything, non sequiturs and blandly cruel judgments, pitiless expressions of self-loathing. Hopelessness, unknowing. Even absent humor, still laughter spills, persistent, as compulsively excessive as the sex acts in Mievske. Wave upon wave of laughing. Nothing is required to make it continue, and despite aches in their sides, soreness in their jaws, tears dripping down cheeks, still they laugh.

When finally it begins to fade, the room has grown darker, the sky beyond the window gone dusk. The women slump together, exhausted, none really sure what started it all.

4.

"Nothing remains pristine. No wish is strong enough
to preserve the smooth reflection of idealized self."
—Viso Mievske, *The Jewel in the Eye*

Every Saturday morning, when Sibyle was very young and brimming with illusion, her Mother made pancakes shaped like moons and stars.

After Mother died, Auntie tried to make them, the way she guessed little Si wanted. No, Si told Auntie, she wanted pancakes from now on shaped like Mother instead.

The new pancakes Auntie made must have been only vaguely person-shaped. Sibyle remembers thinking they looked exactly like Mother.

Sibyle realized the conception of how something ought to look, the certainty of what ought to be, is stronger than reality. It's the same with Si. One stands for the other, without replacing.

Sibyle reclines in the corner of the sectional sofa, friends draped around her. As if boneless, the others conform to her shape. Bellamy and Maud are nearest, Autumn at a slight remove, all of them resting hands upon her skin. Sibyle feels their warmth, the pulsing in their palms.

The view beyond the windows is a new painting, a projection of mind. City, clouds, mountain. None of them real.

Sibyle remembers only distantly how this started. Just a general awareness of unease, a vague, confused worry, which somehow exploded. She loves Lukas, wants him to be truly well, sustained by more than herself. If it makes her a bit uneven, especially at first, isn't that normal?

She allows herself to envision, to remember, the beautiful Si. A vivid clarity, like a solid presence before her, the thing she made from a wish. A construct of mind. She conceives of copper wires, tangled plastic tubes, ozone bubbling in oily transparent blood. A heart of raspberry jam, limbs of pale virgin pine. Between her legs, an overripe fig, split and moist.

None of these things are real.

Si is something made, not born. A doll, a trifle. Not even alive.

Yes, alive. As real as herself, her very own beautiful memory of Si.

The world within the condo moves slowly. The air feels heavy, like breathable water.

"I'm fine now," Sibyle says, standing.

Emotions detach and drift, soft-edged now, floating. Sibyle moves like swimming through air, able to shape her own emotional landscape, if not to change her husband or the wider world, then at least residing now in agreeable, defiant communion with each. She glimpses herself in a mirrored column, hair standing out, dramatically tousled as if for a fashion shoot. "I'm ready for my close-up," she says.

Factors external to us change, and often we permute ourselves, seeking to accommodate circumstance. Don't we? Sibyle's sure that's right, that she remembers it from the book. She has no idea at the moment if she any longer possesses actual feelings, or just holds on to memories of what feelings she once favored. No sense of owning a stake in anything. If any desire is tethered to her, she can't find where it's attached. Certainly nowhere near.

Sibyle's friends, perhaps recognizing this walled-off quality, this lack of need, allow her to remove herself slightly. They let her alone.

Maud and Bellamy go to the piano, trying to play a four-handed piece Bellamy claims to have been able to play perfectly, all by herself, as recently as college. Maud reminds her this was twenty-eight years ago at least, and Bellamy argues a while, until she realizes it's true.

Autumn reclines in the window seat, looking far off as if straining to rise, to float through the window and fly over land and ocean, all the way to Barbados where she was born, where her husband now visits without her.

Sibyle pretends not to see them.

Walking barefoot circles around the piano, Sibyle realizes she's still small, frail, younger than Si. Not an adult at all, but a child who somehow grew up and left Auntie's home where she was dropped off, after Father died first, then Mother. Ventured out prematurely into the complicated world, married, found a home and friends, but without ever having grown large enough to fit her surroundings.

Sibyle pads silently down the central hall. This is her home. She hopes to pass unnoticed, perhaps, but isn't snooping.

Outside the bedroom door she leans, listening. Hears a laugh, or a hint of a laugh. A bright outburst of some kind. So many things could be happening. Whatever it is, the sound's too vague to attribute to either Lukas or Si. She considers walking away, knows that's impossible. Her mind won't rest. She grasps the doorknob, pushes open the door, and neither enters fully nor remains outside. She stands precisely on the verge.

Lukas, reclined sideways on the bed, looks up, seeming embarrassed. Both he and Si are naked, their bodies close but not entangled, apparently not engaged in anything so heated as Sibyle's expectations.

The instant she chose to enter seemed the absolutely necessary, final moment. But she was wrong.

Lukas and Si remain motionless, watching her.

Si smiles, pleased to see the one that made her. "Madame," she says.

Is that what did Sibyle told Si to call her? She can't remember.

The eyes seem human. Deception sometimes lurks behind appearances, Sibyle knows. Si looks like a woman, a familiar one, but every nuance is something Sibyle herself planned, chosen from among all the possibilities she could imagine. It's hard to remember, in her present state. The powder seems to have sharpened her sense of existing within precisely geometric, linear surroundings, while at the same time making details harder to discern, somehow diffuse. It's as if everything material is intangible, and only the air itself has any heaviness. Arrangements, spaces between objects, these possess the electricity of consequence.

What ingredients did she build into this creature, now so intimate with Lukas? What's looking back at her from the bed, thoughts implied behind those eyes? Sibyle's certain she intended Si should care for Lukas, should treat him with gentleness, strive to give pleasure.

In these ways, they're the same.

Something in Si's pose, Sibyle recognizes. A specific inclination of the chin, the possessive way her hand rests lightly on Lukas's chest, fingertips stroking unmindfully the mix of black and gray hairs there. This reminds Sibyle of herself with such potent clarity as to cause a jolt. It's truly as if she's there with him, has been in the room with Lukas all afternoon. Why did she doubt it, need to see with her own eyes? Now Si's hand, so much like her own, resting on her husband's body with the same familiarity Sibyle herself would feel. The sense of observing such a perfect stand-in is unnerving, but also welcome. Part of her feels satisfied, as if she might go now, return to the book group, yet instead she steps further into the room. It's like approaching oneself in a mirror, though at present Si's posture and state of dress match Sibyle not at all. What each sees is not the same. But more than appearance, what Sibyle wonders about is the presence of mind.

Here is self. There is other.

When she looks at me, what does she think?

Sibyle knows her own tendency to think of herself, despite what the mirror shows, as still young, straight and lean, unlined and unworn by the cumulative crush of unmet desires and disappointed dreams, not whittled away by the cost of exchanging a young woman's hopes for the altered landscape of an evolvingly-attractive mature woman, with a brilliant, famous husband and a home atop the city's immaculate summit.

That deferential, accepting look with which Si regards her, is it real in any sense? Is everything a projection of Sibyle's own thoughts, which she knows to be often mistaken? Of course she wishes this made thing should be worthy to share their home, and intimacy with Lukas, should be something more elevated than construct.

On the bed Si curls in upon herself, straight limbs folding so that her outline upon the bed shrinks. "You are my beautiful mistress." She seems intentionally to convey passivity, as if understanding Sibyle's thoughts. "Your husband belongs to you. I belong to you."

Sibyle takes another step nearer the bed. Not only is Si's skin lighter than her own, the pale unblemished ivory of a girl not yet twenty. It seems now transparent, hinting at the flow of blood beneath the surface, the tremor of nerves within, the shift and pull of muscles. Sibyle imagines she can see Si's skeleton, a vague shadow underlying her form. Such inhuman insubstantiality.

How is it Sibyle didn't notice this the night before? Maybe something has changed.

A specific, detailed memory flashes like a fragment of film projected in her mind, throwing her back almost three decades. She can't possibly have seen it with her own eyes, because the image is herself, sitting at an old-fashioned wood desk bolted to the floor in a classroom in Johnson Hall at the University, sun glaring through a tall window. Briefly she is that girl again, waiting for a lecture to begin, having just changed majors from Journalism to English Lit, full of hope, enlivened by having drunk for the first time the water of poetry.

What Sibyle sees, or thinks she sees, causes her to tremble. Happiness, sadness. She's not sure.

Like Si, it's a recurrence of something forgotten. Si lying there, beside Lukas sprawled. Si unfolds one leg, stretches it out, so very long and thin, proportions seemingly unreal.

Sibyle backs into the doorway.

"Don't worry, we're okay," Lukas says. "All three of us."

Sibyle steps outside and closes the door. She recalls her friends in the living room. Probably they've missed her. There's still the book, and the wine, and more talk about Mievske. That's just what she needs.

5.

> "Blood might be transparent
> if not reddened by death's perpetual imminence."
> —Viso Mievske, *The Jewel in the Eye*

The room is expanding, broader than ever, yet the atmosphere has closed in, murky and thick as an opium den. The very air sticks on the lips, molasses brown. Among low-slung furniture full of right-angles, surfaces perfectly flat or vertical, the women recline, Sibyle at their center, the others nearby, embracing one another as if in aftermath of trauma, mutually draped and languidly overlooking the slow movement of the fountain midway between themselves and the outer windows.

How long have the women been stuck, motionless? They were supposed to talk about the book, but Bellamy brought out the inhaler. Time speeds or slows, depending on transient states of mind. Sibyle formulates these notions, concepts carefully worded as Mievske aphorisms. She might stay here, comfortable forever, or at least more willing to remain still than undertake anything else she might imagine.

Without a sound, Lukas enters from the hallway. His hair is in disarray. Silver and black stubble shows on his cheeks and chin.

Sibyle tries to read his eyes, searching for relief, or trouble. She's been thinking of herself, but now scans him with no hint of jealousy. She hopes his suffering will reverse, diminish. Not just that he'll survive, that their life together will continue. That fresh discoveries have not entirely run out.

Lukas lifts the bottles from the piano and raises the lid. He's barefoot, wearing a black suit, rumpled and fitting loose, despite being clean and unwrinkled. His white dress shirt is buttoned fully to the collar, no necktie. This is how Lukas dresses when he performs onstage, though such events have become increasingly rare. Lately, he mostly records, though even that has begun to distress him.

None of the other women have yet looked up.

Sibyle thinks Lukas looks slightly tired, eyes half-lidded. Mellow, perhaps. Certainly not anxious. His anxiety is the state she most dreads.

He starts back toward the hallway. Sibyle thinks he's returning already to the bedroom, but he stops, opens a door in the cabinet at the living room's edge, and takes out a small box of dark wood. This Sibyle recognizes right away: his powder, his private stash. Not the pleasure-giving kind the women just shared. Lukas calls this "creative juice," uses it as a pick-me-up, or more accurately bring-me-down, even on days he never approaches the piano. Sibyle thinks it numbs the mind indiscriminately, kills caring and self-doubt. Certainly it dulls the anxiousness that so plagues him. Lately she's believed Lukas depressed, has wondered whether the dark stuff might be causing problems, not alleviating them as he insists.

Lukas brings the walnut case, a brown so dark it's almost black. Finally Bellamy notices him, then the others.

"Ignore me, ladies." Seeming unusually comfortable and at ease, Lukas roughly places the wooden case directly on the varnished table, heedless of possible scratches. This is new. Usually Lukas protects the furniture almost to the fanatical, even irritating degree he defends the piano.

He opens the box's lid far enough to allow the women to glimpse the

THE JEWEL IN THE EYE

anthracite powder within.

Languidly Bellamy sits up. Her body detaching from mutual contact seems to leave Maud and Autumn bewildered at this shift in arrangement.

Bellamy leans toward Lukas's box, starts to reach, catches herself. "Do we have to ignore this too, Lukas?" She grins, slow-motion.

"You're welcome to it." Lukas gestures, then goes to sit at the bench. "I don't want to disrupt your party."

Something has shifted. Sibyle feels it. His loose-hipped, relaxed walk. The casual offering of the contents of his prized box, the way he dropped it, uncaring. Maybe Sibyle's imagining it, but there's even a hint of confidence in the way he squares his shoulders, facing the piano. Hints of the younger Lukas. Enough to give hope.

Rather than pulling out the bench as usual, Lukas contorts his body, sliding into playing position while the bench remains pushed-in.

Another quote from the book occurs to her, seems pertinent enough that she speaks it aloud.

"The most powerful organ is not the mind, with its infinite depths and myriad confusions, but the eye. With it, into the world we reach. It receives light, and also penetrates."

She feels she's changed her husband, helped and improved him, by sheer intention.

Bellamy opens the box fully. Within, black powder sparkles with silver flecks, finer than obsidian sand. She pinches the powder into the inhaler, puts it to her lips, and breathes in. When Bellamy finally exhales, Sibyle smells a strange pungency.

As Lukas places his hands over the keys, Sibyle wonders how he'll begin to play. Already he's raised the lid, suggesting he intends to coax the most resonant sound from the instrument, not merely knock out a few standards. Most often, he'll perform simple pieces he's learned well, taking advantage of rehearsed habit to satisfy the audience's expectations. It's less adventurous, but helps him avoid nervousness, playing without risk, without worry. Improvisation makes him panic. It's what he considers the true art. Exploring collisions of resonance and room acoustics, beginning a new chord before the last has fully faded. Such interactions obsess him, even as he worries over the risk of accident.

Lukas's eyes settle on the neglected wine on the table, as if he's considering the very question Sibyle wonders about. He leans, reaches toward a mostly-full glass, which Bellamy grabs and relays to him. He gulps it down, gives back the empty.

Bellamy sits back with the others, and hands Maud the inhaler.

The first chord comes easily, a simple C-sharp minor which he extends with another note octaves lower. The sound interacts with the room, so that each note persists after the next is played. With time, and the progression of overlapping long-held chords, the women settle deeper. They seem to subside into the L-shaped sectional, like wrecked ships, decks flush with the ocean's surface, about to drop away into the cold dark. Their only movements are the passing and occasional refilling of the inhaler.

After playing several minutes within safe territory, Lukas veers. The unmet expectation of this swerve startles Sibyle, though she's not sure the others notice. Each subsequent chord ventures further from precedent. Patterns shift from established key. The left hand works at a different slow tempo than the right.

The marble fountain has bubbled away all day, between the sofa, the piano, and the windows. Now Sibyle finds herself noticing the force of downward water into a pool, making patterns rise. Spray, subtle mist. The water bubbles, churns. These patterns make it seem alive, like slow breathing. Must be the music.

What blood flows within Si? Sibyle wonders at her pulse, now that Lukas has left her alone, and come out to make music. Maybe Si is listening from another room.

What does Lukas need? He plays, seeming briefly untroubled. Sibyle hopes he has enough to sustain him. If she could, she'd take away the stabbing despair, would drink off half his poisonous self-doubt. She's not cold or uncaring, nor is she a wife who submerges her own needs. Together, they have only so much time. She monitors Lukas for feedback, often worrying at what she observes.

A chord shifts, begins to fade. None rises to replace it.

Now he seems fully present in the room, upright at the piano in black suit and crisp white shirt, not preoccupied with what happened before, or concerned what Sibyle might be thinking.

After a brief silence, the next song begins.

6.

"Mirrors everywhere, and all the time your eye has carried inside it, unable to spy within itself, the very jewel you seek."
—Viso Mievske, *The Jewel in the Eye*

It's impossible to know how much time is passing. The most obvious sign of change is Lukas leaning closer over the piano. The chords themselves lengthen, and gaps of near-silence extend between the one dying away and the birth of the next. He continues, mouth slack, eyes tired. The slow cadence and long sustain characteristic of his style disguise the occasional mis-timed note. Sibyle recognizes most of what he plays, if not entire songs, then fragments and chord progressions. She knows when he's simplified a complex fingering, diminished an extended chord.

Sibyle stands, trying not to disturb her friends, all motionless, as if etherized. She slips down the hallway, opens the second door. Not the master bedroom, where Si rests in quiet neutrality, but the next. Sibyle knocks on the guest room door, giving the cipher time to come back to life before she enters. The mellow gray room feels like night. She finds the form sitting upright atop of the bed, eyes blankly receptive.

As she leads the thing down the hall, its form beings to shift. First featureless and only vaguely human-shaped, until Sibyle imagines it sharpening, refining. An inch or two over six feet, a broad-shouldered man's build. By the time they reach the living room, its hands have begun to elongate, fingers to taper. Skin the color of flesh, fine hairs breaking through.

Sibyle turns, watches as a face begin to clarify. "They said I should turn you into something."

Her friends look up, barely aware, like playthings brought earlier to life by an imaginative child whose mind has now drifted elsewhere, left them stuck.

Sibyle's focuses her intentions upon the cipher. It continues to change, becoming ever more specific. A blank white screen leaps into colorful life, as if a film is projected upon it. A younger Lukas. Hair shorter, sideburns less wild, less gray.

"We'll call you L," Sibyle says.

Lukas stops playing, twists his torso to see what his wife is doing.

"L, you should play," she says. "Touch the piano just as Lukas does. I remember him, the way he used to play."

Lukas slides out, stands away slowly as if too stiff-backed to fully straighten.

Into the place just vacated on the bench, L slips easily. Fingers hover over keys. His face is blank, as if he's trying to comprehend, isn't sure where to begin.

Then he plays, from nothing at all into a mid-stream performance of the very song Lukas has been playing, but without flaw. The way he makes the song is the version in Sibyle's mind, an idealized collage stitched together from hundreds of near-perfect renditions over recent months. L duplicates not only Lukas's style but his manner, that difficult balance of forcefulness and delicacy, the way he hovers over a chording, seems to waver for an instant as if less than fully certain, then commits with finality, strikes the keys and holds them, pedaling as needed, releasing only when it's time.

Sibyle watches, transfixed, more vitally herself than she can remember. She reaches for Lukas's inhaler, decides against it, reaches instead for wine.

As she sips, something moves beyond the piano. Sibyle thinks one of the other women has stood, is coming around toward the kitchen, but quick glances left and right reveal all three still beside her. The movement is Si, coming down the hall from the bedroom. She wears a stylish green dress Sibyle bought her especially. Her short blond hair is tidy, unlike before, her eyes clear.

We're all different in the bedroom, Sibyle thinks, not just Lukas and me. That's how we all are. We transform.

Si walks barefoot past the piano, behind the angled sofa so Sibyle must twist around to watch. Si's hand trails first along the back of the furniture, then reaches to touch, one by one, the shoulders of Sibyle's friends, all reclined deeply, as if sleeping.

Lukas approaches, seems about to sit at the end of the sectional by Autumn's bare feet, then redirects toward Sibyle. The space between her and Bellamy is narrow, but she scoots over, makes room for Lukas to sit beside her, one arm around Sibyle and the other draped over Bellamy, who seems not to notice.

"Your friends are in fine form," he says, not looking at them, instead watching L perform.

"It's good to have friends," Sibyle says. "If I didn't, what would I ever do?"

Lukas leans forward, takes another abandoned glass of wine and sips, then inhales some of the powder and offers it to Sibyle.

She ignores it, drinks from her glass. "This feels good," Sibyle says. "Doesn't it?"

She's asking herself for affirmation. Lukas, seeming to understand, offers no reply. Here's something beautiful, she thinks. Belonging and closeness, true pleasures. Decadence, no need to participate. Just observe, take in a semblance of life performed by stand-ins.

Sibyle wonders, Is this what we do, now?

L continues playing, Si comfortable beside him, watching his hands. Si glances back at Sibyle and Lukas among the other women, who must be sleeping, now utterly drained of color, Autumn's red hair desaturated to straw beige, Bellamy's deep violet dress drab gray.

L too looks back, as if he's been made aware there's something he should consider.

"Don't worry about us," Sibyle says. "We want to see you together."

After a while, Sibyle says, "L, why don't you kiss her? Her name is Si. Kiss her lips. Later, you can touch her body."

L stops playing. The last chord resounds, harmonizing with overtones on the soundboard, echoing about the room. He turns to Si, looks at her with the familiarity and assurance of long intimacy, and kisses her.

Sibyle and Lukas, a couple married twenty-five years, watch themselves. After a while they stand, move to the fountain, sit upon the marble rim. The room is dim, the sky beyond the windows fallen dark, but the water streams endlessly into illumination from below. Sibyle wants to tell Lukas what she thought about the fountain before, something about blood circulating, but those specific thoughts have vanished.

L resumes playing, Si beside him like a collaborator, moving in tandem, though she doesn't actually play. His hands and elbows move with slow surety. Si shifts exactly when needed, as if she knows when L is about to reach.

The water runs like blood through veins. Blood transparent, uncolored by death.

"That's it," Sibyle says. "Something in the book, about blood. Looming death. Why can't I remember?"

"What book?" Lukas asks.

"Mievske, *The Jewel in the Eye*." Sibyle's certain she's seen him read it. "The book we've been discussing."

"I don't know it." Lukas gestures at Sibyle's friends, bland and personless as ciphers. "Wake one of them and ask."

Sibyle makes no movement. She knows the words, doesn't need to fumble or guess. Sometimes she plays this game with herself. It's a game, isn't it? Pretending to forget, to briefly exist in a world without the mirror. A book is just a cipher, faceless and without color, waiting for someone to project herself upon it. Sibyle knows *The Jewel in the Eye* like she wrote it herself. She's been reading it forever.

THE NEED TO DESIRE

Every time Scott went through this, the agony took him by surprise. He sat by the frost-edged window in the lodge dining room, watching the frozen lake. Others in the room ate breakfast, drank coffee. Because he hadn't slept, it didn't seem too early for a double rye. Morning, a sunlit addendum to night.

The silver-haired waiter approached, immaculate in his apron. He offered a menu. Scott emptied his glass and slid it forward. The waiter raised an eyebrow.

"Trying to outrun a hangover," Scott said. "So far it's neck and neck."

The waiter brought back the rye, placed it at Scott's right hand. An accident of timing, Scott's fault, led to eye contact. The waiter's expression left no doubt how bad Scott must look. Like almost everyone else in the room, the waiter's own skin was solid, yet soft. Flesh-like. Wedding ring on his finger. Forty-one in the room and Scott counted four like himself in various stages of flux. An older man hiding beneath wool sweater, gloves, scarf and ski mask, beside a roaring fire. In a dimmed corner, a trio of college girls, flesh the texture and transparency of jellyfish.

Yesterday, he'd been fine. It was Scott's own fault, all that went wrong overnight. That didn't mean he was used to it.

Scott was working on another rye when Eric and Reese came down from the cabin and joined him by the window.

"Is it bad yet?" Eric asked.

Scott pulled the mitten off his right hand and slid the sleeve of his parka up to the elbow. Diners at nearby tables looked away. Flesh like unpolished crystal, near-transparent fingers colorless as glass. Veins and muscles visible as if in shallow water. Scott poked the skin with the opposite fingertip.

Hard as diamond.

"Just starting." Scott laughed. "Imagine what it's doing to Sirise."

Eric and Reese gave Scott the respect of looking at his hand and forearm without turning away.

"You're the one who started it," Reese said.

"Maybe see about a doctor?" Eric said without conviction.

Only one way to fix this. Scott knew it would happen. Just not how soon, or who with.

Beyond the window, ice crystals glared under midday sun.

Reese gestured at the lake. "Anybody ever fall through?"

"The ice is ten feet thick." The waiter lowered three bourbons. "You'd fall through in April."

The empty glass trembled in Scott's hand.

"Aside from ruining your relationship, bricking your face up like rock candy, I don't blame you," Eric said. "First time Tina's been available. I've always thought she's a prize."

"She is," Reese agreed. "Still a bad move with your fiancée in the next room."

"Just make up with Sirise," Eric said. "It hits women faster than us, and worse. She'll forgive."

They were right. That would be the smart move, Scott knew. "What's Tina doing?"

"Hiding in that back room, the bunk beds." Eric straightened. "If Sirise wants to let you off the hook and blame Tina, go with it. At least long enough to get home, heal up."

Scott's stomach felt wrong. Too much liquor. No solid food.

Reese made a face through his whiskey. "Didn't need that."

"Should've given it to me." Scott stood. No more avoiding the cabin. Eric and Reese followed.

On the walk back to the cabin, Scott's left hand broke free and fell away into the snow. They left it behind without a look back. It would return as soon as Scott recommitted. "You divorced for Donna," he said to Eric. "Maybe Tina's worth it."

Eric produced a flask from his pocket and took a pull. "How does this end, if you keep after Tina? You have a four-hour drive home with Sirise. A house full of her stuff."

Scott kicked a block of snow which looked solid but broke apart into nothing.

"You think this is bad?" Eric indicated Scott's face. "Remember how you got last time." He handed over the flask.

The schnapps smelled like Christmas. All those presents back at the house. Holiday plans with both families.

"Right after we met, Sirise got pregnant. Barely past the boyfriend-girl-friend threshold, we had that to deal with."

"If you're unsure, postpone the wedding. Just don't—"

"It wasn't mine."

Eric walked a few more steps and stopped. "What?"

"Something Sirise said in the car yesterday. I'm driving, Amy mentions something about two Christmases since Sirise's last fling. This guy Peter, her ex. I see in the rear-view Sirise mouthing something to Amy, frantic to change the subject. So I did the math."

Eric exhaled spiral mist.

"I remember her going all jelly. Wondering why's she having this reaction, like somebody's rejecting her, when I'm with her all along." The swirl of possibilities felt overwhelming. All night, all morning, Scott wanted nothing more than something solid to anchor on. Some way to sort conflicting desires.

"Scotty, you're always looking to justify fresh starts."

A tree fallen in loose powder blocked the path. Scott imagined racing ahead to the cabin, finding Tina alone in that room. He could escape. Sirise could find another ride home.

Three pairs of cross country skis were stuck tail-first into the deep powder outside the cabin door.

Inside was freezing. The bunk bed room, Tina's hideout, remained closed. The other three women in their bright skiwear laughed and joked in the kitchen. Reese rebuilt the fire.

"Anything to eat here?" Eric shouted.

"You're at the lodge all day and didn't eat?" Donna asked.

"We're not married yet," Eric said. "Stop crushing my soul."

Sirise approached Scott, the lower half of her face hanging distended like a plastic bag of milky water. The toll of Scott's unfaithfulness. She took his hand and smiled, such as she could.

The other women betrayed no antipathy for Scott. Certainly he'd been the main subject discussed during the day's skiing. Some accord had evidently been reached as to treatment of the Scott and Tina affair. He wished they'd clue him in.

Donna made cocktails for Sirise, Amy and herself, then one more. She delivered it to the closed room, knocked once and entered briefly. Tina followed her out, blond hair disordered from the bed, and stopped outside the doorway looking down at her bare feet. Her skin, especially her face, appeared vital, blood-pink. This was the Tina they'd always known, until her recent divorce led to her mostly covering up. Last night's encounter had worked a quick miracle for Tina's solidity.

"We going to the inner tube runs after dark?" Eric asked.

The question didn't need asking, covert night runs to the hill being an iron-clad tradition, though nobody actually took inner tubes. Instead they drank to the point of insensitivity and slid bodily down the ice chutes.

Reese had the fire roaring. Everyone migrated nearer, seeking heat in advance of the coming venture back into the cold. Sirise stood on her toes, put one hand behind Scott's head and pulled him nearer for a kiss. He tensed, anticipated her mouth. Unsolid as octopus flesh.

The others couldn't help watching Tina's reaction, a neutral smile striving for equanimity. Already her own face glistened, seemingly less solid. She glanced at the still-open bunk room, slid pajama sleeves down over her hands.

Scott wanted to apologize, but he was in the same danger of disappearance.

All he needed to do was turn to Sirise, embrace her. Give himself. Tina would have to find someone new.

He slipped free of Sirise's grasp and lunged at the fire.

The semicircle of friends stood motionless. None of them understood.

Scott's remaining hand melted, faster than ice near flame.

Tina pushed through the others. She knelt over him.

"Look at that." Scott tried to point, but no fingers remained. He meant the moon, visible beyond the window, a luminous circle pure enough to clarify all it touched.

Liquefaction spread. His body seeped through his clothes.

Tina tried to gather him up, soak him up with her fingers. What she couldn't absorb into her flesh, she lapped with her tongue.

"Don't be afraid," Tina whispered. "I've got you, Scotty."

She drank without another pause, hurrying to keep up as the last of him melted. Consumed by her mouth, soaked through her pajama top into greedily absorbent skin, all that was left of him passed into her. A puddle on the floor became a oblong of dampness which rapidly dried.

Tina's skin became radiant, perfect. Scott was part of her now. In the night, he would be reborn, perfected in his own way. Morning would be a new start, as morning should be.

THE BLACK VEIN RUNS DEEP

"One mustn't look at the abyss, because there is
at the bottom an inexpressible charm which attracts us."

—Gustave Flaubert

I

Kinosha (in 11 parts)

1. Unexpected Climb

Any new place can become home. It may take years, or if the place really fits, only a season. All summer I've been working alongside Adi Kye on the west slope of Mt. Hood. Already I feel like I'm exactly where I need to be, or at least, very close.

Returning this evening to Adi's Range Rover after exploring forest land between Triangle Lake and Kinosha village, I assume we're done for the day, and all that remains for us is dinner this evening, me sitting there as always speculating how it might be possible to shift things between us. Should I, shouldn't I? Enjoying the food, a local beer or two, and Adi's company, but too preoccupied to enjoy any of this as much as I should. Too distracted, wishing for some outcome beyond the usual. Thoughts of what else might be possible.

I'm eleven weeks into this routine, leading Adi up and down forest trails, exploring land parcels Adi's development company plans to buy. My geological consultancy work began with quick surveying and loose on-the-fly mapping, while Adi shoots endless digital photos, logs GPS waypoints, and records voice memos. Just the two of us, checking every sub-parcel, confirming public record maps, noting landmarks, utility access, siting possibilities. The geo work's nearly done, but Adi keeps coming up with "man Friday" stuff I can help out with. She knows I need the work, don't have anything else lined up since I left a pretty good job up in Seattle at the office of the City Planner to come down to Oregon. I don't want to go back, but haven't told Adi so, or why. I'm overqualified for what she's been having me do lately, so I'm starting to feel guilty about still getting my regular consultancy day rate. It doesn't really make sense for her to extend me much longer, even if she, or at least the firm, has the money. This supercharged Rover she carts us around in, a personal vehicle, has to be worth $90k. So maybe she can afford this, but the car, our financial arrangement, these are daily reminders. A guy like me, I'm in no position to start anything with a woman like Adi. Despite her flirting and hints, her constant jokes that she's too old for me. I'm forty-four, she's forty-six, so that's nothing, especially since she looks maybe ten years younger. Adi takes great care of herself, despite being a super-motivated "type A" when it comes to business.

So tonight, I'm figuring on Adi driving us back to Thunder Egg Inn, the two of us eating dinner at the Ice Axe next door, same as every evening. Kinosha's a tiny village, so the dining options are limited. Then we'll retreat to our respective rooms, 111 and 112, closed doors facing across the hallway. I'm not sure any part of me is actually ready for more than this, despite all my speculating about scenarios.

But this evening, three blocks before the hotel, Adi turns off Kinosha Loop Road.

"One last stop," she says.

It's pretty common we venture off plan. Always Adi's idea, wandering off for sightseeing excursions on public lands that aren't even part of her deal. If she wants to play hooky half the day, I'll play along, especially since I'm getting paid. I feel the guilt, but I take the money. She guides her forest green Range Rover away from the village center, up the hill into the trees. The road is narrow and unevenly paved, barely more than a trail between metal-roofed lodges raised on stilts against deep snow accumulation to come in winter.

"What's up here?" I ask.

"Top of the big Jones parcel. Been saving it for last." She shoots me a glance as she drives. "Not an official visit, we'll return later. Just sightseeing."

Asphalt disintegrates to rutted gravel, then curves another half-mile up to a barricaded dead-end. We stop.

"This was open past here, long ago, when the mine was active. Sort of a lover's lane." She climbs out, points far up the slope, where sunlight glints off metal. "The entrance to the old mine."

I take the lead, feeling footsore at first, and hungry. Once we're climbing, my body falls back into a groove. I feel in control again. As always, the daily exertion of walking and climbing ends up making me feel centered, more present in my own body. It's a relief, compared to the anxiety I felt before. I left Seattle in pretty bad circumstances. A cloud of pessimism, the conviction my life lacked any point or destination. Every day an identical, meaningless grind. After breathing mountain air these months, exploring the land, absorbing Adi's hopes for her project, I feel enlivened. Even find myself daydreaming about starting over, building something. I wasn't sure what I might find here, just wandered, and managed to stumble across the start of something new.

The only time I still feel that old fear is when I imagine leaving. When all this comes to an end, the need to return to a desk-bound job. That miserable stuck feeling I left behind. A different man, brought low in desperation, consumed with pain. The version of me who walked out at his wife's lowest point, left her with the most hurtful words I could summon so she wouldn't try to stop me going.

I always lead when we climb, even when I'm not sure where Adi wants to go. I'm not sure it would be my own preference to end an eight-hour day on the trails with this extra death-march up a steep, rutted trail, but I can't complain. I'm the outdoorsman. Adi's the city girl, from Portland. So if she's game for this climb, I won't be the one begging off. Besides, anything she wants to show me, I'm eager to see.

"The bacon cheeseburger is what I'm thinking," I say, beginning our usual end-of day game, exchanging plans for food and drink. "With french fries, and two pints of the Amber. You think I earned myself two?"

"Pesto chicken sandwich for me," Adi says. "Two pints, definitely. We're earning it, with this extra climb."

I'd hate to guess wrong about how she thinks of me. Times like now, I feel pretty certain, but jumping to a wrong conclusion would be a disaster. Better to wait. Anyway, it's no good getting my hopes up for something that probably can't ever happen. Scary, wondering where I'll end up. Adi's project won't be truly finished—the land purchases aren't even finalized—but the years of excavating, grading and construction ahead, I probably won't have any part in that. So what next? Sure as hell not Seattle.

The trail broadens, flattens. Adi catches up, walks slightly ahead.

"You were right," she says. "My feet are better since these new boots. My calves still feel kind of tight." She twists, trying to see behind, as if the sensation in her muscles might be visible. She flicks back a long strand of chestnut hair. "Better get strong if I'm going to hike PCT with you next time."

The past week, since I first told her about it, Adi keeps bringing up my Pacific Crest Trail thru-hike from almost fifteen years ago. 2700 miles in a hundred and three days, an ordeal I've never seriously considered repeating. But she keeps mentioning it, insisting she wants to hike it together. It's hard to get a read on her, sometimes. Is she just teasing to pass the time? Maybe that's what I should do next, another long backcountry trek. I doubt she'd really want to go together.

"Sure, why not?" I say, trying to avoid any hint of taking her suggestion as anything but a joke. "First we'll have to toughen up those calves. They're built for looking good, not four-month mountain treks. Have I told you before, the difference between gym fit and mountain fit?"

Adi smirks. "Let me guess. I'm gym fit, you're mountain fit."

"Close," I deadpan. "I'm both."

"All right, I'll work on it." She seems determined, not abashed. "Calves of steel."

2. Missed Signals

As we approach the level of the mine head, the sun hangs low over the opposite ridge. As we climb, Adi keeps glancing back at the horizon. I wonder, as I do countless times every day, what she's thinking.

As if sensing my curiosity, Adi speaks. "Some day, all this land will be transformed." She often speaks in optimistic abstractions, especially when we're actually out in nature.

"You're going to completely change this side of the mountain." I'm not just offering reassurance. It's impossible to spend a summer with someone like Adison Kye, a woman who sees with such perfect clarity the future she intends to create, and not end up sharing that vision. Kinosha needs a rebirth. Adi can give it. "It's hard to believe a gold mine ever operated here, in the past century. I'd love to see what it looks like inside."

"Can't go in, it's condemned. Locked down tight. Imagine, twenty-one dead, never recovered." Adi exhales through pursed lips. "Maybe that's why the old guy's so touchy."

One of the first stories Adi told me this summer involved the 1956 McAttree mine disaster. Whether an explosion caused a cave-in, or the other way around, nobody ever knew. A fire burned underground for almost a year, venting heat and toxic fumes. Everyone evacuated Kinosha village. Most never returned. Now the air's clean, the mine sealed, and Kinosha's just a stopping point on Highway 26 for skiers heading up to Timberline and Mt. Hood Meadows, or a stop for gasoline and snacks on the way to Central Oregon. Nobody mentions the mine any more, but it's the sole reason an early-century boomtown withered and mostly died.

"What old guy?" I ask. "You mean that last holdout?"

She nods. "I'll end up convincing him, but he's so nasty. Maybe in his day, being a rude bastard passed for being a hard-nosed, tough negotiator."

"I miss going underground," I say. "It used to be like home, caves rather than mines, of course. When I was getting my Master's, I spent most of a summer in Logos Cavern, below Rainier. Studying strata, mapping tunnels. Always wanted to go deeper."

Adi makes a boyish snort. "Go deeper." Always first with the coarse double-entendre.

"So, what are we trying to see?"

"Something I've wondered about for years. Not business, just curiosity." She hurries ahead, glances back as if daring me to keep up.

My left foot skids in the gravel down the rut at the trail's center. "Careful. That's an ankle-breaker."

"Funny." She smirks, this playful look she keeps giving me all the time. "Nature Boy, afraid of rocks."

I can't remember when this started. The nicknames, playfulness. Nature Boy.

"It's just a story they used to tell," she resumes. "Not just in Kinosha, even down mountain. People talked of seeing things in the night sky, like shadows or black smoke, supposed to rise, flit around. Probably just kids telling stories. Dark shapes against the dark. Signaling."

"That's spooky. Signaling who?"

"Don't know," Adi says. "Isn't that sad, sending signals, never getting a response? After a while, you start wondering if anyone's paying attention."

The path levels off, follows a jagged rock face toward a jutting outcrop where a square steel frame, almost like a prison door, is bolted down, covered with a grill of expanded metal. A posted sign makes clear the place is off limits.

"We made it," Adi says. "Kind of menacing up here. Scary. I don't remember it like this."

I'm interested in the mine head, been anxious to see it. The idea of exploring underground usually appeals, but a tomb for twenty-one men, that's different.

Behind me, Adi's watching the sky.

"Look." I point out a scattering of bullet casings on the ground.

"Yeah, kids come up here, messing around. See?" She indicates a few sun-faded empty beer cans.

The mountainside drops away before us, the slope appearing from above drastically steeper than it seemed on the way up. It's a trick of perception I've encountered often. A climb may seem difficult, but the slope doesn't look severe until you reach the top, turn around, and look down at the way you came. Especially as dusk falls, and darkness helps distance recede into invisibility.

I find the tiny LED flashlight from my pocket. "You mind if I turn this on, or will it disrupt whatever spooks you're looking for?"

"No, that's good. I'm feeling kind of twitchy. A case of the weird creeps, I guess." Adi's voice softens, and she wraps her arms around herself as if she's cold.

I slide closer, feeling protective.

"Maybe I'm just thinking about what happened," she says. "People lost their lives. Went down, and never came up again."

I shrug. "Mines are just manmade caves. Have you ever gone down, yourself?"

She grins, realizing I've set up the easy opportunity for a joke. For once she lets it pass. "I went through Ape Cave on Mt. St. Helens, maybe twenty-five years ago. Senior year in college I had this hippy boyfriend, Greenwood. He always wanted to commune with nature, listen to trees, sleep in the forest. Back then I thought a lot of it was silly, but he must've influenced me." She turns, looks at me. "You remind me of him, a little. Not so naive, or babyish. I love caves, the idea at least. Quiet stillness, the darkness. A place to escape."

"What do you need to escape from?"

Her eyes flit away to the horizon, then back to me. "I keep remembering stories. You know, down here. Explosion, fire, toxic gas. And ever since then, stories of things coming up from below."

"You shouldn't worry about that part." I'd rather reassure her, than preserve this childhood legend she doesn't seem to want to relinquish. "I've gone deep, dozens of places. You're safer below than on the surface."

"Think so?"

"Sure. Our world's hostile. At least..." I trail off, recognizing something I don't expect. I kneel, examine loose shards of dark greenish rock. Pick up one of the chips, test the sharp, jagged edge with my thumb. Deep green, almost black, maybe Serpentine. Nothing like the dusty, weathered tan-gray all around. "Something like this doesn't make sense here on the surface. Is it possible maybe USGS or someone's going down, doing safety tests?"

"Hmm." Adi remains distant, looking at the horizon. "Not according to what I've heard."

I'm careful what I say, not wanting to suggest conclusions she won't like. "You said it's toxic below, condemned? Nobody's been down in fifty years?"

Adi turns, notices the rock shards. "Definitely. Maybe some rock hound was up here, exploring. Maybe drank those beers, dropped these little gravel bits? I don't know. This gate, it's sealed like Fort Knox."

I examine the bolts, the welds, trying not to think about what's below. "Pretty damn sturdy."

Adi stands, turns back to the overlook. Red-orange sun touches the far horizon. "This will be good for the town. My whole plan, not just the projects on the Jones land, the arts center and resort. I mean, the town really buying in. Infrastructure, utilities and jobs. I really…"

I stand next to Adi, and her eyes find me. She seems grateful, and at least for a moment, vulnerable, unsure.

"You'll do it, what you're planning. I'd never bet against you." I want to say more, stop myself.

That look of uncertainty vanishes, as if my reassurance is all she needs.

3. Falling Escape

Adi leads me away from the gate. We sidle along the wall to where the overlook is less impeded by trees below. She crosses her arms and leans back against the rock. We wait, side by side, for whatever she expects to happen. I can't help looking back toward the gate. What's behind, below? The opening is off-square, the walls and ceiling beyond the grate slightly canted, meeting at odd degrees. Past the first few feet, the tunnel vanishes in darkness.

Adi sees me looking. "County office says the tunnel's completely blocked, a barrier of rock and soil just inside. Shouldn't be anything to see."

I step away, closer to the gate, aiming my flashlight. An uneven mound, as Adi described, slopes to the ceiling. My flashlight finds a gap at the top.

I turn, call back. "The barrier's settling."

Adi comes to my side. "It doesn't really look sealed at all, does it? Just a pile of dirt."

"Yeah." I tug the gate. The metal frame is bolted into the rock with five-point heads.

"These bolts look newer," I say.

"Some government agency must be maintaining it. I'll ask Gwendoline Jones, the owner."

"Yeah, this doesn't seem right. There's a question of—"

A loud, percussive *TING* interrupts me. I'm confused by the sound, and Adi's startled jump, so distracted I barely notice something sting the side of my head. Chips of rock cut loose overhead chitter down over us.

"Fuck!" I blurt.

"What was that?" Adi flattens herself against the gate. "Did something fall?"

The next sound is recognizable, a familiar movie sound effect. A gunshot, and ricochet ping.

Sharpness stings my temple, maybe my ear. Something wet trickles down my cheek.

We huddle together near the entrance. My hand goes to my face, finds blood. Pain, but nothing too severe. Just stinging, and blood. "Adi, I think I'm—"

"Colm, you're hurt!" Adi says. "Is it—"

Three more shots, *TING TING TING*. Adi pulls me back, as if we might shield together behind the gate's outcropping.

Another shot, close overhead. A shower of dust, more rock shards. Not safe here. No protection.

Adi looks down the slope, posture making clear she's ready to go.

"Run," I say, though I'm not sure I can do it. No way I've been shot, but then why this blood? Can't see anything, bad light, trail just a vague line.

My flashlight. Aim it.

"Stay with me," I tell Adi. "Share the light."

Too steep to run, exactly. We scramble, trying to stay upright, just managing our gravity-fed plummet. Pell-mell in darkness, gravel skittering underfoot. Slide, nearly fall, catch ourselves. Keep going.

Overhead and behind us, another bullet pings off the rock face.

Can't see who's shooting. How can they see us? The flashlight reveals us, but we need it. Keep moving, skidding, Adi right beside. We're bounding, trying to slow up, catch ourselves on sudden steeps. Just keep our feet under us, stay upright. Heads down, natural instinct. Wonder, am I still bleeding? At the same time, worrying about Adi. She seems unhurt, in fact she's gliding easily, covering plenty of ground, light as a deer. That's a relief. My heart pounds, lungs protest. Fear, exertion. I'm gasping. Still able to run. Keep going.

A moment of regret, shouldn't have teased Adi. Gym fit, mountain fit. Either way, she's strong.

No more shots. Just our breathing, and skittering rock and gravel underfoot. Still running. Ahead, the barricade.

"Around here," Adi says.

Her Rover.

The sound of another vehicle revving, crunching gravel, already out of view.

"Made it." I want to check my head, my face, whatever this is. I can't have been shot in the head. Probably just a cut, but so much bleeding. I'm shivering, shoulders trembling uncontrollably. Dripping sweat. Maybe going into shock?

Big revving engine, rattle like a diesel pickup, already distant. Dust cloud below, mostly obscured by trees.

I go to the driver's side door, pat my pocket for keys. That's right, not my car.

"Get in, I'll drive," Adi says. "We're not going after them. Just need to find the nearest hospital."

I look at my hands, the trembling. Steady, follow directions. Focus on what Adi needs me to do. Back in control, no more danger. Adi's safe, I'll be fine.

Adi starts the Rover with a pushbutton. Rev hard. Tires spit gravel, as we rip down the quarry road.

"I thought we weren't chasing," I say.

"Not chasing. Just driving," Adi says. Fast, in anger.

4. Call to Gwendoline

Above the trees, the last sliver of red sun settles behind the ridge over Triangle Lake. Almost gone.

Adi punches buttons on her phone. The first ring sounds through the vehicle's speakers.

"Wait, wait a minute," I say. "We need to figure out—"

"I want to know what the fuck that was," Adi barks, adrenalized by the same fear and anger I'm feeling.

Another ring.

"The old lady, Jones, who owns that land, you said she's onboard."

"That's who I'm calling," she says. "She seemed very nice, every time we talked. She knew we were going up today."

"Maybe she has security that didn't hear about our visit?" I wish I was driving. I could grip the wheel hard, try to stop my hands trembling.

Adi glances over, clicks on the console light, and reaches as if she might touch the side of my head.

I check myself in the mirror, see blood trickling from my scalp, definitely more cut than bullet wound.

"It's bloody, but not too bad." She hands me a paper napkin from the door pocket. "You feel okay?"

"Must've been a falling rock. I'll live." I breathe deep, keep flexing my hands. "I'd just love to understand this woman's approach to selling real estate."

A woman's voice through the speakers. "Hello?" Cheerful, and not particularly old sounding.

"Gwendoline Jones? It's Adison Kye."

"Yes, I recognize your number."

"Did you remember, I said we'd be surveying above your place today, taking photos?"

"Of course. You can't be expected to pay that kind of money without your due diligence."

Adi shoots me a look. "Do you know anything about security, somebody following us up there? Anyone who might be shooting?"

"Shooting, like firing a gun? On my land?"

"Yes, gunfire. Definitely aimed right at us."

"Security? No, that's nothing to do with me. I've never been one for fences, or locks. I keep my privacy with wide open space on all sides. Remember, we talked about that, why a buffer zone for me is so important."

"Somebody shot at us," Adi says. "Intentionally. More than once."

Silence.

"Shot at you? Please tell me you're okay."

"Colm was hurt. Not by a bullet. We think maybe some rock shard. He's bleeding and—"

"Kids go up sometimes, drinking. Telling stories, you know."

"Yes, we hope that's all it was." Adi seems puzzled. "Seemed intentional, though."

"You should come up and I'll tend to your man," Gwendoline Jones says. "Colm, you said? I'd like to meet him."

"I have you on speaker, Gwendoline." Adi makes a face, maybe even blushes. Too dark to be sure. That would be something to see.

"I'll be fine," I say.

"Colm's a mess of blood, but I'll get him cleaned up. Maybe we could stop by tomorrow morning, on our way out?"

"Are you sure? I'm just opening a pear brandy. A potent sip will fix you right up. I worked as a nurse, ages ago. I can still bandage a laceration."

I give Adi a look, and just to be sure, shake my head forcefully. My skull throbs, pulsing in my temple.

She nods. "I'll patch him up. We're surveying the south side tomorrow, around Echo Lake to the old bridle trail. We'll see you before we start."

"I wouldn't go traipsing around again until I have the sheriff make sure there isn't some problem up there."

"Don't worry, we're headed a totally different direction. I know you rise early. We'll see you first thing." Adi clicks off.

"What do you think?" I ask.

"That wasn't kids, shooting from a quarter mile away, downslope. Someone wants to scare me off. They don't know me very well."

"We never saw what you were looking for," I say. "Black shapes in the sky."

Adi laughs, then her eyes turn serious. "Some secrets remain. Mysteries for another day."

5. The Wound

In the doorway to room 111, I grasp the doorknob right-handed while my left hand clutches my scalp, sticky with thick, coagulating blood. The napkin Adi gave me is soaked, an iron-smelling mess of red gore. All I want is to hide, clean myself, tend to my wound.

"Thanks, Adi. Thank you." I'm hoping she'll go away, let me take care of this. "Don't worry. It looks worse than—"

Adi pulls the door from my hand, even after I resist letting go. "Come on, dummy."

I'm blocking the doorway, but Adi sneaks playfully past, making a coy swerve of her body. She seems intentionally to linger at the moment of contact.

"I just need soap and water."

"That's silly," she says. "You can't do a decent job cleaning your own wound. Don't you know?"

Normally I'd like to have her in my room. It's something I've imagined often. So many evenings, alone after dinner, wondering what she's doing across the hall. Lying back, musing about somehow ending up together, alone. Not like this, sweat-damp and dirty after an adrenalized, scrambling flight. Not covered in drying blood. Most of the time, I don't mind Adi telling me what to do. Right now, I want her to go.

"It's true." She grins, trying to be disarming. "Let me."

"I can…" Still standing in the doorway, watching her move toward my bathroom. I clutch the doorknob, as if I might take back control. But she's already inside.

"Come on, what's wrong?" She stops, takes a step toward me. "Colm, I want to help."

I let go the knob. Adi shuts the outer door. Just us now. My room.

"This is strange," I say. That doesn't really cover it.

"What, me helping you?" She raises an eyebrow. "Get over it. You've helped me plenty. I owe you. Anyway, it's my fault you're hurt. Adison's big adventure."

"You think we're in for more?"

"Trouble, you mean?"

I nod.

"I'm trying not to think the worst, just yet. First, let's fix you up." She enters the bathroom, flicks on the light. "Come on, get in here."

"All right." I exhale, a profound sense of resignation. Relinquishing, what exactly? No idea. This shouldn't be so difficult. Offering up control, even once I've decided to do so, means fighting my own reflexes. It's not that I don't trust Adi. I do.

She levers hot and cold water on full.

"It isn't that I don't want you to help me," I begin.

Step closer. So hard, remaining motionless. Muscles rigid.

Water rushes into the sink.

Nearer, Adi reaches for my wound. A sting, as she probes. I squint, eyes burning.

"Not too bad." She steps back, my blood on her fingers.

Dark intimacy, pain mixed with desire. Everything confusion, moving forward, back. We must've gone off course somewhere before. Missed a turn. If things between us were going to shift, it should've already happened. Instead we're a couple frustrated teenagers, too awkward to move forward, too insane with desire to give up. Tension so thick, something needs to happen. Some impetus or accident, some outside factor to nudge one of us into the other, so we tumble into proximity before we realize it's happening.

Adi's fingers working. This is what it means to come together. Let myself make a mess of someone. Let her do the same to me.

"You're shaking," Adi says. "Am I hurting you?"

"No." I don't know what to say. "It doesn't hurt."

Stand still. Look at my hands. Stop shaking. Shoulders, up and down my back, muscles running wild, out of control. Not like before, the initial shock. It's anxiety, fear aching to come out. Can't bear thinking of her fingers on me, touching broken skin. Denying consequence of contact, still wanting it. Pressure, pain, her fingerprints penetrating, two pulses intermingled. Intimate proof of Adi's nearness to me. It's real.

Holding breath. Try to let it out slowly, can't gasp, reveal my tension. Breathe slow. Don't look at her. Feel the sting. Astringent cleanse, burning.

Eyes closed. Where am I?

She pulls away. No more contact. "There."

Open my eyes.

Her face, so near. "What would you say if I offered you the two sacred words?"

I look at her, puzzled.

"Ice Axe." She grins. "Couple beers? Maybe an extra, bonus for hazardous duty?"

I take a moment, distracted. Her fingers, my blood.

She plunges hands into rushing water. "Never thought I'd see it. Colman Quinn, not hungry."

Blood fades, thinned into transparency. A clarifying cycle.

Myself, returning. I reach for the towel. "I'm still hungry."

6. The Jones Place

We rise an hour later than usual after Adi insisted I try to sleep a little extra, and meet at the Thunder Egg's dismal continental breakfast table. There we grab a few items, boysenberry muffin for Adi, three chocolate donuts for me. Neither of us have forgotten Gwendoline Jones's offer to feed us this morning, but we're not sure what to expect. Adi tells me Gwendoline's a sweet, earthy old spirit. I'm not sure what kind of food I envision her offering us, so I'm keeping the donuts in reserve.

A few blocks up Kinosha Loop, Adi cuts left at Pied Piper Club and threads behind the dozen businesses on the strip's uphill side. Another left-right jog brings us to Noing Way, a street I've only seen on maps. We break uphill, away from the heart of the village, past scattered tiny cabins and further up, more substantial lodge homes. On the mountain, higher is always more desirable, more expensive. Signs of development, the human imprint, give way to raw nature. In the land around us, I look past sun-bleached rockfalls, slopes bristling with dry pines, soon to be blasted by winter. Superimposed upon this reality, I see Adi's vision. The media arts center and film institute, the resort and spa. In-town condos and offices to replace weather-worn buildings, deteriorated roads, ratty taverns. A new reality.

Why wouldn't every citizen in Kinosha eagerly embrace Adi's offer?

Noing Way begins to crack apart, the edges eroding, chunks of asphalt sliding away into the drainage culvert. The ride roughens, until we bump across a threshold marked with a sign: "Noing Way End."

Suddenly, smooth gravel.

"Gwendoline Jones's driveway," Adi says.

The unnamed drive climbs another half mile to a great pale yellow timber lodge with a galvanized steel roof. The lower parcels, even the big million-dollar lodges, occupy no more than an acre each, but the property of Gwendoline Jones sprawls sidelong and up, attaining a prominent overlook buffered on all sides by open spaces and Douglas Firs and Ponderosa Pines. A pair of detached greenhouses, larger than some of the near-town cabins, stand behind. A stonemasonry waterfall out front descends from the second-story roof, splashing and streaming into a rock garden that seems naturally arranged, larger rocks apparently at rest where they always have been, integrated with decorative stones of lesser size. Within the stillness of the terminal pond, six black, smooth rocks are placed in a circle, submerged beneath the glasslike surface.

"This is what it's about," Adi says. "This land."

The house is more impressive for not seeming intended as a showplace for flashy entertaining, or to attract *Architectural Digest*. Instead, Gwendoline Jones and her late husband designed for themselves a setting for life tastefully integrated with nature.

As we climb from Adi's parked Rover, a woman emerges from the front door, walks tenderly across the gravel, barefoot in green overalls rolled at the ankle, an oversized white fisherman's sweater and wide-brimmed gardening hat.

Adi extends her hand. "Finally, in person. I'm Adi Kye."

"Of course." The woman shakes Adi's hand, then turns to me. "And you're Colm?"

"Colman Quinn. I work for Adi."

The firmness of her handshake surprises me. Gwendoline Jones looks the near side of retirement age, though Adi said Gwendoline was already living in Kinosha with her husband at the time of the mine accident. Even if she married as young as sixteen, that makes her at least seventy-four.

"You seem fully recovered," she says. "I'm glad, though if you'd visited last night, I could've shared my new pear brandy. I get pears and apples from the orchard of a very old friend, down near Roseburg. This morning it's apple fritters, just glazed." She guides us inside, through the tall double doors left standing open.

"A beautiful home," Adi says.

Timbers meet in a peak thirty feet overhead, and high windows facing south and west overlook a view overwhelmingly expansive and deep. The undulating expanse of forest rises west from Triangle Lake to Mirror Lake and the distant cliff faces of Tom Dick and Harry Mountain.

"We'll sit here." Gwendoline deposits us at a great wooden slab, a rustic dining table for eight. The wild wood, planed smooth and transparently oiled, seems still alive. Grain clearly visible, each ring a year. She heads for the open kitchen, visible across stone countertops. "I hope you haven't had breakfast, at least saved room for fritters."

An espresso machine starts growling, hissing steam. Gwendoline brings a silver leaf platter the size of a pizza tray, heaped with red-brown fritters streaked with cinnamon, heavy with chunks of apple, and glistening with sugar glaze. She makes another trip to the kitchen and returns with a lesser platter bearing a glass carafe of dark espresso topped with caramel-toned *crema*, a clay cream pitcher adorned with Inca patterns, a bamboo ice bucket, three tall mugs of blue etched glass, and a tiny antique pewter spice shaker. "I so prefer iced espresso, even in winter. More people like hot coffee, and if I can't change your preference permanently, that's fine. Just indulge me this once."

I watch Adi pour espresso over ice, observe movements of her hands. She takes up the little pitcher, seeming to notice the design. With a splash of cream, Adi lightens the coffee to the color of her hair. She doesn't stir, but loops two fingers through the handle and delicately swirls the glass so the ice blends the liquid. Mannerisms rich with significance teach me of her preferences, habits unknown even to Adi herself. How she grasps an object, uses it.

With fingertips, Adi nudges the spice shaker, delicately sniffs.

"Vanilla powder," Gwendoline explains. "I grow vanilla beans in my greenhouse, dry them myself, and powder them. It's the best way."

Adi sips her coffee, selects a fritter, holds her plate under it. She tears off a small piece to eat.

I'm aware I'm doing this, noticing minuscule details, not participating myself. I stop, follow roughly the same steps as Adi. Sip coffee, wonderfully bitter and dark. "I've always preferred iced espresso," I tell Gwendoline. For a moment I'm back within myself, not obsessing on Adi's every gesture, just taking pleasure in existing here beside her. I can tone down my scrutiny and still remain attuned to her, focused closely like a macro lens, seeking. How Adi carries herself, decisions she makes, small matters which determine her path through the world. These are important.

7. Past Into Present

Gwendoline sips coffee, smiles. Her cheeks flush through mountain tan.

"Adi says much of the land for her project is yours," I say.

"Yes, mostly empty, the outer boundaries to this sanctuary of mine. I'm ready to be shed of all the perimeter, finally. Horseshoe ridge, Laurel Hill, the small lake. The bridle trail. And those ninety rough acres by the quarry, I never know what to call that. Spent half a century buying land, first my husband, then me alone. I've received offers, people wanting to buy, sometimes even the same ones who sold to me, wanting to buy back. Some offers were substantial, but piecemeal never seemed right. Adi's offer made me willing. Not the money, I mean your ideas for using the land. Also, I'm getting old."

"You seem pretty energetic," I say.

Gwendoline smiles. "You shouldn't flirt so, in front of Adi."

I sense Adi watching me.

"Oh, we're... we're just..." I stammer, wishing I could see Adi's eyes, her reaction to this remark.

"I don't mean too old to manage by myself," Gwendoline continues. "I'm doing more traveling with my circle, seeing the world. As my husband went, now I go. Lately I've uncovered destinations worthy of my time. Opportunities for long visits, to immerse myself in different lives. It's like becoming a whole new person. Can you imagine, at my age? Anyway, I used to think the way to set up a life for yourself was to create boundaries, try to stay within yourself. Keep the world outside. But that's no longer sufficient, I think. It doesn't matter what boundaries you set. The only solution is to keep moving. Otherwise, everyone intrudes."

"I think it's worse in cities." Adi turns to me. "What do you think? Colm's just recently moved from Seattle."

"I don't know how things were before," I begin. "But yes, it seems almost impossible now to really define your own way of living. Even halfway up a mountain isn't far enough. I'm not sure where I can go, to find a territory of my own. Avoid everybody else imposing their consensus on me." I smile, at least try to. "But then it's possible I'm just an antisocial bastard."

Gwendoline roars laughter. Adi jumps, startled.

"That's partly just the way things have always been," Gwendoline says. "But things really do change. Would you believe at one time I was a dancer? A showgirl, bit of hoochie coochie. Naughty, I don't mind saying. Such fun, wild times." She looks far away, then sighing, seems to return to the present. "I've lived such a life, first before my husband, then with him, and now another stage. Alone on my mountain, wondering where all the time went. But of course, I have done so much living along the way. We have to remember, and here's my best advice to you, so listen. Don't let your years flit past. Remember always to live. I never visited this mountain until my husband brought me here, but this is where life kept me. I've never left, not for very long. But soon, I think I will. Life keeps moving."

"Where will you go?" Adi asks.

"Warmer places. I like to watch things grow and die, slow change over seasons. That's how you see the world really shift. Watch with a slow eye. That's the only way you'll see it."

I glance at Adi, hesitant to ask. "See what?"

"That the world you find yourself living in isn't the same one you were born into."

Adi leans, touches Gwendoline's hand. "I hope I remember. Not to forget."

"You'll do just fine, I can tell. You're one who lives to create, and transform," Gwendoline says. "You build with the resources you possess. But I wonder what drove you here, to this place?"

"I grew up on the mountain," Adi says. "A little town about ten miles down, Rectory. It's gone now."

"I remember," Gwendoline says.

"I was twelve when my parents moved us to Portland, so nobody around here knows me. But the years spent exploring the trees, listening to streams and birds, seeing weather change through seasons, these imprinted on me. I wanted to come back."

Gwendoline looks pleased, as if Adi has confirmed her hopes. "I knew your vision had to be rooted in loving the land, the way you talked. Protecting forests and lakes, creating natural spaces for hikers and explorers. Not just a business plan. Though I do think money flowing into the area is a good thing."

"I'm trying to bring together nature and culture, something like Sundance or Taos, in Oregon. Not exclusive or too elitist, though I don't deny there are business aspects to the project, a desire to make money. And to do that, we have to convince people to come, give them a reason to invest or at least visit and spend." Adi seems to catch herself. "But you're right, Gwendoline. The impetus for this project goes back to something early, probably my childhood. We left the mountain, like I said. My parents died, one after the other, as soon as I left for college in Eugene. By the end of freshman year, I was alone. They left me enough to finish school, and after graduation I moved to Portland, got involved in real estate. I bought some properties in The Pearl, that's a district downtown, near Powell's Books. I owned a derelict warehouse and some empty lots, at exactly the time when the condo boom happened, a real gold rush in The Pearl. Commercial developers were buying everything. I was twenty-two, not really experienced yet, but decided to hold out. I wouldn't sell outright, only agreed to trade my properties for shares in their planned developments. So I learned the ropes with very smart people, and turned my inheritance into some real money."

"So then you started looking for a dream project, up on the mountain where you grew up?" Gwendoline asks.

"Not yet," Adi says, hesitant, as if she can't quite remember. "Turning forty, maybe I had a mid-life crisis or something. Feeling like I haven't amounted to anything. Money was accumulating, but I was still the same person. Working ninety-hour weeks, grinding away. All I knew, I didn't want to end up like one of those old guys, my mentors. Tired millionaires who can't let up, never retire, enjoy life. Eighty years old and still working deals every day, over lunches at Wildwood, dinners at City Grill. Of course, some of those same men are helping back my project, so I'm not saying I don't respect them. It's just that I don't want to end up exactly the same. I need them for this. I don't have quite the money or clout myself, not yet. I decided I didn't want to wait."

Adi sets down her empty plate, sips the last of her coffee.

"Anyway, you said you have work planned for today." Gwendoline stands. "Don't let this old lady keep you."

"Old lady," Adi laughs. "Gwendoline, you're the farthest thing from that." Gwendoline considers. "I hope that's true. Except when it suits me."

8. Two Into Nature

Our days always start with business. Back in the vicinity of the Thunder Egg, we park near a mid-town trailhead we've avoided until now, despite passing by it daily. Beginning with more than a mile of public forest trail, we approach the boundary of the first of various lower parcels held by Gwendoline Jones. The pleasantly cultivated trail starts us off toward Laurel Hill, nearest of our day's planned destinations, from which we intend to loop around toward town, passing several other parcels in the next five hours or so.

I'm distracted, mentally compiling all the new information gained this morning about Adi's past. Until a few hours ago, all I knew was that she grew up somewhere nearby the mountain, moved away to Portland, later attended University of Oregon, then returned to Portland after graduation.

"The southeast corner, point eleven on your C Parcel map, is right up here." I compare written coordinates to my GPS. I've done this so many times, I can accomplish it without too much thought. My mind drifts. "We ought to detour. Down here, the footing's better. Then loop up, find the ridge point. It kind of angles—"

"I see it," Adi says. She's wearing her usual outfit, snug black lycra shorts and long-sleeve shirt of neon green microfiber. I've never understood why it's always long sleeves for her, even on hot days like today. Some people are shy about revealing their bodies, but then she wouldn't wear the ass-grabbing shorts. I don't see her having any flaws, but you can never tell why somebody might gladly reveal some parts of themselves, while keeping other aspects hidden.

We approach an unmarked boundary, the westernmost point of all Gwendoline's properties. Portland is sixty miles away, too far to see from here, but I sense its presence. Maybe Portland is where I'll end up. It's sort of Seattle's mellow cousin, and Oregon's biggest city. Also Adi's home. I wonder if she feels it pulling her back?

Adi shoots photographs and I mark GPS waypoints, and sketch in a Moleskine notebook with the Japanese 0.3MM no-bleed marker I use for small maps. Adi carries a digital voice recorder and a Leica digital viewfinder camera with a deep optical zoom. Both recorder and camera take the same XDHC memory cards, which Adi carries in such abundance, I wonder if she intends these expeditions to last forever.

We leave behind the delta-shaped prominence at the base of the first parcel, quickly document the flat and featureless upper portion, then return to the narrow dirt path which leads north toward the old bridle trail. For over a century, the trail has been mostly abandoned, used only by rogue mountain bikers making long descents from Timberline to mid-mountain towns like Rhododendron and Zig-Zag. Sections of the bridle trail are alleged to have carried pioneer wagon trains, despite occasional rockfalls and small cliffs which apparently necessitated lowering the wagons on ropes. Later, some of the flatter portions became railroad right of way. The path now crosses back and forth between public and private land, and though some of it degenerates into near-impassible overgrowth, most of it remains a pleasant circuit below Echo Lake. The mid-point of the trek gives us access to Parcel F, the smallest Jones plot. An unnamed side trail weaves through weird old valleys behind Kinosha, downhill from Gwendoline's place. We'll loop up under Echo Lake and pass by a couple more minor parcels on our way back into town.

Nature exists in many variations, and while I once obsessed over caverns and tunnels, I've learned to see forests, especially on the mountain, as the most nearly perfect form of wilderness. Especially in the Northwest, where forests are made of such noble trees, forming a canopy beneath which thrives lush green in infinitely varied shades. Trails like this one, surrounded by so many vines and ferns and mosses, soon grow over in the absence of foot or bike traffic. In places, stems, leaves and unidentified brush lean over. Little sprouts shoot up from the verge, threatening to take hold, to make this into something other than a trail. More than once, we have no path to follow, can only hope the lowest hint of a previously rutted place will eventually give way to a reemergence of the way.

Viewpoints are usually high places looking down, but as we near the bottom of this valley, curve across trickling streams, contend with sections overgrown almost to waist depth, we finally descend to what opens into a lower clearing. Past a thin screen of trees, the ground drops away and the sense of being at bottom is relieved. The world continues, lower still. A rush of tiny waterfall at the trailside lends a soundtrack to the wide unexpected space below, a swooping valley carved from hillside, as if some titan extracted a city-sized divot out of wild forested land, and the wild green returned to cover what had been stolen.

At this view we pause without speaking, then resume downward, toward the bottom newly revealed. Places like this, so deep, remain mostly dark, even on summer afternoons. The waterfall disappears, rushes near again, becomes a stream, gurgling instead of hissing. Black rocks, lush with moss, adorned with droplets of water, tiny lenses magnifying the green threads upon which they stand. All this might have been here for eons, the same tiny droplet lenses focusing back on an earlier time, undisturbed, when the water was born.

Later the trees thin and the trail is more nearly dry, a ground more brown than green, comprised of disintegrated bark and wood, needles and cones. Patterns of light and shadow make a camouflage pattern over which we pass, the blotchy uneven light rendering us invisible against this background. In such wide and deep places of nature, I sometimes imagine myself seeing visions, or being overcome with an experience I can only refer to as ecstasy. I waver at the verge of bright, hopeful inspiration, and plummet into abysmal terror at the scale of things. Submerged in oceans of wild green, standing within such abundant beauty, the greatness swamps my senses. It's hard to describe as pleasurable, even in retrospect, yet I've often believed this may be the reason I love the outdoors. I pursue it like a drug, though it's terrifying while it's happening. Like staring from the precipice of this life into what comes after. This transcendent quality is rare, yet I continue chasing, never knowing when it will come again. Like Ahab circling the globe, willing to sacrifice everything, even when years have passed since he's seen his white whale.

I don't mean ecstasy, the way it's often used. My visions are dark, compulsions more like a swooning, smothering opiate dream than some luminous heaven.

My wound burns. I'm convinced I'm bleeding again, touch my wet scalp. Fingers come away damp with sweat. Not blood. The fear reminds me of Adi's fingers on my scalp, our closeness beside the rushing sink. Pain like severed nerves, her fingers pulling away, glistening red, the blood of my life.

She holds her fingers, extended for me to see. Here. This is you.

Thousands of pine cones, fallen to the ground from hidden tops of trees, varnished with a resin like the glaze of Gwendoline's fritters. Exotic crusts of silvery amber flecks glisten in refracted sunlight.

"Are you ever going to tell me what happened in Seattle?" Adi asks.

I hesitate. "What do you mean?"

"Some people move away from places. It seems more like you evacuated."

I'm frozen by her words, the prospect of revelation both terror and urgently desired opportunity. I hate to wreck a day so blissful with talk of painful realities, but Adi wants to know me, wants to hear more about my life before. She thinks I've been holding back. That's true.

9. What I Left Behind

"I left behind a disaster." I sigh, wondering how deep to go. "I was married, officially still am. Our divorce isn't final, but everything between us is dead." Already I'm afraid I've poisoned things, been a blunt, honest fool. What could she have expected, that I came from some immaculate, uncomplicated background? A man my age, lacking adult entanglements?

We continue without speaking, not terribly long, but my mind races. What's Adi thinking? The things I've said, maybe she needs time to absorb. I hear her walking, breathing, behind me.

Finally, she speaks. "What broke down between you? I know sometimes we get stuck, sometimes just so incompatible. A person doesn't even hear the words we say." She pauses, seems to reconsider. "I mean, I don't know how it is for you."

"Paula had serious problems," I begin. "Not just incompatibility. Addiction problems, and mania. This single-minded focus on her paintings and music, blocking out the rest of the world, including me. I'd disappear for long adventures outdoors, she'd vanish into the basement. Often weeks would pass, not seeing each other, maybe not even talking. That sounds crazy. Somehow, years passed. I was working for the City of Seattle, so there were benefits to being married. And Paula liked having a husband, as weird and radical as she was about everything else."

"Everyone needs stability," Adi ventures.

"Having a husband with a salary and health insurance, a house to live in, meant she could stay disengaged from the world. Free to swim around in this… delirious dreamland. Mostly painting. She gave up singing, but still wrote lyrics. This was never easy, but it functioned. We kept going, managed to pass a decade. I think all the time spent apart functioned as a release valve for the pressure that would build up. After time apart, we kept drifting back together."

I glance at Adi. She's staring forward, as if thinking. When she notices me looking at her, she nods.

"When Paula turned forty, suddenly she wanted to be a woman, not just a girl. Her words. She wrote all these poems about motherhood. That's something we never talked about before. Daydreams of my future never included a child in the scenario, you know? But it immediately became Paula's highest priority. She tried cleaning up her act, trying to convince me she was capable. Stopped her sleepless binges. She might still work all night, and crash at dawn on the basement futon, hands and face all smeared with paint. But no more pills, or harder stuff. Really, the picture of domesticity, compared to before. I mean, not too different from many of our friends.

Still very dependent on alcohol, and weed."

The trail here is smooth, nearly flat. It's as if we reached a place like this where I could just talk, without being distracted by finding the way.

"Remember she's forty, but that's not my biggest concern. Women can get pregnant at forty. But she's been diagnosed with severe psychological problems, which she's halfway managed with medication, as well as some kind of serotonin glitch. You know, a serious solo drinking problem, even used heroin off and on. Those are reasons not to have a child, not to mention it's not something I ever really wanted. I tried to make myself, believing Paula seemed to need it. So I finally said it was something that I wanted too. Maybe if I'd just told her the truth, that it was something I was willing to try, for her. I said I wanted it too. Maybe that's the thing that bothers me most. I just gave in."

"Wow, I had no idea she was so wild," Adi interjects.

"If you saw her, I doubt you'd picture us together. I mean, she was attractive, used to sing for a band that was popular then, called Languish. She became so thin, skeletal like Kate Moss. All angular bones. She liked that, the way her body looked. She'd wear short tank tops and panties, walk around like that in the basement, bare feet all dirty, hands black with paint. A waist I could encircle with my hands. Tiny breasts, like a thirteen-year-old waif. Had kind of a fashion model look going, when she was younger. Past a certain age, though, all that wear and tear. The scars accumulate. She started tattooing her arms to cover needle marks, got addicted to body ink. Started covering herself, hands, arms, shoulders, all down her chest. Started working her way up her legs."

"You don't like tattoos on women?" Adi says.

"I like them just fine," I say. "It's just that by now, I can't stand anything about Paula at all. I realize when I describe her, you must be able to see on my face how I feel. Hate, disgust, whatever." I exhale, try to start again. "Anyway, she wore me down. I went from absolutely opposed to telling her I wanted it too."

The trail broadens and Adi catches up to walk beside me. "You wanted a child?"

"I said I did." I consider, trying to be fair. "So, we tried, but it wouldn't happen. I figured she wasn't capable. Her body too worn out. Just because she wanted it didn't mean it was going to happen. I thought she'd drop it, move on. Sometimes, Paula would briefly become obsessed with some new idea, then just as quickly forget it. She went through this with meditation, I Ching, archery, Kaballah. We didn't speak about it for weeks, stopped having sex, so I'm thinking that's over."

"But it wasn't."

"One day I get home from work and Paula announces she's been to a fertility clinic. The doctor proposes treatments, not covered by insurance. So, our financial situation… Paula never worked. Sometimes she sold a painting or two, but mostly she spent a lot. Weed, pills, a basement full of candles. And these handcrafted liquid oil paints, you wouldn't believe. Ninety bucks a jar. These fertility treatments, we had to pay out of pocket. $7,000 to start, another $5,000, another $2,000."

I glance at Adi, who's watching me with a combination of amusement and horror.

"I know, I'm making the bitter face," I say. "Let me get it out."

"It's okay. Go ahead."

"I'm unhappy about the money, but at the same time glad it's not happening. Finally I resolve to say we need to stop. That's when she tells me she's pregnant, but she's upset, terrified. She was the one who changed her mind, didn't want to let me down. We both had second thoughts, but never spoke up. She said, Fuck this. Look what it's already doing to my body. She wanted an abortion, after spending $20,000 to get pregnant. I realize she's drunk on wine, crying, talking nonsense. She runs for the bathroom, vomits all over herself, falls on the floor and pisses through her panties onto the tile. I leave her there a while. I don't know, maybe thinking she'll learn a lesson. I go to bed alone, she comes in crying, still drunk, smelling horrible, climbing all over me, all slippery with tears and snot and… Fuck, anyway, she says, I do want it, I changed my mind. Goes on describing this vision she's had. It's going to be a beautiful girl, she wants to name her Annabel. Paula knows exactly what Annabel will be like, tells me everything, the whole life path of this unborn child. An hour ago she wanted an abortion. I had great reservations about going ahead, but she pulled me along. Can you believe that? After everything. So skip ahead, she grew a big belly. Overall she mellowed, became almost happy. Smiled more than I'd seen, at least. She'd wear light-colored clothes, which if you knew her... Paula Quinn in lime or bright yellow. Like yours." I point at Adi's shirt, and immediately regret comparing her to Paula in any way.

"Then another drama, another collapse on the bathroom tile. Blood all over the bed, the carpet. Lots of screaming, laughing, crying. I thought she'd harmed the baby on purpose."

"Oh no." Adi reaches, lightly touches my arm.

"At the hospital, they said spontaneous miscarriage is common, women her age. After, she really swerved. First night back from the hospital, started cutting. Then branding herself, burning with hot metal heated over candles. One night, I woke up, felt cold air blowing through the house. Found the back door open, Paula in the backyard. Pouring rain, she's sprawled naked, asleep on the grass. And endlessly ranting about suicide, saying Annabel knew she wasn't wanted. That if Paula had really wanted her, the way normal women are supposed to want beautiful little girls, Annabel would've been born. She said Annabel must've heard our hateful thoughts, and died of heartbreak." I hear the way I'm speaking, high-pitched, painful in my throat. I take a few breaths, and go back to my own voice. "It's better this way."

"I know what it's like," Adi says. "Not that situation, exactly. But emotional extremes."

"Paula wasn't someone who could cry it out, then bounce back. She spiraled, darker, more depressed. Paula hated herself for feeling broken, hated me because I couldn't fix things. Things became so awful in that house. Poisonous. Maybe half of it was me. But the last thing is, I reached a point where she really needed help, maybe needed to be committed. Do husbands do that?"

"Maybe," Adi says. "I know that's hard."

"I can't explain how bad. I was right in the middle. Don't you think there must be something wrong with me? Swimming through so much poison, maybe there's no climbing back out."

Adi shakes her head emphatically, as if trying to fling loose something stuck to her. "I've been with someone who always maintained a fake version of themselves, all the events in their life. Nothing was true, not even close to the way things really were. You can't force a person to see, if their perceptions are so different that they don't even see the same world around them that you see. All you can do is try to leave, and you did. Maybe you were too tolerant, should've left before. Your tolerance let her continue along, when maybe on her own she would've had to see the way things really were. You're only guilty of carrying her along. Accepting a person who would leave your bed, go out to sleep naked in the yard, and instead of leaving, you would say, Come back inside."

"Yeah. But I did leave."

"Good. I'm glad you did. I understand, I've experienced similar things. I mean, nothing is similar. But feeling you're half of the problem, when the other person is not meeting you halfway. That, I understand."

Adi's acceptance seems impossible. Can it be, that not only are my failings reasonable, my flaws relatively ordinary, but maybe it's even fair to believe I'm not fifty percent to blame for Paula's demons? Maybe it's true, and I'm worthy of moving forward, trying to be happy. Maybe I'm good enough to be here now, beside Adi. A man, walking with a woman, talking about our lives. So many days we've shared, yet I never imagined myself Adi's equal. I feel like she's just granted me permission to conceive of myself that way. As if that's how she thinks of me.

"Being half a rotten relationship doesn't make you half rotten," Adi says. "Maybe you're guilty of bad judgment. You wouldn't be the only one. Truth is, I'm talking about myself. Terrible things happen behind closed doors."

"How do I know what blame I really deserve?" I'm not playing games, trying to be let off the hook. I'm genuinely wondering. Damage lingers even now, despite small hope gained by Adi's words. Painful wound carried for years, since long before any talk of babies. Guilt, like a chronic illness. The burden of failed investment. Lost years, wasted possibilities. Worst of all, the fear I contributed to Paula's collapse, that I've never been capable of taking care of a woman, let alone a child. So desperate to start over, aching to believe in the possibility of new beginnings, yet terrified at the prospect of trying.

"How did it end?" Adi asks.

I consider, unsure how to summarize. "I got tired of being in a state of permanent heartbreak. I became angry, without really trying. Frustration built up, until I realized I blamed Paula. Then I admitted I never wanted it in the first place."

"The child," Adi says.

"Paula kept asking, What do you mean? Over and over, wailing in agony, throwing herself on the floor, hysterical, hitting herself in the face until her nose bled. Finally I said it."

Adi walks along beside me, with me. Doesn't ask, just waits.

"I admitted it," I said. "The truth. Part of me was glad. I never wanted a child."

10. The Unmarked Path

My forest, ours together. We'll always have this time. Better look around, remember.

Emotions flood, a tide released. Incomplete fragments in constant alteration. A shrinking, tentative fear. A rush of fullness, unanticipated. A sense of perfect, centered completion.

"I should have done better," I say. "Either helped her, or if she was beyond help, gotten myself the fuck away. Much, much sooner."

"I don't know," Adi says. "You can't reach a new stage of life before its time. You had to feel that to become who you are now. Soak in cumulative pain, until it's too much. Now it's time. I envy your freedom."

"Freedom?" The word surprises me, so far removed from how I feel. "Is that me, what I have? Freedom?"

"Of course. Maybe it's scary. You remember what Janis Joplin said? Maybe you're not old enough to have heard that one." Adi gives the first semblance of a grin since my story. "Now that you've got it, what will you do?"

Nothing left to lose? I wonder. We're still walking, just like always. What's different is that everything feels calm. That high-alert sense of anxious anticipation, I don't feel it any more. My heart thumps, but only from the effort of climbing a short rise. The sky above, trees around us, all seem changed. Indifferent to my past, my future.

I've shown Adi the worst of Colman Quinn. Somehow, the world hasn't fallen apart.

"You deserve things to get easier, Colm. You've helped me a lot. Taught me a lot."

"Taught you? Like what?"

Adi shrugs, looks me in the eye, and ignores my question. "You have a chance to start over. Build yourself a new life. No overhead, no obligations. Nothing to tie you to your past."

I consider. "Phrased that way, it sounds pretty good. From where I sit it's frightening."

"Sure, but that fear is much better than staying safe and secure in a bad situation."

"It's a relief to have left that, but I left security too. The city job was dull, but I always knew what was coming next month, next year. Now I'm wondering what comes next. I've saved money this summer. You've kept me so busy, I've barely spent a dime. I have a head-start. But where will I be in a year? I'm almost middle-aged."

"Not almost." Adi giggles, shaking her head. "Colm. You won't have any problems. Unless you want to."

I almost laugh, but she doesn't look like she's joking. Does it seem that easy to her? I want to remind her my job's coming to an end. But I'm afraid. Maybe if I don't say anything, it can just continue like this. If I remind her, the spell will break. "That just isn't how things work in the real world."

"Oh?" Adi seems amused. "How don't they work?"

"We can't just drift forever, always exploring side trails, going off the map. We can't walk all day until we're hungry, then sit down and find food and drink provided by magic."

"See," Adi says. "You're stuck."

"Stuck? You just said I'm free."

"You're free, unless you remain stuck, believing nothing has changed. Thinking your world's the same as it was before you left your wife. You didn't just end a marriage, or leave a city. You began a new self, starting when you came here. The old Colman Quinn is dead. As soon as you realize it, everything's new."

I consider, as we walk. Sometimes in the woods, especially in the mountains, or places far removed from cities and people, where nature and exertion combine to create powerful distortions, all the troubles and worries of my life, no matter how magnified they seemed before, all recede before the unavoidable recognition of the scale of the world. The smallness of a single man's place in things, yet at the same time, that certainty that everything else, all the massive measureless unseen and unknowable expanse, belongs to me just as certainly as the ground beneath my feet. Is time stuck, or am I capable of racing ahead, glimpsing alternate futures? I can imagine it, myself with Adi in some new place, a world so changed from this one, I recognize nothing of the new realm that surrounds us. That word again, one I hesitate to use. Ecstasy. The terrifying, sickening visions, life-shattering. Not just glimpses of future. Reassurance of the possibility of escaping time. All pleasure and pain, bound together, enlarged, pulsating, all-encompassing. The entire scale of everything magnified, life no longer mundane, but too much, too great. The cup overflows. Sanity teeters.

Having seen this, I know it must come true. Not foolish hope, but certainty, absolute.

"What's wrong?" Adi asks. "Your face."

I can't describe what I'm thinking, not yet.

"I'll tell you what bothers me most of all," I begin, realizing I can change the subject, just like Adi. Tell her the truth, just not the answer she asked for. "I knew Paula was defective, or at least wrong for me. Yet when I ended things, it hurt so much. I think it hurt me more than it did her, even though I was the one leaving. Fear so intense, like something was being wrenched loose from me. Why is that? Pain should mean something."

"We're blind to what we're living through at any given moment," Adi says. "We only see it later. But you're right, it's not easier, being the one to leave. We convince ourselves they'll never survive without us."

I don't know what Adi experienced herself, to have such thoughts ready at hand, as if she's spent time contemplating scenarios not too different from my own. I'm glad not to be alone. There's some relief, thinking all the outlandish, wrenching pain of leaving Paula behind derived not from actual harm I perpetrated upon her, but my own misguided vanity.

Adi comes to a stop at the side of the trail, stands looking up. I'm so consumed in my own thoughts, a moment passes before I realize why she stopped. She's staring at a towering, uneven monolith of black rock. The base is several steps down the slope, yet the top of it towers well above our heads.

"That's amazing," Adi says.

"Dave, I have a very bad feeling about this," I say.

"I always believed rocks had roots, like trees reaching down," Adi says. "Big rocks, at least. Giant trees have roots that reach deeper than the tree is tall. A big monument like this probably has toes that dig way, way down deep. You could never uproot something like this."

"In all my geology studies, they failed to mention any of that. Or else maybe rocks don't work like that."

"Are you sure?"

Grasping roots descending, comprised of some matter variant on the above-ground stone. A different texture, purposed to reach into Earth's foundation, and grab hold.

I don't answer.

"I saw *2001*, you know." She grins. "Bet you thought your Dave Bowman reference flew right by."

"Nah, older woman like you, I figured you must've seen it."

Amusement brightens Adi's eyes, the opposite of age. She'll live a hundred more years, at least. Never grow old.

For the first time, I wonder if I'm in love with Adison. Maybe the idea has drifted to mind before, but I've always dismissed it immediately, a question too awkward and doomed to consider. Some part of me now wants to proclaim this possibility, shout it out, share with Adi the giddy, preposterous statement. Or is it still a question?

We wander through such beauty. So abundant, I feel less present myself, as if my identity is fading. I'm becoming anonymous, a personless carrier for observant eyes, rather than a thinking, worrying, judging man with too many desires of my own.

A tiny waterfall from a swollen pool burbles down, spills over rocks to another pool. The water continues this way, alternating stretches of movement onward and downward, with intermittent rests. In the barely moving crystal water, green moss hangs weightless, delicately arranged. Illumination reflects off lighter rocks on the stream bed, passes through translucent verdure and glimmers the surface as if through the lace mesh of a veil.

We're both carried away. Wandering, camera and GPS ignored, Adi's notebook at her side. She walks, eyes raising to the canopy of trees, falling to affirm the trail surface. No more work. Adi doesn't appear to care. I blink, and this valley floor seems very dark, so deeply shaded we might find ourselves blind if we didn't transition in very slowly, gradually.

Adi stops. "Are we still on the bridge trail from Echo Lake to the bridle trail?"

I find her staring at a trail sign, old wood, weathered like the rest. Beneath the word TRAIL, the number is eradicated. Someone has used a knife to chip away the trail number, leaving the rest of the sign intact. They could have cut down the sign, uprooted it, knocked it over. Instead they left it standing, proof the way has been lost.

Trail zero. Nothing, nowhere.

"If I wanted to," Adi says, "I could see that as sort of terrifying."

No trail, no name. How is it possible to be anything but lost? Could two people be erased from the world, transported elsewhere, just by scratching out of numbers on a sign?

So easy to fall loose. To stray from paths.

"Which way?" she asks.

"Follow me." We're not far at all from where we're meant to go.

Adi walks beside me, close. She hip-bumps me, then elbows me slightly off the trail.

I'm on the uphill side, so I don't fall, just trip through the ferns. "Clumsy girl."

"Any idea where we are?" Her voice, an airy whisper.

"There's no way to tell," I say. "Trails here are unmarked."

"There are no maps."

"Even lost like this, you know what I'm thinking of?" I ask. "Even when time and geography are unmarked and unreckoned, what's the one thing, the eternal force that continues?"

She answers without a pause. "You're thinking about eating."

"After a tiring adventure like this, is anything better than imagining food and drink? It's important to choose correctly, of course, so there's that reason to think about it in advance. But the real point is the extension of the pleasure."

"Anticipation," Adi says. "You're right. Thinking about doing a thing is almost as good as the thing itself."

"Almost."

"But just talking about it forever wouldn't be enough. At some point you have to reach the finish line."

"Sure." I'm always mindful of how Adi's looking at me. Something has changed, I feel certain. Her position in relation to me. The way her eyes look through me, focused not on my true face but some nearby conception of me. A projection of mind. So much like the way I look at her.

Such surreal closeness, communication without words. Things expressed by moving nearer, holding eye contact an instant longer than usual. Bumping elbows playfully, shifting our weight into each other, like playful children. An awkward yet naturally comfortable give and take, as real and intimate as anything between two people. It might not look like much, if someone saw us. No bare skin, no secret intimacy. But I know where this is headed. We both know.

Things continue, this sort of long-held dream made real, until we're back at Adi's car. First I'm afraid the presence of her Range Rover, the dark metal shell, a symbol of practicality, of business, might somehow break the spell. But she unlocks it, we climb in, and before she starts the engine, Adi looks ahead, rests her hands on the wheel and breathes deep. It's like a sigh, the sound she makes. A release of tension, a lessening of worry or anxiety. Relief.

Adi looks at me and there's no question, we're still together in a new place. Past the threshold, no going back. Something new is underway.

11. Discovery in Room 111

Flush with excitement, overstimulated with possibility, with overwrought potential, we return to Thunder Egg Inn. In the car, Adi makes hints, flirts more overtly than usual. I can't stop smiling. It feels like the conclusion of a very exciting first date, but we've known each other much longer. Hard to believe, after how much I dreaded admitting the truth about Paula, that Adi's response made me feel more certain than ever. It all seems so different, after so much time spent together, all the work outings, the dinners. Returning every night to the hotel.

Adi keeps glancing at me as she drives. I'm not imagining it. A high tension between us.

I see Kinosha differently now. That golden tinge of idealism that normally colors my view, it's been influenced, I know, by my idealization of Adi. After such an intimate day together, feeling closer than ever before, I'm surprised to return and see the town more faded and depleted than I wanted to see. Not that I think less of Adi, but that now she's more a woman to me than an ideal.

So often in the course of our mornings, afternoons and evenings, I'm mindful of the way Adi looks at me. What's she thinking? Now, I'm reassured at the undeniable intensity of her focus, like a mirror, my own gaze returned. At times I've conceptualized myself as awkward teenager, unsure how to move closer to a girl he likes. The truth is, I've had plenty of experience, before Paula. At least when I'm not paralyzed by anxiety, I recognize what it feels like, this electricity with two people.

We're at the hotel, out of the car, and breathless rounding the corner toward the hallway to our rooms. As we approach the facing doors, we're side by side, close, not hurrying. There's a shared anticipation, a new tension, the usual polite distance and reserve replaced by a tremulous force of attraction, like a powerful magnet poised near metal. I think of touching Adi, or taking her hand, but we're almost to the rooms.

Inside that door, everything will change.

I don't even look at my own room, just stand beside Adi as she finds her key. The door to 111 is ajar, already unlocked, and pushes open. A disorder of trash, shredded fabric covers the floor and bed. Adi's room is always tidy, nothing like this. Scattered everywhere, clothing, towels, pillows, curtains. Adi enters ahead of me, staggers in shock from desk, to bed, to chairs.

Amid the destruction, nothing seems to be missing. Adi's laptop and mobile printer remain on the desk, cracked apart as if struck by something heavy. Expensive business clothes and less formal outdoor gear are both part of the destruction. All her luggage lies empty, open on the bed.

Adi's wristwatch, some expensive designer platinum thing I haven't seen her wear since we first met, seems to be undamaged on the desk. Next to it, an open book of matches, none missing.

"That smell," Adi says.

"Gasoline."

Adi points. "Check 112."

Across the hall, my door remains locked, closed. I open it, find nothing disturbed within.

"Lucky for you," Adi says, coming up behind. "They assumed we were together, just one room."

The things I could say, openings for innuendo, suggestion. I let these pass, not because of the old fear and awkwardness. We're looking at each other, wondering what this means. So much has changed. Everything. That giddy, disorienting excitement, just moments ago. Now vanished, replaced by dawning fear. This intrusion isn't a scene of burglary. It's threat. Intimidation.

"Pack up." Adi crosses the hall, back to her own room.

My things are already mostly together. I zip my my razor and toiletries into their bag, retrieve my old laptop and several maps from the desk, stow everything in my day pack. I check under the bed, just making sure I left nothing behind. I never realized how attached I feel to this room. I consider calling Adi back, suggesting we share my room, but decide against it. Not because I'm trying to keep secret my desire for her. I won't hide that any more. But this is her room, at least she's paying for it. If she wanted to stick around, she would've said so.

I carry my pack to Adi's room, find her sorting items into two piles. A few items not shredded or gasoline-soaked go into the suitcase, everything else into the trash can.

"Almost everything's wrecked," I say.

Adi turns, half-shrugs. Then she straightens and reaches for my forearm as if needing support. "Time to relocate."

"There's no other hotel in Kinny, just those hostel rooms over the diner. You want to go up to Timberline?"

"Down the mountain." Her expression shifts, as if she's remembered something. "Are you still hungry?"

I laugh, unsettled rather than amused. "No."

"Liar. You always were."

Another laugh, lighter this time. "I admit it, Adi. This bothers me. You're in danger." Immediately I wish I'd said *We're in danger*, but she says it for me.

"We both are. As long as you're still running around with me."

"I am. And I will be. I'm not through with this until you say so." I inhale deep, hold it, look at Adi. She's scared. "Now that you mention it, we might as well eat. You have in mind the usual?"

"Yeah, what we talked about," Adi says. "Nothing has changed. I mean, everything has."

"I know what you mean. We'll be safe at Ice Axe, then…"

She nods. "Then we go. Bring your stuff."

II

Hood Highlands (in 11 parts)

12. Hood Highlands

The window overlooks a golf course, brilliant green under afternoon sun. I'm alone with my laptop, doing online research, and otherwise watching golfers finish the ninth hole. After dinner last night, Adi moved us ten miles down the mountain to Hood Highlands, a golf resort and spa. This morning she headed out to undertake her own research. I offered to go along, but she said she also needed to buy new clothes to replace the damaged ones, and if we worked separately one of us might uncover details the other missed.

Compared to the Thunder Egg, Hood Highlands is a whole different level of luxury, something I never could've afforded even back in Seattle. Adi's paying the tab. On many occasions this summer, she told me she wanted to demonstrate commitment to Kinosha by remaining present, proving her devotion to improving conditions around the village. So there we stayed all summer, even weekends. After what happened, we're both relieved to be at a safe distance, at least until we understand what we're up against.

After spending three months geared up for trails, I'm desk-bound. Google ninja, research assistant for Adi's development project. I'm adept enough at online detective work, checking public records databases, searching for archived news articles. It's just so different from the way I've been spending my days.

The cut on the side of my head, nearly forgotten yesterday, is aching again. Beneath the skin, I feel a localized burning and pulsing. Something deep within. I'm starting to worry about infection.

The 36-hole course, surrounded by tall trees and great mounds of ancient rhododendrons, seems an entirely different world. The quiet atmosphere and rolling grass is pleasant, but I find myself a bit intimidated by the many prominent signifiers of affluence and material superiority. Maybe I'm just wishing I had more, myself. Anyway, at least here we won't have to dodge gunfire.

As for Adi and me, it's not that things have reverted to how we were before. But after last night's surprise, we were both a bit rattled. We're still in two separate rooms, next door rather than across the hall.

So I'm working at a table in the lounge, heavy wood varnished gold-blond. It reminds me of Gwendoline Jones's great slab of a dining table. I'm using my stuttering old laptop, and a printer Adi rented from the resort's business center. For my reference, Adi left behind a few banded and clipped papers. These were in the trunk of her car at the time of the Thunder Egg room invasion, and luckily most of the big green and black topographic contour maps remained safely in my room the whole time. These I've unrolled on the table, curling corners held down by empty wine bottles borrowed from the bar. To my left, a fire crackles within a stone hearth, despite the heat outside. From where I sit, the course's first, ninth, tenth and eighteenth holes are visible. Dozens of foursomes have begun and ended rounds, heading out fresh-faced and enthusiastic, trousers and golf shirts pressed, only to return sunbaked, sweat-damp, looking beleaguered and dehydrated. This tempts me to consider golf as some kind of metaphor for life itself, but the sport doesn't interest me enough to devote that much energy into pursuing such a line of thought.

Though golfers cycle past steadily all day, the dining room empties after the lunch crowd. A single female bartender covers thirty-two empty tables plus my occupied one. She emerges to clear my lunch plate and deliver fresh iced tea with lemon. Her name tag says Robin. She reminds me of Paula, tattoos from wrists to elbows, hints of damage in her eyes, or at least an abundance of pain in the rear-view mirror. Funny how it's so easy to recognize now. I never recognized it in Paula until years in.

I glance up. "Thanks, Robin." Check my watch. Almost 3:30.

Robin lingers. "Stuck, waiting for your wife?"

I'm startled by this. How does she know about Paula? "You know my wife?"

A playful grin, like maybe she figures me for one of those married guys who pretends to be available. "Tall and slim, good legs. Hair like a movie star?"

Adi? That's right. I remember the unfamiliar twist she put into her hair before heading out this morning. A different style for her, after so long spent in a mode of outdoor casual, after months of mountain life. I wonder, is that how she looks normally, working from her Portland office?

"Right, Adi. She's not my wife. I work for her."

Robin shifts, doesn't move her feet but adjusts her body subtly closer. Her hip leans against the edge of my table. Detached as I am, her body language interests me. What's behind it? That little smile, a hint of thoughts in motion. "Not a bad gig, if you don't mind being alone. You get to work in a place with a view."

"She'll be back. We're working on the same thing, just from different angles."

Robin drops the girlish playfulness, becomes more serious. "What kind of work do you do?"

It strikes me belatedly, so focused on Adi. This young bartender, attractive in her way, seems drawn to me. It feels alien, some strange misapprehension she just hasn't yet realized. I should be pleased. Newly separated, essentially unattached. Haven't been with any woman in such a long time. Months before I left Paula. But I don't feel unattached. I can watch Robin's center of gravity, shifting nearer. Her excited, confident forwardness flipping into uncertainty, when I don't react as she anticipates.

Is this how I used to twist and turn, worrying about Adi?

I realize one thing about Robin. It's not that she reminds me of the Paula I left. She resembles the appealing version, from our earlier years, when Paula seemed full of edgy confidence. The strange mystery of the artist, a hint of darkness. It seemed within her control, then. Before I knew how deep it went, the abyss that loomed beyond the visible edge of the cliff.

Her question. What kind of work do I do for Adi. Most of what I was hired for is finished. I've become a sort of general assistant. It seems so obvious. She's keeping me around, doing me a favor. Even two weeks ago, I might've considered there was still enough work to justify my place. But for what she's paying me? Adi could easily get an assistant to do the same work, much cheaper. Certainly her development company has support staff.

"This and that," I say. "I just try to free her up to focus on the project she's assembling, around Kinosha." I stop myself, figuring Adi wouldn't want details divulged. Once it's in motion, the development will be known all over the mountain. But it could be considered competition for Hood Highlands, even ten miles down the highway.

Robin says something polite, returns to her work. I wonder how I appear to her, what conclusion she's drawn. Then I drop it, and resume searching public records. The ability to unearth digitally archived information from a loose mountain of search index data has become the modern equivalent of deep education. Once, knowledge meant having information at hand, delving into one's own gray matter. Now it's more about understanding how search algorithms function, how to utilize terms neither too broad nor too narrow.

I've marked twenty-two articles and eleven digital photos, and begin printing these out.

Adi's plan is to email me from her cell phone once she's on her way back. I'm impatient for her return, keeping one eye on my inbox.

A thousand and one times I check my email, then a message pops in.

"Back in about an hour. —A"

13. The History of Ownership

The dinner crowd surged in early, and already begins to disperse by 6:30. Robin, replaced by another bartender and supported by several dining room waitstaff, has been lingering, sitting on the edge of my table, not too intrusively looking over my work. I can't tell if her shift is over, and she just wants to chat before departing, or she's supposed to still be helping behind the bar, and instead leaving everything to the new guy.

At movement within the open entry to the lobby, we both turn.

Adi enters, carrying a messenger bag, gray felt with a black leather strap, over one shoulder. In each hand, a large brown paper shopping bag with a waxed twine handle. At first, I'm not sure she sees me. She seems contained within herself, as if participating in some conversation I'm not part of. Then she reaches for her ears and removes a pair of headphones so unobtrusive I hadn't noticed them. Thin black wires trail to her pocket. She's dressed in black leggings and a snug summer sweater, sage green with a wild feather design in black. It's strange, seeing her dressed more city. She looked like this when we met, before she started dressing for our outdoor work.

Adi notices me and smiles, broader than usual. Either she's learned something encouraging, or she's glad to see me. Both, I hope.

"Red House Painters say hello," she says, "and something about the void. I think it's supposed to be encouraging." She raises an eyebrow. "Who's your friend?"

Robin stands, smooths her skirt. "Just making sure he's taken care of." For the first time, she seems awkward. As she departs for the bar, I'm mindful of the mismatch, her tattoos and Betty Page bangs offset against the preppy Hood Highlands uniform, khaki and light blue.

Adi faces me, yet I can tell she's appraising Robin as she walks away. Evaluating, weighing possibilities. Not that I want to make her jealous, but I do enjoy the idea of Adi considering me at least capable of drawing a woman's interest. Probably she'd be shocked at the narrowness of my focus.

"Find anything?" Adi asks. "You first."

"Yeah." I glance at the printouts and maps, not necessarily intending to read from them for my response, just resetting my mind to the day's subject. "If I trace back far enough, before the mine disaster, ownership of virtually all private land in the Kinosha area was at one time held by McAttree Mining Company, or individual members of the McAttree family. The disaster nearly bankrupted them, and they seem to have survived by gradually selling off almost everything they owned. Parcel by parcel, this continued for almost a decade. They retained three family homes, and some smaller acreage west and south, without much value. They held lumber rights on some of the bigger acreage they sold, and logged it aggressively. The very last piece sold, which was also by far the largest dollar value sale, was the Jones A Parcel, the one near the mine. That seemed to be the tipping point, the trick that got them solvent, and they stopped selling. Still, most of their empire shifted toward Central Oregon, despite Lewin McAttree keeping very much in touch with Kinosha. The old man rents a place in the village, just to allow him to remain on Kinosha's council. The address seemed familiar, so I looked it up. It's a room in Thunder Egg Inn, though he never stays there."

Adi nods. "So, McAttree. That confirms what I found."

"One other thing, not sure what you'll think." I pause, looking for any hint Adi knows what I'm about to say, but see none. "Gwendoline Jones's son, Perkins Jones, works for McAttree. Not directly, but he's employed by one of the McAttree family lumber divisions, down in Roseburg. Structural wood products, beams and joists." Another pause. "Are you sure Gwendoline is what she appears? She seemed perfectly sweet, and very charming, but—"

"I'm sure enough about Gwendoline." Adi slides out a chair, sits beside me. "I turned up the same connection, Perk Jones and McAttree. Perk, that's what he goes by. No, Gwendoline's not our problem. She has every intention of selling me the land, straightforward enough. Lewin McAttree's the one that stinks. I keep thinking it's got to be something about the disaster, wanting to keep people away. I don't know, maybe prevent anyone finding what really happened down there. It's a different world now. Environmental concerns, disaster liability. This roadblocking isn't about Lewin McAttree wanting to remain top dog in Kinosha. He has something to hide."

I scan my papers, not sure what more I have that Adi hasn't already found for herself. "I've got other McAttree family businesses here. Timber, other wood products. Even road construction, going way back. All the stone walkways around Multnomah Falls, the Lodge, the lower bridge. You know that stone bridge, where all the tourists stand and crane their necks, trying to see the top of the falls?"

"Sure," Adi says. "I grew up here, remember?"

14. Digging Deeper

"So, seriously." I nod at the shopping bags. "What have you got here?"

Adi peeks down into one of her bags, even seems to consider showing me what she bought. "I just went as far as Troutdale, at the end of the gorge. Grabbed clothes and gear at the outlet stores there."

"I thought you'd go into Portland," I muse. "Sak's, at least Macy's. Girl like you, all fancy."

Adi grins, but doesn't protest. "I used to be a bit of a brand snob, I admit, but lately I find myself reformed. Probably it's all our time spent roving through the trees." She lightly smacks the back of my arm, and changes the subject from her clothing. "The library in Sandy was a dead-end. Mother used to take me there when I was little, nineteen-seventy-whatever, nearest library to where we lived. I doubt they've added to their collection since then. But the librarian there tipped me off to the Mt. Hood Historical Center. Should've just gone there first, in fact I can't believe I never knew of the place. Right under our noses, behind the liquor store in Kinosha. Spent most of my day there. Tons of old newspapers, books, microfiche copies of public deeds. Old maps. Pretty cool."

"Sounds like it."

"Swung by the Gorge Society reading room, in Troutdale, near the outlet mall. Two birds, one stone."

"Columbia River Gorge? How's that connected to the mountain?"

"You mentioned Multnomah Falls? Something I found in the Kinosha archives led me toward construction of the Gorge Scenic Highway. Before the McAttree family ever started mining, they were blasting tunnels through hillsides, flattening grades for rails and roads. At some point around thirty-three, the Governor's office called in the Army Corps of Engineers, who were down the gorge surveying and prepping for construction of Bonneville Dam. The Army's guys discovered the McAttree excavating crews were operating beyond the scope of projects for which they'd received government contracts. Falsified work progress reports had been filed. Not only were they working outside boundaries designated on plan drawings and land surveys. Some of the tunnels went off at strange angles, away from the planned highway. McAttree's own foremen played dumb about the errors, claimed to be lost, and were taken off the project. And it goes back even earlier."

Adi digs out a plain paper copy of an old photograph, slides it toward me. In the corner, the date November '11 is scrawled in coarse pencil. A gang of men pose before a blasted-out tunnel, a yawning open space in a hillside, amid mules and wagons and jagged mounds of dynamited rock. Dust-gray faces stare, grim and frozen.

"There." She points.

One man stands before the others, arms crossed. He resembles photos I found of Lewin McAttree.

"That's Artemire McAttree," Adi says. "Founder of McAttree Mining Company, or at least that's the name on the earliest documents I could find. Might be father of Lewin McAttree, or grandfather. Records are unclear."

"Artemire. Jeez, what a clan."

"I read three contradictory histories of the disaster. One, the mine exploded out of nowhere. Two, a sinkhole opened and everything collapsed, which caused a fire. Or three, maybe gasses rose from deep in the mine, and some fled while others died below. All agree, Kinosha had to be evacuated, remained empty for many months. Another thing, the same in every version. The McAttree family always owned that land, going back before the township, the mine, even Kinosha settlement. Maybe back to the days of Barlow Trail. Pioneers, wagon trains, all that."

"Crazy," I say. Adi's findings confirm my own, yet extend wider in scope and deeper in time.

"Some of this I had from before," she says. "I guess another reason I trust Gwendoline is that her late husband Eliot Jones used to be McAttree's number one, up until the disaster. After that, Eliot broke from McAttree. Seems like there were some hard feelings. Eliot gave up what seemed like a very lucrative position with McAttree, and turned down other opportunities within McAttree's other ventures, which soon thrived beyond anything the mine had ever accomplished. For whatever reason, Eliot stayed in Kinosha."

"So what did Eliot do for a career, the last half century of his life? He and Gwendoline obviously accumulated money somewhere."

Adi shakes her head. "Not sure. Gwendoline says Eliot travelled a lot, mostly without her. She seems completely uninterested in McAttree, or any kind of related agenda. As for the son, Perk Jones, I actually called down to the wood products mill near Roseburg. Asked their payroll person to confirm employment of Perkins Jones, and she said, Sure, Perk Jones, he's on our payroll, but never actually shows up at this facility. The woman I spoke to, she's worked there thirty-some years. Quite cheerfully she told me she always wondered why the second highest-paid man on their ledger lives four hours away, and she's never met him."

"Interesting. So maybe McAttree figures if you never end up obtaining Gwendoline's land, he might be able to get it back through the son?"

"Another thing, Perk Jones seems to be in a relationship with McAttree's granddaughter. Isn't that perfect? The old man's own daughter and sons are dead. The granddaughter's all he has. Must must be our age, roughly. But if this is all a big fix-up, one thing doesn't make sense."

"Yeah. How does Lewin McAttree keep the mine protected."

"A man almost ninety, waiting for Gwendoline to die, so Perk and Grand-daughter McAttree can inherit the land? Lewin McAtree's fifteen, twenty years older than Gwendoline."

"That's a lot of puzzle pieces. You think this old man might kill to regain a piece of land he sold decades ago?" I frown. "Sounds like an episode of Perry Mason."

"Maybe it's some long game. Just keep the status quo, everything secret, until Lewin McAttree is dead. The last McAttree connected to the accident." Adi leans back, stretches in her chair, then pushes it back and stands. She rubs her eyes with one hand, rests the other on my shoulder. "I'm sorry, I'm wiped out. I didn't sleep much, after we checked in last night. My mind just kept going over everything. I should try to rest."

"Sure." I hate to see her go, but I understand.

"I'll call Gwendoline tomorrow, but mostly, I want to talk to McAttree. For now, I'd better sleep."

"I'll go along," I say. "To Kinosha tomorrow, I mean, not to sleep now. If that's okay?"

Adi nods, blinking tired eyes. "We'll shake something loose. Good night."

She squeezes my shoulder before she turns, and leaves the lounge. I consider doing some more work on my own. Robin's still lurking around the end of the bar, watching. I shut the laptop, power off the printer, and gather my papers.

15. Confronting Lewin McAttree

Adi asks me to drive up from Hood Highlands to Kinosha. She barely speaks on the way. It feels strange going back, after just two nights away. To me, this place is summer. Days blurred together, waking to work, meals then sleep. Then everything changed. Someone shot at us, then what happened to Adi's room. I never imagined Kinosha could ever feel dangerous. Always before, everyone in town seemed friendly, welcoming. Maybe I was blinded by my desire for a perfect place. This village, nestled into a prime spot on the most beautiful mountain I've ever seen. What flaws, what dangers did I miss?

We veer off Highway 26 onto Kinosha Loop Road. Most of the village's businesses cluster around the center of the strip, where Multorpor Road cuts away and crosses an ornamental stone bridge toward Ski Bowl, the small resort just across the highway. At that corner stands the oldest and grandest of Kinosha's structures, sprawling over an entire block, four stories high. Ground level is all retail. Market, liquor store, post office, and a shop that rents skis, snowshoes and mountain bikes. Upper levels house administrative offices for local utilities, and the many support businesses, such as maid services and concession contractors, that work here in town and at the recreational resorts nearby and up the mountain. Also, a handful of public offices include rooms for the Clackamas County Sheriff, Hood Tourism Board, and our destination, the Kinosha Village Council.

As I park outside, Adi seems to come awake, blinking as if startled. Something in her face appears strained. Her lips press together, thin and pale. For the first time I've seen, she looks her age. Nothing at all like the Adi I know.

"Okay," she says, "time to press on."

In front of the market, on our way to the side stairs, we pass a pair of gray-faced mountain types. They walk hunched, slump-shouldered. At first, I take them both for middle-aged women, almost identical. Clothes rumpled and sun-faded, gray hair tangled with leaves and dry grass, as if they've spent many nights sleeping out in the trees. The two share the same uncomfortable, shuffling gait and improbably forward posture, leaning out as if searching the ground for something lost. The women both appear somehow sick, or damaged.

"Something in the water around here," I say.

Adi glances up, sees the two. "Yeah." One eyebrow lifts. "Sometimes they come down, they try to sleep up in the rocks. Especially in summer. The mountain has a lot of secret places. Even still."

The gray, faded pair look back over their shoulders at us, as if listening. Though they appear identical in shape, I now see one is clearly male, his face spiked with a week's white stubble. They shuffle down access stairs toward the sidewalk, and Adi leads me the opposite direction, around the corner of the building.

The encounter makes me uncomfortable, in a way I can't imagine how to explain to Adi. I don't want to appear to judge the people here. How many times have I failed to notice similar things, overlooked discrepancies, superimposing what I expect to see in place of the actual. So entranced by my imaginary version of Kinosha—Adi's dream—I may have missed the truth of it. Everything has seemed so wonderful here, not just the land itself. The staff at our hotel, just a block away, always pleasant. And the Ice Axe, where we always enjoyed great food, and friendly, personal service. All the wait staff knew me and Adi by name. And the other patrons, all of them seemed just like us. Enjoying the atmosphere, the setting. Then again, many of them weren't locals, but just passing over, or visiting briefly.

How many people have I passed, without really looking? Kinosha has always seemed charming, pleasantly quiet, at worst a faded, slightly impoverished little town. Now it feels perilous, somehow implying concealed secrets. That charm, a facade. People come down from above, their faces strange and frightening, seeking food or begging change, hoping they won't be truly seen. Somehow they pass for normal, relying on those like me, who fail to look, too focused on what we're hoping to find.

Adi stops outside the Kinosha Council offices.

The only thing she told me in the car was that she'd heard Lewin McAttree is supposed to be found here most weekday mornings, despite now living far outside town. An old habit, apparently. I can only guess what draws him back to Kinosha.

"Ready?" Adi seems nervous, but doesn't hesitate. She pushes open the door.

A single open room, divided by barrier rows of brown filing cabinets into quarters, each given to a single desk. The younger of the two old men, sitting up front, responds as we enter.

He's at least sixty-five, wearing a light blue polyester suit. His thin combed-over hair is dyed mud red, several shades darker than his silver-orange mustache. "Help you two?"

Adi ignores him, focusing on the man we came for. Lewin McAttree rises in the back corner, recognizable by the thick, perfectly white hair he shares with his father, or maybe grandfather, Artemire McAttree. What defies expectation is McAttree's upright cowboy posture, and crisply new Wranglers. Denim work shirt, tan suede jacket and cowboy hat complete an outfit far too heavy for the day's heat outside. The office is super-cooled, at most sixty degrees. McAttree watches Adi approach.

"Hold up there!" Blue polyester guy tries to block.

Adi steps around, makes for McAttree with such urgency, she barely stops short of running him over. Her arms held out, tense at her sides, as if ready to grapple. "Lewin McAttree?"

McAttree swivels the too-large hat, then straightens it. "Young woman. Coming up to me like that."

Adi lowers her arms. "I'm Adison Kye. I'm wondering if we have a problem."

McAttree breaks eye contact, glances at me. "Kye. I've heard the name."

"I know what you're doing." Adi shifts slightly, back into his line of sight. "Your family's got history, and you don't want anyone getting near enough to find it. Mistakes, recklessness. Maybe Artemire's, maybe your own. Quite a few lives lost."

McAttree cocks his head. He reaches to straighten his hat, but stops himself, seeming to realize he's just done so. He loops both thumbs over the front of his belt. He chews as if working a toothpick, though none is visible. "Miss Kye. Going through life, so hot-fired with passion, based on so many wrong conceptions. If ever you stumbled accidental-like upon a single correct thing, you'd never recognize it in time."

"You can't stop this happening," Adi says, all calm and confidence now. "This area's going to be remade. Visitors will come to the mountain from all over the world. Everything in Kinosha will change. Whatever ancient malfeasance you're trying to protect, that's no longer relevant. My project will go forward."

"That so?" McAttree glares, seeming to hold in reserve some encrypted truth.

"Maybe I'll tell Gwendoline Jones about her son's connection to you. Let her know maybe you plan to get the land back that way."

McAttree's mouth opens slightly. "I'll not stand here." He shakes his head, moves to leave.

Adi motions, trying to block him, wave him back. McAttree doesn't stop. I shift into the way. The old man nimbly sidesteps. I don't want a physical showdown, especially not with a man twice my age, but I raise an open hand as if I might grasp his shoulder. Without hesitation, McAttree grips my upper arm and spins me. I'm disoriented, facing the other way, wondering what happened.

Adi's tone changes. "I'm just trying to help Kinosha."

We follow McAttree outside, around the corner. It's clear he's angry, muttering. He moves quickly down the stairs. At ground level, outside the market, we start to gain as he approaches the parked cars.

Adi shouts after him again, exasperated rather than angry. "Mr. McAttree, I don't understand."

McAttree's trembling, anger in his eyes, disgust on his face. "That's right, you don't. And acting without understanding, that makes you dangerous." He unlocks the door to a red pickup, swings the door open. Gets in, starts up, revs the engine. McAttree backs out, spins tires like a show-off teenager. The pickup disappears, toward the highway.

I'm angry, so frustrated, I have to do something. "Let's go after him."

I move toward Adi's Rover.

Adi takes out her phone. "Wait."

We both turn at the approach of a much smaller vehicle, which pulls into the spot just vacated. A tiny green Honda hybrid driven by Gwendoline Jones.

16. The Rest of the Council

Adi leans close to me. "Should I tell her about Perk?" she whispers.

I shake my head. Gwendoline climbs out, shuts the door.

"I was just going to call," Adi tells her.

Gwendoline, nose wrinkled in disgust, waves a hand at the hulking yellow Humvee in the next parking space. "Would you believe this monstrosity, a gift from Councilman McAttree to Councilman Spence. That's small-town politics. No concern at all for the appearance of undue influence."

"McAttree just roared off," Adi says. "I think I upset him with my candor. I was about to call you, maybe go in and speak to the other one. Spence?"

"Let's go." Gwendoline walks between us, steadying herself, one hand on each of our arms. The arrangement seems more a gesture of friendliness than a need for support. When we start up the stairs, Gwendoline climbs just fine with no help from us, and she leads us back to the same offices we just left.

Councilman Spence, he of the blue suit, starts to protest at our entry until he sees Gwendoline. "You may as well come in, sit down." He throws up his hands.

The scuffed plastic guest chairs resemble surplus from an elementary school of my childhood. Adi and I sit, Gwendoline standing behind. We all look at one another, appraising. There seems to be unspoken agreement to start over from a place of civility.

"Now first off, I know why you're here. Trying to push Lewin McAttree on your development plan. Of course he knows who you are, what this is about. Now listen." Spence pauses as if preparing to start choosing words with greater care. "There's no way this transaction of yours can be forced on the village. You may as well go back to Portland. My own thinking on this isn't important." He pauses, makes a point of casting an eye at Gwendoline. "What Lewin McAttree wants, everybody around here knows, that trumps everything else. It's good as law, really."

Gwendoline sighs. "Oh, such bullshit."

Spence's eyes widen. "Listen, Miss Kye, some around here like your plan, at least in certain respects. Maybe some of us like to believe it's not too late for a new Kinosha. But what a man like me thinks personally, that's a separate matter from official endorsement by Council."

"We're not here to persuade you, or McAttree," Adi says. "But it's useful to know he's already dead set against the village endorsing my plan. The deal is going to be done. Gwendoline owns eighty-eight percent of the land I want to buy. After everything's built, when people in Kinosha realize they can take part in it, share the benefits, we'll see if people here really want to resist, and watch all the money flow around them."

Spence shrugs. "All right. Just don't bother trying to argue with McAttree. He's in charge. He's the big hat."

"Where's he going from here? Can we track him down?"

"Just goes to his place, down past the reservation. Sizable complex he's got out there, almost to Madras, all metal buildings, radio dishes, technology. Cuckoo kind of stuff, I might think, but that doesn't change the one thing. That's him being the big hat. That's what he is. No matter what I think on the plus or minus side of any ledger you've got, with regard to Lewin McAttree, I'm not no way going to cross him once his mind is set. You can try, but you won't get anywhere. Not in Kinosha, or down to Bend, or anywhere far as Roseburg, really." Spence keeps looking to me, rather than Adi or Gwendoline, though he clearly understands Adi's the one buying Gwendoline's land. "You want my advice, your play here is to look for ways to get as nearly as possible what you want, without needing anything from Lewin McAttree. That's the blunt goddamn truth. That's what I'd do."

I wait for Adi to escalate, try another angle. She's just listening.

"What's McAttree doing out there?" I ask. "You said, all this technology, radio dishes?"

"Even if he gave you a close-up look at all those items, it wouldn't add any clarity for you. I've seen it, and I sure to hell don't know. One thing is, the radio dishes aren't aimed up at the sky, where they'd find satellites. They're aimed at the mountain, here at Kinny itself. But what he's listening for, I don't know."

Adi rises, goes to stand in the doorway. I follow, and we look down at the street. Behind us, Gwendoline takes the seat Adi vacated and tries talking to Spence in a familiar, almost intimate tone. Spence seems more friendly, at least. "I know McAttree's business has become too weird, and I'll say it. Too foreign. It just isn't something any of us can stop."

Gwendoline stands, summons us back.

Spence stares at Adi. "You're from Rectory?"

Adi seems stunned. "Rectory? When I was little. Who told you?"

"You knew about Nomon House?"

Adi shakes her head.

"Not a real house, just a pile of old rocks. Shape of a house, or church. The stones weren't gathered there by men. They fell together, at the instant of a lightning strike, and landed just exactly as they're now arranged. Before the whites came, even before Indians, others lived on the mountain. Kinosha settlement, Mountlake, Rectory. All stayed away from Nomon House."

"Why?" Adi asks.

"Grandmother used to tell, I don't know, must be sixty years ago, Nomon House stood in the low point of a dry lake bed, where long ago all the water drained down, overnight, drunk up by something below, something that lived there, down in the rock, far longer than people have settled around. How long is that, I don't know. Millions of years."

Gwendoline laughs lightly, shaking her head.

"Thing comes up, some occasions," Spence continues. "Some full moons, some not. Maybe years pass, but always it sweeps up from that rock like a wind. Blowing through, overnight. Come up, take somebody back down. Grandmother called him a name, thing that lived there. I don't remember it. He's a blind shape, she said. Knows everything, remembers everything. When he wants to, walks up out of lowest rock the way you or me might stroll through a wind."

"Why are you telling us this?" Adi asks.

Spence's face changes abruptly, as if he's let slip a secret. "Often wondered about Rectory. Everyone near there left the mountain, all at once. Haven't seen one soul among that number, nor heard from any, must be thirty-five years." He stands, face stoic, rigid. "Thought you might know something, is all."

"I'm sorry, I don't," Adi says. "I was young when we left. My mother, my parents never returned here."

Spence says nothing more, just nods. Our meeting is finished.

I follow Adi and Gwendoline out and down the stairs, a few steps behind.

"Gwendoline," Adi begins, "I want to make sure you understand the interest Lewin McAttree still has in your land. He may have sold it long ago, but he's watching over it, trying to prevent it changing hands. I'm concerned he'll try to get it loose from your son. Maybe act against you, then everything's left to Perk. McAttree has influence over him."

Gwendoline is visibly shocked, hearing her son's name this way. "My son would never put in with violence." She looks within herself, seems to reconsider. "Not against me."

"I believe you." Adi touches Gwendoline's arm, grips it. "That won't stop McAttree doing something on his own. You have to be careful."

17. Room 111 Revisited

We reach the sidewalk, and stop at the curb before Gwendoline's Honda and Spence's big Humvee.

"It's true what you said," Gwendoline says. "Perk's employed by a McAttree company."

Adi takes a different approach. "Who else would want to keep us away from the mine head? I keep thinking back to that specific place, because of the shooting. Did anyone ever investigate the mine, the cause of the accident?"

"Investigate?" Gwendoline shakes her head. "Not really. It was a different world, that time. Every family nearby lost somebody, or knew someone. All received settlements, and that ended it."

"When you bought the upper parcel, was anybody else trying to buy it? Maybe other bidders who might still be angry you beat them out?"

"I doubt there were other potential buyers. We purchased it directly from Lewin McAttree. He's bounced back financially by now, and then some, but at the time he needed money. All those settlements. These days, if he wanted, Lewin could buy himself another mountain all his own. Back then, he liked the idea we had, to leave the land raw, untouched. A buffer zone surrounding our home. I think at the time Lewin felt he owed Eliot something. Maybe believed he might some day get him back into the McAttree businesses."

"You haven't spoken of your husband. I wondered how he went from being highly placed with McAttree Mining and split off, completely on his own."

"You might think the accident precipitated things, because Eliot broke from McAttree soon after. But earlier, maybe 1953, his reading made him want to explore new directions. We first spent time in Mexico, then Central America, Curacao and Belize. Always vacationing down there, while Eliot was working around the mine. Not digging of course, but above ground management. He earned lengthy vacations. We kept venturing south, Peru and Brazil. Finally Eliot became enamored of Buenos Aires, the Argentine writers. He became obsessed with metaphysical time. We'd go down there, live very differently for a few weeks, and when we returned, Eliot would obsess over dreams of making a new life. That part of the world, he felt connected to the ancient. I argued with him, there's plenty of that here. This mountain." Gwendoline gestures, in case we've forgotten where we are. "But after the mine closed, he made his own way. Business opportunities, separate from McAttree's world. Eliot wanted to break free of that. Not just mining. The whole connection, McAttree, all his cronies. Called it the 'old Northwest cabal.' Eliot wanted to start life anew, but didn't seem to believe we could. I told him it was possible. Later he said he never believed it, much as he wanted it. Only considered the path open once I said those words. I gave permission, he said."

At this, Gwendoline looks as if emotions might overtake her. Adi's face also changes, as if moved in sympathy. I want to take Adi's hand.

"Anyway, we bought the land from Lewin McAttree. He said he liked that I wanted to leave the land raw. To him, that was just as good as keeping ownership himself. The McAttrees were already involved in road-building and timber. There was certainly more money in those things than mining. They shifted at just the right time."

"But if the mining was done, what keeps McAttree coming around?"

Gwendoline shrugs, sighs. "Kinosha was a ghost town for years. Boarded up, decaying. In winter, nobody plowed, except the highway. Twelve feet of snow on this loop road, can you imagine? Still Lewin McAttree kept coming, all along. He's never bothered me, though, about the land. A few times, he joked he'd buy it back one day. Mainly I think he wanted to make sure nobody would build condos on the upper slopes."

"I wonder if that's what he thinks I'm trying to do?" Adi muses.

"Oh, I can't see how, but Lewin McAttree's a weird old man." She stops, chuckles at herself. "Listen to me, old man. Not ten years older than me." She steps down toward her car, rests her hand on the door. "I'm sorry I can't help more. I think everything can still work out, whether or not the Council's onboard to start. Once the town sees construction reshaping the hill, everyone will see it's inevitable. They'll want to share in the benefits, I'm sure."

Adi shakes her head. "I'll keep working. I'm glad you showed up. I was about to call you."

"Oh, I saw your Range Rover on my way down. Heard of problems at the Thunder Egg, and worried about you two. Wanted to be sure you were safe. Such a relief, seeing the pair of you standing there safe and sound, behind your big lug of an SUV." She smiles, disarming.

Adi and I look at each other. We turn in sync to look down the block, toward the Thunder Egg.

Two Sheriff's department vehicles out front. Yellow tape strung everywhere.

"What kind of problems?" Adi asks.

"Let's walk down," I suggest.

As we approach, a Sheriff's deputy comes out and waves at Gwendoline.

"I was a little concerned," Gwendoline tells the deputy. "These friends of mine, they were staying in the Inn all summer, until a few days ago."

"Two nights ago," I say. "Someone tossed our room. Her room."

"You never filed a report?" The deputy doesn't seem to require an answer. "Well, this is plenty worse than B&E. Couple guys killed. Pair of mountain bikers from Portland, sharing a room." He raises an eyebrow. "Sliced up into pieces, in their bed. Luggage contents all shredded."

"What room?" Adi asks.

The deputy glances back. "Ah, it's 111."

Standing at the front fender of the Sheriff's truck, I see past the fluttering crime scene tapes, down the front hall, and through the open doorway into the room. The interior is dark, obscure shapes barely discernible, other deputies moving. A flash bursts, a photographic moment illuminated. Scene of horror, so much blood. Raw flesh, bone. Limbs contorted, impossible angles. Visceral shock of human gore. Sickening.

I glance at Adi. Her face displays the same horror I feel, that nightmare flash image reflecting in her eyes, echoing. An instant is more than enough.

I take charge, guide her away. Gwendoline follows.

"Can I borrow your cell?" I ask Adi.

She hands it over. I dial.

"Ryan, it's Colm. I'm up on Mt. Hood, Kinosha village. I need your help."

Adi stares into the distance, attention slowly drifting back from what she saw, what she must be remembering, to the three of us walking slowly back toward our vehicles.

Ryan says he'll come, just needs to know details. Where and when.

"Thanks. I'll email directions. Bring everything." I click off.

"What are you doing?" Adi asks.

"Helping you," I say.

18. Respite at Hood Highlands Lounge

Adi and I have been watching the gradual settlement of night over the golf course. Fairways and greens, sand traps. A man-made lake, and perimeter trees. All vanished now, invisible. Finally we turn away from the window. The lounge is nearly as dark, illuminated only by tiny candles glowing on dining tables, and a row of halogen pinpoints behind the bar. In the corner nearest us, a piano player plays inoffensively, nothing recognizable. Small groups, mostly older than Adi and me, sit in clusters around the room, drinking expensive bottles, wine, cognac, and single malts. Vintages selected from weighty, leather-bound lists.

Adi and I order the same drinks and food. Maker's Mark doubles, Hopworks IPA drafts. Sourdough pizzas with wild chanterelle and oyster mushrooms, sun-dried tomato, roasted garlic and olive oil.

"See that?" I point out the huge mural hanging above the bar. "Yesterday I spent the whole day in here, broad daylight. Never even realized it was there."

"Maybe you were distracted by that bartender girl of yours." Adi breaks into a grin.

Tonight, the bar is tended by a pair of older men. No sign of Robin.

I shrug. "She was just flirting a little," I say. "I could tell there was nothing behind it."

"You did notice, at least." This seems to satisfy her.

"What do you mean?"

"Nothing." She smiles broadly, as if at some joke she gets to enjoy without me. "Usually you're just… less perceptive when it comes to these things."

I'm still focused on the painting. "The canvas is murky, sort of vague, at first glance. Look like nothing but texture. But it's actually complicated."

Adi shifts her gaze to the mural. "Sure. There's plenty going on, if you look beneath surfaces."

"You can sit here in front of it, and barely notice. Then, focus. Look into it. See that? What are those?"

"Feet and legs, in rows. They're much taller than the house. Is that a house?"

I finish my beer, look into the glass. "I might want another one of these."

"We'll get another round." Adi finishes her own beer. "You sit long enough near a picture like that, I think it starts affecting your subconscious without you ever realizing."

"All sorts of symbolism in there. That house."

"You think that's us, humanity? We're inside a house, just trying to live, and the whole time there are giants outside, looking down?"

"That's one possibility. The legs are all in rows, tall and straight, like trees. But they have feet. Maybe the trees can walk around."

"Do you remember my theory? Big rocks, how they're like trees?"

"Sure. Roots reaching down. Gripping with toes."

She nods, makes a quick gesture to one of the bartenders.

"I remember," I continue. "Did that idea of yours come from this painting?"

"No. I've never been here before. But you wonder. Maybe everything we know is wrong. It's stones that have roots. Trees walk around on legs."

The bald bartender places two more pints. His white-haired partner delivers two Maker's Marks.

I sip. "Everything we know is wrong. I like the sound of that, it fits. You know, brand new universes are starting up all the time. Just study the symbols, interpret to see what we've got, and what's lacking. Whatever we need, just dream it into reality."

"I think one of us is getting drunk," Adi says.

I consider. "Two of us."

"So, is that what you think?" Adi swallows half the bourbon. "That's the way dreams work?"

I consider. "Thoughts are powerful. I mean, not just every fleeting idea. But concentrated thoughts. Intentions with real focus. Yeah. I think that can change your reality."

Adi sits quiet, seriously appraising. "I hope so."

"The creative will is strong. Nothing quick, or easy. But a mind that's intent. Dreams, waking visions, whatever. See the change with enough clarity. Focus long enough, hard enough."

"You've said things like this before, little hints, here and there. I always wondered if that was your philosophy."

"Philosophy, I don't know. That makes it sound formal."

"Everyone has a philosophy." Adi lifts her beer, sets it down without taking a drink. "Most people, it's just simple ideas, like you should tell the truth, keep your family safe, that sort of thing. Other people. You really think about things. How to make the life you want, find a way to exist in this world. Ideals, specific to yourself, based on chunks of your past. Memories too big or stubborn to dissolve away." She shakes her head. "I'm not criticizing what you said. Not at all. I'd love to believe you're right. It's almost optimistic."

"Optimism, I don't know. I think it must be from Emerson. I read a lot of him, on the trail." I shrug. "Or, maybe it's just idle bullshit, invented to pass time while I wait for dinner."

"I've waited with you for a hundred dinners," she says. "This is the first time you've talked like that."

I shift in my seat, hand moving automatically to the bourbon. "Things are changing."

Adi gives me a look.

"I'm not saying anything's easy." I lift my beer, sip. "Nothing ever is."

She nods. "Nothing."

"We've just got to keep pursuing it," I say. "As if it's already a foregone conclusion."

"What? Specifically?"

"Whatever it is we want."

She looks down. "There are things you want?"

"Sure. Of course. And even if everything in the world has to shift to allow that to happen, it will."

"What if two people want contrary things?" she asks. "Whose version wins?"

I can't help thinking of those working against Adi. Her life, her safety. Can't help wondering whether this project is really the best thing to pursue. It's no longer just about us. Factors are moving, chess pieces hidden from view. Two dead, Thunder Egg room 111. Could've been us. There's no longer any question someone's trying to stall Adi's deal. Drive her away, or worse. We're just lucky they've been clumsy. So far.

As if she hears these thoughts of mine, Adi speaks. "I'm scared, I admit it. That doesn't mean I'll stop." Her hands squeeze into fists. She stares down. I can see her concentration, trying to force herself to relax. Her muscles tense, seeming beyond her own control. "I'd like to run, hide. Part of me at least."

"But you won't."

Her eyes show alarm, worry, as if she's considering apologies for the danger I'm in. Maybe letting me off the hook.

"Don't worry," I say. "Nobody's forcing me. I know what I'm part of."
I finish the bourbon, savor the smoke-tinged burn. "We're both scared,
stressed. That's okay. We have these drinks, and fancy pizzas with wild
mushrooms on the way."

"Bourbon and beer. To kill the fear." Adi grins at the rhyme, clinks my
empty glass, and sips.

19. Time to Fly

"I'm starving." Somehow it always makes me feel at ease, telling her so.
Hunger, the need for drinks, constant touchstones for us. Something to
think about, briefly, outside ourselves.

Our pizzas arrive. Bubbly crusts charred to the perfect degree. Beautiful
texture, airy softness inside, the exterior crisp. The scent of garlic, basil and
wild mushrooms.

"You've got that look," Adi says. "Like yesterday, when you said you felt
out of place here."

"I'm definitely not complaining. I might just feel a little bit under-re-
fined."

"That's dumb," Adi says. "You belong here, as much as anyone in the
room."

"This place is amazing. The drinks, the food. Beautiful setting. But for
me, there's an invisible line. I don't need to see the line to feel I'm on the
wrong side of it."

"What is it, just a class thing? I grew up dirt poor, always hungry. I'm
the same person, now, just not poor any more. So do I belong here, in the
lounge of this nice resort? Or do I not I belong, because as a little girl I lived
in a drafty, falling-down house, and had to piss in a wood shack outside?"
Adi's features compress, burdened by some unpleasant recollection.

"I don't know. Maybe it's that I can't pay my own way here. I'm constantly
afraid someone's going to ask for my ticket, or some kind of membership
pass I don't have."

Adi looks hurt, disappointed, and I'm afraid I seem ungrateful.

"I'm sorry," I say. "You said your parents left you money. I didn't really consider what it might mean, them both dying young."

Adi starts to take a slice of pizza but exclaims at the heat, yanks away her hand. "I'm forty-six. Mother died, thirty-eight." She takes up fork and knife, starts to work on the pizza. "The situation was more complicated than what I told Gwendoline."

I have questions, but consider carefully. "Your mother died, but not your father?"

She keeps her eyes down at her hands, folded on the table, as she speaks. "I never knew him. Barely ever caught a glimpse of the man, even. He visited only on certain nights, my mother marked them on the calendar. Moonless, rare. No sign of him for months. Sometimes years."

"I can't imagine how that was for you."

"Sometimes I'd wake up. The sound of him, with her. I'd sneak out of bed, see them together. If I rushed in, she'd put me back to bed, so I learned to hide. Stay quiet. It was the only way I could see him." She looks up briefly, back down. "I realize how that sounds. He was the most beautiful… like a demigod, or fallen angel from some classical painting. I read in one of my books, sometimes angels would come down, mate with human women. I thought that's what he was. Such long black hair, past his shoulders. And eyes so green, they didn't even look human."

"That's where you got your eyes."

She looks surprised. "I suppose, if he was really my father. There's so much I never knew. I've idealized him, imagination filling in the blanks. He was always so young, so elegant. The longest eyelashes I've ever seen on a man."

"You never spoke to him?"

"No, never. And Mother never referred to him as my father, when she did speak of him. Sometimes she'd use his name. *When I see Abracsa…* Finally Mother said, next time Abracsa visits, she's going to make a bargain. After that, everything changed. We abandoned the Rectory house, moved to the city. He never visited again. When Mother died, just six years later, I was surprised what she left behind. I always guessed she'd asked him to help us move to the city. But there was much more than that."

"I understand, you've said enough." I'm worried at the sad, hollow look in her eyes. "Thank you for telling me all this."

"Okay. That brings us back to what you said, about belonging. I came from nothing, from a shack rotting in a field. Later on, money came from somewhere. I was still myself, whether in the old house in Rectory, the new place in Portland, in college in Eugene. I want you to sit at this table with me. We don't need to have exactly the same." Something in Adi's face churns, searching, trying to process. "Or is that what you—"

The piano stops, startling in its abrupt absence. The player stands, empties his tip jar. He loosens his bow tie, heads to the bar for drinks.

"Silence can swerve you a bit, when you've gotten used to leaning on the music." I look into Adi's eyes, trying to get her to look back at me.

Another round arrives. That gives us something to grab hold of. Both of us, trying to get reoriented.

Sinatra's "Come Fly With Me" starts up, over the speakers. Instant mellow energy.

Adi smiles, equal measures happiness and sadness. "Frankie's trying to tell me something."

I settle back, relieved. "You like it too? I do love Sinatra." This beer tastes cold, crisp. That and the bourbon, starting to make everything better.

Adi nods in time with the tune. "When this deal's done, and I don't mean years from now, when everything's all built. Just when the last necessary document's been signed, two or three weeks from now. I want to fly somewhere to celebrate."

"Where?"

"I don't care, just go. That's the thing. Where would you go? Anywhere you feel like seeing? I'll take you."

"Wait, you're flying somewhere and want me there? You're going to fly to Maui, and I bring my GPS along to navigate for you?"

"No, wise-ass." Adi laughs. It's nice, seeing her ease up. "Maui, you said. Is that where you want to go?"

"I thought this was about you wanting to celebrate your deal closing. Why ask where I'd want to go?"

"Colman." She looks at me, like she knows what I'm trying to draw out of her, but isn't going to play along. "Doesn't it sound good, flying some-where? Especially hearing Frankie sing this."

I pause, not sure how I should respond. In the past I've always backed off, played dumb with her. That's never gotten me anywhere, just led to frustra-tion. After all these drinks, can't I just say what I mean? "I'm trying to figure out if you're actually suggesting I travel somewhere with you, or you're just going somewhere yourself."

"For such a smart man, you're lousy at reading signs. Anyway, why would I want to travel alone? Somewhere like Maui, just fly there, hang around? Snorkeling, by myself?"

Another gap of silence. When the music stops, we both pause, wait for it to continue.

"Who's controlling the music?" I ask. "Our moods are at your mercy, oh great invisible hand."

Over the speakers, "In the Wee Small Hours" begins.

Adi wrinkles her nose. "Still Sinatra, but oh. This is a weird, downbeat one. Yeah, I know this. The Sinatra suicide plan."

"I love that about him, the swings. I mean, usually Sinatra's on top of the world, fucking Lana Turner—"

"It was Ava Gardner."

"—or Marilyn Monroe or whoever, but when he wasn't, the man immedi-ately went full-dark. I mean, suicide watch, drowning in bourbon. Exactly like us, right now. How fucking awesome is that? Sinatra, he's like, no one cares. I've got nothing."

"What about Mia Farrow? Frankie tapped that." Adi snickers into her whiskey.

"You just said, tapped that." I finish the bourbon, slide my glass away. It tastes good, but the sensation is growing dull. I need another, many more. "Anyway, Mia Farrow doesn't do it for me. Thing is, I know Frank bounced back. He always did."

"I might be getting drunk." Adi looks into the bottom of her glass.

"Finally. I've been drunk for forty-five songs now."

"No, you're not. I don't mean Mia Farrow from today, like post Woody Allen. I'm talking waif Mia, like nineteen. *Rosemary's Baby*, pixie cut. Frank went there."

"Yeah, he tapped that. You said."

"Yeah." She nods. "Fucking right he did."

"It's great, seeing you get like this." I'm determined to drink more, catch up with her. "If we're talking nineteen-year-olds from classic cinema, I'm thinking Lauren Bacall. *To Have and Have Not.* That's a proper woman. *Key Largo.* Classy, but something in her eyes. Awareness of night time, and sweat, you know? A mature mind. Whiskey and cigarettes. Sex."

Adi frowns deeply, almost a pout. "I don't like cigarettes."

"I know, I hate them too, really. I mean movie cigarettes. Those aren't the same, they don't hurt your lungs any." I gesture as if inhaling an invisible cigarette, and exhale with exaggerated drama. "They just look cool on the screen, you know? The way you hold the cigarette, black-and-white cinematography. The lights create a magic glow, smoke circling around your face. That's cool. Glamour, you know. If cigarettes were really like that, I'd smoke them. You know, our personalities change, our voices, when we're drinking."

"I'd smoke them too," Adi agrees. "Movie cigarettes. You're right about that. So you're a Bacall man?"

"Sure. What man isn't?"

"I've had men tell me I resemble a young Lauren Bacall. Betty was her name."

"They tell you that because you do look like her. You look a whole lot like her, even without movie cigarettes. It's your jawline, and the shape of your mouth. An angular face, good angles. Eyes that can look at a person, keep a person subdued. Frozen there."

"You make me sound really pretty good," Adi says.

"That's easy. You are pretty good."

Her smile is bright, as if savoring something I said.

20. Hands Touch

The bartender delivers glasses, moves away. Two more bourbons. Drafts I don't remember ordering.

Music changes, a new song. Same orchestration, and languid, midnight pace.

"What's this?" Adi asks.

I glance up. "'Mood Indigo.' They're playing the whole album. Not just Greatest Hits."

"I love this. Everything's jazzy and grim tonight. Sinking away into dark."

"Yeah, this suicidal depression is the most excellent variety. We just have to split before 'I Get Along Without You Very Well.' That's a sentiment I don't need to hear tonight."

So many pleasures tonight. Food and drink, words and music. Adi, so close. All factors collaborate, nudging us together. I think we both feel it, now. Leaning in, hands touching across the table.

"Colm, you know I'm…" Adi stops, shakes her head.

I want to hear what she was about to say, can tell it was important. "Don't stop. Come on, I told you about the mess I left behind, all that background noise that was ruining my brain."

She says nothing, still hesitant.

"I showed you all the stuff that made me feel maybe I was too messed up. So you'd better tell me."

"Okay. I won't give all the gruesome details, just this one, gruesome fact." She lifts the glass, eyeballs as if measuring, then gulps down the whole shot. "I'm married. In fact, it's far worse than that, much more fucking pathetic, actually. It's just the most defective, broken-down domestic nightmare. Somebody should take my marriage down to the lake and drown it. But somehow, I can't seem to get free." A despairing look crosses her face, like a wish she could unsay it all. "There, that's more than enough. Now I know what you meant before. Any sane person would be put off by so much ugly, complicated bullshit. My half-assed mess of a life."

"I'm not put off," I say. "Technically, I'm still married too. But not together."

She narrows her eyes. "Right. That's something."

"But I'm moving toward getting a divorce," I say.

"I've tried." Adi's eyes flare, hinting at the prospect of argument or protest, which quickly dies away. "I'm always trying, but he's manipulative. He thinks as long as he avoids signing those papers, just maybe, he might get me back. Somehow, he always manages to keep stretching things out." She looks weakened, exhausted by futility.

I lean in, wanting to show I'm sympathetic, even if I don't yet know enough to understand. I reach across the table, touch her hand. Such a simple thing, hands clasped, a seemingly minor intimacy. Yet when I cover the backs of both her hands, her trembling abruptly stops. I feel like an enormous obstacle has been knocked over. Movement together. Fingers interlace, clench. Adi's face changes in visible relief. Her shoulders relax, giving in.

My mind rushes. A sense of attainment, breakthrough. But we've moved this direction before, seemed ready to go forward together, only to find ourselves interrupted. Gunshots, a trashed hotel. Nights sleepless, afraid and separate. Maybe I've turned away too easily. Been too uncertain.

Caution isn't what she needs from me. No more holding back. Tonight, I won't turn away.

Adi's eyes, liquid with emotion, focus on my hands covering her own. She seems on the verge of tears, looking back and forth, from our hands to my eyes. Then she turns her palms up, so I'm not just covering her hands. She's grasping mine too. The curve of her palm, a perfect fit with my own. Our hands designed this way, each for the other.

"I'm so relieved." Her eyes, more raw and naked than I've ever seen her. "God. To finally tell."

"That's how I felt on the trail before. It was painful, admitting about Paula. Risky. After, though, I felt stronger. Like I'd cut loose some horrible, dead appendage, left attached far too long."

"You shouldn't have worried. At least you managed to end it, start to move on."

I hesitate, not sure I'm ready to delve deeper. "Because we didn't just agree to split up. It felt cruel, like I held her responsible. And maybe I did. But sometimes we carry blame for things that aren't our fault. The opposite, really."

"I guess I do feel better. So much is still fucked." She laughs. "But I'll get through. I've got you. I mean, not to presume." She covers her eyes with one hand. "Must be the bourbon."

"You do have me." I'm sorry she doesn't know. It's my fault she doesn't realize.

"That helps. Makes the barriers seem lower, at least. Maybe surmountable." She squeezes my hand.

"My head's spinning, too. Not just the drinks. Talking like this. Two days ago on the trail. Just now."

"Part of me is relieved." She shakes her head. "But God, you still don't know. It's just impossible."

I turn her hands over in mine, trace her palms with my fingertips. So much of consequence, negotiated by the boundaries of hands. Imposition of touch, nearness of fingers. "It's going to be okay, all of it," I say. "Maybe there's plenty I still don't understand, but I'll do what I can. I'm with you now. Even if I weren't, you're strong enough. You're the smartest woman I've ever known. Smartest person."

"It feels like there's so much to lose," Adi says. "But also, I can feel myself letting go. This sense of calm. Like nothing can really touch me. Everything to lose. Nothing to lose."

I know what she means, and feel the same. "Maybe some of the details that you're clinging to can be cut loose. What you really want, just the core. What matters most. Focus on that. Forget the rest." It's powerful, and freeing. More at risk, yet no going back. We can't control everything, so stop worrying and move forward.

"Yeah. The checklist seemed long, just weeks ago. I can feel complications falling away." Adi leans closer, extends across the table until her face nears our hands. So awkward, this obstacle between us. She stands, moves around to my side of the table, sits beside me, leans her shoulder into me.

Her eyes loom, so present, right in front of my own. So close. It's almost a kiss. Soon it's going to be. Her breath, proof of her nearness. She grins, sits back.

"What?" I ask. "What's wrong?"

"Time to go." Adi slides back her chair, fingers of her free hand still locked with mine.

My thoughts spin. What could possibly have come up, knocked us off the tracks? Somewhere we have to go. Maybe we've forgotten some bit of work. "Go? Where?"

Still grinning, Adi lifts an eyebrow. No question what she's suggesting. "My room."

I stand, knees weak, trying to think what to say. My mind races, tracking back and forth. Scenarios opening, new possibilities. Desire, a compelling rush. A flood.

"Come on." She's pulling me along. She doesn't have to pull.

I want to follow.

21. The First Movement That Changes Everything After

We fall together, a trajectory from dizzying heights, through clouds. In Adi's room, everything moves fast. Shoes thrown off, belts unbuckled. Falling sideways, onto the bed. Adi unbuttons pants, pulls them down, reclines decadent and sidelong in her panties, one bare foot kicking off the pant leg.

She pauses, still wearing the long-sleeved shirt, gives me a final look. Then she pulls her long-sleeved top over her head.

"Wow," I say, too stunned to say more.

The front of Adi's torso is adorned, pelvis to collarbones, with a tattoo so large and dramatic, my mouth drops open at the sight. It's an intricately rendered tree, ornately textured trunk rising in black striations from her belly, thrusting branches upward, between and around her breasts, to culminate in a flurry of leaves, the crimson and orange of fire. At her navel the trunk splits downward into an elegantly tangled network of narrowing roots, pink and silver. From above, the intensely colorful leaves scatter, moved by invisible winds in swirling patterns among the complex unfurling of the limbs, and settling among the nerve-like root network. The leaves form a backdrop of color, like a wild spattering of blood, interspersed with the blade-sharp angles of larger black birds ranging as far as her shoulders and upper arms.

Adi looks shy, uncertain. "After what you said, Paula's tattoos, I hoped you wouldn't—"

"This isn't the same. This is you. Every part of you is perfect." I step forward. It's time to touch, to finish undressing.

So much pressure, a tension almost painful. An accumulation of passion, a response to stress and to fear. Both of us, out of our minds now, leaving prior selves behind. Not tender exactly, at least not gentle. More an unbearable pressure seeking anxious release. Boiling over.

When I'm above Adi, the wild tree is part of her, as much as her face, her eyes, the feel of her skin. Proximity to her fire, powerful enough to kill everything that ever obstructed me. I need to seize this, tame it. Last chance to control my life. Our lives. Out of long-building frustration, urgent need, powerful as anger.

Together we clutch, we sweat. Her body, already familiar. I've known her all along.

After, resting together, breathing, the room feels enormous. An expansive private universe, perfectly stable, motionless. A great ship, floating quiet in a placid ocean. So distant from everyone. The old world gone now, not just out of reach, but obsolete. We're isolated, together.

I return to my body, the room. Notice the broad headboard, gold-brown wood the length of the wall. Hanging lights made of curved bamboo dangle like inverted kites from thin metal cables.

Such relief. Adi's face reflects the same. For the first time, everything feels settled. As if we've fallen so far, finally hit bottom. Not landed, but broken through, continued falling, fearless at last. No more sense of impending loss. Adi's here beside me, exactly where we both want to be. Something I've wanted so much, it seems impossible it could be true.

Everything after this moment, this place, will be different.

Our bodies outlined. Shapes of us, melded. Together we're comfortable, warm. Playfully flirting, teasing. I am nothing but our two bodies, half of her. Our minds settling in, relaxed. Happy. Adi's cheekbone on my shoulder, her hair sprayed across the pillow as if designed that way.

"Do you realize this is the first time? Almost three years. God, that fixed everything." She squeezes me. "So good, I wish we'd…. Well, if it sounds bad, I don't care. I wish we'd done it sooner."

"No. That doesn't sound bad."

"I was never sure you were interested."

"Of course I was," I say. "I didn't know what you'd think of a guy like me."

"What does that mean? More status bullshit again? That's stupid." Adi whacks my chest with the back of her hand. "You have a Master's degree. You've had real, grown-up jobs." She makes a crude raspberry sound in dismissal.

"I may have been insecure, after my life broke apart. I was never unsure about you being desirable, just didn't know if you were available."

Adi shakes her head, sighs. "Available."

"Sorry." I sit up slightly, still in contact. "I didn't want to wreck anything."

"No, not you. It's just I'm not sure I'll ever be available. It seems unattainable, somehow. How do we get so brainwashed. Things are worse than I told you, much worse. Three fucking years." Her demeanor changes, suddenly serious, as if she's remembered something. She sits up, stands, unselfconsciously naked. She crouches beside the bed over her clothes and purse. "You know, fuck him. It's not fair, him doing that to me."

"What are you doing?"

Adi comes back to bed with her phone, dials a number. She attends to the phone, not looking at me. "Do you know who this is? You recognize my voice? That's right, I never call you. I never have anything new to say. I try to have my lawyer do that, but we both know how well that works. You don't listen to him, don't listen to me."

She pauses, mouth open as if anxious to jump back into the argument. Briefly she flashes me a look.

"How many times did I tell you? The words don't even mean anything anymore, so I gave up telling you it's over. You tried to ignore my right to decide, stop me moving on, but this is it. I'm through. No more manipulation. No, you always say that. This time, my answer's different. I do have someone else, a good man. You can't. It's true, I'm with him right now. He's listening to this. I don't know, he probably can't believe how pathetic you are, probably wonders why I'd ever be with someone who wouldn't appreciate me. You always said you didn't believe me, because I hadn't moved on. But I was alone because I was working too hard, not because I was waiting to come back to you."

Adi's face transforms, listening moment to moment, visiting a sequence of emotions. Pain to frustration, amusement to indifference.

"Flaunting my infidelity? Seriously, did you actually use that word? No, it's not. It's just that you don't realize it's been over. When was the last time we slept under the same roof, let alone together? You call yourself married, but you think it's just been a little while? I do know, over two years. I've told you hundreds of times, letters, emails, voicemails. My lawyer. Still you pretend. You run out the back door to avoid being served. This is real. I'm through waiting. This is the last time you are ever going to hear from me, do you understand? Yes, I'm angry. I'm furious, and fed up. I don't need you to let me go. I'm gone."

Adi hangs up, drops the phone. Her eyes go vacant, and she's far away for a moment. Then she remembers me, drops beside me on the bed. She starts breathing hard, as if just come up from a deep underwater dive. Her face distant at first, then gradually returning.

"I'm sorry, I shouldn't have." She looks at me, then away. "I promise, I wasn't using you to pry him loose."

"I know."

"If I was only going to sleep with someone, to make a point—"

"You could have done that any time." I prop myself up on my left elbow, and touch her shoulder.

"The man's hopeless. Before I separated my finances, he paid for escort services on my credit card. Said he did it as a gesture for my own good, for the good of our marriage. To make me understand the pain I was causing him, withdrawing my affections." Adi laughs, pushes back her hair with a trembling hand. "Problem with that angle is, he started in with the prostitutes before I ever withdrew anything. He's hopeless. I'm stupid to have let him hold on. But Colm, I don't want you thinking I only wanted you to help me pry him away."

"No," I say. "I know it's not that."

Adi stands from the bed again, leans and grabs her clothes. "It's not too late for a drink. I feel a whole new something-or-other coming on." She turns, gestures for me to get up.

"I'm just noticing how you look at me," I say. "It's different now."

"Yes." Adi comes around the bed, pulls me up by the hand. "Everything's different."

22. Last Call

Adi puts on the same pants, but a different top, one I've never seen before. The off-shoulder cowl neckline swoops low to reveal the uppermost portion of her body art, mostly a swirl of birds in their courses. Though only the uppermost part of the tree is revealed, I remember everything hidden below. The whirlwind of leaves. The roots, reaching down.

"If you'd worn something like this before, I'm pretty sure I would've guessed about all that ink you're hiding."

Adi gives me that eyebrow raise, her signature move. "Just bought this yesterday. Had kind of a feeling the time was right."

As we enter the Hood Highlands lounge, the lone bartender tells us, "Last call." Bart, the name tag says. Gray handlebar mustache, old-fashioned vest.

Beyond the windows, all is black. Almost 2 AM. Nothing to see outside. We sit at the bar.

"No way I can sleep. My head's spinning. Something with coffee." Adi sits beside me, and the negotiation of territory of personal space is different from ever before. So quickly, everything's new. I wait for Adi to order, expecting it, but she's just looking at me, herself waiting.

I lean in. "Bart, what do you recommend for two people who just had an evening so nice, they'd like to keep it going until sunrise?"

Bart nods, fills two highball glasses with crushed ice, then starts pulling espresso shots. A swig of heavy cream over the ice, two espresso shots each, then a long pour of syrupy red liqueur from a crystal decanter.

I smell cherries, and ferment. "And that is?"

"Bit of a secret ingredient, special of mine," Bart says. "Cherry brandy from Croatia, high octane."

He pours, stirs, and after he presents the drinks, steps away to the end of the bar.

I sip. Not just cherries, but a tingle strong enough to cut through the espresso.

The orange glow of candles permeates everything.

Adi leans in, hand on her glass. "Even if we stay awake, the night eventually will end." Her voice sounds tired.

I'm surprised how vulnerable Adi seems, until I remember the phone call. For her, this is like the night I drove out of Seattle, planning never go to back. I squeeze her hand.

She seems to appreciate this, even smiles a bit. "I've gone my whole life feeling strong. Unstoppable, but not now. Why do you think that is?"

"Because you finally don't have to be quite so strong."

"I don't want to be alone." She sighs, leans against me. "Also don't want to sleep."

"You don't have to. Either one."

"Good."

"Tomorrow morning, there's something I have to do. You don't need to be part of it, but you need to know."

"Anything you're doing for me, I'm part of."

"There's danger."

"I don't care."

"You're still drunk."

"We both are."

My drink burns. Tartness intensified by fermented sweetness. A burn deeper than alcohol.

"I'm talking about going in there, the mine. At least far enough to see what's going on. I have a friend who'll help. He understands dangerous places."

"I'm going too."

"You keep saying the project will still go forward, even without McAttree."

"Yes, but if Kinosha buys in, things will really fly. Whatever's going on, I need to know." She leans heavily against me, eases back, and leans in again. It's like she's testing me for solidity, shifting this way. Or just feeling it, realizing I'm there, fills some need for her.

"You should stay here. Let me go in with Ryan."

"No."

Bart moves near, signaling time.

"You said last call," Adi says. "How about just more espresso?"

"Just coffee, no alcohol, sure."

"Lots of it," Adi says. "Enough to get us through to morning."

Bart pulls enough shots to fill two tall glasses. A glass pitcher of ice. A pint of half-and-half. I pay Bart, tip him twenty on top. Bart smiles, starts away, and comes back. He hands over a clear plastic squeeze bottle with something dark inside.

"Chocolate syrup," he says. "You stay in the lounge long as you want. Fireplace'll die off by itself, another two, three hours. These doors stay open twenty-four and seven. Just nobody but front desk and room service is on duty."

"Have a good night," I tell him.

Adi waves Bart goodbye, then gives me a wink. "Gwendoline was right about one thing. The iced espresso. That's the way to do it."

We huddle together, rattling ice in our glasses. We talk through stories we've told before, inconsequential things, but tonight given a different angle from our newfound intimacy. Later, jittering with too much caffeine, wired drunk and laughing, despite anticipation of what's to come. Overstimulated by so many changes. More coming.

When the night has gone very late, so late it's almost early, Adi stands. She takes me by the hand, just like earlier, when she led me to her room.

I guess she's changed her mind, wants to try to sleep before the morning comes.

"Let's go," she says. "Outside."

We venture out the front door, down the broad stone steps and onto the golf course.

"I'm thinking about how happiness works," Adi says. "You have to build it."

"I'm starting to remember."

"What was in that cherry stuff?" Adi says.

"I was already reeling," I say. "From everything else."

Soon we're beyond the reach of the resort's exterior lights. Through manicured grass, we reach a vacant pavilion. Rough, natural timber beams standing on stout pillars of stone and mortar. It resembles an ancient place, where people very different from us might have met for ceremonies long ago. The remnants of a wedding left behind, tattered and destroyed. A torn banner, confetti stomped into the ground, sodden with spilled punch and intermixed with broken glass. An empty punch bowl rests on a table without chairs. A single white bow made of ribbon, twisted into knots.

This is another kind of beginning.

The night draws us outward, toward trees. We undress on the run, carrying clothing and shoes as we remove them. We both understand, when we find a place secluded enough, this is the place to leave our bundled things hidden. Unencumbered, finally, we run naked and laughing through deserted fields beyond the resort, into untamed woods. Running out of our minds, away from time, into new places, unexplored and dark.

III

Seeking Below (in 7 parts)

23. Going In

Adi and I sit idling in her Rover, eyes bleary and minds tired. I've given up on coffee, not sure my stomach can take any more. At least fatigue softens anxiety's edge.

"Who's this guy we're waiting for?" Adi asks.

"I know him from Northwest Cavers. He lives in Portland, does consulting work on contamination scenes."

"Contaminations, like what?"

"All kinds of biohazard. Mostly gas or chemical."

In the side mirror I watch the sky lighten with coming dawn. Finally, headlights approach. A tall white Sprinter van pulls in. Ryan climbs out, wearing a white hazard suit with the hood pulled back. He's very tall, thinner than I remember. Black curls on top, shaved close on the sides, and black rim glasses. He resembles an elongated Buddy Holly.

Adi and I get out. I introduce Adi and Ryan, they shake hands. Ryan opens the van's rear doors, one decorated with a "Cavers Go Deeper" sticker, and lifts out two white duffels. He hands one to me, the other to Adi.

"Biosuits." He looks Adi up and down. "Yours might be too big. You're smaller than Quinn told me."

Adi turns on me, mock offended. "What did you say?"

"He did refer to you as slim," Ryan offers.

"Get it, Slim?" I ask Adi. I tell Ryan, "We were talking about *To Have and Have Not*."

Ryan nods approval. "Bacall. She's lovely."

I unpack my hazard suit.

Ryan brings out an aluminum equipment case. "GPS won't work below, satellites can't reach. Got various tools, though. Laser rangefinder, infrared viewers—"

"You're geared-up like Ghost Hunters," Adi jokes.

"Oh, sister," Ryan groans.

"You hurt his feelings," I say.

"Seriously, we need to be careful today," Ryan says. "I can handle most varieties of mess, but can't do anything about collapse or explosion. People die in places like this."

"People already have," Adi says.

"Last chance." I face Adi, hands on her shoulders, as if lecturing someone younger. I don't mean it like that, but she's inexperienced underground. "You've said your deal can proceed with or without McAttree. You don't have to go."

"Oh, I'm going down." Adi grins. "I was born to go down."

"Okay, then." Ryan laughs, surprised. "Let's do some caving."

"It won't be what we're used to," I say. "But if we can crawl through icy streams and over mounds of bat shit, we should be able to deal with engineered walls and floors."

"You might wait to put on your suits until we've climbed up," Ryan says. "I'm used to mine."

"You sure we need these?" Adi asks.

"Damn sure," Ryan says. "Waiting until you're exposed, then putting on the suit? That'll get you dead. There could still be dangerous stuff below. Even clean mines are dangerous. I've got canary sensors that'll screech if they detect certain toxins, radiation. But there's still a hundred potential risks I can't detect."

"Let's go," I say.

"Cowabunga," Adi says.

We climb. This part's familiar.

Halfway up, Ryan leading, he looks back. "Figured old man Quinn would still be in decent shape. You, Adi, I'm impressed." He nods approval. "You're doing great."

"I've been getting myself fit," Adi says. "Planning a Pacific Crest Trail hike."

"Oh yeah?" Ryan asks.

Nobody speaks again until we reach the level area outside the gate.

Ryan opens the equipment case slung across his shoulder, takes out an impact driver, and eyes the bolts on the gate frame. "You said penta-star, five or six millimeters. I'm guessing five." The first try fits. "Five it is." He quickly extracts twenty bolts and places these in the plastic lid of the driver bit case.

Ryan and I lift off the door while Adi finishes fastening her oversuit.

"Hoods up," Ryan says.

"Will this be enough?" Adi indicates the breathing filter.

Ryan looks surprised. "Respiration tanks are heavy, and don't offer much breathing time anyway. I'll test for gasses, and if there's any uncertainty, we'll go back for the SCBAs."

Adi nods. Ryan flicks on his head-mounted lamp, Adi and I follow suit. We move inside, toward the soil and stone blockade ramp.

I scramble up first. "See this?" I demonstrate the looseness of the soil up top. "From the gate, it looks like permanent fill, but it's sandy."

Ryan goes down for the case just inside the gate, returns with a collapsable shovel. In less than a minute we've widened the gap enough to crawl through. I go first, then Ryan. The light from our headlamps barely seems effectual against the deep, profound dark.

Adi sticks her head through the gap. "I guess chickening out at this stage would be bad form, since you tried talking me out of this."

I pull her through. "You insisted."

Ryan waits below, where the berm meets flat interior ground. "All kinds of footprints. You said this was shut down."

"Supposed to be," I say.

"Have I mentioned I dislike this suit?" Adi asks loudly, voice muffled by the mask.

"What's wrong with it?" Ryan asks. "I live in mine."

"Not complaining, I appreciate your help," Adi says. "But it already feels sticky in here."

"If these things breathed, they'd be no protection at all," Ryan says. "You okay, Quinn?"

"Mild strangulation is preferable to quick death by poisoning."

Seeming excited to proceed, Ryan hurries down the tunnel. Soon he's twenty feet ahead, then thirty. Our headlamps illuminate a clean tunnel, ten feet wide and barely taller than Ryan.

"Let's stay clustered," I suggest.

Ryan stops, glances back. "Sure, sorry."

The tunnel's perfect, orderly squareness surprises me. No sense of hazard. Passages open, walls and floor smooth, clear of debris. "After hearing of twenty-two dead, explosions and cave-ins, I'm not sure what I expected."

"Not this." Adi comes to my side. "This tunnel looks like it was dug yesterday."

Ryan's getting ahead again. "See here? A side tunnel, an offshoot." He continues.

I peer down the right-angle digression, venture in slightly. The floor slopes down ten or twelve feet, then the side tunnel dead-ends. Adi stays with me, just behind. "This one's filled in." I turn, shout down the main tunnel. "Ryan, come back here, look at this."

Ryan jogs back to us. "There's another like it, further along. Looks nothing like any cave-in I've ever seen. Too squared-away."

"The dead-ends aren't just loose rock," I say. "It's stabilized with concrete. Let's keep going. See about getting deeper."

In the main tunnel, Ryan pauses to check a wrist-mounted sensor and a larger electronic device, like a big stopwatch worn around his neck. "I'm getting no traces, nothing at all to worry about. Totally clear. Maybe someone just did a great job decommissioning."

"No," I say. "Nobody's supposed to have been inside at all, since everything went to hell."

We continue past several more evenly-space sidecut shafts, about a hundred feet apart, each like the first blocked by a wall of scrap rock sealed with concrete. I'm starting to wonder if this is all we'll find.

Further down the tunnel, a glow of small lights.

Closer, I see. "An elevator."

Within a sturdy frame and hinged gate, a small elevator car waits, all pristine yellow-painted square tubing and expanded metal. Against one outer wall of the frame is a desk and attached panel of lit-up electronics. A rack-mounted Dell server and array of display panels mounted in rows comprise a surveillance workstation.

Ryan leans over, scrutinizing. "This gear ain't fifty years old."

"Not even ten," I say.

"We've got Samsung monitors like these in my office," Adi says.

Each is split to display views from four different surveillance cameras.

"Other tunnels." I point. "Stairs. A whole world down here."

"Also, the entrance." Adi points out the monitor showing the gate we just dismantled, the door off its hinges. "That explains how they knew we were here, the night they shot at us."

"Wait, wait," Ryan says. "Somebody shot at you here?"

"Outside." Adi's voice is flat.

"Somebody's still using this place," I say.

"All along," Adi says.

"This makes no sense," Ryan says. "New surveillance gear, this elevator, but no conveyors. Nothing for drilling, moving ore, no heavy gear at all. I'm no expert, but this doesn't seem like a mining operation."

"I knew something was happening," I say. "Those rocks outside the gate, those came from deep." My scalp wound throbs, memory of that night recalling the sting. I feel the wound pulse, a burn like infection. Every time I think it's starting to heal, the pain returns.

"Gwendoline Jones and her husband have owned this land half a century," Adi says. "They thought it was just empty acreage, and the whole time, someone's sneaking down here?"

"Speaking of someone," Ryan says. "Shouldn't we assume this surveillance feed's being watched? They probably know we're here."

"Yeah, maybe it's time to go." I'm feeling anxious, maybe even afraid, but also curious. "First, though, don't you want to understand what's happening?"

I turn to Adi. We look at each other without speaking.

Ryan shakes his head, unconvinced, but says nothing more.

"We're already in," Adi says. "I want to continue."

My fingers tingle, my spine feels chilled. Even within this suit, I can feel the closeness of the air. Though of course it must be impossible, I'm sure I can smell something else, some tinge of scent I can't identify.

24. Downward

The controls are simple, three buttons for up, down, and stop. The narrow cage must be intended to carry only three or four. Ryan latches the gate, I press the button.

The descent is smooth, without ratcheting or strain. The cable unwinds, the motor whirrs. Walls of the shaft, close on all sides, seem to vibrate. It's a sensation of claustrophobic blindness, like hiding in a coat closet. Air rushes past, flutters the plastic biosuit against me, but can't penetrate to cool my skin. There's nothing at all to indicate we're moving. No perspective, no scale in any direction. I'm placeless, hovering.

Nobody speaks. How much time passes?

A darker side opening flashes past the elevator, some crosscut or drift. I look to Adi, wondering should we stop, go back up to that passage? She's staring straight ahead.

Ryan is watching a readout on wrist-mounted gear. "You two feel warmer yet?" he asks.

"Should we?" Adi asks.

"Air increases in density, further down," Ryan says. "Opposite of air thinning at altitude. Thin air is cooler, deeper means dense, warmer air. More than the air, the rock heats up."

"I'm sweating like mad," Adi says. "Thought I must be getting excited, or afraid."

"We've been going down so long," I say.

"How fast you think this elevator drops?" Ryan looks around, as if he might gauge the speed at which the shaft walls are flying past. "I want to say 10 feet per second, does that sound right? Not sure that figure applies to an elevator like this one."

"What's it been?" Adi asks. "Ten minutes?"

"Not that long," I say, though I don't have any better guess. "That'd be six thousand feet."

Ryan cranes his neck, trying to see up through the grating. "That's a huge coil of cable. Still plenty to let out. We're nowhere near bottom."

"How deep could this go?" Adi asks.

None of us know. We ride in silence. The rushing air feels damp and hot, like ventilation from a clothes dryer, but that's my imagination. This suit is airtight. I squint, seeking Adi's eyes within her hood's visor. Something seems different, some shift in her features. Didn't she say she's afraid? Her eyes dart, an anxious twitch, like when she was angry at McAttree yesterday in the Council offices. I don't trust myself to interpret what I'm seeing. Some part of me keeps looking for the strange, expecting to find it everywhere around me. If I'm convinced the world is menacing, that we're all constantly under threat, I'll find confirmation everywhere I turn. So tired. Just want to sit.

Then I remember we haven't slept.

Adi nudges me. "I saw maps indicating the mine went down a thousand feet or so."

"I remember seeing 1,500 feet max," I say.

The repetitive clicking of descent, a hypnotic metronome. My wound still burns. The ache in my temple blurs my vision. Both eyes water.

Adi touches my arm. "Would you rather get out of here? Find some backup, return in daytime?" Then she catches herself. "Oh, right. It's still morning."

"Down below," Ryan says, "the brightest noon is still pitch black."

I know Ryan well enough to recognize he's being a good sport, would rather turn back. I'm still curious, though. Adi must be, too. We've come so far.

The elevator slows, then jerks to a stop. The sudden absence of motion is jarring.

Ryan checks his wrist display, glances at me and nods. "The bottom."

I open the gate and stumble out. Another straight tunnel, indistinguishable from the last, except no surveillance desk. The only light emits from our headlamps.

"It's hot," I say.

We all notice another difference at once.

"Someone's dug into the walls," Adi says.

Though floor and ceiling are entirely smooth, the walls have been intermittently chipped away, though nothing so deep or large as the side tunnels above. I shine my headlamp, see thin cracks hollowed out. Traces left behind of some black mineral substance, shot with shinier flecks. I start to reach, wanting to touch, then realize my hands are within the protective suit.

Adi kneels at my side. "What's that, coal?" She points.

The fissure glistens, darker than the common blue-gray basalt. Something like graphite combined with a wet-black component, and the odd glitter or sparkle. Most of the substance has been scraped out, leaving a gap, but what traces remain are neither dull enough to be coal, nor sticky like tar. This complex amalgam wanders a diagonal crease, contents mostly carved out, to a depth of several feet.

"Is this the whole game?" Adi asks. "Pulling out, what, a few pounds of this stuff?"

"Maybe some rare earth," I guess. "There are minerals more precious than gold, that we'd never recognize."

Adi stands, removes her headlamp, unfastens her hood and lifts it over her head. She does this before I realize what she's doing, before I can stop her. She breathes deep, face trickling perspiration.

"Adi!"

She exhales, inhales again. First she savors the air, then her nose wrinkles as if in recognition.

"What?" I ask. "What is it?"

"Just a smell." A look crosses her face, like fear she's made a mistake, or recognition. "Sort of pungent."

"Adi, put it back on," I say.

"Seriously," Ryan says. "I brought all this gear to prevent you dying down here."

Adi inhales deep, expands her lungs, holds it in. Seeming satisfied, she exhales. "It's okay, just strange at first. A wild funk. Maybe like truffles or something."

I can't stop what she's doing, but she's scaring me. "Don't. Adi, please.

She looks fine, relieved to be free of the restrictive hood, and fastens the headlamp band onto her forehead. "Take off your own, you'll see. Seriously, the air's fine." She laughs, lighthearted, almost giddy.

I consider. "Obviously people have been coming in here." I lift off my hood. Breathe.

"Jesus, guys," Ryan says. "This was not the plan. I can't drag two of you up from here."

"I think she's right," I say. "That it's safe, I mean. But also the smell. I've never encountered ambergris, but this is how I imagined it." A strange, enticing balance, foulness somewhere between rot and excrement, with a beguiling, exotic undercurrent. Where does it come from? The walls are clean, dry. It's such a relief, having that hood off. I turn to Ryan. "Sure you won't join us?"

Ryan shakes his head, moves past me, down the tunnel.

I follow, feeling weird excitement and affirmation. Adi and I have both been afraid, but we've faced our fears. Confidence surges, inexplicable but impossible to deny. The euphoria is almost drug-like. Maybe it's the thrill of being so deep, but I don't recall ever experiencing anything like this before.

"Let's get a sample." Adi indicates the seam. "You've got tools, Ryan?"

Ryan turns to the crack, scrapes loose a few pieces, which drop to the ground. Adi picks one up, Ryan another.

Adi looks at hers close, as if considering popping it in her mouth. "So strange."

"What?" I ask. "The rock?"

"No." Adi smiles wide, exuberant. "How I feel."

It may be lack of sleep, or the surprise of finding this place. Maybe our breakthrough experience last night. Adi looks dreamy, strange. I know what she means. This intense, heart-pounding abundance of possibility.

"All right, you're both putting your gear back on," Ryan insists.

I realize I'm scratching my scalp. "My head's burning. It itches, not just where I was injured. Must be heat rash, from the hood."

"Did you hear that?" Adi turns toward the darker end of the tunnel, away from the elevator. Her eyes go wide, mouth open. She scrambles back several steps, toward the elevator. Instinctively, I follow.

Ryan watches, wary, unsure whether Adi's kidding. "I didn't hear anything. You guys are freaking me out."

"Come on, Adi," I say, motioning. "Let's stay together."

"Okay, let's go ahead." Ryan leads us down the tunnel. "See what we need to see, then we can go."

Adi beside me, we follow, adding our headlamp beams to Ryan's. I see no shapes, just a vacant tunnel devoid of features. But the walls shift, almost shimmering. The angles may be straight, yet contours seem to vary slightly, to waver or seethe. At the light's farthest reach, just before it fails against the darkness, movement teases the limits of my perception. Nothing tangible. Just a hint.

I point, but say nothing. I'm sure the others see it. Nobody speaks.

I feel the first tingle of fear. Terror of the dark, of what might be lurking unseen, like the panic stirred in imagination by a fireside ghost story. So deep, so lost. The projected fear, much more real than the daylight world left behind. Fear is a manifest presence, a projection of mind running wild, frantic with apprehension of the unknown.

A sudden certainty, no single reason I can name. I want to get out. Back to the surface.

I look to Adi, expecting to see in her a sudden swerve toward fear or the thrill of excitement, either of the two extremes I've experienced since we reached bottom. Her eyes are wide, posture slightly hunched. On high alert, like a wild forest creature that heard a twig crack beneath a hunter's boot. Ready to bolt, unreasoning victim of hormonal surge and electrical impulse.

Behind, a metal clank. We spin in unison.

Adi gasps. "What's that?"

Long echoing reverberation from the shaft. Headlamps illuminate the elevator car starting to rise.

"It's going up." I run. Before I reach the base of the shaft, the cage is gone from view.

25. Far Below

Air swirls within the tunnel. The echoing metal racket heightens my panicked sense of urgency, as I look for controls, a stop button, anything. There's nothing here. The only controls are inside the elevator itself, already vanished.

"Oh, fuck!" Adi laughs. "Unbelievable."

"Don't panic," I say, trying to convince myself.

For several seconds there's no sound but our breathing and the diminishing whirr of the elevator.

"Wow," Ryan says. "This is really, really not at all what I bargained for. You realize how far down we are?"

"No," I say. "Exactly how far?"

"Exactly doesn't matter." Shaking his head, Ryan starts pacing back and forth. "What matters is, we're way, way too fucking deep to ever climb out."

"Whoever called the elevator up, maybe they'll come down," Adi says.

"What if they don't? What if they just want to strand us here?" Ryan gestures with both hands. "Then we're dead."

I can't accept Ryan's conclusion, but I'm angry too. We left ourselves vulnerable.

Adi stands between us. "I'm so sorry, both of you."

"It's not your fault." I reach for her shoulder, though we're both in suits to our necks.

"You're down here for me," Adi says flatly. "My project."

An ocean of stone. Billions of tons of resolute earth between us and the sky.

Ryan's pacing is already driving me crazy. "Come on," I tell him. "Please stop."

"Whether we're a mile down, half a mile, doesn't matter." Ryan's breathing is hard and shallow, rasping audibly through the mask as he continues back and forth. "Even a quarter mile, no way we're climbing out. We need that elevator."

"Would you please stand still," I insist. "We need to relax. Think clearly."

"God damn, it's so hot. I'm stifling here." Ryan glares at Adi and me, as if casting blame. He unfastens the front of his hood, pulls it up and off. His face glistens red, dripping sweat. Wet curls lie flat on his scalp.

"The air's fine," I insist. "It's the least of our problems."

Adi looks at me, seems to remember. "Let's huddle, come up with a plan."

"Search for controls," I suggest. "Communications gear, any kind of equipment we've missed."

We search this featureless tunnel, find nothing. All there is to see is the gated cage at the bottom of the elevator shaft. No electronics, no controls. Just a dead-end at bottom.

I examine the gate. "Looks like we needed to keep this open, to prevent the elevator being called back up."

Ryan stops pacing. He and Adi look at each other, then at me.

"Doesn't matter who shut it," I say, though I know it wasn't me. "Anyway, there's nothing we're missing here. No elevator controls, no way to communicate with the surface. We agree on that?"

Adi leans against the wall, measuring breaths, looking down.

I stand near Adi, while Ryan examines the elevator cage. Minutes pass, wordless.

"We can climb the inside of the frame," Ryan says. "Not all the way up, but maybe far enough. Find a side tunnel."

I walk over, look up the shaft. "Thousands of feet, up painted metal. Just one slip."

"The next level is maybe…" Ryan says excitedly, calculating, then trails off. "Yeah, way too far."

I lean against the wall at Adi's side, immediately feel the warmth of the rock through my suit. Ryan watches, seeming to measure what closeness exists between us. I haven't lost hope, feel no risk of giving up, just curiosity about what will come. Something has to happen. It's impossible Adi and I finally came together only to end up stranded the next morning. That reminds me again, we haven't slept. This morning is just an extension of last night, the most important night in my life so far.

Time passes, indistinguishable increments.

I wonder, does Adi feel the same? I could tell her not to worry. I assume she understands. Just to be sure, I reach for her hand.

She looks unsure, but not afraid.

"A place like this, it's supposed to be in my comfort zone," Ryan says. "Got to admit, this fucking scares me."

"Warmer," I say. "Warmer all the time."

Ryan glances at a rubberized orange device. "Hundred ten. I wouldn't lean against the walls, the rock's warmer. Air cools, circulating up and down the shaft." He squats on his heels, elbows across his knees.

"I have so many great memories, being in caves," I say.

Ryan looks up, doesn't quite smile.

"The elevator will come down." I feel calm certainty. "Meantime, let's check out this tunnel."

"I should be more afraid." Adi's voice is strange. Her eyes distant, as if remembering. "I thought I knew what McAttree was doing, but I was wrong. It's something else."

"Come on, let's see where this tunnel goes. Who knows, maybe there's another elevator." I can't think of any reason to justify the expense of a second elevator so near the first. "Remember the surveillance? We saw ladders, stairs."

Ryan seems hesitant. No, he's not hearing me. He's listening. "The elevator stopped."

A clang from the shaft, a long feedback of echoes. Another tone, distant.

"Hear that?" I hold my breath, trying to be silent. "It's coming back down."

26. Confrontation

The metal frame vibrates.

Adi looks at me with desperate hope. "It's definitely moving."

Ryan laughs, briefly exultant, then stops, turns away as if thinking. "So, now we get to ponder who might be coming down."

"We have some idea." I understand Ryan's emotional swing, from relief to new fear.

"I'd prefer a confrontation," Adi says.

"Sure, anything's beats being left for dead," Ryan says. "Mostly I'd prefer to make it home in one piece. I told my girlfriend I'd be home to grill steaks for dinner and watch *Guardians of the Galaxy* on our new TV."

From down the tunnel, away from the elevator, comes a sound.

I turn. Something like whispering. "You hear that?" I try to direct my headlamp beam. Nothing tangible. Just a hint of motion at the edge of my light's influence.

"Colm," Adi says. "What is it?"

I take a few more steps. Watch, listen. "Nothing." I turn back.

Ryan leans against the gate, as if ready to leap aboard the moment the elevator returns.

Adi comes to my side. "Nothing there?" She squeezes my shoulder. "You sure?"

The rattling and vibration from the shaft is impossible to ignore. The elevator's arrival seems imminent. Adi and I return, stand behind Ryan. All of us watch the vacancy at the bottom of the shaft. Muttering voices reach down. Our feeble lights shine up, find nothing in the vertical shaft. Finally brighter spotlights probe down from above. The cage descends, stops.

The gate swings open. Lewin McAtree emerges, flanked by two younger men. None of the three wear any protective suit or mask. The larger men behind him carry electric lanterns, a backlighting which renders the old man a dramatic silhouette.

McAttree, in his beige cowboy hat, inhales deep, as if enjoying a lungful of fresh mountain air. "Who might we find down here? Even an old man can guess."

"You, in the white jeans." Adi addresses the one to our right. "You're Perk Jones. Does your mother Gwendoline know what you're doing?"

Perk Jones offers no response. Along with the white jeans, he wears cowboy boots and a black T-shirt with the words "Say what the fuck?" in italics. The third guy, bald with a handlebar mustache, wears jeans and a leather vest without a shirt.

McAttree steps forward, adjusting his hat. He twists it off-center, then back. "Thought of leaving you down here. Be easy enough to hide the traces, tow your vehicles. But that's not the way I work, no matter what you figure me for."

I squint against the lights. "You shot at us."

McAttree angles his head, a dismissive half shrug, then gestures at his men. "Them, not me. Anyway, nobody got hurt. Just scared you two into jackrabbiting that hill. They could've shot you, but they didn't. Generally they hit where they aim. Thing about me is, even when someone imposes their goddamn curiosity upon my business, I still don't put an end to that person. I care about lives of human beings. Even those that put a pain into my ass."

"You almost destroyed Kinosha," Adi says. "Half a century everyone suffered, from a disaster that never happened. Now you don't even own this land, yet still you're—"

"A closed mine, on property I don't own, that's an arrangement with advantages." McAttree leans back, seems to be trying to stick out his belly. "So I invented a disaster. Kept folks away."

Adi gapes. "But twenty-two men died."

"It's an easy thing, convincing a man to leave a job half-likely to kill him. Offered two years wages, every man without exception was happy to giddy up elsewhere. A fresh start, money in his pocket."

"So it's always been safe?" I ask.

"Oh, no. There's times it's safe," McAttree says. "You can watch the sky for signs. Still, there'll always be mysteries. Down here, everything's different. You have no idea. Right this moment, we're perilous close to rare veins, old ones, run down deep. Nobody understands why some mountains, not others. Never mind that. Let's all of us get the hell up, where it's safe. In town, I'll treat everybody to dinner, that place you like. I can't tell you everything, but more than enough to convince you this plan of yours, it's busted. Get you back to your business, nice and city-like, in Portland."

"You're the one finished on this mountain," Adi says. "I'm not letting some old lunatic roadblock my plan."

McAttree presses toward Adi. He burns her with his glare, then shifts to me. "Both you have seen the things down here, moving in shadows? Not solid things enough to grab hold. You can only keep moving, get yourself back out, before they settle in. Nobody deserves that. No matter how much you might itch my balls."

"What are you actually talking about?" I ask the old man. "What's down here?"

McAttree shakes his head. "All you need to know, it's not for you. I've kept a tight lid on everything. This particular vein, it's rare. A man who discovered this drug, he might grow wealthy, selling overseas. There's a cost, though. Cost runs in the blood. Soaks into a person."

I stare back, hold McAttree with my eyes. Something shifts in the shadows behind us. I sense it, but don't turn. Movement, like swirling leaves.

"No, we can't believe anything you say." Adi glares at McAttree. "You lied to everyone."

McAttree shoots a look at Perk Jones, then addresses Adi. "Stop worrying yourself over what's not for you." He looks behind, into the elevator shaft, then the other direction, at the tunnel past us. "Shut your mouth for once, you might still get out of here. Move now, time's up." He motions everybody to move.

Handlebar mustache steps to the elevator gate.

Anger flares in me. McAttree ordering Adi around, implying threats. He's still standing close. I press forward, up against McAttree's chest. The old man's eyes widen. Perk Jones observes this, sets down his lantern, reaches behind his back. He comes up with a chrome pistol, shows it off a moment, doesn't aim, just ratchets back the slide. The metallic sound seems muffled, almost dull in the strange, heavy air. With his free hand, Perk Jones separates me from McAttree. Not a hard shove, but a slow, firm push back. There's no scuffle. I don't want one. I only intend to show McAttree we're not afraid, not going to be bullied off the mountain.

"Get on the damn elevator," McAttree croaks. "Last chance."

"It won't hold six," Ryan says.

Perk Jones grabs my arm. "Get in!" He waves his gun.

That movement again, much louder. The air, swooping.

Behind McAttree, handlebar mustache screams, falls back.

Unsure what's happening, I glance at Adi, thinking she must have seen something. She seems as confused as me. McAttree realizes it's one of his own men screaming. Handlebar mustache, sliding on his back toward the elevator, dragged by something we can't see.

"Watch out!" Ryan raises both arms wildly, as if shrugging off an unwanted blanket thrown across his shoulders.

Warmth pushes through us, half-solid.

"What's happening?" Adi asks.

"Ahh! Ahhhh!" McAttree rasps, harsh, crow-like. Arms flailing, he takes small, jittering steps, seeming to fight against nothing. The strange dance reminds me of something I saw on TV as a child, an auto racing pit crewman, burning with invisible flames from some exotic fuel. Though whatever he's fighting against remains unseen, his desperation is clear. His cries become a shriek, and he stops jittering, bends sideways at the hip as if straining to reach down, touch his his shoe. He lets out a grunt, his leg folds sideways at a gruesome angle, and he slumps to the floor, moaning.

Perk Jones rushes to McAttree's side. McAttree clutches his thigh in a panic, as if trying to keep a severed limb from dropping away.

"One went through," Perk Jones says.

Shivering convulsively, McAttree begins to hum. The hum sustains, builds to a growl.

Perk Jones looks at us, gestures. "Everyone, stay still!" he barks.

Confusion all around, sounds lacking visual cause. Invisible feet shuffle. Jostle of a murmuring crowd. Pit of rattlesnakes seething.

"Something's here," Adi says.

With a guttural cry, handlebar mustache is lifted into the air, arms flailing, as if trying to brush spiders off himself. Near the top of the elevator car, where it meets the shaft wall, he scrabbles at the steel grating with desperate fingers. The man's screams turn ragged as his body squeezes through too small an opening. The elevator car jerks, displaced slightly as the body is forced through, limbs fracturing. The man's body is lifted upward, vanishes up the shaft.

McAttree still on the ground, Perk Jones beside him. The rest of us, backing away.

A ragged whine rises in the tunnel, pressure hissing from a ruptured tank. So much cold air circulating, as if a turbine has been switched on somewhere below. Unexplored connections must be open to ventilation.

"This way." Shivering, I start down the tunnel.

Adi follows, then Ryan. Staggering, then walking.

The elevator. The only way out, our last hope for escape. We leave it behind.

"What happened?" Adi appears stunned, confused.

"Not sure," I say. "Try to run."

Ryan surges past, pressing ahead into the dark. I chase after, one hand in the small of Adi's back.

Another scream, far behind.

I try to run, but my legs are confused. All I want is to escape the screaming.

27. Confusion in Darkness

We press ahead, headlamps barely penetrating the darkness. The tunnel curves, no sharp corners, just gradual alternating bends. The screams subside. Safe distance.

Ryan abruptly stops, and we bump into the back of him. His chest heaves, each breath a sharp, throaty whine. "Something brushed past. Did you see anything? I felt it."

"That same smell," Adi says.

"Wait a second." I turn back, listen. Nothing behind us.

"Keep going," Adi urges.

We move again, headlamps bouncing random, divergent beams. From a mayhem of unexplained violence into a mapless quiet. One confusion for another. Adi's right about the smell, stronger than before. A strange atmosphere, burning cold. So long through fatigue.

On and on, jogging, bumping each other, running into walls.

Me, Adi, Ryan. The three of us made it.

No, just two. I've been running, thinking it's Adi beside me, but that's not her. Too tall. It's Ryan.

"Wait." I stop. Can't concentrate. Can't focus.

Turn around, start back. I can't be sure who's who. This blind scattering, so many bodies. All that screaming.

No, wait. I can't hear the screams any more. We're safe.

My heart thuds, ready to burst. Pressure in my temple. Infection burns. I'm going back—

"Colm! Colman Quinn," Ryan barks. "This way." He's behind me.

"Where's Adi? She was just with us." Wasn't she? Adi wouldn't go back, toward McAttree. She wouldn't leave me, not on purpose. Most likely she's ahead, leading the way. Which direction was I headed? So disoriented. "Sorry, I must've turned around. But we need to catch up to Adi, find where she went. Was there a split? Some side tunnel passed in the dark?"

"I thought she was here." Ryan seems confused, looking around like she just vanished.

I move again, following someone's headlamp bobbing. Fighting this constrictive suit. At least I'm going again, but I feel out of control, like I'm drunk.

"Adi!" Trying to yell, I barely gasp. Stumbling, tripping.

"Wrong way," Ryan says. "You're all turned around. What's wrong with you, Quinn?"

I'm trying to breathe. Can't get enough air.

From out of the perfect darkness down the tunnel, a whisper. "Come on." Adi's voice. "Let him go back. This way. You and me."

"Adi?" I ask. "Is that you?"

Where the voice came from, there's no light. She must've lost her lamp. I aim my light, probe the tunnel. "Adi!" My voice, a stage whisper. "If you're there, please—"

"Maybe she's back at the elevator," Ryan suggests. "We should go back."

"Didn't you hear, just now?" I ask. "It was her. She's nearby."

"There's nobody." Ryan starts moving, back toward the elevator. "The best thing we can do is go back, go up to the surface. What if they've got her? Come on."

"I'm sure I…" So confused, pulled in opposite directions. I heard Adi beckon me. But why would she hide?

Think about what Ryan's saying. Maybe she's alone, back there. We have to go.

"We'll go back, see if she's there," I say. "But if she isn't, we come back, keep searching."

"Agreed." Ryan starts back.

His headlamp's more powerful, so I follow. He'll see obstacles better than I would. It can't be too far, down here.

Around the next curve, a hint of illumination. No voices, no movement. We creep forward, moving for stealth rather than speed.

The elevator, visible in the distance. Nearer, a body slumped against the tunnel wall, sitting flat on the ground. A man, legs extended in white jeans, soles of cowboy boots worn through. The slogan, "Say what the fuck?" on his t-shirt matches his gaping mouth and wide-eyed astonishment. Bloodless chunks missing from arms, torso. Not cut. Burned deep.

"Perk Jones." I kneel out of reach, just in case. "So pale." I'm afraid of what we'll find near the elevator.

"Leave him," Ryan says. "Keep going."

Outside the elevator cage, McAttree's body, lying on the ground beside his tan cowboy hat. We approach cautiously.

"Hear that?" I ask.

A sizzling sound, like bacon popping in hot oil, but very quiet. No movement. Dead eyes.

"Yeah. We can go up now," Ryan says.

"I'm not leaving without Adi. You go up if you want." I turn from the elevator, start down the tunnel.

"God damn it, Colm."

Ryan runs up alongside me.

Eyes adjust. I struggle to aim my light. Soon we're around the first curve. Ozone, chemicals burning, and that other smell, the one from the black crease. The elevator's forgotten, far behind. I don't care about going up, have no idea where I am. Just want to find Adi.

28. Becoming Lost

I repeat her name until the sound makes no sense. Forward, always forward, trying to stay straight, avoid walls. How long have we been here? This tunnel never changes.

Then, a variation. I stumble over something unseen, unevenness on the ground. Beside me Ryan falls hard, lands with a grunt. His flashlight clatters, broken. His headlamp goes dark. Ryan lies writhing, moaning in the beam of my headlamp, the only light remaining.

"What is it?" I ask, trying to avoid conjuring whatever hurt McAtree and his men.

"My ankle!" Ryan groans. "It's broken. Oh, shit, shit. It's bad. Bad."

"Are you sure?" My light finds Ryan delicately probing his lower leg through the suit.

"I feel bone coming through. Oh, fuck this." Ryan puffs between pursed lips as if fighting hyperventilation. "You got to go up. Use the elevator. Get help, come back. For Adi too, not just me. God, I'm sweating bad." He shakes his head wildly, as if trying to wish this away.

I grip Ryan's trembling hand, try to meet his eyes. He won't look at me. I want to do something to alleviate his pain, stabilize the leg, but there's nothing. I don't want to leave him, but Adi's already alone. "I'm not going up, not yet. Not until I find her. We'll come back for you." I brace myself, one hand on the floor. "The rock, it's so hot."

Ryan's eyes blink rapidly. "Hurry if you can. I'll be okay. Not going anywhere." He laughs, unconvincing.

I stand, remove my biosuit, and let it drop. "Don't need this." My clothes beneath are soaked with sweat. Unsure what more I can say, I hurry down the tunnel, don't look back.

Very soon, the last of my small light will leave Ryan behind.

"Adison." My voice, a rasp. "Adi, I'm coming."

Alone for the first time, facing the dark. The headlamp beam helps, but so much resists the light, fighting to remain unrevealed. I'm surprised how afraid I am. Not just worried about Adi, but frightened for myself, for whatever I might encounter. I've been underground a thousand times before. This is different. Voluntary exploration, knowing I can go home any time, that's nothing like facing the abyss. Wondering if there's any way back.

Is Adi lost, or am I? I don't understand where she could've gone. Everyone's left behind us, all dead but Ryan. Ryan's tough, he'll hang in there.

Maybe he can drag himself out. Probably not, with a compound fracture.

Down endless tunnels, my dim lamp hints the narrow way. Can't trust these angles, this sense of leaning to one side, like the wall to my left might corkscrew around, suddenly become the floor. That's the problem with perception. Senses are the only way to apprehend the world, but senses lie. Worse than tricks or distortions. They're a false projection, a flat diorama that fakes the illusion of depth, and never conveys the causative potential lurking hidden beneath.

Alone already, so soon after Adi and I found each other. Before we ever really had our chance. We were on the verge of becoming the reality we wished into being. Something was coming, made by both of us, and now—

This jagged hallway. The floor broken, uneven. Sharp cobblestones, bricks set at wrong angles. Too difficult to walk, let alone run.

This tunnel leads nowhere.

Legs tired, feet aching. My hands tremble, fingers vibrate on frayed nerves. I'm meant to turn back, not wander aimless, alone forever.

My light fades, battery half dead. Where did confidence go? Hope dwindles so quickly, breaks down at first disappearance of the sun. Here, don't forget, night is forever.

I want to talk to Adi. On the trails, I walk ahead of her, talk without seeing. I know she's there. I speak, knowing she'll hear. "Onion rings at the Ice Axe. Pub fries poutine, if you want. We can share. All the beers, two each. More than we can ever drink." My voice feeble, sick. Barely audible.

I wait, listening. Nothing returns. An echo in my skull.

"What about you, what first? On hot days, you get the blonde ale. I like amber or porter usually, but not now. I'm so thirsty."

See the surface, sky ahead. Over the dirt barrier, push open the metal grate, exit into infinite sunlight. I only have to climb out, emerge again. Fresh air. Adi waits.

"Is it night or day, Adi? How is it where you are?"

Here it's late. Black shapes flit and dive out of corners of memory.

I cower, try to rest. A bed of sauna rocks, next to heat death. A flood of sweat. Night passes, so deep. Passes without ending. Freezing, shivering delirium.

No straight halls, right angles. Just dead-end stairs. Blockades, half doors. Crawlspaces circle to where they begin. Confusion isn't a straight line. It's complicated as the mind can make it. Night endless. The void may drop away suddenly. True deepness. Is this shock, delirium? No way out, only down, down. Led deeper, misled by eyes, suffocated, starved of light. False eyes, deranged hints. Deep gray phantoms forever out of reach.

If I had different eyes, I could see.

29. True Dark

Huddle against hot stone, invisible in delirium.

Have to move, try to crawl. Fingers find an opening in the wall, a crease. Not like the other black seams. A trickle of water, tiny and cool. I lean, drink with brittle lips. Not water, something else. Impossible, cool brightness. Such relief. Don't know what I'm drinking. Don't know where I am. Should be afraid.

I was afraid, before. Left it behind.

Stop, wipe my face. My head clears. Sit up, feeling myself again. Feeling transformed, energized. Can't see myself to confirm it's still me. Hands touch my face. My own hands. I feel the same. I know I'm changing.

A voice.

"If you drink without seeing, you drink whatever you imagine."

Still thirsty. Too thirsty to see.

The same voice, directionless.

"You can heal. You can create."

I struggle upright, stand on wobbling legs. Impossible to walk, not without sight. Yet I find myself moving. Feel a corner with my fingertips, navigate to a new branch. Further along, a hint of light. Something against the wall ahead. The outline of a tree, a simple design, radiance in the dark. Every other branch is ornamented, a white sphere glowing from within. Count branches, twenty-two. Two branches share each sphere. There are eleven.

I see this, though I'm nowhere near. Perception far outreaches the eye.

What do I see?

Perk Jones, Lewin McAttree, charred by burning mouths. They never reach the surface. Night approaches. Black flares against the sky whisper, *Come this way, can't you. Try to rise up, take back your world.*

None of this is anywhere near me. Not this world. None of them. None of us.

I'm somewhere. Not above ground. Not walking past a glowing tree.

Both of us went below, Adi and me, trying to understand. So much remains hidden. That single truth always holds. More remains hidden.

I can imagine a perfect story, a dream crafted to unfold the ending I desire. I only need to wish. What light is this, tiny illumination dimmed to orange? Almost nothing at all. My headlamp, dying. Flick the switch. That's where I am.

I'm in the tunnel.

So cold, freezing. And this fear, where do I put it?

No one to tell, no one to share—

This dark is perfect, naked skin warm and smooth. Adi's body. First time we touched, hurried to her room, found ourselves. It was a night.

And now—

Black liquid seeps. Precursor to coal glistens, component of diamond, meant to become gleaming pinpoints. Liquid, poisonous brain-eating tar overflows my dreams. The smell of it floods. How long have I been asleep?

Can't crawl, only hide. Lost in tunnels all night, or is it gone around to day? It's a very old problem, the fading of hope. Didn't I say you can manifest desires? Something's still out there, listening, making note of my plans.

It found me—

Exhausted heart still pounds. Skull rock-struck, dripping blood. Old wounds, inadequate to end me. I lie terrified, shivering, the memory of heat still fresh, but no consolation against the freezing depths.

Is this hallucination? Madness?

So much uncertain, unknown. Surmounted by infinite stone. Enough rock to build another world, enough mass to create gravity. A world lacking monsters, a place of ideal forms, pure conceptions. A house in the forest watched over by giants. Only their legs are visible. Legs resemble trees. The giants are a forest. I could make a world like that. That place is not far.

I keep slipping, terror of hot death and undoing. Fear of dying alone, too soon, before lagging hopes catch up.

So long running. Run until sleep, then dream only of running. I spent many years frozen, always thought I was trying to get away. Dreams of starting over aren't enough. Had to break my past. And who deserves to find someone perfect, so soon? Someone designed for me, before I realized what I wanted. Now lost, tethers cut, becoming forgotten. Like the face of a dead child, never known.

I drink from this bubbling spring. The voice says I'm intoxicated, drunk on these words, transformed by this place.

Remember Adison, our hopes. Union in dissolution.

There are many gods underground. New gods rise, others fall away. When their time comes, they swirl and rise or else slumber. Immaterial bodies have no respect for stone, only water, fire and air. The number only grows, never counted, never seen.

Memory grasps, seeking future.

Hands clutch in the dark, find nothing. Hands alone.

IV

Black Dawn (in 4 parts)

30. Awaken Changed

I wake. A voice murmurs nearby, unseen in persistent darkness.

"Colman." A woman's voice. "Open your eyes."

A moment of panic before recognition. I know her. My hearing distorts, confused by blindness, the strangeness in the air, alternating extremes of heat and cold. I drift into awareness, lacking memory, out of nothing. At the instant of birth, between one awareness and the next, the slate is blank. I've never been awake before, don't recognize this place. No context, no self.

"You're awake," she tells me. Adison Kye. Adi.

My own voice replies. "I must have been dreaming."

"Colm."

"I heard a voice. I couldn't see who it was. It said, *My name is knowing.*"

"Knowing?" she asks. "Colm, it's me. Open your eyes."

I try to sit up. "A nightmare. It must have been. She said, *I am silence that is incomprehensible.* Those words, and others like that." My fingers grasp, find nothing. Flat stone.

"She? A woman's voice?" Adi's hand touches mine.

"I was dreaming. Unless it was you, talking to me?"

Adi leans so close, I feel her breath when she whispers. "*I am silence incomprehensible. I am substance immaterial. I am union in dissolution.* Is that what she said?"

"That sounds familiar." I can't see, wonder at my surroundings. "Where does it come from?"

"I heard it too, when I was exploring. I heard a voice, more than once, different places." Her voice is gentle, unhurried.

"I can't see anything." My voice, a tremulous whine, full of fear. This place

309

confuses me. "Everything's so dark."

"Your eyes will adjust," she tells me. "Mine did."

That voice and her touch are all I know of her presence. These are enough. I don't have to see her hand to recognize it. Skin soft. Shape, like a face I recognize. The feel of it comforts me.

"There's no reason to fear, Colm. Try opening your eyes." A waver in her voice. The version of Adi I imagine speaking to me changes. "Open them slowly, or it'll shock you."

She's right, my eyes are closed. They've always been closed.

I finally see Adi, standing there before me, dim gray. "It's you." I have to blink.

Now I remember. Ryan, with Adi and me. We entered the old mine. We found--

"Don't ever be afraid again." She gushes excitement. Her fearless ease convinces me. "Just look."

She helps me stand. Weak, unsteady legs.

"Your face," I begin. Have her features changed, or my perception? The air shimmers. Eyes are affected by pressure. Yes, still the Adi I've known. Her face is a permanent thing, even with slightly different lines, new angles. Especially around the eyes.

I want to ask about the changes. "I'm cold," I say instead.

"First I was dripping sweat, then freezing. Now I'm used to it." Adi removes her jacket, hands it to me. The jacket is my own, the one I gave her yesterday morning. Or whenever that was, when we left the Highlands. Maybe more than a day. "I've found so much. Come on."

I haven't lost Adi. She's really here, wants me to follow. If she seems different, it's only because of everything that's happened.

I'm able to walk, slowly at first. Adi leads me by the hand, down subtly curving tunnels, always seeming to know the way. She was right, we don't need a lamp. Atmosphere swirls, stubborn hallucinations pressing against my eyes. A sense of thickness to the air, everything compressed, amplified by this titanic gravity. This is how right ways become wrong. Angles bend, distances distort. Vision lies, a broken lens.

I remember. "We found bodies, Ryan and I did. Ryan's hurt."

"I've seen everything," Adi says. "But not him. Ryan must've found his way out."

As we walk, recollections flow back, an incoming tide. Sudden violence. Racing down tunnels, Adi lost. Our return, bodies near the elevator. "I left him. He was trying to help us."

"I know," Adi says. "It's impossible to predict how our other lives will unspool."

"I looked for you." I don't want to remember. Remembering is pain. I want to stay here, in the present. Memory is too potent. "You were lost, or I was. I wanted to find you, then go back for Ryan. But I couldn't. I stopped. I must've slept."

Adi looks at me, understanding, still walking. "I know." Her look conveys the same determination I've always seen in her. Sympathetic, but resolute.

The slope is a gradual decline. The way curves gradually. Stone surfaces glossy black, like the skin of a buried leviathan.

"So deep," I say.

"The way was never flat," Adi says. "We were always going down."

31. Impossible Tunnels

Left, left again, then straight. I recognize this, though I've never seen it. The floor briefly inclines, rough and uneven like shallow stairs. Obstacles clearly visible now, but running here, sightless in the dark, anyone might stumble.

On the ground, two discarded biosuits, crumpled white plastic. I expect to smell our stale sweat inside the suits. There's no smell, no hint of moisture, as if they've been here a long time.

"I dropped mine. That must be Ryan's." No sign of Ryan himself. "He broke his ankle." I remember. Agonized moans, hyperventilation. Left helpless, alone, trusting me to return.

"You had to see," Adi says. "So we can leave this behind."

"But we're—"

"Do you remember what you used to tell me, on the trails?" Adi asks. "The only way to handle a long trek? Always keep moving forward. Never stop. Don't look back and measure. Always forward." She seems about to continue, but stops herself, watching me.

"I remember," I say, and mouth the word, *Forward*. "I remember."

So we continue. I don't understand where she wants to go, what knowledge she might have gained in our time apart. I can't recollect how I passed those hours. Sleeping, delirious.

We keep passing turns, unexpected splits, backtracks, digressions. At every such divide, Adi makes her choice without hesitation. So many potential routes, infinite possibilities. What I imagined as a straight path is really a labyrinth.

"These turns," I say. "I ran past them, never saw. Just kept running. How could McAttree have dug all this?"

"This is the way I found," Adi enthuses.

"What about the elevator?" I ask.

"Let me show you," she says. "You'll see."

"Wait." I grab for Adi's arm, try to get her to stop.

Adi keeps walking, just out of reach. "We don't need the elevator." She leads, possessed of enough certainty for both of us.

All summer, we followed her plan, even when I was the one leading on the trail. Back then, fresh from my split with Paula, I needed to follow, keep decisions simple, until I regained confidence. It took a while to remember. By then I knew Adi needed me, knew some vacancy existed down here. Something Adi needed to find. Finally I felt capable of a decision. Now I'm back to following.

"Mother used to talk about the true birth," Adi says. "Becoming something new."

Of course Adi knows more than she's telling. She's seen more than I have. I'll continue to follow, because I trust her. I still don't understand.

"We both searched," Adi says. "Separately, we could wander forever. Together, different ways are open."

I'm still trying to follow, but my balance shifts off center, my gait uncoordinated. Focus slips, vision a parallax blur. "Adi, my eyes." I stagger, hands outstretched, feeling for walls. I shake my head, trying to clarify. "A minute ago I could see."

"Don't remember, don't switch back," Adi whispers. "Being down so deep exerts pressure on the mind, on the air itself. It's not your fault."

"Adi—"

"I keep remembering things Mother said. This smell." She breathes deep, fills her lungs. "What does a shadow leave behind when it slips through stone? An empty shadow is enough to change all you see, all you think, everything you feel."

Adi turns to the wall, finds a dark crease, one of many we've passed. She reaches in, scrapes with her fingernail, then shows me, holds it close so I can focus. A black trace held between fingertips. "Here, see this? Open your mouth."

I stand bewildered. What's she doing? It's Adi. Her eyes fix me, her gaze heavy, expectant. One hand offering, the other hand on my chest, stabilizing. Her touch, more than familiar. Intimate. I remember our night. We fell out of the past, into some future unknown until we landed. Fell together.

I open my mouth.

She slips fingers between my parted lips, spreads the weird, tangy paste on my tongue. It burns, a sizzling organic ferment like kimchi or vinegar.

"Oh." I understand.

A radical clarifying. Abstract shapes, poetic forms. Baudelaire's hypnotic darkness, Whitman's ecstasies of atmosphere, a deeper spectrum beyond color and shade. Vision sharpens, so bright. More than simply the clearer sight of what existed before. The emergence of new elements. Hidden truths arise within every seemingly vacant interstice.

"Now you see," Adi says. "The gaps were never empty."

32. New Eyes

After too long spent within claustrophobic confinement, we pass into a wider tunnel. The distance lengthens from one turn to the next. The ceiling, before just out of reach, gradually becomes higher. While before it was featureless, first irregular roughness appears, then the protrusions are more pronounced. Finally, the roof overhead is repeatedly thrust through with uneven squares of a character and color different from the stone around them. I remember something Adi said on the trail once, realize now what she meant. These great downward thrusts of rock are the striving roots of great monoliths that reach above, deepest extents of ageless bodies of standing stone, acting as conduits between the surface and the depths.

The path declines, always more steeply.

After long silence, Adi speaks. "You wondered how McAttree could create this," she says. "A man like him could never build such complexity, could never tolerate such depth. He wasn't seeking this. His tunnels only delved as far as the very tip of the vein. What lay below didn't interest him."

"That smell, like trees," I say. "The forest around Triangle Lake. I miss that place."

"Remember," Adi says. "Our old lives are behind us."

Adi's right. I've always wanted movement, the possibility of discovering myself somewhere new, far from where I began. I wanted that for myself, but somehow failed to keep after it. I don't remember when my priorities broke down. Long years with Paula, deluded into believing we still had a chance. Monday through Friday I worked my job, weekends I ventured out, went climbing or hiking or caving without my wife. I kept busy, so thought I was going somewhere. Constant motion, endlessly treading the same ground.

Time counts. I've wasted too much.

I'm relieved to be here, with Adi. Not just working together, more than day hikes and meals. Real proximity. This is the outcome I wanted. I'm through protesting, wondering why.

Adi turns to me, breathless with excitement. "This is what I found. It's familiar to me. I might have been here when I was young."

A cavern opens, ahead and below. Like the forest hike, when I thought we reached a valley floor and discovered the way went deeper still. All around us is openness.

Has this place always existed? I want to ask Adi. I suspect she knows.

"This place, it's him," Adi whispers. "I recognize his way."

"Him?"

"My father, Abracsa."

I remember what she said at the Highlands, about her childhood. She implied her father was nothing but a mystery to her. This seems to be as much a discovery for her as for me.

Adi strides out ahead, into the open. I follow, all narrowness and convolution left far behind. No more barriers, no restraints. Without walls, it's difficult to gauge proportion or distance.

"I'm surprised there's no groundwater, so deep," I say. "We're not far from Triangle Lake. Something's draining away the water." What did Councilman Spence say in Kinosha, about Adi's home town? Rectory, vanished now, all the residents dispersed. Nomon house. Something below.

"There's always some deeper gap." Adi points. "Look there. Water."

A low spot in the rock accumulates moisture into a rough oblong pool. The surface reflects, a perfect mirror.

My face. So strange.

"Maybe you're thirsty," Adi suggests.

I kneel, lean down, touch lips to the quivering surface. The water smells clean. I taste, drink. It's wonderful. Splash my face, wash arms and hands.

Adi kneels. "We should both clean up."

Water cools my mouth, refreshes, rinses away the sweat and dirt from my skin. I feel completely clean, new.

"Look around." Adi stands. "Everything's here."

I straighten, still kneeling, and look. The arched ceiling, many times my height. Far off, an opening into misty illumination. Through the haze, an upward slope. A hillside of trees.

"Are we still below?" I ask, disoriented. This seems impossible.

"Don't worry," she says. "We're together."

She's right. Being with her is what I've wanted, what's most important to me. It's just that I imagined a different future, possibly in Portland, some merging of the best aspects of Adi's life and my own. Hikes on the mountain, adventures around Oregon. Make plans, eventually share a home. We'd cut away everything from before that bothered us, like Paula, and Adi's husband. But all these aspects are bound together, difficult to escape.

"What are we doing here?" I'm certain of Adi, but afraid of leaving everything behind. Even aspects of my life I hated, like my city job, Seattle, and

Paula. These things, all the pain and frustration and anxiety, they're part of what formed me.

Adi watches, waiting. Her eyes convey trust, care, even love. "I'll go wherever you are."

"That's what I was going to say," I answer. She's what I want most.

"Something new, then," she says.

"Are you sure about leaving? What about your dream of changing Kinosha?"

"I wanted transformation, thought that meant buildings, roads. But I don't care about those things."

"Can you really let everything go, after wanting it so long?"

Adi walks a while without saying more, then finally speaks. "Remember when you told me about hiking the Pacific Crest Trail? You said it taught you lessons you never knew you needed. You started off on one trail, chasing one goal, and never left the trail, but ended up somewhere else."

"Yeah." I'm surprised she remembers details from all my rambling trail stories. I always wondered if she was bored, listening to talk of blisters and fire and trail philosophy. "You can't find in the first mile. Whatever I gained came on the last few days. Maybe last few steps."

"I was serious about trying it with you," she says. "From Mexico to Canada."

"When you mentioned it, I wondered."

"So instead of a trail you already walked, let's try something else." Adi slows, takes my hand. "The woman who dreamed of developing the mountain above Kinosha, that wasn't me. That was someone else. This place is familiar to me. It explains so much, clarifies so many stories, connects the dots in old memories."

"What memories?"

"Our house, the forest in Rectory. Such impossibly tall trees. And one lightless midnight, the sky outside starless and black, all the crickets silent. Mother whispering in the other room, demanding he let us off the mountain. I heard him answer, *Only if the girl returns.*"

"You came back," I say.

Young Adison, a girl I never knew. I see her wandering, alone in the forest, looking for whatever her future intends. She must've felt the mountain's pull, heard the trees whisper, as I have. And me, I've been preparing just as long, seeking in caves and on trails. All my failures, my wandering in avoidance. Adi's learning, her ambition and pain. Neither of us knew what would carry us.

I squeeze Adi's hand. Don't need her to pull me along. I know the way. "The moment I forget, my past is destroyed." I want what she wants. We belong to no place, no time. Wherever we go becomes all we require.

33. The Seeping Egg

Banks of mist hover in scalloped rows overhead. A subterranean sky, expansive atmosphere adrift with subtle clouds. Immeasurable open space, tall and deep and vastly broad. As we move toward the far silver horizon, I start to believe the light through the mist comes from the glowing of a distant sun.

"I told you," Adi says. "There's always more."

So difficult to gauge size or scale. Not a sun, but something oval or egg-shaped, nearer. It expands and contracts, fluctuating as if under the influence of observation, the way time and causality vary in dreams. On the floor of this yawning abyss, visible through shifting vapor, lies a giant, cracked egg. The semi-transparent gold and yellow surface pulsates, luminous from within. Still distant, yet so massive, so overwhelming in scale, it seems close.

See Paula's face, as if she's here with us. Her tears, her desperation to play Mother. And within her, an amniotic sac, throbbing with proximate pain, doomed by the madness of a poisoned womb. A child never meant to glimpse our world, or any other.

I tried to want you.

"We're born too small," I whisper.

New life coalesces, growing. Biology quivers with aspiration, yearns to challenge a patient, malicious universe. A foundry of one budding to infinity, emitting heat in its slow shift from embryonic potentiality to imminent ego-actor, awhirl with creative ambition and causative intent, soon to crack through the fragile shell of this tired Earth, shrug off ruptured shards, and like a chrysalis shed our obsoleted world.

"It's very slow," Adi says.

"What was it called?" I ask.

"Nobody knows. The name is old, maybe lost."

The egg's surface is deeply cracked, a jagged diagonal like the seams we discovered in tunnel walls above. Dark effluent seeps from the black vein, the familiar vision-inducing, fragrant poison. From here it spreads in its slow, pestilential reaching. An impulse of change, devouring the past. Infinite futures seeking return, foaming through cracks, the blackness surging outward through creases, down toward the molten core, up toward the open boundary of sky. It vies outward in all directions, inevitable and impossible to resist. Movement so slow, it resembles immobility.

What absent maker left behind this imminent god, I wonder?

"You shouldn't be afraid," Adi tells me. "I'm home, and you're with me. All this is ours."

I keep thinking Adi appears changed. I look at her closely, see familiar features, chestnut hair, tattooed birds on her shoulders, and across her chest the very top of the tree. Beautiful now, like before. Maybe more natural, more self-possessed. We're comfortable together. The same Adi, here at my side. New ways of seeing, modes of creation. Circumventions of birth, and what else? Here, all possibilities exist.

"I'm afraid of change," I tell her. "But I need it."

Adi grins. "Another thing Mother always told me."

"Change is the true birth." I walk closer to her. As long as we walk, we seem no nearer the greater center of this place. "But you're still Adison Kye."

"No." She shakes her head, face solemn, not sad.

"I'm still Colman Quinn," I insist without certainty, prepared to be told otherwise.

"Those are just names, stuck in memory."

Then how have I changed? I believe it's true, but can't see it for myself. I need Adi's eyes to reflect me back.

"There's so much always hidden." My voice sounds fearful, not what I meant to convey. I may be afraid, but want to deny it. Fear's been within me as long as I can remember. I'm not sure it's something I'll ever leave behind, but I need to try. At first, pretend. Ignore the fear, until maybe I learn to forget.

"The hidden can keep us busy a long time," Adi says. "Maybe we'll go back up. Maybe we'll forget."

"Why me?" My last question. "I've only followed along. You've given me everything."

"No," Adi says. "You don't notice what you give me because it comes from you naturally. I was stuck. You brought me here."

This way she's looking at me, it's a look I recognize, but never managed to understand until now. It's taken me too long to trust. I was foolish to doubt the part of me that grasped what was underway. Up there, we spent each day talking, climbing. Down here, maybe it will be the same. Ground supports ground, stone under stone. More than enough open space. Heat and light radiate from the center. The egg pulses in expansion, waiting for the birth of a new serpent to replace one vanished to crush other worlds.

Think about birth. A father never met, a child never born. I want to tell Adi about my daughter. She has no eyes, but I think she still watches me. Everywhere, always.

I don't have to tell. Adi knows.

She leans into me. I feel her breath. "My father's eyes are sun, moon, stars."

An explosion is coming. I don't know what it will yield, a singularity or multitudes. Until that outburst, Adi and I will explore, discover with hands, observe with eyes, transform with intention. Of course an ending must come. A rupture of violence and pain, a disarray of burst memories. Tears of loss intermingled with blood.

No matter how long it builds, the transformation will arrive too soon.

PUBLICATION HISTORY:

"The Lure of Devouring Light" appeared in *Apex Magazine*

Far From Streets first published as a limited chapbook by Dunhams Manor Press

"Arches and Pillars" appeared in *Black Static*

"Diamond Dust" appeared in *The Grimscribe's Puppets*

"No Mask to Conceal Her Voice" appeared in *Lovecraft eZine*

"The Need to Desire" appeared in *Phantasmagorium*

"Dreaming Awake in the Tree of the World," "The Book of Shattered Mornings," "The Accident of Survival," "The Jewel in the Eye," and *The Black Vein Runs Deep* appear here for the first time.

"A lavish, sumptuous tapestry of luxurious surrealism and strangeness."

—*The Horror Fiction Review*

AN ANTHOLOGY OF ORIGINAL STRANGE STORIES at the intersection of crime, terror, and supernatural fiction. Inspired by and drawing from the highly stylized cinematic thrillers of Argento, Bava, and Fulci; American noir and crime fiction; and the grim fantasies of Edgar Allan Poe, Guy de Maupassant, and Jean Ray, *Giallo Fantastique* seeks to unnerve readers through virtuoso storytelling and startlingly colorful imagery.

What's your favorite shade of yellow?

Trade Paperback, 240 pp, $15.99

ISBN-13: 978-1-939905-06-2

http://www.wordhorde.com

In his house at R'lyeh, Cthulhu waits dreaming...

WHAT ARE THE DREAMS THAT MONSTERS DREAM?
When will the stars grow right? Where are the sunken temples
in which the dreamers dwell? How will it all change when they
come home?

Within these pages lie the answers, and more, in all-new stories
by many of the brightest lights in dark fiction. Gathered
together by Ross E. Lockhart, the editor who brought you
The Book of Cthulhu, *The Children of Old Leech*, and *Giallo
Fantastique*, *Cthulhu Fhtagn!* features nineteen weird tales
inspired by H. P. Lovecraft.

Format: Trade Paperback, 324 pp, $19.99

ISBN-13: 978-1-939905-13-0

http://www.wordhorde.com

ABOUT THE AUTHOR

Michael Griffin has lived in Portland almost his entire life, even before it was the coolest American city. He's worked over 23 years in a factory that cuts huge chunks of steel into smaller ones, and spends as much time as possible running, mountain biking, roving on beaches, and skiing, snowshoeing and hiking on Mt. Hood. He's also an electronic ambient musician (as M. Griffin, and half of Viridian Sun) and founder of Hypnos Recordings, the ambient music record label his wife helps run.

His stories have appeared in magazines like *Black Static*, *Apex*, *Strange Aeons* and *Lovecraft eZine*, and such anthologies as the Shirley Jackson Award winner *The Grimscribe's Puppets*, the Laird Barron tribute *The Children of Old Leech*, and *Chulhu Fhtagn!* His standalone novella *Far From Streets* was published by Dunhams Manor Press. He recently finished his first novel and is anxious to begin his second. His blog and other information can be found at griffinwords.com and he's also active on Facebook and Twitter.

CPSIA information can be obtained at www.ICGtesting.com
Printed in the USA
LVOW10s1620100616

492100LV00006B/553/P

OCT 2 5 2016